SPEAK of the DEVIL

The Devil's Hand Series

J. LYNN MILLION

Speak of the Devil
Book One of The Devil's Hand Series
Published by Imagination in Bloom Publications
1761 West Main St #1057
Troy, OH 45373
www.jlynnmillion.com

Publisher's Note: This novel is a work of fiction. Names, characters, businesses, places, events, locales, and incidents are either the products of the author's imagination or used in a fictitious manner. Any resemblance to actual persons, living or dead, or actual events is purely coincidental.

ISBN 979-8-9935561-2-3 hardcover
ISBN 979-8-9935561-1-6 paperback
eISBN 979-8-9935561-0-9 epub

Library of Congress Control Number: 2025922729

Cover and interior design by Shonda Ramsey www.shondaramsey.com

Printed in the United States of America
First Edition 2025

10 9 8 7 6 5 4 3 2 1

11252025

DEDICATION

To my mom, thank you for sharing your love of reading with me. From reading to me every night the She-Ra books, including the origin story (even when you were tired), to weekend trips to the bookstore and library sales, I was never without a literary world to escape into. It's one of the greatest gifts you've ever given me. I love you!

To my best friend, soul sister and fellow author Shonda, I am so grateful to you for supporting me through this journey of publishing my first book. As you know, this process started at a time in my life when I wasn't sure what was next. I probably would have given up and never shared this story or any others with the world if it weren't for your encouragement and love. You are to me what Francine is to Jackie: the friend that makes everything seem possible and that I'm ridiculous for even thinking it wasn't. What's more is that it IS always possible when you are rooting me on. I love you to bits and pieces, my dear friend.

LETTER FROM THE AUTHOR

Dear Reader,

I'm so honored that you picked up my debut novel *Speak of the Devil*. I've been a terrible chicken when it comes to sharing my writing, though I have been doing it for a long time. It would mean the world to me if you left a review for my book when you finish it so that hopefully other readers can find it and enjoy it as well.

This story does contain some religious references, but is not a Christian fiction story, nor is it based on any religious teachings. Personally, I am more spiritual than religious. I feel strongly that people of all religions, sexual orientations, races and ethnicities have a place on this earth and therefore have a place in my stories. The focus of my stories is the romantic connection of the two main characters and, in the case of this story, a bit of mystery. There are some spicy scenes in here as well. If any of this goes against your personal beliefs or feelings, I may not be the author and storyteller for you. However, you're missing out on a great story!

As a writer, part of developing my storyline and characters is putting together a music playlist. Some of it is vibes, some of it is background story, and some is how they connect with each other. On the next page, I have shared the link to the playlist on Spotify as well as the playlist itself in case you subscribe to another platform. I hope you enjoy this little insight into my creative process.

Most of all, I hope you love Kyle and Jackie's love story. They really surprised me. Originally they were only going to be side characters in Francine's story, but the more I worked on their backstory, the more I realized they needed to have their own book. I know it sounds strange if you're not a writer, and I know they are fictional people, but I genuinely feel that they chose me to write their story, and I am so pleased to do so. I hope you love them as much as I do!

Happy Reading!

J. Lynn Million

TRIGGER WARNING

- Infertility
- Blood
- Vomit
- Heart Attack
- Hospitalization
- Weight Loss
- Death
- Gun Violence
- Kidnapping
- Car Accident
- Imprisonment
- Murder/Attempted Murder
- Suicide

BOOK PLAYLIST

For the playlist on Spotify:

Song Title	Artist
Lost	Maroon 5
Don't Speak	No Doubt
Angels Fall	Breaking Benjamin
Rise Above This	Seether
Better Than Me	Hinder
Stay (I Missed You)	Lisa Loeb
Everything Changes	Staind
Broken	Seether & Amy Lee
Without You	Hinder
Give Me A Sign	Breaking Benjamin
Let Me Go	3 Doors Down w/Jack Joseph Puig
Waiting for Superman	Daughtry
Need You Now	Lady A
Untitled (How Could This Happen To Me)	Simple Plan
Far Away	Nickelback
Never Stop (Wedding Version)	SafetySuit
Light On	David Cook
Little Do You Know	Alex & Sierra
Sorry	Buckcherry
All of Me	John Legend
When We Were Young	Adele
Never Too Late	Three Days Grace
All I Want	Staind

CHAPTER 1

Arrivederci Chicago

Jackie
May 1, 2017

I t had been almost five years to the day since I had picked up everything I owned from my childhood home in Brooklyn, New York, to move with my grandmother Nonni to Chicago. We left to escape the fallout of my parents' illegal actions that had decimated their investment firm.

Nonni and I had hoped to start over in a new city. For her, that new start was with a new gentleman and for me, it was going to school to fulfill my dream of becoming a teacher. Now, five years later, both of our plans for a fresh start have been dashed.

It wasn't often that Chicago reminded me of Brooklyn, but on this day, there was something about the way the air blew between the buildings that reminded me of home. That wasn't exactly true...the day reminded me of the last time I saw *him*.

A chill raced down my spine at the memory as I opened the door to my attorney's office. I had taken the day off from my job at the bakery to discuss Nonni's will and make the arrangements for her final expenses to be paid out. When she had a stroke two years ago, they sent her home under my care with hospice aid to live out her final days. No one expected she would make it a year after suffering the stroke, but she held on.

My attorney, Mr. Driscall, was chatting with the receptionist, Donna, as I approached her desk. When they looked up from their conversation, both smiled at me warmly.

"Good afternoon, Miss D'Marco," Mr. Driscall greeted, gesturing for me to follow him.

"Good afternoon, Mr. Driscall," I replied, smiling to mask the butterflies swarming in my stomach as I followed the man.

When we arrived at his office, he invited me to take a seat first and closed the door behind us.

"It's lucky your grandmother kept such meticulous records," Mr. Driscall remarked. "We only had to wait for all her medical bills from her care over the last year to complete things for you. There was enough in the estate escrow to cover them, but I'm afraid once we finish those, that will leave only enough to cover my fees."

"I'm just grateful that Nonni's insurance covered as much as it did," I sighed, though I truly meant the words.

There was a twinge of disappointment in my chest. I knew it was too much to hope that there would be anything left for me to finish school. Besides, whatever money left had to be split between me, my uncle, and his two sons back in New Jersey. Any way I looked at it, getting the money to finish school was going to be a pipe dream at best.

"Just a few more pages to sign and that will finalize your grandmother's estate," Driscoll said, shuffling papers toward me for a signature.

With a few swishes of my pen, everything was in order and Mr. Driscall walked me back out to the receptionist's desk. Handling someone's final affairs seemed like it should be more momentous somehow, but now that it was done, I needed to figure out what I would do next.

"Thank you for everything," I said, giving the man's hand a shake for the last time.

"Good luck with everything, Miss D'Marco," he smiled and pivoted back to his office.

As I left Mr. Driscall's office, something had shifted in the air once more. A warm breeze that hadn't been there when I first walked in had replaced the chillier one. It was welcome and felt like a good omen somehow. Maybe just because the weight of finishing up with Nonni's final business had lifted? It was hard to say, but I was grateful for it all the same.

The sounds of the city at lunchtime created a symphony around me as I made my way back to my car, Nonni heavy in my mind. The woman was small but intimidating. Her word was final and no one in our family dared to go against it. She made me swear to her I would start living again when she was gone. It broke her heart that her illness had forced me to put a hold on school. She wanted me to get back to it even before she had passed, every day asking me what time I'd be leaving for school. It was hard to watch such a tough woman wither away to nothing.

"Jackie! Oh my God, Jackie, is that you?" a familiar voice called from behind me as I approached my car.

The hair stood up on the back of my neck as though I was in the presence of a ghost. I turned and there she was, dressed in an expensive royal blue pants-suit: Francine Carrollton. Her face broke into a wide smile as she confirmed it was me. Her strawberry-blond hair whipped in the wind as she rushed to me.

"I can't believe it's you!" she cried, wrapping me in a tight hug.

I returned her embrace and stifled the tears threatening to fall. She pulled back just enough to see my face but left her arms wrapped around me and her eyes roamed over my face, as if cataloging the toll the last five years had taken on me.

"Francine, it's so good to see you," I smiled sincerely, "I've missed you."

"Whose fault is that?" she teased, squeezing my sides playfully. "You're the one that moved, not me!"

My face fell in shame. She was right; I was the one that had left without a word to anyone. Looking back, it didn't have to be that way...though at the time, I was certain it was the only way it could happen. If I had known how lonely my life would be over the last five years, I would have chosen to stay and face the fallout.

"Is this where you've been this whole time?" she asked. "I come to Chicago all the time for work!"

"Yeah, I moved out here to live with Nonni," I explained.

Francine nodded in understanding. Surely, she knew what my parents had done by now, which is why that answer must have satisfied her.

"Excuse me, Francine?" a young Indian woman called out. "I need to get back to the hotel for a meeting. Do you want me to call a car, or are you coming with me?"

Francine released me from her embrace but hooked her arm through mine and pulled me along toward the other woman.

"No, please take the rental. I'll get a car later," she said, handing the keys off to the young woman. "Shreya, this is one of my oldest friends, Jackie D'Marco. Jackie, this is my good friend and colleague, Shreya Bhasin."

"Nice to meet you," I smiled.

"It's a pleasure to meet you too," Shreya smiled back. "I'm sorry, but I have to get going."

"I'll see you back at the hotel this evening," Francine called as the other woman rushed through the crosswalk to get to their car.

Shreya waved in response and took off in their car for her destination.

"What are you doing right now?" Francine asked, turning back to me once more.

"I was about to head back to Nonni's apartment to finish boxing up some things. I need to move out of there soon."

"Great!" she said. "I'm coming to help you."

"What? No," I insisted, "I don't need help."

"You may not need it, but you're going to get my help. Anyway, I am not letting you out of my sight until I get a working phone number for you and convince you to come back to Brooklyn with me," Francine replied, taking the keys from my hand and unlocking the car so that she could get in.

She settled into the passenger seat, and I stood on the street, just staring at her through the windshield, dumbfounded. I had left her behind when I left Brooklyn without a word. Why would she want to help me move?

Stubbornly, she waved for me to get into my car. When I still didn't move, she reached over and pressed the horn, which shocked my legs into moving again. I plopped myself into the driver's seat and fastened my seatbelt before starting the ignition.

"You come to Chicago a lot for work?" I asked as we drove back to Nonni's apartment.

"Yeah," Francine boasted, "I work for a tech company that sells customer resource management solutions to businesses. I am a sales and onboarding specialist, and I'm damn good at it!"

"That's amazing," I replied with a laugh. "I always knew you'd find something that you loved."

"How is school—I assume you're working on your master's by now?" she asked.

Everyone that knew me knew I had wanted to be a teacher my whole life. It stung a little not to be that far into my dream with the time that had passed.

"Actually, with Nonni falling ill, it set me back a bit in schooling," I admitted.

"Oh, I'm so sorry. How is she?" Francine asked sympathetically.

"She passed away," I replied. "I dropped out of school and had been taking care of her over the last year of her life. I just met with her attorney to finalize her estate."

Francine let out an audible gasp and turned to look at me. I could see the sadness on her face.

"Jackie," she breathed out, "If I'd known..."

"I know you would have come," I smiled ruefully, "I didn't think I deserved it after leaving Brooklyn without a word."

"Maybe not," she conceded, "but I should have been given the option to be there for my friend."

We pulled into the parking lot of the apartment I shared with Nonni and got out of the car.

I nodded, considering what Francine had said. It made me feel worse than I already had by cutting her out of my life, but if she would have been willing to come, then maybe he would have been too....

"How is your family?" I blurted out as I unlocked the door to the apartment.

She gave me a look as if to say; *I know what you're not asking.*

"My dad had a heart attack about a year ago—don't worry, he's fine!" she assured me, seeing the panicked look on my face. "He's doing great, actually. He and Mom retired early and sold me their house."

"Wow," I replied. Francine had always wanted to buy her childhood home from her parents if they would agree to it. There were few lots in Brooklyn that had much of a yard, but her parents had bought the lot next door after the house had burned down beside theirs. It was perfect for Francine, who loved to garden.

"My brothers are all grown up—can you believe baby Ben is 18 now? He's working for the firehouse and goes on runs all hours of the day and night," Francine smiled proudly. "He and Jason got an apartment together when I bought my parent's house. Jason's an EMT."

"That's amazing," I replied. It was hard to imagine Ben and Jason as young professional men now. They were 13 and 15 respectively when I left. I turned 23 this year and still had no clue what I was doing next. I'd missed so much and had been stuck in one place far too long with nothing to show for it.

Francine turned and picked up a flattened box and started folding and taping it into shape.

"Oh my God, Francine!" I cried, "Your suit! You shouldn't pack stuff with me in that beautiful suit. Let me lend you something to change into before you ruin it."

"Thanks," she said, following me down the hall to my bedroom, which I'd been putting off packing until last.

I pulled out a baggy shirt and leggings and handed them to her. She was one of the few people I'd ever been able to share clothes with. We were both plus-size girls and usually ran about the same size, but looking at her again, it seemed she had dropped a bit in size.

I left her to change and began packing unnecessary items from the kitchen. I hadn't found an apartment yet, but I was quickly running out of time on what I could cover in this apartment. I needed to be ready to go as soon as I found a new place.

"Before we get really started," Francine said, coming back into the living room in the change of clothes I had offered her, "what is the new address you are moving to and your current phone number?"

"My final destination is still TBD," I explained, taking her phone from her hands and putting my number into the contact she had saved for me.

"But you're already packing?" she asked, confused.

"I'm almost out of time on my lease, and the landlord has someone else lined up to move in soon, so I have to be ready to go as soon as I find a place," I elaborated.

"I know the perfect place!" Francine said, "Come live with me!"

"You can't be serious," I replied with a laugh. "I don't have a job lined up in Brooklyn."

"Actually, I may have one for you—at least a short-term gig until you line up something else," she said.

"Oh really? What would that be?" I asked suspiciously.

"I'm having gastric bypass surgery in a few weeks, and I'll need someone to help me with things around the house until I'm released for full activity by my doctor," she explained.

"You're getting a gastric bypass surgery?" I asked, astonished.

Francine had always loved being a curvy woman. She dressed and carried herself so well that no one made snide comments behind her back the way they had done to me. Everyone saw me just as the nerdy, fat girl whose rich mommy and daddy bought her expensive clothes in a failed attempt to make her more popular. Well, everyone except Francine and...

"Yes," Francine replied, pulling me back from my wayward thought, "when dad had his heart attack it really got all of us thinking about ways to improve our health, so I started working with my doctor and this is the route we decided on."

I sat down on the sofa quietly to contemplate her offer. I had no real ties to Chicago anymore with Nonni gone. At least in Brooklyn, I would have my best friend back and be closer to what remains of my family.

"Please say you'll do it," Francine pleaded, sitting on the sofa next to me, wrapping her arm around me and shaking me as she drew out the word "pleeeaase" in time with her shaking.

I laughed at her ridiculousness and replied, "Alright, I'll do it."

She squealed and tackled me in an enormous hug. "I'm so excited you'll be coming back with me!"

"Wait," I said pragmatically, "we need to iron out some details first."

"Jackie, while you're helping me, your room and board will be covered, as well as your moving expenses. What other things could we possibly need to iron out?" she asked.

I thought about that for a moment.

"That answers my most urgent questions, actually," I replied.

"Does it?" she asked, surprised.

"Yes?" I replied in a question, unsure what she was getting at.

"Really, I thought you'd have one more detail to iron out," Francine replied innocently.

"School?" I guessed at her meaning.

She shook her head and gave me a patronizing look.

In that moment I knew what she was getting at, and my heart pounded in my chest as his name escaped my lips on a breath. "Kyle."

CHAPTER 2

Jackie. Fucking. D'Marco

Kyle
May 15, 2017

It was 500% cliché, but I sat in my police cruiser in line at the bakery I worked at as a teenager, Holy Cannoli, waiting to get a donut and coffee on my way to pick up my partner to start our shift. The line was moving exceptionally slow, so I began looking around at the cars in line ahead of me, noting that the little red sedan with a patch of rust in the shape of Tennessee just above the license plate in front of me had Chicago plates on it.

"You're a long way from home, aren't you?" I muttered to myself, tapping my thumbs against the steering wheel in a steady rhythm to stave off my boredom.

When I reached the call box to place the order, I soon realized why the line was moving at a snail's pace. They placed the new kid, Ricky, on order duty.

"Holy Cannoli, what can I get for you?" Ricky's disembodied voice came through the call box.

"Hey Ricky, it's Officer Carrollton, here for my usual," I replied.

"I don't have an order for you, Officer Carrollton. Did you place it on the app?" he asked.

"No, Ricky, I come here every day and order the same thing...a large black coffee with two sugars and a raspberry jam donut," I explained patiently.

Jackie. Fucking. D'Marco | 13

"Woah, woah, one sec," Ricky's voice pleaded through the speaker. "That was a large black coffee, and what?"

"With two sugars and then a raspberry jam donut," I said.

"We're out of the jam donuts," he said.

I let out a sigh—I knew it was bullshit—the owner, Janice, always made sure to make one for me and set it aside.

"Ricky, is that Kyle? Kyle, is that you?" Janice's disembodied voice came through the call box.

"Yes, it's me," I replied, unable to help but smirk.

"Your usual will be ready at the window, sweetheart. Go ahead and pull forward," Janice called.

"Thank you, Janice," I replied and pulled up behind the red sedan to wait my turn to pay and get my order.

When it was finally my turn at the window, I could hear Janice giving Ricky an earful for not knowing my order.

"Janice," I called to her, hoping to stop her from actually picking Ricky up by the ear so that he could hear her better.

She smiled at me and pushed Ricky toward the window to ring up my order.

"Sorry Officer Carrollton, it's my first morning on the drive-thru," he mumbled sheepishly.

He started to hand my order out to me without taking my money and gave me an expectant look, like I should be pulling away.

"Uh, Ricky, you haven't asked me to pay for my order yet," I said, holding out my card for him.

"Oh yeah, the car ahead of you paid for your order and hers," Ricky said. "Oh man, Aunt Janice is going to kill me! She paid for both orders, and I forgot to give her the donut for her order because I was thinking it was the one for your order."

"Here, give it to me. I'll track down the lady and get it to her," I replied.

"Thanks, man, I owe you one!" Ricky smiled in relief.

"See you tomorrow," I called back with a wave as I pulled away to track down the red sedan. I had seen it turn right out of the parking lot, and luckily morning traffic still had the roads a bit congested, so she couldn't have gotten too far.

Once I pulled out onto the road, I could see the sedan three lights ahead of me turning right onto Pennsylvania Ave. I turned on my lights and siren to be able to catch up to the car before she got too far ahead. I wanted to thank her for breakfast and make sure she got her donut—can't have a Chicagoan thinking we New Yorkers cheated them somehow!

As the cars before me pulled over into the other lanes so that I could get around them, I closed in on the Chicago plate and Tennessee-shaped rusty bumper. I followed her car to the curb as she pulled off to the side of the road. I'm sure by now she was thinking she was going to get a ticket for speeding or blowing through a red light or something, none of which she had done.

I peeked into her donut bag to see what she had ordered—bear claw— great choice. I rolled the top of the bag back down and approached the car from the driver's side. The window was down, and I could hear the girl cursing herself under her breath for getting pulled over. I almost laughed out loud at her litany of curses and decided I wanted to mess with her just a little.

Turns out I was the one who was being messed with that morning. My God...Jackie. Fucking. D'Marco.

Her mouth hung open in surprise—clearly, she recognized me as well. I cleared my throat and pretended I was so far past her I didn't recognize her.

"License and registration, please, miss," I asked, defaulting to my routine line of inquiry.

Jackie turned and pulled the documents from her handbag sitting in the passenger seat and held them out to me.

"One moment, I'll be right back," I said, taking her documents and the donut back to the car with me.

My blood boiled beneath my skin where our fingers touched ever so slightly when I had taken her documents from her. After disappearing without a fucking word five years ago, here she was....

What the hell was she doing here? Where was she staying? When did she get here? Had she been here all along? I needed a moment to gather myself. I wasn't the lovesick puppy of a boy she had left behind. I was a calm, cool, and collected officer of the law, and I needed her to know that her being back would not have any effect on me.

I just needed a moment with her papers to answer a curiosity—where she had been. I pulled up her records on my in-car system and found that she still had no criminal record, no outstanding warrants...last known address was in Chicago. Six months ago, the car's registration was transferred to her.

To both my relief and disappointment, I had nothing to arrest or detain her on. For some reason, I truly wished I did at that moment, even though I could barely stand to be in my skin, let alone this close to her. I was so relieved to see she was alive and well that I wanted to hug her and so angry she had left without a word to me that I wanted to shake her at the same time.

I looked up at the ceiling and took three deep breaths before picking up her documents and the damn donut bag that started this shitshow of a day and headed back to her driver's side and handed back her documents but held onto the donut bag.

"Thank you for your cooperation," I said. "I'm letting you off with a warning, but I must impress upon you how seriously we take what you did here in Brooklyn, ma'am."

"I don't understand," she stammered, "w-what did I do?"

"It is a crime to order breakfast and drive away without your donut," I said, holding the bag up in front of her, "especially when it is a donut from Holy Cannoli. Don't let it happen again."

A laugh burst out from her in relief, and she covered her mouth with her hand. Her laugh pinched at a space in my heart. I hadn't heard it in so long, and it was just as beautiful as I remembered it.

"Drive safely," I said, holding the bag out closer to her, frustrated with how traitorous my heart had been just a moment ago.

16 | Speak of the Devil

She took her hand from her mouth, schooled her features, and gave me a somber nod.

"Have a good day, ma'am, and thank you for buying my breakfast," I said, turning and walking away as quickly as I could.

"Be safe, Officer," she called back, but I didn't acknowledge her.

As I sat back down in my cruiser, my cell phone rang with a call from my partner. I looked at the time and saw that I was late to pick him up.

"What?" I barked in answer to his call.

"Good morning to you too, Sunshine. My, my, did you wake up on the wrong side of the bed this morning?" Oscar Romero, my partner, chirped in my ear.

The son of a bitch was always in a good mood. It was disgusting.

"I'm on my way, just made a traffic stop on the way to you," I explained, my tone unnecessarily gruff, even to my own ears.

"Okay see you soon," he said, ringing off.

I pressed the speed dial for my sister Francine as I pulled the cruiser back onto the street, aiming to pick up Oscar. I had to see if she knew anything about the return of Jackie D'Marco.

"Kyle! Is everything okay?" Francine asked—she was chipper this morning too.

"Yeah, everything is fine. I just thought you'd like to know that Jackie D'Marco is back in town. I just pulled her over," I announced.

"I know she's in town. Wait, you pulled her over? Please tell me you didn't give her a ticket," she sighed.

"What do you mean, you know?" I demanded, my blood pressure spiking again.

"I ran into her in Chicago a couple weeks ago and asked her to come back and live with me while I recover from surgery, so my superhero brothers don't have to take time off from saving the lives of others to care for their one and only most favorite sister in her time of need," she replied, laying the guilt on thick.

"How long has she been here?" I demanded.

"She and I just made it back late last night. We took her car with her more personal items, and the moving truck should arrive any time now," Francine explained. "By the way, do you have anything in your old room that you left behind? I was going to set her up there since it's got an ensuite bathroom."

"Do not give her my old room!" I growled.

"Why? It's not like you are going to move back into it," Francine shot back.

"Put her in your old room," I ordered.

"It's my house, Kyle, and I will let her have any room I please," Francine argued defiantly.

"I don't have time for this. I need to be focused on work, but don't think this conversation is over." I warned her.

"It is over, but you're welcome to stop by and have dinner and a different conversation with me tonight if you'd like. Jason and Ben said they could make it over, and I'm sure they'd love to see their big brother. Be safe, Kyle, and let me know if you can make it or not," she said.

"I'm not coming over to have dinner with my ex-girlfriend!" I bellowed as I pulled into Romero's driveway.

"Fine, don't then, but do be safe. I love you," she said sincerely, knowing that it would deflate my blustering attitude.

"Love you too," I grumbled back to her as Romero took his seat next to me.

"Aw, Carrollton, I love you too," he said, pretending he was going in for a hug.

I gave him a shove to keep him off me and gave him a menacing stare.

"What? Too soon?" he laughed.

"Too soon," I replied with a huff.

"What happened?" he asked.

"It all started with a donut," I replied, taking a petulant bite of the raspberry jam donut for dramatic effect.

CHAPTER 3

Unpacking the Past

Jackie
May 15, 2017

Kyle Carrollton, the love of my life, pulled me over in his patrol car and...and...he didn't know who I was! The man who had occupied my heart and mind—my very being—since we were teenagers didn't remember me! The dagger of disappointment pierced my heart and twisted, making it hard to breathe as I made my way back to Francine's house.

Tears streamed unwanted down my cheeks the last few miles back to Francine's house. This whole idea was a mistake. I could stay with Francine for a week or two, just long enough to get her through her surgery, and then I'd need to leave...again.

Pulling in front of Francine's house ahead of the moving truck, I cried even harder. This house used to feel more like home to me than the one I grew up in. I thought I would get to put down roots here once more. Now, I might not have another chance with Kyle, and that left me feeling like the ground had been ripped right out from under me.

I stayed in my car just a few minutes after parking to pull my emotions together. As I put my hands over my eyes for a moment, a series of maniacal knocks came from the window beside me and the passenger side window. I pulled my hands from my face and shot a startled look in both directions. My heart pounded first in shock and then in excitement at seeing Jason and Ben Carrollton, Kyle and Francine's younger brothers. My face broke into a smile as Jason opened the driver's side door and pulled me out of the car and into a big bear hug.

"Oh my God, look at you!" I squealed as I hugged him tighter. I leaned back and ruffled the thick beard he had grown, eliciting a modest laugh from him.

"My turn," Ben called out, shoving his brother out of the way and crushing me in a big hug of his own.

I laughed and squeezed him back as a car rolled behind us.

"Come on, you goons, let's hug somewhere that is not in the middle of the street," Francine called from the sidewalk.

Ben pulled back from our hug with a wide grin on his equally bearded face and pecked a kiss to my cheek. "We missed you, Jackie."

"I missed you guys too," I sighed, my heart slightly warming back up from my earlier disappointment.

Ben and Jason took a box each from the back of my car and carried them into the house. I took another and followed them, listening to them chatter back and forth between each other.

"Where are we taking your boxes, sis?" Jason asked me over his shoulder.

"Francine's old bedroom," I answered.

"Actually, I thought you might like being in Kyle's old bedroom better," Francine suggested in a hurried manner. "It has an ensuite bathroom."

"Wouldn't that make more sense for you to have during your recovery?" I asked suspiciously.

"The master has one too," she replied, urging her brothers toward Kyle's room.

"Really, Francine, I'd be more comfortable in your old room," I insisted.

Her brothers looked at her and after a pause, she nodded in acquiescence, so they trudged the rest of the way to Francine's childhood bedroom at the end of the hall and put their boxes down.

"Okay boys, now for some heavy lifting," Francine rubbed her hands together, "Jackie's got a few bits of furniture that are special to her on that moving truck—don't hurt them when you bring them in and don't run into my plants in the foyer."

They nodded and dutifully headed back out to get my furniture. When they were gone, Francine turned to me, and her face crumpled in concern.

"Have you been crying?" she asked, "What happened?"

"You'll never believe it..." I sniffled. "I ran into Kyle, and he had no idea who I was."

Francine bit her lip to stifle a smile, but it didn't work, and a laugh burst through.

"Trust me, my brother knew exactly who you were," Francine assured me, still laughing.

"No, Frannie, I swear! He didn't even know me after I had given him my license and registration!" I insisted.

"Kyle absolutely knew it was you," Jason said with a grunt of effort as he put down the heavy wooden dresser that had belonged to Nonni.

"Yeah, he gave Frannie an earful about it 15 minutes ago," Ben agreed, wiping sweat from his forehead with the back of his hand.

My heart pounded in my chest...so he was just pretending he didn't know me? To what end? What kind of game was he playing?

"She even invited him over for dinner tonight," Ben added before Francine elbowed him in the ribs, eliciting a grunt.

"You invited him to dinner?" I demanded of my friend.

"Yes?" she replied, confused by my reaction.

"Were you going to tell me?" I shrieked.

"Yes?" she replied again, with a question and a weak smile.

"Why are you answering as if you're asking a question?" I shouted.

"Because you're really scary right now and I don't know what you wanted my answers to be!" she shouted back.

I walked in a small circle between the three Carrollton siblings, who were all way too close to me at this moment of panic. I could see the three of them exchange worried glances, but that didn't stop my pacing and hyperventilating.

"Ben, why don't we go get those other pieces of furniture off the truck?" Jason suggested.

"Good idea," Ben replied, following his brother out of the room.

Worry still wrinkled Francine's brow.

"Jackie, please talk to me," she pleaded.

My feet stopped moving then, and anger flashed through me.

"What game are you playing, Francine?" I accused, "You want me to take Kyle's old room, have dinner with him...are you playing matchmaker?"

"Maybe?" she shrugged. "Is that such a bad thing?"

I gave her a glare, huffed, and began pacing again. Was it a bad thing? Was it a bad thing? Ha! It was the thing my heart desired most of all!

"Why would you do that?" I demanded, a tear trickling down my cheek.

"Why wouldn't I do that?" she asked, perplexed by my question.

"Because I don't deserve the man he's become," I replied, my answer bursting forth from somewhere deep within me. "I'm such a hypocrite! I've done nothing with my life other than care for Nonni and work in a bakery. You know the last conversation he and I had?"

Francine shook her head no.

"I told him that his bakery job wasn't good enough. He needed to grow up and get a real job," I replied miserably. "Then, of all places, I end up working at a bakery because that's the only job I could get and still take care of Nonni."

"Jackie," Francine sighed sympathetically, "as harsh as what you said to him was, he needed to hear it. He loves being a police officer, and he's so good at it."

"Francine, when I saw him in the uniform, I was so proud and sick at the same time. I knew he would choose something that helped others, but I can't stand the thought of losing him to this job."

"There it is..." she said, pointing to me, her face breaking into a wide smile.

"There 'what' is?" I asked.

"You do still love him! I knew it," she grinned widely.

"Of course I do! I'll always love him, but that doesn't mean we should be together," I replied.

"I know...but don't you think you both owe it to yourselves to find out?" she asked hopefully. "Kyle was a wreck when you left. It took him a long time to get his feet under him again...becoming a police officer did that for him. It gave him a purpose."

"What if I'm not strong enough to be by his side?" I asked weakly.

"Then you'll know for sure that he's not the one and you can both move on," Francine replied pragmatically, "either way, it is evident that the two of you have been on pause for five years and it's time to hit play again."

I took her words in and stayed in the room, putting some items from my boxes into the dresser the boys had brought in while she went to find what was keeping them. Francine was right. I had been living, but my heart had been on pause the whole time. I hadn't even tried to find love after moving to Chicago. The closest I had come was a misguided study session in which my partner thought it was a date. It was totally embarrassing for both of us.

I heard the Carrollton siblings coming down the hallway with another piece of Nonni's heavy furniture.

"Jason, make sure you let Ben know when you're going to turn it!" Francine scolded. "You guys almost dropped this!"

"Why don't you get in here and give us a hand, then?" Ben shot back, "This thing is heavy, and your screeching about it isn't helping."

I smiled—bickering was the way the Carrolltons showed their love. If they weren't bickering about something, they were trying to wrestle each other or something equally ridiculous.

"Frannie, I'm sure the boys are doing fine," I said, moving out of the room so that they could swing the desk in without an extra body to work around.

"They are not paying attention to where they are going, though," Francine complained. "They almost knocked down my plant stand in the foyer."

"Why not move it somewhere else for today?" Jason grumbled, "Walking past it fifty times, it's likely to get damaged."

"Not if you're careful!" Francine reasoned.

The boys got the desk shuffled into the room and both leaned against it to rest for a moment. I had tried picking that thing up to get something that fell under it and couldn't lift it at all by myself. Thank goodness the Carrollton boys were on the job. They were often mistaken for big lazy boys, but all three of them made time for the gym even when they were younger. They just loved food as much as the gym and didn't always eat the best.

Francine leaned down and picked up a file folder from the floor in the hallway.

"Jackie, I think this fell out of the desk," she said, handing the file to me.

"Thanks, I thought I had packed all the files separately—this must have been stuck behind the drawer or something," I replied, noting Nonni's elegant handwriting on the tab at the top.

We moved all Nonni's files to a storage unit in Brooklyn, where we kept my parents' investment firm's records. I didn't remember seeing a missing file; this one was dated February 2011. It was strange that I wouldn't have noticed it missing when I was boxing her things.

I flipped through to see what it was and found that it was documents from my parents' firm, but this wasn't what I remembered seeing in the files that the police had taken into evidence to convict my parents. They were similar, but the e-signature code used to sign off on the transactions was mine! I didn't even know I had one in the company system, but there beside the code was my name: Jacqueline Christine D'Marco.

I didn't understand how this was possible, but I heard Francine and the boys coming back again with another piece of furniture, so I shoved the file in the desk's drawer and decided to dig into it later. Something was wrong...I just didn't know what yet.

CHAPTER 4

Penny's Diner for Your Thoughts

Kyle
June 9, 2017

I avoided Holy Cannoli for two weeks and skipped dinner with my siblings after learning that Jackie D'Marco was back in Brooklyn, but it didn't matter. I'd seen her nearly every day since. It felt like the walls of the city were closing in on both of us.

"What's soured your grapes, Carrollton?" Oscar asked, glancing over at me brooding in the passenger seat of our patrol car.

"Jackie D'Marco," I growled, her name burning my tongue.

"Was that her name? The redhead you took out last week. I thought her name was something like Brittany. So, it's over already?" Oscar chuckled.

He could afford to chuckle, I suppose. He and his beautiful wife Maria had been married for ten years and had three kids with one more on the way. They were always so happy with one another it was almost sickening, but Maria was such a great lady I couldn't hold it against them.

"No, I canceled the date with Brianna," I replied, correcting him with the name.

"Why? She was hot!" Oscar asked curiously.

"Jackie D'Marco," I answered in agitation.

"So, you went out with Jackie instead?" he asked, confused.

"No, I ran into Jackie D'Marco when I went to buy condoms for my date with Brianna," I explained.

"So?" Oscar asked.

"So...Jackie D'Marco is my ex-girlfriend that disappeared five years ago. She's been popping up everywhere since she's come back," I complained.

"And that's why you canceled your date?" Oscar asked, still not following.

"Right. It's the same reason I have been coming to your house for coffee every morning instead of going to Holy Cannoli," I explained.

"And here I thought you were trying to put the moves on my wife," Oscar teased.

"Then I went to get my hair cut two days ago, and who was there?" I asked, ignoring his insinuation.

"Jackie D'Marco?" Oscar asked, feeding into my diatribe.

"You got it!" I replied, "I can't go to dinner at my sister's house because Jackie is staying there until she gets a place of her own."

"So come to dinner at my house," Oscar offered. "Maria cooks way too much food, anyway."

"That's not the point!" I shouted.

"Well then, get to the damn point, Carrollton," Oscar pleaded. "You're giving me a headache with this nonsense."

I sighed, "Every day for two weeks, Jackie D'Marco has been everywhere I have been, and I don't want to see her. Somehow, I think if I planned to come to your house for dinner, she'd be there too."

"Maybe it's a sign, man," Oscar replied with a shrug.

"A sign..." my mind raced with the suggestion, "a sign for what?"

"I don't know...a sign you need to talk to her?" Oscar suggested.

"What could we possibly need to talk about?" I demanded, "She left me without a word—not even a note or an email. I was a good boyfriend to her. I didn't deserve that!"

"I'm not saying you did, man," Oscar reasoned, "but maybe she didn't have a choice in the matter, and that's what you need to know. Have you ever thought of that?"

I turned my head to stare out the window, and Oscar waited quietly for me to absorb what he had said. We'd been partners for two years, and he'd learned that sometimes I just needed quiet to sort out my thoughts.

Oscar's last words rang through my mind over and over. Did she have a choice, or was she forced to leave without a word to us? Was our last night together too much for her? Had she run to someone else instead of me? Why was it so easy for her to leave me behind?

I loved her with all that I was. As the weeks turned into months, I was overrun with so much hurt and anger that I didn't have the capacity to consider all that could have driven her decision to leave. For a long time, I just wanted to know that she was safe. I went door to door and begged anyone who would listen to help me find her. There was no light switch moment, but somewhere along the way, my concern grew into anger. That anger kept my heart safe from being hurt by anyone again, and I wasn't sure I was ready to let it go just yet. Still, I couldn't help being curious about what had happened.

After a good five minutes of silence, Oscar started whistling a tune I didn't recognize. He was doing it because he knew it annoyed the shit out of me and would make me talk again just to make him stop whistling.

"Are you ready to go for lunch?" I asked, deciding whether food might temper my mood and make his awful whistling stop.

"Are you buying today?" Oscar smiled innocently.

"If it makes you stop whistling, then yes," I replied, crossing my arms over my chest in irritation.

"Ah, is that all it takes to get free lunch?" Oscar laughed, "I will start whistling every day when you start to get hangry."

"Where do you want to go?" I asked, trying to keep the growl from my voice.

"Don't you want to pick?" Oscar asked, surprised.

Any other time, yes, I did want to pick. Oscar had terrible taste when picking restaurants. Not to mention, with the luck I had recently, whatever place I picked, inevitably we would run into Jackie.

While I was starting to think Oscar was right about needing to talk to Jackie, I wasn't ready yet, so I thought it best to let Oscar pick—even if he picked the crappiest place in town.

"No, man, you pick," I conceded.

"Famous last words," Oscar chuckled.

I was nervous about what he would pick, but Oscar pulled into Penny's Diner, a place we frequented because we both liked the food there. It was nothing to write home to your mother about, but they gave us a generous discount when we came in. They had hearty soups and big sandwiches on their lunch menu that would fill you up for the rest of even the toughest of shifts.

I suddenly remembered why Oscar said it would be famous last words for me—he loved their fish sandwich and onion rings. Whenever he ate them, the cruiser smelled of it for days because it just kept sweating out of his pores until it finally worked its way out of his body.

"Come on, Romero, order something else," I pleaded as we walked into the diner and waited to be seated.

"You said I got to pick," he reminded me in a singsong tone.

My shoulders sagged as I resigned to my fate. Maybe I could get the server to make a 'mistake' and bring him fries instead of onion rings. He was too nice to send it back to the kitchen.

A cute blond server came to seat us.

"Good afternoon, officers. Table or booth?" she asked.

"Booth," Romero replied.

The server gestured for us to follow her, and I fell in step behind her. She was a cute blond girl, maybe 19 or 20. I admired her figure as she led the way to the table, providing a welcome distraction to my earlier thoughts of Jackie. I wasn't going to ask the girl out or anything, but I could appreciate a beautiful girl.

I took the seat facing back toward the direction of the door we came through, and Oscar sat across from me. When I glanced back at our server, I noted her name tag 'Lauren' and the extra button that was no longer buttoned, revealing the top of her lacy pink bra as she bent forward to put a menu before each of us.

"Do you know what you'd like, or do you need a minute?" she asked with a widening smile when she caught the momentary focus of my gaze.

"I know what I want," Romero chimed in, his charm flashing from across the table.

"What can I get for you?" she turned to Oscar and took down his order as he rattled it off.

"And what about you?" she asked, turning back to me, intentionally putting her pad down on the table so that her chest was basically in my face.

"I'd like the chicken tortilla soup and the Turkey club," I replied.

Romero was texting his wife, so I took the opportunity to collude with the server while he was distracted.

"Hey, can I see your pad and pen?" I asked in a conspiratorial tone.

She smiled and handed both to me. The poor girl probably thought I was going to write my name and phone number for her. Instead, I wrote her a quick note that there was an extra 20 dollars in it for her if she brought Romero fries instead of onion rings.

She looked down, and her face fell slightly, but then she looked up at me. With a smile and a wink, she headed off to put the order in with the kitchen.

"Carrollton, I'm surprised at you," Oscar scolded. "Here we are on the job and you're giving girls your phone number."

I just laughed, pretending he had caught me. He fell for my trick.

"Here I thought you were hung up on this Jackie Dominico," he said.

"D'Marco," I corrected without hesitation.

The bastard had the nerve to smile back, as though he had gotten me to admit to still being in love with her.

"I'm not hung up on her," I added quickly.

"Really? You talked about her practically the entire morning. I guess I misread the situation," he replied, feigning innocence.

"You did," I replied. "Jackie is in the past."

As soon as those words crossed my lips, a flash of chocolate brown hair flipping over the shoulder of a customer seated at the bar caught my eye over Oscar's shoulder.

"You've got to be fucking kidding me," I muttered loud enough for only Oscar to hear.

"What is it?" he asked, glancing over his shoulder.

I slid my hand over my face in exasperation and admitted, "She's here."

"No shit?" Romero perked up excitedly, looking around the restaurant, desperate to get a look at the girl that was driving me crazy.

"Would you stop?" I hissed at him. "You're making everyone nervous that you're looking for a hardened criminal in here. We're in uniform, remember?"

Oscar turned back to me and let out a huff of laughter.

"You're the only one nervous, Carrollton," he smirked. "Why don't you go say hi to her?"

"Now? What? Why?" I asked, panic forcing the questions to come out in a staccato fashion.

"Because clearly you need some answers to truly move on," Romero said compassionately. "Even if you don't want to be with her again, you clearly need some closure with this one."

Did I need closure? What did that even look like? How would that conversation even begin?

I must have asked at least the last question out loud, because Oscar replied to it.

"Usually 'Hello, can we get together and talk sometime?' is a good place to start," Oscar encouraged.

Taking in a few deep breaths, I nodded and got up from the booth to walk over to where Jackie was seated at the bar, conversing with one of the servers about their coffee selections. Both women laughed at something I couldn't quite hear. Hearing Jackie's laugh again after so many years softened my resolve to keep her at a distance. What I hadn't admitted to anyone, including myself, was how much I had missed her.

As I came up beside her, I took the stool next to her and cleared my throat. She whirled in my direction, her laughter stopping so abruptly she began coughing. When she finished, her dark brown eyes, wide as saucers, locked in on mine.

"Hi," I said.

Her mouth moved, trying to put together words, but nothing was coming out. It was cute.

"I swear I didn't follow you here," she offered in apology for being here.

"It would be really hard for you to...I got here after you," I answered calmly.

She nodded and took in my words.

We sat quietly, neither of us sure what to say, but the energy between us was buzzing madly. I'd dated and flirted with more women than I even remembered over the last three years, but none of them gave me the feeling the woman beside me did while saying nothing at all.

"Jackie," I asked, "do you think we could just get together sometime and clear the air?"

"Yeah," she cleared her throat and added, "Yes, of course."

"Good," I replied, a brief smile flashing. "Let me give you my phone number."

Nervous energy radiated so thickly between us I wasn't sure how much was coming from her and how much from me. Her hands shook as she fumbled through her large purse for her phone. She unlocked it and handed it to me.

I recognized the waft of perfume that lifted from her bag—Miss Dior. I bought that perfume for the last Christmas we spent together. The hint of florals was perfect when combined with the scent of her skin. She should wear nothing else.

I shook myself out of that thought and punched in my phone number and then pulled up her text messages and sent one to myself from her phone so that I would have her phone number before handing it back to her. Our hands brushed ever so slightly, sending chills up my arm.

"Thanks, I think it will be good for both of us," I said with more composure than I felt. "Talk to you soon?"

She nodded mutely, her hand frozen in the position I had put the phone into.

I stood and gave her shoulder a light squeeze, unable to resist the urge to touch her once more before turning back to find that Oscar had switched seats with me so he could watch the whole exchange without being conspicuous. He gave me a thumbs up and a wide grin.

I would have punched him, but my hand still tingled with the memory of touching Jackie's shoulder, and I wanted to savor that feeling a bit longer.

Right on cue, Lauren delivered our meals to the booth with fries instead of onion rings, per my request. Oscar looked down at his plate and back at me before mouthing 'asshole' in my direction, and I laughed a bit louder than I meant to.

I felt good after exchanging numbers with Jackie. We could set up a time to talk and finally leave the past behind us. Not to mention pulling one over on Romero was my favorite pastime.

I was no longer facing where Jackie was sitting, but it was suddenly clear that she had looked my way when she heard my laugh. I could feel her eyes on me. I always loved knowing when she was looking at me, like we had this invisible tie between us. The feeling now felt familiar and yet at the same time foreign. I wasn't sure I could ever get back to where we were, but something about still knowing when she looked at me made me feel off balance.

"Lauren," I said as she placed my order before me, "can you add the bill for the brown-haired woman at the counter to our bill? I'll make sure to tip you and the other server separately."

Lauren's head shot up, and her eyes traced their way over to the woman in question. I could see a look of disappointment cross her eyes, but I knew a woman like Lauren would move on and not think twice about this moment.

She nodded and headed to the counter to tell the other server. Oscar and I dug into our meals.

"So, you're paying for her lunch," Oscar jabbed at me with a wiggle of his eyebrows. "Smooth move."

"It's not a move; I'm just returning the gesture. She bought my breakfast the other day, remember?" I said and casually sipped the broth from my soup spoon.

"Right, I forgot, you don't have moves," he grinned and bit into one of his French fries.

He dropped the fry in his hand and pounded on the window beside him. Oscar's reflexes in his moves were so quick I almost took cover, but all I did was drop my spoon into my soup, which splattered some on the table.

I looked out the window and saw Jackie's beautiful face looking horrified. Oscar just waved at her and then held his hand up to his ear like a phone and then pointed at me.

"Call him!" Oscar said, over-exaggerating his mouth movements to make sure she understood him through the glass.

I was horrified at my partner's childlike behavior, but she laughed and gave him a thumbs up. Her eyes met mine and she waved to me before continuing on her way.

"See that, she's going to call you," Romero crowed as he picked up the fry he had dropped and shoved it into his grinning mouth.

"Carrollton! Why do you let your partner out in public?" A familiar voice boomed from behind me.

Pete Billings, my mentor on the force and good friend, walked up to our table, his arthritis giving a slight limp to his gait.

"They tell me it's unsafe to leave him alone in the car for extended periods of time," I grinned, extending my hand for the man's firm handshake.

"Hey, Pete, it's been a long time. How's retirement?" Oscar asked, scooting over in his seat to make room for Pete.

"It's miserable," he grumbled, taking the seat next to Oscar.

Romero and I both laughed at the older man's honesty. Secretly, I was grateful to Pete for stopping by and breaking Oscar's laser focus on the topic of Jackie.

"Start watching some telenovelas, they play on TV during the day," Romero suggested.

"I retired; that doesn't come with a lobotomy," Pete barked. "I started working as a chauffeur, driving rich people around town just so I didn't have to accept that torture."

"Judy let you?" I asked, surprised.

Despite Pete's commanding presence on the force, his wife Judy definitely wore the pants in their relationship.

"She insisted," he laughed.

As I was taking the last bites of my turkey club, I felt my phone vibrate against my hip. I pulled it out to find first the text from Jackie that I had sent:

> **Jackie:** Jackie D'Marco's new number

Then another text from her just a minute ago:

> **Jackie:** Thank you for buying my lunch. Maybe we can get together after Francine's surgery?

> **Kyle:** Sure. We can do that.

Francine's surgery was coming up soon enough. Waiting until afterward to hear something I likely didn't want to hear in the first place would be soon enough for me, anyway.

"Is that your girl?" Oscar asked in a singsong voice.

"Carrollton's got a girl?" Pete echoed.

"It's Jackie, if that's what you mean," I replied nonchalantly.

"Jackie who?" Pete asked. "Did you check her record?"

A laugh burst from my chest at Pete's protectiveness.

"Jackie D'Marco," Oscar answered for me.

"D'Marco?" Pete's brow furrowed, and he stroked his mustache thoughtfully. "Isn't she the one that got away?"

"She came back for our boy," Oscar crowed. "You just missed it, Pete. He's smitten."

"I'm not smitten," I grumbled, shoving my phone back into my pocket.

Heat crept up my neck and across my face. It was too soon to know what I felt, but smitten sure as hell wasn't it.

"I see smitten all over your face," Oscar insisted. "Look, his ears are turning red."

"Smitten or not, you should still dig into her before you do anything," Pete warned.

"Her record is clean, Pete," I replied, frustrated with two men now on my case.

"What is she doing back here?" Pete asked, his tone sounding a little angry rather than curious.

Oscar and I exchanged looks, both of us uneasy with Pete's tone.

"She moved back to help my sister for a bit and to be closer to her remaining family," I answered cautiously.

Pete nodded and stood abruptly from the table.

"It was good running into you both, but my order is ready at the counter," Pete said and made his way to the counter for his order. Oscar and I both watched him leave before we looked back at each other. My partner looked just as confused as I felt.

"Was that weird, or is it just me?" he asked.

"Definitely weird," I replied.

CHAPTER 5

Snack Attack and Dinner Invitations

Jackie
June 29, 2017

Francine was snoring loudly in the passenger seat of my Ford Fusion on the way home from her gastric bypass surgery. She had insisted that her brothers all go about their days and come to see her later. They agreed to come after they'd had dinner, since she was on a restricted diet post-surgery.

I glanced over at my friend and noticed how well she had done losing weight prior to her surgery, and a twinge of jealousy tugged at my heart. She was beautiful, even with the extra pounds she carried. She had even turned down modeling jobs offered by several plus-size clothing lines. For her to want to change her body was a big deal. I was certain her dad's heart attack must have really gotten to her, and she wanted to do better for herself. I was so proud of her for that. I just wish I had an ounce of her willpower with baked goods—they were my weakness.

"Jackie! Don't let the Doritos get me!" Francine mumbled urgently in her sleep, her arms twitching in her lap.

"They won't get you, Frannie," I assured her with a laugh, "we're driving away from them now."

She seemed to be reassured by my words, and went back to snoring, her arms relaxing once more. Our talk about all the food she would miss before she was taken back for surgery must still be on her mind.

When I pulled into the driveway at her house, I woke her by gently nudging her shoulder. Her eyes opened, but barely.

"Where are we? Did we get away from the Doritos Gang?" she asked groggily.

"We're home," I replied confidently. "We left them in the dust."

"Good, 'cuz my feet are getting too sleepy to run anymore," she muttered.

"Well, your feet just have to be awake enough to walk inside the house and to the couch," I replied, getting out of the car and crossing over to her side to help her walk in.

"Why?" she whined.

"Because you can't stay out here in the car. It's too hot," I explained, as though I was speaking to an obstinate toddler.

"But what if the Doritos Gang teams up with the Cheetos Bandits? How will we get away?" she asked as I lifted her legs up and out of the car.

"We don't need to worry about them. I fed them all to Jabba the Hutt," I replied, playing into her story.

"Oh good," she said, wrapping her arm around my shoulder so that I could help her stand.

"Come on, Frannie, we're going inside now," I cajoled her.

Francine walked with me slowly from the car, up the three stairs of her porch and to her front door. As I dug through the pocket of my purse, she leaned forward and rang her own doorbell.

"Jackie, I don't think anyone is here. Maybe we should come back later," she suggested. "Can we go home now?"

"Honey, this is our home. I just didn't have the keys pulled out," I told her, putting the key in and opening the door.

"Oh!" she squealed in delight as though she had won the house on The Price is Right. "I like what you've done with the place."

"Thanks," I laughed as we walked from the foyer into the living room.

"Hey, wait, isn't this my parent's house?" she asked suspiciously as I helped her sit on the couch.

"It was, but you bought it about a year ago," I reminded her.

"Oh yeah," she laughed. "Would you tell my mom that I want my fuzzy socks and my comforter, please?"

"I'll get them for you," I said, helping her lie down on the couch.

"Thanks, Jacks...you're good people," she said, squishing the pillow under her head until it was to her liking.

"Stay here. I'll be right back," I ordered.

"Aye, aye, Captain," she replied before starting her even pattern of snoring once more.

I rushed to her bedroom and grabbed her blue fuzzy socks from the bench at the end of her bed and the king-sized comforter from her bed and went back out to tuck her in and put the fuzzy socks on her feet.

When I got her settled in, I made a nest for myself on the second couch with the quilt Nonnie had made for me and fell asleep, too. We'd gotten up at five this morning to get over to the hospital for her procedure, and that was a bit early for me. Besides, I was close enough to her that if she woke up and needed something, it would wake me, too. Well, at least that's what I had thought.

I was so sound asleep that I didn't hear Kyle Carrolton at all. He had come in through the front door using his key, used the bathroom, changed his clothes, and poured himself a glass of water, all without waking either of us. The move that finally startled me awake was him sweetly tucking the quilt back up around my shoulders as it had started to fall on the ground. I gasped loudly in surprise and jerked back quickly. He held up his hands as if I were holding a gun.

"Sorry," he whispered, lowering his hands, "I was just trying to keep the blanket from hitting the floor."

I sat up and pulled the quilt back up over my shoulders as I shifted to an upright position. My heart raced in my chest as I looked at him. He was so handsome with his neatly trimmed beard. I shook away the thought and sleepiness and allowed myself to respond.

"I just didn't hear you come in," I explained. "When did you get here?"

"About 15 minutes ago. I didn't mean to wake you," he apologized again.

Apologies or politeness seemed to be all we could manage at that point. I hated the awkwardness that seemed to loom between us like a rain cloud.

"It's okay," I assured him. "I didn't mean to fall asleep so hard. It was an early morning."

He nodded and asked, "How did everything go?"

"It all went fine. She's having some funny reactions to the anesthesia, but they said everything went according to plan." I smiled.

"Funny reactions?" he asked.

As if on cue, Francine mumbled out loud, "Marshmallows are on the attack! We need to deploy the Rice Krispies to trap them."

Kyle turned back to me with his dark eyebrow raised. My mouth shook, trying to hold in my burst of laughter, and his mouth slid into the easy grin I've always loved so much. We both burst out laughing and woke Francine.

"What are you two laughing about?" she asked, annoyance coloring her tone.

"We heard you fart in your sleep," Kyle said, being the pesky brother that Francine brought out in him.

"If you heard it, it wasn't a fart...I'm a lady," she replied and then added, "it was probably you."

He and I looked at each other and burst out laughing again. We didn't expect that to be her response. When we were kids, Francine would claim that she doesn't fart at all or that when she does, only glitter and rainbows come out—something ridiculous.

"So along with half of your stomach, they re-routed the rainbows and glitter that used to come out?" he asked suspiciously.

"Well, I don't see any, do you?" she asked, sitting up and gingerly rubbing her eyes.

"Hard to say. You have a comforter big enough for six people wrapped around you—maybe it's stuck in there somewhere," he replied, sitting down beside her and lifting the edges of her blanket as if he was checking for it.

"You're a jerk," Francine sighed, punching his shoulder and then wrapping her arms around her brother's middle, snuggling into his side. "You're supposed to be here taking care of me, not teasing me."

He gently put his arm around her shoulder and squeezed. "Yes, but I can do both proficiently. I'm that good."

"Oh God, help me," Francine cried out, looking up at the ceiling.

Watching Kyle and Francine together brought on a rush of memories. Time spent in this house over the years: fighting with the boys like they were my brothers too, then growing to love Kyle and sneaking out of Francine's room to kiss him for an hour or two before I returned to her room while Mr. and Mrs. C. slept, peaceful and unknowing across the hall.

An ache filled my chest as I remembered taking pictures with the two of them in our caps and gowns on graduation day, promising to come over to their house even though I knew I wouldn't be there. Tears welled in my eyes, but I refused to let them fall. I stood abruptly, and they both looked at me like I had jumped out of the bushes at them.

"Do you need something, Frannie?" I asked suddenly, desperate for something to do. Kyle's protective energy was so close it overwhelmed me, and I needed some space to breathe.

"No, I'm fine," she replied, snuggling further into Kyle's chest.

My heart melted as I watched him rest his chin on top of his sister's head. I'd seen him do this only once before, after he, Jason, and Ben had beaten the crap out of Francine's ex-boyfriend, Jared, when he made a very public spectacle of dumping her at our homecoming dance sophomore year. It was one of the things that made me fall in love with him all those years ago.

I nodded and walked out of the room to at least stretch my legs and use the bathroom. I couldn't stop thinking about all the things that made me love this man. He was so easy to love. At the same time, I knew he deserved to move on from us if that is what he wanted to do. After the way I left, I had no right to hold on to him. I would have to accept that before he and I had our 'talk.'

As I finished up in the bathroom and washed my hands, I could hear Ben's boisterous voice as he entered the house, announcing that he and Jason were there. The Carrolltons used to joke that Jason had let Ben take all the words. Ben could talk until he went hoarse and kept ongoing. Jason, on the other hand, was quiet and studious. Francine and Kyle were somewhere in the middle but often at each other's throats—being only about nine or ten months apart, they were often competing for their parents' attention, starting at a very young age. It was nice to see them cuddled on the couch earlier. I'd even heard Kyle say 'I love you' when Francine had him on speakerphone one morning. That was new for them—their family was very loving, just not verbally so.

I returned to the living room to find Ben and Jason flanking Francine, and Kyle sitting on the couch with my neatly folded quilt draped across the back. In the accent chair sat Francine's coworker, Shreya, who I had met back in Chicago.

"Wow, full house," I smiled.

"Hi Jackie," Ben smiled back. "How did everything go?"

"The doctors said it went well. She's been funny coming off the anesthesia, but aside from that, no side effects so far," I replied.

"What a relief," Shreya said.

I smiled at her and nodded in agreement.

"Did you get to eat?" Jason asked, abruptly changing the conversation.

I hadn't even thought about food all day, but suddenly I felt my stomach rumble a reminder. The nearest vending machine had been out of order, so while Francine was in surgery, I just had some coffee, and I guess that tricked me into feeling full up to that point.

"No, not yet," I admitted, putting my hand to my belly, hoping to quiet it.

"Why don't you go out and get something?" Ben suggested. "We can stay here and keep an eye on Frannie until you get back."

"I was getting ready to head out, anyway. I'll walk out with you," Kyle offered.

"You didn't have dinner before you came?" Ben asked.

"No, I came here right after work to check on our sister," he replied pointedly.

Instinctively, I began to ask Kyle to go to dinner with me but held my tongue. He probably just wanted to go home and rest after a long day. I desperately wanted to know what his home looked like, but that would be even more inappropriate to ask to see than asking him to go to dinner with me.

"Are you coming back after?" Francine asked, though it was a bit muffled as her face was stuck halfway in the crook of Jason's neck.

For a moment, I thought Francine was talking to me until Kyle spoke.

"Not sure. If I don't, I'll come check on you tomorrow," Kyle promised.

"Okay, I love you both. Please be safe," Francine said.

"We will," Kyle assured her, giving her knee a squeeze and then walking past me to the door.

"I'll be back in a little while," I announced unnecessarily.

"See you soon, sis," Jason smiled at me.

Outside, Kyle was pacing by the driver's side of his car, which was parked behind mine.

When he saw me, he stood stone-still and locked eyes with me.

"Do you want to just come to dinner with me?" he asked. "The way our luck has been, we'd end up at the same place, anyway."

We both laughed. My heart was going to explode out of my chest, but I did promise to have a conversation with him to 'clear the air' after Francine's surgery. Dinner seemed like a harmless way to do this. Even though I was not ready, we needed to talk.

"Okay," I replied, and as I walked to his car, he made his way over to the passenger side and opened the door for me.

As quickly as my appetite had appeared earlier, my nerves about the situation devoured the feeling. I don't think I could eat a thing if I tried. My hands shook as I pulled my seatbelt down and across my lap, but I couldn't get it to fasten. Kyle took it from my hand and pushed it into the clasp with ease.

"Now you're stuck with me," he teased, but there was more there. A spark fired in his light brown eyes that I recognized from when he used to love me. My body tingled in long suffering silence, remembering the way his thick fingers used to trace all his favorite parts of me. Chills raced down my arms, standing every hair on end. Was that love for me still in his heart, hidden beneath the hurt and all the things we hadn't said? Could what I have to say heal the hurt and bring our love back into the light?

I sucked in a deep breath, certain he could see all my thoughts as they raced through my mind one by one. Instead, he just calmly started his car and backed out of Francine's driveway. When I let out the breath I was holding, a peaceful thought washed over me: wherever we were going, we were going there together.

CHAPTER 6

The "Talk"

Kyle
June 29, 2017

This conversation was going to happen on my terms, so I didn't even ask where she wanted to eat. We were going to the restaurant we went to before prom, Chevy's Steakhouse. It would bring both of our minds back to the moments leading up to her decision to leave. I hadn't been back to Chevy's since that night, and it was time to exorcise this ghost from my life once and for all.

I unbuckled myself and looked over to see if she needed a hand, since the buckle on that side could be tricky. When I looked at her, the neon sign illuminated her beautiful face in alternating red and green hues as the sign flashed against the darkening skyline ahead of us. Despite that, I could see that the tone of her skin had gone green too.

"Jackie?" I asked, "Are you okay?"

A tear trickled down her cheek as she continued to stare forward at the sign flashing ahead of us. Her fingers pinched and tugged nervously at the bit of fabric that was loose closest to her knee but said nothing.

"Jacks?" I asked again, using her old nickname, this time putting my hand over hers.

She startled and met my eyes with her beautiful browns, tears pooling on her dark lower lashes.

"Kyle, this is where you took me for prom," she whispered.

The bittersweet memories of the night flooded into my mind, and I wondered if it might have been a bad idea to bring her back. Instead, I waited a few seconds for her to say more, and when she didn't, I replied, "Yeah...is that okay?"

She nodded yes, which allowed two streams of tears to slip down her cheeks. She wiped at them with a huff, embarrassed.

"Are you ready to go in?" I asked gently.

She nodded again, wiping her cheeks once more to make sure there were no more tears there. She unbuckled and got out of the car. Knowing that I had made her cry broke down the toughness I had come in with. We walked past the glass front of the building to the entrance. I desperately wanted to take her hand to comfort her, but couldn't bring myself to do it. We were close enough that we brushed against each other; it would have been easy...instinctual.

When we got inside, the smell of steak and freshly baked bread permeated the air and flooded me with more memories of the last time we were here. I had made reservations, and we had a special table on the rooftop surrounded by rose petals and candles. It cost a fortune to reserve, but the look on her face was worth every extra shift I had picked up to pay for it myself.

We stood at the podium and waited to be seated. They had remodeled the bar area with dark wood cabinets and a black top since our last visit. It was beautiful before, but the warm wood tones really brought out an atmosphere of romance and sophistication that Chevy's didn't quite have before. I wondered if they required a jacket or tie now.

"Hi folks, just two of you tonight?" the older host asked us.

"Yes, just two," I confirmed.

"Follow me, please," he smiled.

Reflexively, I put my hand against the small of Jackie's back and guided her ahead of me as we weaved between tables in the busy restaurant. I couldn't help but watch her hips as she walked. The sway as she walked mesmerized me despite my best efforts to keep my distance.

I followed to her side of the table and held out the chair for her to sit before taking the seat facing her. The host handed each of us a leather-bound menu.

"Would you like the wine menu, sir?" the host asked me.

I made eye contact with Jackie, asking her with just a shrug of my shoulders. She shook her head no...guess we were doing this one sober. Okay.

"No, thank you," I replied to the host.

"Very good, sir. Your server will be with you shortly," the host smiled and left to return to his podium.

We sat quietly perusing the menu while we waited for our server. Awkwardness hung in the air like summer humidity, making it feel like you were trying to breathe air that was too thick for your lungs to process.

"The last time we were here, we were too young to order wine," Jackie remarked, breaking the silence that had been hovering between us.

I set my menu down and smiled at her, grateful that she had said something first so that I could relax into the conversation she had started.

"Hard to believe it was that long ago," I agreed.

She nodded. "But it was a great night."

My body tensed—was she just saying that? I thought it had been a great night. She looked like a queen that night—my queen. She had pinned her soft brown hair back from her face, leaving a mane of curls flowing down her back from the top of her head. Her dress was black and sparkled with dark red gemstones over the top of the gown. We got a hotel that night and made love for the first and last time. She left the next day, right after graduation. I always wondered if prom night was part of the reason she left without a word.

"So, I didn't hurt you?" I asked, desperately wanting to know the answer to the first and most important question. The one that had weighed so desperately and heavy on my mind when she left.

Her hand clutched mine quickly on top of the table, her forehead furrowed in sympathy as she reassured me, "Oh, Kyle, no! That night was the best night of my life. You were so sweet to me."

I let out the breath I had been holding, and she released my hand when the server approached our table.

"Good evening," the young man said. "What can I get you to drink?"

"I'd like a Coke, and she'll have ice water, no lemon," I replied, my reflexes once again taking over.

The server nodded and rushed off.

"Shit, I'm sorry. I should have let you order your own drink," I apologized to Jackie.

"It's fine; that's what I wanted," she smiled. "You remembered."

I felt the tips of my ears heat with embarrassment. I remembered everything that had to do with Jackie D'Marco.

The server came back with our drinks and asked what we would like to order.

"Can I have the chicken cordon bleu with green beans and roasted red potatoes?" Jackie asked.

"And for you, sir?" the server asked me.

"I'd like the ribeye steak medium rare with roasted red potatoes and green beans," I answered.

"I'll get that over to the chef for you," the server beamed before scurrying back to the kitchen.

Jackie picked up her water and took a sip, her throat working with the action. She was nervous. Hell, so was I! Her chest heaved a heavy breath in and out of her lungs, steadying herself for the conversation ahead.

"You probably already know some of this, but the police arrested my parents for embezzling money from their company and clients for a little more than a year. About halfway through our senior year, I suspected something was going on with them and asked Nonni what she thought since she had helped Nonno with the business side of the restaurant before he passed away." She began.

I nodded. I knew her parents had been arrested shortly after Jackie had left Brooklyn. Through my mentor, Pete, at the police department, I learned Jackie was not accused or convicted in relation to any of the crimes they committed, but Pete either couldn't or wouldn't tell me how to find her.

"Nonni and I became informants on the case, turning in evidence of the suspicious activity that ultimately led to their conviction," she continued. "Nonni was planning to move to Chicago after I graduated. Her new boyfriend had moved there to revive a bakery that was failing because of his son's mismanagement. She insisted I come with her and go to school there and work at the bakery since my parents' names would be in the news for years and no one would want to hear or see the name D'Marco here."

My blood boiled in my veins. Nonni knew I had planned to propose at my graduation party the day after graduation, so her D'Marco name wouldn't have been a problem for long. Nonni was worried I would get Jackie pregnant before she finished school and she would have to rely entirely on me, a kid that had been working at a bakery for two years with nothing to show for it. Yeah, I knew where 'Jackie's opinion' of my job came from.

"I applied to schools in Chicago just in case I decided to go," she explained. "I didn't know what would come of the case, and you know how much I wanted to be a teacher. I was accepted at the University of Chicago, among others. I waited to see what would happen with my parents."

Jackie continued, "The police waited until after the graduation ceremony to arrest my parents. They seized all our bank accounts, including mine and Nonni's. They needed to see if any of the stolen funds traced back to our accounts. Nonni called her boyfriend, and he wired money for us. We took what we could to Chicago. My uncle came later and got Nonni's furniture and moved it into storage until she could arrange to get it. I had no choice but to go with her that night."

"You could have come to me," I growled. "You know that I would have made sure you were safe and had everything you needed."

The server came back with our plates and, feeling the tension at the table, fled quickly after placing them before us.

"You're right, I could have," she admitted, "but I was so ashamed of what my parents had done. Your parents invested with them too, and I'm sure they lost a lot of money. Not to mention, as soon as the news broke, Nonni and I—even my uncle—began receiving threats from people that wanted their money back. It was so scary."

"I would have protected you," I insisted stubbornly.

"And who would have protected you?" she asked, frustrated with my obstinate attitude toward her very real concerns. "You have no idea how many threats we were getting on a daily basis. Email, social media, messages on our cars, phone calls, bags of dog crap set on fire on the porch step at the restaurant. It was terrible."

I felt the furrow in my brows soften toward her at the thought of my tender-hearted Jackie getting messages that upset her to the point she left behind everything she knew and loved. Back then, I was just a dumb kid who thought he had his life figured out: marry my girl, put her through school, have a family. Would the news and the threats have separated us even if she hadn't gone to Chicago? I wanted to think I was all she ever needed to be safe and happy, but would I have been?

"You're right, I had no idea," I sighed, my tone softened as I began cutting into my steak, "but Jackie, Francine and I were so worried about you. We requested the police do a welfare check on you."

"I know. They did, and when I explained to them what was going on, they suggested I continue to keep my distance at least until after the case had gone all the way through the court system. They told me they would at least assure you both that I was okay and would reach out as soon as I could," she replied, wringing her napkin with her hands.

"Yeah, well, they didn't," I complained, "and you never reached out. The only reason you're here now is because Francine happened to pass you on the streets of Chicago!"

"You're right," she bowed her head in shame, using her fork to push her food around her plate now. "I made choices in the face of what was an impossible decision. I can see now that they were all the wrong choices, and I wish I had chosen a different path. There are not enough things I can do or say to make it right, but I knew I at least owed you some answers. When

I saw Francine, I realized it was time to stop running, stop hiding, and come home."

We sat quietly for a while, taking a few bites of our dinners—mine would have been delicious if it weren't for the acid in my stomach creeping up my throat. I was sad. Sad for the girl I loved, who saw her family crumbling before her eyes. Sad about the loss of time we should have had together. Sad for the people that were stolen from. Sad for the boy who told himself that love was a lie for the last five years to protect his heart from the biggest loss he'd ever experienced. Sad for the girl who had lost everything she cared about.

Above all, I was angry. Angry at her parents for their crime. Angry at Nonni for taking Jackie from me. Angry at Jackie for agreeing to go. Most of all, I was angry at myself for not searching to the ends of the earth for her. My wounded ego wouldn't let me do it, and now I regret I hadn't just set it aside to be with her at all costs. Sitting at this table, as awkward as it was, was the only place in the world I wanted to be—near Jackie D'Marco.

"Does that mean you plan to stay once Francine is back on her feet?" I asked as casually as I could manage.

She looked up, startled by the sound of my voice breaking her thoughts.

"I was planning to. There's really nothing for me in Chicago," she admitted and then added in a smaller voice, "Unless you want me to go?"

My eyes locked fiercely on hers, and I told her my truth. "No, I don't want you to go."

I saw relief and the faintest of smiles draw over her face as she replied, "Then I won't."

I nodded, feeling we had settled that. We went back to eating silently. Jackie ate at a more normal pace, which made the tension ease from my shoulders a bit.

Jackie cut several pieces of her chicken before resting her knife on the side. She scooped up a piece with her fork and placed it on the side of my plate and then went back and stabbed the second piece for herself.

I couldn't help but smile at her gesture as I stuck my fork into the piece of chicken she had given me and raised it to my mouth. It was perfect. The breading was crispy, the chicken was tender, and the ham was a nice salty contrast to the creamy cheese filling. I would have moaned out loud if I were eating at home—it was that good.

When I looked across the table at Jackie, I found her eyes on me and her lips pinched together to keep from laughing.

"What, did I get sauce in my beard?" I asked, picking up my napkin and wiping over my face.

"No," she giggled, "you just looked like you were having a moment with that chicken, is all."

"Oh, well, I was," I admitted as I laughed too, "that is really good."

"It is," she agreed. "How is your ribeye?"

"Amazing," I replied, holding out a bite on my fork to her.

She took my fork from me and brought the bite to her mouth and moaned a little. My heart raced at the memory that sound brought forth of our one special night together.

"That is amazing," she agreed, handing my fork back to me. "Have you tried your potatoes yet? So good!"

I nodded and pointed to the green beans on the plate with my fork. "Wait til you get to the green beans. You may never be the same."

She grinned and stabbed a few with her fork and lifted it into her mouth. When the flavors hit her tongue, she shimmied her shoulders in her chair in the little dance she did when something was tasty.

"Oh my God, yum!" she said, continuing to dance in her chair as she stabbed more and shoved them in her mouth.

"Good, right?" I laughed, digging back into mine.

"So good," she agreed.

We were both lovers of food. It was good to see this side of her come back out. The awkwardness that had hung between us before this date seemed to lift. Wait, did I just say date?

"You remember the tiramisu we got here last time?" she asked, interrupting my wayward thoughts.

"Yes, we should get some," I suggested.

She nodded vigorously. "I could bathe in that stuff! It was so good."

Now there was an image my already snug pants did not need for two reasons: a naked Jackie covered in tiramisu…I cleared my throat and did my best to rid my mind of the delicious mental image.

Thankfully, she didn't notice my discomfort as she went back to eating her dinner. When the server popped by to check on us, we ordered the tiramisu. I finally calmed down and began eating again, too.

"Can I ask you something?" She looked up.

My mouth was full, so I nodded and took a sip of my Coke.

"What made you decide to become a police officer?" she asked. "When we talked about different jobs you were interested in, it wasn't one that came up."

She was right. I loved my job at Holy Cannoli. I thought I could hold on to that and work my way up to manager so that I could pay for our housing expenses while she got through college. Janice even considered training me to take over the business when she was ready to retire.

"When I was working at Holy Cannoli, there was an officer who came in almost every day and ordered the same thing. Officer Pete Billings. He came in one day when we were being robbed. The kid robbing us freaked out when he saw Pete in uniform, turned around and shot him. I didn't want anyone else to get hurt, so I tackled the kid while his back was to me. The kid dropped his gun, and I kept him pinned down until more officers could get there to apprehend him," I said.

Jackie's eyes grew large. "Kyle, you could have been killed!"

"Subduing opponents with weapons was something we practiced when I took martial arts as a kid. It all came back to me. I was never so grateful that my dad wanted his children to grow up to be the Teenage Mutant Ninja Turtles," I continued, brushing aside her concern, "Pete was fine—he was off duty for a few months recovering but Janice gave him free donuts for the rest of the year."

"I don't know if that is a fair trade-off for getting shot," Jackie sighed.

"Probably not, but you have to admit they are damn good donuts," I smirked. "When Pete was recovering, he would come in and we would talk about different takedown techniques and stories about his police academy days. It became the thing I looked forward to most every day. One day Pete asked me when I was going to apply to the academy, and it really got me thinking that I should. I was tired of feeling like a loser still working the same job since I was sixteen years old, so I asked him to get me the information. When I got my badge number, I knew I was right where I was supposed to be."

"Why? What's your badge number?" she asked.

"55228," I replied.

"Our birthdays..." she said in a whisper.

I nodded. Mine is May 5th; hers is February 28th.

The server set the plate of tiramisu between us with two clean forks.

"Enjoy," he said and left the bill at the end of the table.

I snagged it and put my card in the folder.

"You don't have to buy my dinner, Kyle," she said, but her smile told me I had done the right thing.

I waved her off with my hand. "Shut up and have some tiramisu."

Her smile widened, and she picked up the fork on her side of the plate. I waited while she slipped her fork into the dessert and lifted the bite to her mouth. Her eyes rolled back into her head with pleasure. Damn, this girl was going to kill me!

Instead of thinking about that any further, I took a bite of the dessert on my side and had a similar reaction. Chevy's had the best tiramisu in Brooklyn. Hands down.

The server came back and took my card with him to process payment for our meal while we finished enjoying the coffee-flavored heaven we'd been served.

When the server brought back my card, I put it in my wallet, signed the slip with a generous tip, and walked Jackie back out to my car.

I helped her with the belt again and started up the car. She looked over and pointed to my keys hanging from the ignition.

"You still have it?" she asked. "The Saint Christopher keychain I got you after you wrecked your car junior year?"

I looked over and nodded. "It's kept me safe. I haven't even had a speeding ticket since you gave it to me."

Jackie smiled at that and began digging in her purse. She pulled out a black velvet bag and handed it to me.

"What's this?" I asked, opening the top of the bag and carefully pouring the contents into my palm. It was a similar medallion, but this one was on a long, thick silver chain.

"This is Saint Michael, the patron saint of police officers. I bought this before I left Chicago when Francine told me you had become a police officer. I wanted you to be protected," she explained.

"Thanks, Jacks," I replied, slipping the chain over my head. The medallion rested right over my heart.

"You're welcome," she smiled. "We'd better get back now. I'm sure Ben and Jason want to get on with their days."

I nodded and took off for Francine's house. We were quiet during the ride home, but this was a more comfortable silence between two people with full bellies than the awkward silence we'd had before our dinner.

When we pulled in, I walked her to the door. It felt strange walking her up to the door that had been my home for so long, but I could feel the buzzing energy of desire to kiss her at the door. She must have too because she turned around to face me before opening the door.

One kiss wouldn't hurt, right?

As I leaned down toward her, my idiot brother Ben opened the door and ruined the moment.

"Oops, sorry, kids!" he said to us before turning back to the group in the living room and yelling, "Frannie, Jason owes you five bucks!"

"Five dollars for what?" I demanded, following Jackie into the house.

"That you two actually would come back from dinner together," Jason grumbled, slapping a five-dollar bill into Francine's open palm.

"Ben would owe me five dollars too if he hadn't gone and interrupted the kiss that was about to happen," Francine beamed.

"There was no kiss about to happen, right Kyle?" Ben asked hopefully.

"Nothing happened," I seethed.

At the sound of my words, Jackie wilted a little, but it was true. We had dinner and cleared the air. We made room to be friends with each other again. The idea of kissing her was just a reflex—it didn't mean we were back together or on our way to being, right?

I turned on my heel and stormed out of the house, leaving the sound of my siblings' laughter behind me. I really needed to see my family less.

CHAPTER 7

Grown-up Girl Talk and Crushes

Jackie
July 4, 2017

I'd been dying to talk to Francine about my dinner with Kyle for days, but I knew I was here to care for her and that was what I was going to do. She had been a dulled-down version of herself since her surgery but finally seemed to be returning to normal.

"How are you doing? Can I get you anything?" I asked as Francine shifted her position on the couch.

"Can you bring my supplements and a glass of water, please?" she requested.

I went to the kitchen and brought the glass of water and supplements back to her.

"Thank you," she said, taking them from me.

I sat on the couch beside her and picked up the TV remote to see what we could watch next. She swallowed her supplements with the aid of the water and then turned her sharp focus on me.

"Now, I want to hear about your dinner with my brother," she giggled like when we used to talk about the boys we had crushes on in middle school.

With a laugh at her giddiness, relief washed over me as I turned and folded my legs Indian-style so I could face her on the couch. She clapped her hands in anticipation, knowing I was going to share the scoop about the evening with her. My heart beat a quick, steady tattoo, excited to finally get to share what happened that night with my very best friend.

"Kyle took me to Chevy's Steakhouse," I began, "SOOO good. They had these amazing green beans..."

"Jackie! I don't want to hear about the food," she complained.

"Oh sorry," I winced, remembering she was still limited on what she could eat, and she hadn't been feeling very good to boot, "anyway, we got there and when we were being taken back to our table, he put his hand on my back and pulled out my chair for me."

"Aww!" Francine squealed. "Then what?"

"Then I spilled my guts about what happened with my parents and why I left and why I didn't communicate with you guys," I continued.

Francine made a circle with her hand for me to continue on to the good stuff.

"Okay well, it was quiet and awkward for a little while after that, until just out of habit, I cut a bite of my dinner and put it on his plate, and he smiled. He smiled, Francine," I gushed.

She squeezed my hands, excited for me, and I squeezed back before releasing them.

"It was like that one small thing unlocked our old rhythm. The rest of the night felt so natural, like no time had passed. I even gave him the pendant I bought him in Chicago. He put it on right away," I smiled.

"That's great!" Francine cheered. "Are you guys going out again soon?"

"Well, that's the thing," I replied, puzzled. "When we got back here, I thought for sure he was going to kiss me goodnight on the porch until Ben opened the door. But the way he acted when we came in, I think I may have just been wishing for something he wasn't ready for. He hasn't called or sent any texts. Maybe he is just content now that he knows what happened and wants nothing else to do with me?"

"Jacqueline Christine D'Marco, you know my idiot brother shuts down when someone catches him being mushy. With Ben's big mouth announcing your near kiss, Kyle just got rattled. I'm sure if you talk to him, he will agree to go out again."

I knew that about Kyle. He had his romantic moments, but each of those was balanced with at least two emotionally constipated moments. Still, I couldn't help but wonder if every gesture that night was just a reflex from when we were together. I knew he had at least dated other girls, which hurt so much. I desperately wanted to know what his situation was, but at the same time, I didn't.

"Francine, are you sure he's not with someone at the moment?" I asked, taking a deep breath before I continued. "Shortly after I came back to town, I bumped into him at CVS, and he was buying condoms."

Francine burst out in laughter, "Let's just say they didn't get used."

I wrinkled my brows. "Are you telling me Kyle told his one and only sister about not being able to perform on his date?"

Francine's laughter turned into a cackle. "Oh my God, no! He called his one and only sister to tell her to keep her best friend on a leash because that was the third time in a week that he had run into you. A few days later, he told me he canceled the date because he was afraid they would just run into you while they were out. He was probably right—I think you guys ended up running into each other that day with whatever his alternate plans were."

I sat quietly with that information, twisting a loose thread on the couch around my finger. Just because he canceled one date with this woman doesn't mean they weren't an item. Then again, a date beforehand was not required for sex. Didn't people in dangerous lines of work like this have a bevy of beautiful women ready for booty calls at all hours of the day and night? He could have several women just waiting their turn for him. I wasn't sure which idea was worse...Kyle having one special woman in his life or a harem of women to meet his every fantasy.

"Jackie, look at me," Francine ordered.

When I met her blue eyes, they flashed fiercely.

"Kyle has not been on a date or had sex or whatever you may be imagining with anyone since he pulled you over," Francine assured me.

"How do you know?" I whimpered, desperate for her words to be true.

"Because he was bitching to Ben about it, and Ben told us when you left for dinner. That's why we made the bets," she grinned widely.

For some reason, that made me feel better, but it didn't fully reassure me. Just because there wasn't someone special right now, it didn't mean he hadn't had someone special in the years I was away. What if he loved her more than he loved me?

"Listen, it may take some time," Francine said. "He was really hurt and confused when you left. Give him a little while to process your conversation."

I nodded. I knew she was right. Kyle had a hard time working through big emotions. He just needed time. I had nothing but time to give. I just hoped that the time would lead us back to one another.

"Now, I have been dying to know: what are all these papers you've been shuffling through?" Francine asked, pointing to the accordion file that I had been sorting through over the last week or so.

I blushed—I didn't realize she had noticed since I usually did it while she was napping—but I thought maybe she could help me.

"You remember when that file folder fell out of the desk when the boys were moving it in?" I asked.

Francine nodded.

"Well, I looked at the documents in the file and they look like a few documents that Nonni and I had collected and turned into the police as evidence in my parent's case," I continued, "funds transfer documents to a random Swiss bank account and one in the Cayman Islands."

"Okay, so Nonni kept a copy. What's so weird about that?" Francine asked.

"That's what I thought at first too, but when I looked at the e-signature, it had a pin number like theirs to verify the e-signature, but the signature on there was mine. As far as I know, my parents never signed me up in their system, so it looks like they were trying to frame me for the embezzlement," I explained.

"Then why keep the filed copy you guys turned into the police with their e-signatures?" Francine wondered.

"I don't know. It doesn't make sense, right?" I asked.

"Not to me, anyway!" Francine agreed with a shrug.

She sat quietly for a moment and then grew excited with an idea.

"You should ask Kyle to come look at this stuff with you!" she said with the widest grin her face could stretch into.

"What? No! I'm sure he doesn't want to do police work after his long day is over," I replied dismissively.

"Are you kidding? He loves that crap 24/7," Francine insisted. "You should call him. Do you want me to call him?"

She began pulling out her phone, and I held up a hand to stop her. My heart raced, and my hand shook with nervous energy. Of course, I wanted to see Kyle again. In the first weeks of being back in Brooklyn, it hadn't been a question of if, but when I would see him. Since we had dinner, nothing. Granted, I had been home more with Francine, but I still managed to go outside of the house at least once a day for something. Catching glimpses of Kyle felt like playing bingo with Nonni: every time I saw him was like getting one daub closer to winning. Here, Francine was giving me a valid reason to see him, but we weren't in middle school anymore. I knew I needed to be the one to reach out to him.

"I'll ask him myself, but if he is not interested, promise not to push him to help with this," I warned.

"Pinky swear," she said, holding up her pinky finger.

I hooked it with mine and quickly released it so that I could grab my phone from my pocket to text Kyle.

Jackie: Good afternoon, Officer.

Kyle: Hi. What's up?

Jackie: I need your help.

Kyle: Is Francine okay?

Jackie: She's fine. Can you come over and look at some documents I have from my parents' case?

Kyle: Sure, tonight?

Jackie: If you're free.

Kyle: Okay, see you then.

Butterflies blasted off into flight in my belly as I put my phone down.

"He said he'd look at them tonight," I told Francine.

She cheered as though she had won a bet. "I told you he would."

I shook my head at her smugness.

"Listen, if I need to make myself scarce, do we need a code word?" she asked, "because I love how close we are as friends and that you are willing to help me in the bathroom and stuff but I draw the line at knowing what either of you sound like in the throes of passion."

"Dear God, Francine! We're going to be looking at paperwork; how does that get passions stirring?" I asked exasperated.

Secretly, I wondered if it could. I was pretty sure a swift breeze could stir my passion for Kyle, but I didn't want to get ahead of myself.

"Again, I don't judge you or my brother for your respective kinks, I just don't want to know what they are or when they are happening," she insisted, "with the code word I disappear and plug in my noise canceling headphones for the night."

"You are too much," I laughed. "No code word needed. Nothing will happen."

"Says the girl who didn't think he would even come look at her mysterious papers," Francine teased.

When I was caring for Nonni, I often thought that what I needed was Kyle's loving embrace and I could make it through another day, but on the days that nearly broke me, I missed Francine. She had a way of making an impossible situation not only seem possible but that I was ridiculous for thinking I wouldn't come out of it smelling like a rose. What's more, when she was involved, I always did.

Thankful for my crazy friend, I leaned forward and hugged her, careful not to squeeze her too tight. She looked surprised but wrapped her arms around me and returned my hug.

"What was that for?" she asked when we released each other.

"I just love you. I really missed you when I was in Chicago," I replied.

"I missed you too, but I hope you know I was always rooting for you, wherever you were and whatever you did," she said, a tear trickling down her cheek.

"I was always rooting for you too," I smiled and hugged her once more.

"Good, now that we've got your love life sorted, let's talk about mine," she laughed and took hold of my hands. "There's this trainer at the gym I've been going to. His name is Seth..."

Even though we were talking about things so silly and girlish as who we had crushes on, I listened as though she was telling me state secrets. Francine had always held a huge chunk of my heart. Being near her always fills me with peace, and I am so grateful to have her back in my life. I never wanted to take what we shared for granted again.

CHAPTER 8

A Happy Wok Down Memory Lane

Kyle
July 4, 2017

I pulled into the driveway of Francine's house behind Jackie's red car with the ever-present Tennessee-shaped rust spot and noticed that she had swapped out her Illinois plates for New York State plates. She might have had them the last time I was there, but this was the first time I had noticed them. The blue and yellow plates belonged on the back of her car, like a sign of hope, as if it meant she was one step closer to staying here permanently this time.

After our dinner last week, I went home and soaked in the day. I almost kissed her, but did I actually *want* to kiss her, or was it a reflex? Avoiding her until I knew the answer seemed like the right thing to do at first. It was strange, though: when we didn't run into each other at all over the last few days, I felt anxious, like she was going to pop out from around the next corner, but when that didn't happen, disappointment filled me. Getting her text earlier 'to come over' gave me the excuse I needed to see her again. The problem was, I still wasn't sure about whether that near kiss was reflex or desire.

I got out of my car and grabbed the bags of takeout from her favorite Chinese restaurant, Happy Wok. I should have called her to make sure she hadn't made other dinner plans, but Chinese is just as good the next day, so it would be fine either way.

"Freeze," Jackie called out from the open front door. "What is in the bag, sir?"

Freaking adorable–telling a cop to freeze. Desire one, Reflex zero.

"I come in peace," I called back, holding the bags up, "and bearing Happy Wok."

"You may enter, but if you forgot the duck sauce, I will send you back," she warned as she let me in the door.

"What kind of monster do you think I am?" I asked, setting the bags down on the coffee table and pulling out the handful of duck sauce packets I had swiped on the way out of Happy Wok.

"Good man," she laughed, "Frannie's taking a nap. Do you want something to drink? I think the only soda she has is Sprite."

"Sprite is fine," I replied, pulling the various cardboard boxed dishes out of the bag and lining them up on the coffee table.

"Do you want a plate?" she called out from the kitchen.

"Nah," I replied.

She came back with the Sprite and some real forks from Francine's kitchen. We both could manage chopsticks but found them too tedious to bother with.

"Thanks," I said, taking the fork she held out to me.

"I can't believe you brought Happy Wok!" she gushed. "I haven't had this since I came back home."

"You're kidding?" I asked over a mouthful of crunchy cashew chicken.

I felt genuinely surprised. Happy Wok used to be a regular on our date nights. It was hard to believe she wouldn't have gotten it as soon as she got back to town.

She shook her head. "Frannie had diet restrictions before and after surgery, and they don't have a sit-down area, so I kept going for other things."

I nodded and opened a container of fried rice. Its delicious aroma filled the air as I held it out to her. She took a bit on her fork and tasted it.

"Mmm, I missed this!" she sighed contentedly and then looked longingly at me.

The air in the room thickened with the things we weren't ready to say. I knew what she wanted to say. She missed me too. I nodded and felt the corners of my lips turn up in a small smile.

To break the tension of our gaze, I looked down at the rice container still in my hand and shook it in front of her, inviting her to take another bite. She smiled, taking another forkful of rice. I took a forkful as well and enjoyed the combination of flavors. With that, air returned to the room, and we popped open the other containers and took turns taking bites of everything. Sharing was a reflex, so the score was even: Desire and reflex were one to one. That was until my wayward thoughts wondered if the mix of dishes tasted the same on her lips as it did five years ago, bringing desire up to two points.

It wasn't long until we agreed we were full and packed everything back up for the fridge. I suddenly remembered the reason I was there.

"So, what is this paperwork you found? Do you still want me to look at it?" I asked.

"Right, yes, come out to the kitchen with me," she said, carrying one bag of empty containers and one with leftover containers going into the fridge.

I followed her and opened the fridge door so she could put it in without having to juggle the bag in her other hand. She smiled her thanks up at me and put the bag on the empty shelf in the fridge. I took the bag of empty containers from her and pushed it into the trash compactor.

Jackie picked up a folder of papers that was sitting on the counter and handed it to me. I flipped through it and noted that it was a series of bank transfer statements that had Jackie's e-signature as the requester of the transaction.

"I don't understand. What is unusual about this?" I asked, still scouring the document for the oddity.

"A couple of things..." she said. "First, in my parents' system, you needed a PIN to e-sign requests like this in their system. I never received one, but this document appears to be signed using a PIN created for me."

A Happy Wok Down Memory Lane | 79

"Is it possible they created one for you that summer you were going to work for them, but you came to work at Holy Cannoli with me instead?" I asked, picking up the next paper to examine.

"I thought about that, but this document is from almost a year before that. That was the year I had planned to go to that summer program for future educators, so there would have been no discussion of working with them for the summer at that point," Jackie said, stepping closer to me so that she could point to the date.

Jackie's sweet perfume wafted to my nose and set my heart beating faster. Dammit...I wasn't sure if that counted as reflex or desire or both? All I knew was that there hasn't been a single woman in the last five years who had gotten my heart racing like this just by standing close.

"Oh, that's right," I replied, clearing my throat and my thoughts, "the program was canceled a couple weeks before you were supposed to go. I remember how pissed your dad was that they took off with the money and he never got refunded."

"Ironic, huh?" she asked ruefully.

"Sorry," I winced, "I really wasn't trying to take a dig at your dad."

"I know," she smiled reassuringly, "the other thing that's weird about this is that I remember turning in an identical stack of documents to the police, but the e-signatures on them were my parents', not mine."

"Do you still have copies of the documents?" I asked, eager to compare them.

She nodded. "My family has a storage unit at Brooklyn Storage Warehouse where the records for Nonno's restaurant in Jersey and my parents' financial records are stored. I still have access to it; I just haven't stopped over there yet to see if I can find the box from when these transactions took place."

At one time, Brooklyn Storage Warehouse was in a decent part of town, but over the years, the area had become overrun with mostly juvenile delinquents that made money stealing catalytic converters and enjoyed tagging anything they could in their spray-painted symbols in a criminal game of tag. No, it wasn't the artsy kind that improved the neighborhoods and gave a regional flair. I appreciated that kind of art. This was the childish boobs and penises and racial slurs that made everyone feel unsafe. Thinking of my sweet Jackie getting caught up in any of that made my skin crawl with worry. Shit...did I really still think of her as mine? I'm calling it: reflex and desire are neck and neck again.

"You really shouldn't go alone," I warned. "Why don't we set a day and time that I can go with you?"

"Kyle, it's just a storage unit," she laughed dismissively. "I've been there tons of times with Nonni and my parents over the years."

"Exactly, never by yourself," I pointed.

She crossed her arms and gave me a look. I crossed my arms over my chest and mirrored her look. I was determined she would not do this alone.

"Uh oh, I've walked into a classic Kyle and Jackie standoff," Francine remarked, startling both of us from our stare down.

"I was just telling him I could go down and pick up some more files from Nonni's storage to show him the documents that were sent to the police, and he doesn't want me to go," Jackie complained to Francine.

"That's not what I said," I argued. "I simply told her she shouldn't go by herself. She should wait until we can go together so that she stays safe while she's looking."

"That's actually a good idea, Jackie," Francine agreed. "That storage facility has gotten pretty seedy since you were last in town. There are a lot of sketchy-looking people there now."

I was surprised and relieved that Francine agreed with me. Growing up with a sister that was 11 months older than me meant that she often opposed me just for the joy of being my nemesis. While we had grown closer as adults, it still surprised me when she took my side in an argument.

Jackie looked between me and Francine for one of us to cave, but neither of us did.

"Fine, he can come with me," Jackie huffed, throwing her hands up in surrender.

"Look, if you don't want me to go through anything in there, I completely understand, and I can just stand outside. I'll feel better if I can at least stand and keep watch at the door until you're done," I reasoned with her.

Her rigid posture softened at that reassurance. I wasn't sure what she thought I would find digging around, but I could respect boundaries. I just wasn't used to having any with her.

"Thank you," she said. "Maybe over the weekend?"

"Sure, just text me," I replied.

I looked over the documents again to see if I could find anything that might help us uncover any further clues about the origin of the documents I was holding.

"Hey Jacks, do you remember the name of the guy who set up the PIN numbers for the e-signatures? Maybe he could say when or why you would have had a PIN number set up?" I suggested.

"I don't, but I think I remember seeing it on a company roster in another folder. One sec!" she said before rushing back to her bedroom to get it.

My eyes followed her down the hallway, past my old bedroom and into Francine's.

"You're not going to follow her?" Francine baited me.

"No, she said she was bringing it back here," I replied, not feeding into Francine's well-meaning meddling.

"Don't you want to see what she did with the room?" she asked innocently.

"Nope," I replied, though I did desperately want to see it.

Did it have a huge bookshelf with all of her favorite dragons and fantasy novels like it had when we were kids? Had she grown out of those things?

"Your brothers have both seen it," she prodded.

"Enough," I grumbled.

Just then, Jackie rushed back into the room with the roster.

"It was Mitchell Herrington," she said.

"Do you know what happened to him after they shut down your parent's firm?" I asked.

"He took a job on Wall Street...I think he may have even opened his own firm," Jackie replied.

"Mitchell Herrington," Francine announced, reading from her phone in hand, "former employee of D'Marco Investments, now owns Red Fish Financial Group in Manhattan."

"Write down the phone number," I ordered. "Jackie, why don't you call him tomorrow and set up a time to see if he can look at the documents with us?"

"Us?" Jackie asked as Francine slapped a grocery list page from her notepad into my palm with the phone number.

"Yes, us. You should not go see this guy or do anything related to this case on your own. If someone is or was trying to frame you, it could make you look like you actually did it and are trying to cover your tracks," I explained patiently.

"Fine," she conceded. "What if he can only meet us during your working hours?"

"I'll make it work," I replied confidently.

"What about me?" Francine asked.

"What about you?" I asked, confused.

"Can I come too?" she asked.

"No," I replied. "This is related to official police business, not a Girl Scout meeting."

Now it was Francine's turn to cross her arms over her chest and give me a look.

"You're not coming. You can stay with Ben or Jason until we get back." I insisted.

"Fine," she grumbled and turned on her heel to go sit in the living room.

I turned to Jackie, and she looked uneasy. I raised my eyebrow as if to ask her what was wrong.

"Official police business?" she asked nervously. "Does it really have to go on the record?"

I crossed closer to her so that I could whisper and not be heard by Nosey in the living room. "No, we just don't need her tagging along."

I watched as the tension left Jackie's body. I loved that my words still did that for her.

"Is there anything else you want me to take a look at tonight?" I asked.

"No, so far that's all I've found," she replied.

I nodded. "Good, in that case, I'm going to head home and get some sleep. When you get in touch with Herrington, send me the meeting details."

"Thank you for helping me with this, Kyle," she said. "There's just something about it that isn't sitting right with me."

"It's definitely unusual, but I'm sure we can figure it out," I assured her.

CHAPTER 9

Something is Fishy

Jackie
August 4, 2017

Kyle and I opted to take the subway to the Red Fish Financial offices in Manhattan to meet with Mitchell Herrington. It took weeks to get an appointment with the busy man. Actually, I don't think he really wanted to meet with the child of his former employer that nearly destroyed his career in the financial industry. Who could blame him?

Francine let me borrow the gorgeous blue suit she'd been wearing the day she found me in Chicago. It wasn't my usual style, but I had had little need for these types of clothes in the last few years, and what I had either didn't fit or well...didn't fit. I'd packed on weight, no question about it. Living off bakery scraps for the last year hadn't done my figure any favors. Even her lovely suit was snug on me, but it would work for the occasion.

On the subway seat next to me, Kyle's elbow brushed my arm as he fidgeted, loosening his tie a bit. I looked over at him and couldn't help but admire him with appreciation. His dark beard was neatly trimmed and just a bit shorter. A day or two earlier, he'd gotten a fresh haircut, so the baby hair that grew at the base of his neck had been shaved off in a neat row at the nape of his neck. He wore a navy-blue blazer over a powder blue and white pin-striped shirt, a solid navy necktie, and khakis with brown dress shoes and belt. He looked so handsome it made my breath catch.

Kyle must have felt my eyes on him because he turned and caught me staring.

"Do I look alright for this place?" he asked nervously, "They're not going to kick me out for looking like a bum, right?"

I couldn't help but smile. "You look good."

He smiled and let out a breath in relief. "Good. So do you."

Kyle stopped fidgeting in his seat, but my nerves took over, and I started running my nails over the edge of the accordion file, feeling the click of each section against them. I wondered if he was just being kind since I had complimented him first or if he really meant that I looked good. I wished I could see behind the mask of professionalism he was wearing. He'd been all business since he'd met me at the subway station earlier, and this was the first crack in his armor.

When we got to our stop, I teetered slightly in the heels I had borrowed from Francine. Kyle got out first and held out his hand to me to help me step out of the train and onto the platform.

"Thanks," I said, my hand tingling from the contact.

His hand was warm and strong, just the way I remembered. As soon as I was steady on the platform, he let go. It took everything in me not to reach out and take it again.

"Here, let me take your file so you can hold the handrail up the stairs," he offered, taking the files I wanted to show Mr. Herrington.

I was grateful for his suggestion. Using the handrail, I climbed the steps leading us to a busy sidewalk in Manhattan, about four blocks from Red Fish Financial. Kyle took my hand again, and we weaved together through the crush of people going in all directions around us. My heart soared to be in physical contact with him. It set my nerves at ease even though the excitement set my body on fire. His keen sense of direction and broad battering ram of a body got us to the lobby of the building where Red Fish Financial Group did business in no time at all.

He let go of my hand to hold the door for me so that I could walk in first. The loss of physical contact left my legs feeling shaky again, but I took a deep breath and walked up to the reception desk with him following into step behind me.

"Hello, we are here to see Mitchell Herrington. I'm Jackie D'Marco and this is my associate Kyle Carrollton," I said to the receptionist.

"Mr. Herrington will be out to see you shortly. If you'd like to take the elevator to the second floor, there is a waiting room. Help yourself to water from the mini-fridge if you'd like," the woman at the desk replied.

Kyle and I entered the elevator, and I pressed the button for the 2nd floor and stood shoulder to shoulder with him in the small space.

"Are you ready?" he asked, handing the files back to me.

I nodded. I was hoping Mr. Herrington would have the answers to my questions. When we reached the second floor, we followed the signs to Herrington's office, past a bullpen area where investors were buying and selling stocks at a frantic pace.

The fast-paced environment was familiar and set off a chain reaction of memories. The look of horror in my mom's brown eyes when she was being arrested alongside my dad flashed before me as though I was living it again. They had been equal partners in the firm that they had built from the ground up.

"Jackie," my father had pleaded, "you know we would never do this."

At that point, I had more than enough evidence to believe I had never known my parents at all. I had never felt so betrayed in all my life. Holding the documents with my signature on them made the feeling of betrayal resurface. Were they really intending to frame me in this and run off to the Cayman Islands to live out the rest of their lives with the millions they had taken from people? It made me sick to think.

"Jacks?" Kyle asked, concerned. "Are you okay?"

When I returned to the present moment, I saw the worried look in his eyes as he guided me to a firm but cozy accent chair in the waiting area. I sat down, grateful to be off my feet.

"Sorry, just in my head," I apologized, rubbing the tension from my temples with my fingertips.

He held out a small bottle of water to me from the mini-fridge in the waiting room. I took it gratefully and opened it up to take a sip of cool water. I needed to focus on the present. I needed answers, whether they were what I wanted to hear or not.

When the double doors to Mitchell Herrington's stately office opened, his secretary invited us to enter. Mitchell was a little older than my parents... probably in his late 50s or early 60s. His hair, once a vibrant light auburn, was now dulling into a dirty strawberry blond color on its way to turning what would likely be white as he aged further. He had more freckles and wrinkles than I remembered, likely from spending too much time in the sun on his annual family vacations to the beach. Judging by his orangey tan, they had been there recently.

He stood and shook each of our hands.

"Jackie D'Marco, it's been a long time," he remarked.

"Yes, sir, how have you been?" I asked politely.

"Doing well, all things considered. The mess that your parents left behind gave me an opportunity to go into business for myself. The scandal displaced all of their employees. I actually brought on as many former employees as I could," he boasted.

"I'm so glad you could," I smiled tightly.

Since they were the reason we were meeting with him, I wasn't surprised he took the opportunity to dig at my parents. Still, I had hoped he wouldn't start so soon.

"What is it I can help you with? You mentioned you found some documents?" he asked, noting my unease.

Mr. Herrington invited us to sit in the two chairs on the opposite side of his desk, and he sat in his desk chair.

"Yes," I replied, taking the documents from the accordion file and placing them in front of him, "I came across a set of documents that didn't match the set of documents from the evidence the police had collected. The most notable difference being that this set has a PIN for me complete with e-signature. To my knowledge, one had never been set up for me."

"Hmmm," Mitchell hummed, "there are a couple of other discrepancies here as well. Minor things in the legal jargon on the form but nothing that would significantly stand out unless you were looking for it."

"Like what?" Kyle asked, sitting forward a bit in his seat.

"Well, I personally wrote the statement that went on these forms, and I often reviewed the statement with clients when they committed to investing with us and, again, no significant changes, but just a few words different. Almost as though someone that also reviewed this statement with clients was summarizing the statement rather than reading it word for word. For example, where it says 'Transfer Date' on the original forms, it would say 'Date of Transfer.' Little things like that," Mitchell explained.

"So do you have any idea how or why these documents would have a PIN and e-signature for me when I never worked for my parents officially?" I asked, desperate to understand that piece of the puzzle.

"Well, I seem to recall that your parents had asked our IT guys to set one for you when you turned 16. They had learned of a tax break they could take if they put you on the payroll for the filing work you did while you were waiting for them to finish their workdays. They planned to invest the money and set it aside for you for school. Though it was never designed to approve documents like this. Only their e-signatures met the criteria to release funds like this," he explained.

"So, this document would still have required an additional signature from one of them to be a valid transfer request?" Kyle asked.

"Right, one or both of Jackie's parents would have had to sign off on it as well and as you see, this document does not reflect that," Mitchell pointed to the empty signature portion at the bottom that required one of the co-CEOs completing the request.

"In other words, they couldn't have framed you without implicating at least one of themselves," Kyle said to me.

"Then I don't understand why this copy is even here?" I asked him, "What's the purpose?"

"I can't even begin to guess," Kyle replied.

We both turned back to Mitchell, hopeful he had some kind of insight, but he just stared back at us like a deer caught in headlights.

"I'm sorry, kids, I really don't have any idea what purpose this could even serve. Without one or both of their signatures, the transfer could not have occurred," Mitchell said with a shrug.

"My parents claimed their innocence all the way through the trials. Do you have any reason to think that they could have been telling the truth?" I asked hopefully.

Mitchell leaned back in his chair and folded his hands, resting them on the hump of his beer belly in thought.

"For a long time, I wanted to believe they were," he admitted. "They had always been good to me and the other employees. The staff that was left when the news broke went through hours of auditing and mountains of paperwork. As much as we wanted to believe them, the evidence pointed to them every time. I'm so sorry."

I deflated after hearing his statement. Kyle squeezed my hand in sympathy, and our eyes met.

"Jackie, I'm happy to help answer any questions you have if you find anything else. I can give you my fax number and email address if you like, but I think you're going to find that your parents did this, as shocking and unbelievable as it is," Mitchell offered, kindly handing me his business card.

I couldn't describe the dismay I felt upon hearing his words. I so desperately wanted to believe they were the people I had grown up loving and not the money-hungry monsters they were accused of being.

"Thank you for meeting with us," I said, standing and shaking his hand.

Kyle did the same, and we left the office with no more hope than we had come in with. In the elevator, Kyle's eyes searched my face as if trying to read how I was feeling in that moment. The truth was, I didn't feel any one thing, so my face didn't know what to do with itself. I was sad, angry, relieved, and probably several other emotions I hadn't even processed yet.

"Do you want to go back home now?" he asked.

"Yeah, there's nothing more to do here right now," I replied, defeated.

"Listen, Jacks, this doesn't have to be the end of the road," Kyle said as the elevator doors opened on the ground floor.

I gave him a puzzled look as we walked from the elevator to the exit.

"You have a storage unit full of boxes. We can go through them box by box if you want," he offered.

"We?" I asked.

Was it possible that he really thought my parents were innocent? I wasn't sure how anyone could after hearing what Mr. Herrington had to say on the matter.

"Yeah," he replied, "I got to know your parents pretty well back then, and I don't know if the cautious, generous people that I knew could do this. I think I could help you look into this."

My heart soared. "You think it's possible they didn't do this?"

"Anything is possible," he replied. "Don't you owe it to yourself to see if we can prove it?"

"Okay, let's keep digging," I smiled, my resolve renewed.

"Good, and hey, at least we made a contact today that can help us understand the practices of the business that would mean things either make sense or don't," he cajoled.

I nodded; my spirits were officially lifting. Being any kind of "we" with Kyle Carrollton made me feel like I could conquer the world. I loved him for saying "we." I loved him for believing my parents could be innocent despite the mountain of evidence to the contrary. I just loved him.

CHAPTER 10

A Moment of Silence, Clarity, and Hope

Kyle
September 11, 2017

Every year, at 8:46 am, all cars observe a moment of silence for our fallen brothers and sisters in blue who lost their lives in the 9/11 attacks. The scanner in my kitchen was turned on so I could hear the call. The dispatcher's disembodied voice called out, "All units, please observe a 1 minute silence for those we lost in the 9/11 attacks."

Oscar and I were off duty and planned to hit up the gym. He knocked on the door of my apartment after dropping his kids off at school. Stepping into my apartment, Oscar pulled his crucifix necklace out and held it in his palm as he bowed his head. I mirrored him, holding the St. Michael pendant necklace Jackie had given me as we observed the minute of silence.

When the minute had passed, Oscar put his hand on my shoulder and prayed, "Dear Lord, please be with the families that live on without their loved ones today. Our job is dangerous, but we ask you to stand behind us and our brothers and sisters in blue. Fill us with courage and wisdom to keep our community safe. Through it all, be at our side so that we can return home to our families tonight and every night. Amen."

"Amen," I said in reply.

Oscar was solemn on 9/11. He was about to turn 37. September 11, 2001, happened his rookie year, and he said it was a day that he will never forget. If I had seen the aftermath of that day as a rookie, I probably would have quit. I certainly wouldn't be the cheerful bastard he was after seeing that firsthand.

"Living a good and happy life in their honor is the best way to remember them," he said to me, same as he did every year.

I nodded in understanding.

"Having a good woman by your side goes a long way to that," he smiled, noting that my hand was still wrapped around the charm at the end of the necklace Jackie had given me.

"I'm sure it does," I said, letting the pendant fall back to its resting place over my heart.

"How are things in that department?" he asked. "I notice you're not showing up at my house as often for dinner."

Dinners had been with Jackie nearly every day this week since we met with Mitchell Herrington. Afterward, we would go through documents with a fine-tooth comb looking for any clue that could prove her parents' innocence. What we put aside as suspicious left us with more questions than answers.

"Is it possible that you miss me, Romero? You see me every day," I teased.

"Maria has been asking about you," he replied nonchalantly, opening my refrigerator to take one of my pre-workout drinks. As he closed the door, my cat, Toby, rubbed his body in figure eights around Romero's legs.

"Ah, yes, your good woman is asking about me...better watch out," I barbed.

"Please, you would drive her insane with your brooding," Oscar replied, "besides, we know the only pussy you are getting right now is from your furry little friend here."

I smirked as Romero leaned down to scratch behind Toby's ears.

"Though you've been brooding less...maybe I should worry a little," he laughed.

Oscar literally had nothing to worry about. He and Maria were so in love it was disgusting, but he was right. The only one snuggling with me at night was my cat, Toby. I never called Briana back to reschedule our date that I canceled months ago when Jackie caught me buying condoms. Truth was, I really wasn't interested in anyone at the moment. I just wanted to help Jackie find the answers she was looking for in regard to her parents.

"Nah, I've been trying to help Jackie figure out the weird paperwork she had uncovered when she was moving. At first, it looked like someone was trying to pin her parent's crimes on her. But it looks like once they tried, they discovered there was a safeguard her parents put in place where at least one of them had to provide the final signature to allow the funds transfers to go through. So, trying to use Jackie's PIN would be a bust," I explained.

"But they kept copies of their failed attempts?" Oscar asked, his brow furrowed.

"Yeah, it was in a file that was in her grandmother's desk drawer. Seems odd, right? Why wouldn't they shred the copy that failed to approve the money release?" I was puzzled.

Oscar shook his head and shrugged his shoulders in response. We stood quietly, letting the puzzle work through the gears of our well-trained minds.

"Didn't D'Marco's brother work for the company for a little while?" Oscar asked.

"Jackie is an only child," I replied with a shake of my head.

"Not Jackie—her father," Oscar clarified. "His brother was suspected of conspiring in the case, but there wasn't enough to even press charges. He might know something."

Of course! Jackie's uncle works at the family restaurant in New Jersey now. It was only about an hour from Brooklyn. Maybe he would know something from his time working for his brother.

I had not met her uncle. My family insisted I be with them for the holidays until after graduation, and then I could decide where I wanted to go, so I never ended up attending any family gatherings with her. Was it bad that I hoped he was the one responsible so that her parents could go free?

"Why did they suspect him?" I asked curiously.

"Around the time the money went missing, he suddenly had a silent partner that was making improvements to the restaurant, big-ticket items. It just seemed like odd timing," Oscar explained, "but we eventually traced the source back to an existing corporation that has made video games since the late 70s—a totally reputable company just looking to diversify. Last I heard, they were still partners."

"Seriously? Video games and authentic Italian food?" I shook my head at the idea.

"To be fair, they had invested in other sectors too: a wing of Brooklyn Memorial Hospital, a local hardware store chain, and something else. The thing that really forced us to drop our investigation on that end was the silent partner had lost a few million dollars in the D'Marco deal too," Oscar recalled.

"I didn't know you worked on the case," I remarked.

"I didn't," he shrugged. "I was on desk duty at the time because of an injury and heard a lot of the details in the bullpen."

That made sense. As capable as Oscar was as a police officer, he was terribly accident prone and had served desk duty on several occasions over his career.

"Let's get going. We need to get our workout in," Oscar suggested.

I nodded in agreement and threw a toy for Toby so that he would chase it and not try to follow us out of the apartment. As we made our way down to Oscar's car, his words floated in my mind. What he shared with me didn't sound right. Why hadn't the company that invested in the family restaurant pulled out when they lost money due to the D'Marco's misdeeds? Jackie and I needed to dig into this angle of things. My fingers itched to text her, but I knew Oscar would have something smart to say about it.

"So, when can we have you and Jackie over to dinner?" Oscar asked.

"What?" I asked, surprised by his question.

Why would Jackie come to dinner with me and the Romeros? She didn't know them.

"Come on, man," Oscar laughed. "You are dying to text her right now, aren't you?"

I turned to face him, my brow wrinkled. Was I that obvious?

"You tell me you have missed dinners with your friends and gym time to sort through a box of old documents with her on a case that's already been prosecuted. You haven't complained about seeing her everywhere in weeks, you haven't hooked up with any other girls and yet you've been in a good mood..." Oscar ticked off on his fingers, "You're telling me that's not code for hooking up with Jackie?"

I sputtered before I could finally put together the words, "We're not hooking up."

"But you want to?" Oscar asked, leading me.

Taking a deep breath, I let it out in a long, suffering sigh. Honestly, I didn't know. I loved being near her, hearing her laugh, her voice, smelling her soft floral scent, having dinner with her, touching her...oh shit. I wanted to hook up with her.

"I'll take that as a yes," Oscar grinned triumphantly.

"I didn't say yes," I argued.

"You didn't say no either," he pointed out, "so I'll ask again, when would the two of you like to come over for dinner? Maria could give Jackie pointers about being the romantic partner of a police officer. It's difficult for them, you know."

I did know how that felt, but not in the way he suspected...when Jackie left, I spent the first year wondering where she was, if she was safe, if she would come back to me. Francine was the closest to knowing what I was going through, but I don't think she even got the full extent of it.

"If we get to where we are romantic partners again, I will let you know about dinner, fair enough?" I growled, trying to get Oscar to back off.

Jackie had broken my heart before. I wasn't ready to hand her the pieces I had stitched back together just yet. I wasn't sure I would ever be. Remembering how it felt not knowing what had happened to her, I wasn't sure I could go through it ever again.

"Listen, Carrollton, what are you hoping to accomplish by keeping her at arm's length? Are you trying to give her the chance to leave you before you fall for her again? She told you she's back home for good. Are you trying to punish her or yourself?" Oscar asked.

"Myself?" I pondered, "for what?"

"For letting her get away the first time? For not continuing to search for her once you became a cop? For not knowing what she was going through while you were apart? I don't know man. That's a question you have to ask yourself," Oscar suggested, "but you better try to figure it out before she gets tired of being kept at a distance and decides to move on."

"Or run away again," I huffed.

Oscar nodded in acknowledgment. I sat quietly and thought about what he had said. Was I punishing myself by keeping her at a distance? I knew I never wanted to feel the way I did the day after graduation. Sick with worry, the news of her parents' arrest was all over the news, and I couldn't find her or reach her no matter how many times I tried. The weeks and months of waiting for a phone call with any news at all only to hear nothing. It was torture.

"What happens if I can't forgive her?" I asked.

Oscar looked at me with compassion. Clearly, that question had been too vulnerable, but I needed to know what he thought.

"You know what you need to do in that case," Oscar replied solemnly, "but if you decide to forgive her, forgive her completely. You can't hold it over your relationship for the rest of your life. I made a mistake in my relationship with Maria early on, and I am grateful every day that she chose to forgive me."

"Maybe what you did wasn't as bad," I reasoned.

"No, it was worse," he said pointedly, "but every day, I showed up and showed her I was willing to put in the work to mend things. It seems to me that Jackie is trying to do the same."

Oscar wasn't often mysterious, but when he was, I knew he was not willing to elaborate further on the situation, so I let it drop there.

Maybe the nights of looking through box after box of paperwork together was our way of recommitting to each other, as strange as it seemed. I went over almost every night after work to dig into another box with her, have dinner and talk. Did we even find anything else at this point? Nothing concrete, but we kept looking.

It was then it occurred to me what we were looking for in those boxes....
Hope. Hope for us. Hope for a chance to start over. Hope that we can make
it this time. Hope.

CHAPTER 11

Masso Misconceptions

Jackie
September 11, 2017

y Uncle Tomasso had the strangest silent partner in a tech giant, Reese Clearwater, who was the CEO and founder of Clearwater Gaming, a well-established video game systems and programming company. No one had expected the tech magnate to invest in a family owned restaurant, but D'Marco's Italiano was nearly unrecognizable since the last time I saw it.

Mr. Clearwater was very savvy when it came to business and took my grandparent's sweet little Italian restaurant and decked it out in tech. Each table had a card reader so that you could pay at the table without asking the waitstaff for the check. You could even order from it if you wanted a dinner with minimal interruption from the staff.

The walls that had once been pesto green were now a Tuscan yellow with beautiful hand-painted murals of the Tuscan countryside. Even the menus, for those that preferred a more traditional restaurant experience, had been beautifully re-done with professional pictures of our signature dishes. They were truly stunning.

Uncle Masso joined me at the table, giving me a hug and a kiss on each cheek before sitting across from me. I was relieved to see that he had welcomed me the way he had since I was a child. He was offended that I was named executor of Nonni's will, but he had honored her wishes.

"Jackie, it is wonderful to see you," he beamed.

"Uncle Masso, it's been so long. How are the boys?" I asked.

"You can ask them for yourself," he smiled, and stood up and gestured to the door.

I stood also and turned toward the door I had come through earlier to see my cousins Robbie and Drew.

"Cousin Jackie!" Robbie called out, running to me from across the restaurant. "Where have you been?"

Robbie, Drew, and I were all the same age, but Robbie was mentally the age of about a 7 or 8-year-old. His rounded facial features were characteristic of the Down syndrome he was born with. His brown hair was cut just long enough to allow his wavy curls to show, just as it had been when we were children. Robbie wore a green D'Marco Italiano shirt and khaki pants with sturdy black work shoes. His boisterous greeting had heads in the restaurant turning our way, but I ignored them. Robbie was the sweetest and should be allowed to be exactly who he was anywhere.

"I was living with Nonni in Chicago until she passed away. I just moved back to Brooklyn in May, so I can come visit more often," I said, giving him a hug and a peck on the cheek.

Behind him was my cousin Drew, Robbie's brother. He'd been placed with Uncle Masso at birth but not officially adopted until Robbie and I were two. He was only a few months younger than the two of us.

Robbie turned to Drew and said, "Drew, Drew, look! It's Jackie."

"I see her buddy," Drew smiled. "Remember I told you I had a surprise? Well, she was the surprise!"

"Drew," I smiled and hugged him, "It's so good to see you."

When we separated, he smiled widely at me, his dark-rimmed glasses slightly big for his face. His dark hair was long and curly on top with a gentle fade down his head. He was clean shaved and just had a nerdy hipster vibe about him. He had grown into such a handsome man.

We all sat down and put in our orders. Robbie sat beside me, and we held hands like we used to when we were kids. He always wanted to have physical contact with the person sitting closest to him, and his childlike innocence made me love him even more. I wondered how I had made it five long years without seeing him more than just for Nonni's funeral.

"So, Jackie, you said that you had some questions?" Uncle Masso prompted.

"Yeah," I replied, pushing the file folder across the table to him, "I was moving Nonni's desk, and this file fell out of it. I didn't think much of it at the time, but when I looked through the papers to see where I could file them, I found it was a form requesting a funds transfer to a Swiss account and two in the Cayman Islands."

"That's where your parents had the embezzled money transferred, so why would this seem odd?" he asked, not picking up the file.

My heart sank a little at that. Masso seemed to believe this without question. It was a punch to my gut that he didn't even care to pick up the file. Perhaps my curiosity regarding this was unhealthy, but didn't a small part of Masso want to believe his brother and his brother's wife were innocent?

"The documents were e-signed by me," I explained.

"How is that possible?" he asked, finally flipping through the papers.

Some of the tension left my shoulders, and I explained what was going on.

"That was my question too," I agreed. "I had a police officer friend of mine look at them, and he thought it looked like my parents were trying to frame me."

"Why would they do that?" Masso asked, putting the file back down on the table and sliding it back to me.

"A fallback plan in case they got caught?" I theorized.

"Why you, though? There were plenty of employees they could have used to take the fall if that was their intent," Masso countered.

"Exactly, so my friend and I tracked down Mitchell Herrington to see if he could tell us how I even ended up with a PIN and e-signature before I ended up working for my parents later that summer. He told us they had created it when I turned 16 because they learned of a tax write off. It would allow them to 'pay me' as an employee and turn around and invest that money to give me more money toward college when the time came. So, the theory that they were the ones who were trying to frame me for their crime seemed wrong. But what if someone else did it and was trying to frame me instead?" I asked.

Uncle Masso sighed heavily and gave me a pitying look. I instantly felt like a little girl in his eyes.

"Jackie, you and your Nonni turned in countless documents that showed that your parents did this. Why on earth are you wasting your time and energy trying to find evidence to the contrary now? Aside from these misprinted documents, have you found anything that would even make you think your little theory is correct? It's long overdue that we all put this behind us and move on with our lives."

His words stabbed through my heart like a dull, jagged knife.

"Uncle Masso, do you really think they did it?" I pleaded.

"Yes, I do, based on all the evidence I have seen," he replied obstinately.

I heaved a sigh of my own and sagged, defeated, in my chair. Maybe he was right. Maybe they did it, and the set of papers here means nothing at all.

Robbie leaned back and slid down in his chair next to me. He leaned over and whispered to me, "I don't think they did it, Cousin Jackie."

"Thanks, Robbie," I whispered back, the tiniest of sparks lighting up my hope.

"You're welcome to stay for lunch and visit with the boys," Masso said, throwing his napkin down on the table. "I'm done with this conversation."

"Dad," Drew called, trying to reason with his hot-tempered father.

"Let him go," I said to Drew. "I should have warned him this is what I came to talk about rather than springing it on him."

"He's just worried that you're digging back into things with a police officer. It could mean that they want to investigate him again," Drew explained.

"Again?" I asked. I wasn't aware that the police had investigated Uncle Masso as well.

It was starting to make sense why he didn't even want to entertain the conversation. Perhaps whoever committed the crime was trying to take down my whole family in this scandal, but why?

Drew nodded solemnly. "Dad partnered with Mr. Clearwater just before everything went down with your parents. His investments in the restaurant were all made through an LLC to protect his other assets. At the time, Mr. Clearwater had not revealed he was Dad's business partner. The investigators thought Dad was part of the scheme your parents were convicted of, and that's where the money had gone. When Mr. Clearwater finally came forward, the police dropped the investigation."

The waitstaff brought out our order minus Uncle Masso's, which must have been taken to him in his office. My cousins and I dug into our dishes. To my relief, Nonni's recipes had not been altered in the partnership with Mr. Clearwater. It was like she had cooked family dinner again. I smiled as I watched Robbie twirl his spaghetti using the fork and spoon method Nonni had taught us when we were little. For all the things he had trouble with from a dexterity standpoint, he had no problem getting the spaghetti into a mostly neat ball on the end of his fork.

I used the same method on mine and was grateful for the new memory with what remained of my family. Uncle Masso had behaved strangely when I asked him my questions, but it was understandable. Robbie needed lifelong help, and if his father had been arrested unjustly because of the scheme my parents had orchestrated, I don't know what would have happened to him. He probably would have ended up in some kind of group home.

"Drew, are you going to school?" I asked.

"No," he replied, smiling proudly, "Mr. Clearwater brought me on as an intern right after I finished high school. Afterward, he decided to hire me on permanently. I work on developing new games for his gaming division now."

"Oh, that's perfect for you!" I grinned. "You must love it."

"I do," he agreed, "plus they let me bring Robbie in to beta test the ones he can."

What a great situation! Robbie always wanted to be with Drew. For them to work together in any capacity was just amazing.

"Yeah, Cousin Jackie," Robbie interjected excitedly, "I tell them if the game is good or not."

"Yeah? I bet the ones Drew makes are great," I said, so proud of them both.

"The first one wasn't," Robbie argued with his patented brutal honesty. "The monkey kept falling into the banana trap."

"But I fixed it, didn't I?" Drew asked good-naturedly.

"Yeah," Robbie conceded and continued eating.

We all settled back into the comfortable rhythm of eating as a family once more. I hadn't realized how much I had missed this until I was sitting here in the restaurant with my two cousins. They were my childhood playmates.

One of the servers cleared our plates when we finished eating. I was about to suggest that I go home when Drew said something that stopped me.

"Jackie, can I look at the files you showed my dad?" Drew asked.

I nodded and handed them across the table to him. Ever excited to help, Robbie got up and stood behind Drew as his eyes scanned over the documents.

An uneasy look flashed over Drew's face as he read through page after page.

"What is it?" I asked.

"I think I did this," he admitted.

"What?" I asked, stunned by his admission.

"I think this is a sample document I made when I was playing businessman years ago," he said, "back when my dad used to work for your parents, he used to have copies of a contract like this and he yelled at me and Robbie for playing with his official documents, so he told us we could make documents to play with and he would print them for us. We were due to see you soon, so I made documents that were e-signed by each of us so that we could all play."

"Seriously?" I asked.

My stomach sank. These documents had been the most promising clue that my parents could be innocent. Kyle and I had been through hundreds of documents and, despite flagging a few as suspicious, none of them offered any clear sign that it could be a set-up.

He nodded grimly. "I'm so sorry. I really hoped this was a sign that your parents were really innocent. Uncle Davide and Aunt Susan were such kind people, it never made sense to me that they could do it, but maybe my dad is right. Maybe they had us all fooled."

His words echoed in my mind. I had prayed night after night for an answer to this riddle, and now that it was before me, I wanted it to go away or at the very least be untrue.

I fought back tears as I said goodbye to my cousins. I needed to go back to Brooklyn. It seemed to be the only place that the earth felt steady beneath my feet.

CHAPTER 12

Personal Records and Paramedics

Kyle
September 11, 2017

O scar's junk was entirely too close to my forehead as he spotted me while I was trying to set a new personal record—400 lbs. He looked concerned watching me try this lift. My muscles burned as I lowered the bar down to my chest and strained to push it up.

"Come on Carrollton, you've got this," he encouraged.

I felt my arms quivering with the effort as I pressed them back to a fully vertical position with the added weight, but eventually I felt my elbows fully straighten, gave a 3 count in my head and then rocked my arms back to allow the weight to settle back on its hook.

I sat up and saw myself in the mirrored wall. My face was beet red from my effort, but I couldn't help the cocky grin that was on my face as Oscar patted me on the back.

"Damn, that's a new PR for you, isn't it?" he asked.

"Yeah," I replied, still winded.

"I'm getting too old to keep up with you," Oscar said, removing weight from each side of the bar.

"Come on old man," I teased, trading places with him so I could spot him as it was his turn to bench. "You should give it a try."

"Thirty-seven is not that old," he grumbled as he hefted the barbell from its hooks.

He did five full presses with his significantly lighter weight before he returned it to the hooks.

"Not too shabby, Grandpa," I laughed, giving him a congratulatory slap on the shoulders.

"Shove it," Oscar said with a chuckle.

I pulled my phone from my pocket and read the previewed part of the message from Jackie that I had missed earlier.

> **Jackie:** Headed home now. Family lunch didn't go well.

I frowned at the message on the screen. When I swiped the screen to text her back, I saw a message from Francine.

> **Francine:** Can you pick up Gatorade, bananas, and a loaf of bread for me when you get done at the gym?

> **Kyle:** Did you mean to send this to me?

> **Francine:** Yes. Jackie isn't back from NJ, and I'm miserable. Been sick.

> **Kyle:** Fine. Anything else, Your Highness?

Francine: That will be all for now, peasant.

I couldn't help but chuckle at my sister as I put my phone back in my pocket.

"What's next?" I asked.

"Pull ups," he replied, pointing to the pull-up bar two stations over from where we were.

"Whoever does the most gets out of doing reports for a week?" I suggested.

"Deal!" Oscar replied, slapping his hand against mine.

I dried my hands with my gym towel and took a slight leap up to grab the bar that was just above my hand height. Once I settled into my hold, I began counting out my pull-ups every time my chin lined up with the bar. At around twenty, my arms couldn't hold my weight anymore, and I had no choice but to let myself drop back to the ground.

"Does someone like paperwork?" Oscar mocked.

"Show me what you've got." I swiped back, knowing he would likely beat me out, but holding my breath that a cramp from working the other stations first would take him out.

I received another text notification and figured it was my sister with another request from the grocery store, so I pulled my phone out. To my surprise, it was Jackie again.

Jackie: Francine just said she's still sick. Maybe we should get together another night.

Kyle: She just asked me to pick up some things.

Jackie: She must have thought I was further away. I just pulled into the driveway

.

I heard Oscar call out 22 as I shoved my phone back in my pocket. Damn it!

"And that's how it's done, son," he crowed, dropping back down to the floor. The onlookers clapped at his achievement.

I shook my head and let him have his victory. The music cut out again, indicating another text coming through. I pulled my phone out of my pocket once more.

"Are you crying to your momma about your defeat at the hands of Oscar Romero, the pull-up master?" he baited.

"No," I replied, "Something's up with Francine. I'm going to have to cut it short. Sorry, man."

"I hope everything's okay," he offered, his tone mirroring the concern I felt.

"I'm sure she's just being dramatic, but I better go check on her," I said, picking up my towel and water bottle.

"Of course, see you in the morning," Oscar called after me as I made my way back to the locker room.

I held out my arm in my rushed version of a wave goodbye. I was never so grateful we hadn't been doing leg day because I was able to quicken my pace to the locker where I had stored my bag without stumbling over abused leg muscles.

As I was buckling into my car, my phone began ringing. It was Jackie. I answered, sure that my sister just needed something else from the store and didn't think I would get it for her because of that peasant comment. She was probably right.

"Hey, Jackie, what does Princess Francine need?" I asked.

"Kyle," she sniffled, "I got home, and Francine was unconscious. The ambulance is on the way."

"Jesus Christ, what happened?" I asked, my heart thudding in my chest.

"I don't know. I came in and she was just lying on the floor of the bathroom," Jackie sobbed. "They're here now. I have to let them in."

"Go do that, but stay on the phone with me," I ordered.

I could hear a flurry of muffled voices through Jackie's phone as the paramedics came into Francine's house.

"Jackie, can you ask them what hospital they are planning to take her to? I'll meet you there," I said to her.

I heard Jackie's muffled voice asking a paramedic where they would take Francine and a mumbled answer.

"Brooklyn Memorial," Jackie said into the phone, "I'm going to ride in the ambulance with her."

"I'm going to hang up now," I said, "but if anything changes, call me back, okay?"

"Okay," she whimpered, "be careful."

"I will," I assured her.

I put the magnetic lights on top of my car and took off down the road at break-neck speed, weaving around the cars that had pulled over to make way for my emergency lights. When I finally pulled into the emergency parking lot at Brooklyn Memorial ten minutes later, I pulled my phone out and called Ben first. He was likely asleep from being on call last night.

"What?" Ben grumbled into the phone.

"Ben, Francine is being taken to Brooklyn Memorial Hospital. Jackie got home and found her unconscious on the floor," I said without pause.

"What happened?" Ben asked, alert.

"We don't know yet," I said. "They were taking her by ambulance, so hopefully by the time they get here, they'll have some kind of idea what's going on."

"I'm on my way! Did you call Jason yet?" Ben asked.

"I'm going to as soon as I get off the phone with you," I replied.

"Okay, I'll find you when I get there," he said, hanging up.

I hit my speed dial for Jason.

"Kyle, I'm already on the way. The EMT's on site called me at home," he said in greeting.

"Good, Ben's on his way too," I replied, walking toward the emergency room doors.

"Have you gotten any info on what's going on?" Jason asked.

"Jackie found her passed out on the floor when she got home. Other than that, no," I replied.

"The EMT's haven't been able to revive her yet," Jason explained, "they checked her blood sugar, it was super low, which could be part of the problem, but when they gave her some glucose tabs, her sugar improved but she's still unconscious."

"What does that mean?" I grumbled.

"It likely means that the blood sugar isn't the only problem, and they need to run more tests to find out what's going on once they get her to the hospital," Jason said.

"Fine, well I'm here. I'm going to let the reception desk know who I am and see if she has made it here yet," I said.

"I'll be there in about five minutes. I'll come find you," Jason said. "If you get to see her, tell her we all love her."

"She knows," I said, "but I will."

Jason and I hung up. As I entered the gently lit waiting room, I saw Jackie pacing distraughtly with her arms hugged around herself.

"What happened? Why aren't you with her?" I demanded, holding her still by the shoulders.

"They asked me to wait out here while they run some tests on her to find out what's going on," she sobbed.

I pulled her into my chest and hugged her tightly, her tears soaking my sweaty gym shirt. I stroked her hair, and we rocked back and forth in a comforting sway.

"What happened?" Jason asked, Ben following on his heels.

"They asked us to wait out here while they run some tests to see what's going on," I explained to my brothers, but not releasing Jackie from my embrace.

"Let me see if I can find out anything," Jason offered, heading to the desk.

Ben paced back and forth with his fingers laced together on the back of his head. Worry and exhaustion were evident on his normally jovial face. When he paced close enough to me, I reached out and pulled him into a hug with me and Jackie.

"She's going to be okay," I insisted, squeezing them both reassuringly.

When I released him, Ben nodded, and he sniffed back a sob. We all loved our sister fiercely.

I felt Jackie's legs shake against mine.

"Come on, sweetheart," I said to Jackie, "let's sit down."

I guided her to a bench against the wall, and we sat together, my arm wrapped around her shoulders, holding her face against my chest. Her sniffles grew to include hiccups as she tried to hold in her tears. Whatever condition she found Francine in must have been pretty bad.

Ben took a seat next to us to wait for Jason to come back with any news. It felt like he had spent an hour at the desk before he came back to relay what he had learned. He pulled a chair over from another section and sat across from me and Jackie, with Ben on his left.

"Unfortunately, they don't know everything yet, but she regained consciousness shortly after arriving here. They discovered Francine had been vomiting so strenuously that she tore open the incision from her gastric bypass, and they believe she is leaking stomach acid. They've taken her back for surgery to repair that and are pumping her with fluids and anti-nausea medicine to keep this from recurring," Jason explained.

"How serious is that?" Ben asked, wincing in sympathy.

"They won't know until they get in there and clean things up, but it sounds like she has been vomiting pretty regularly since the procedure. Jackie, did she tell you?" Jason asked.

Jackie's head shot up in surprise. Her lip trembled as she replied, "No, I had no idea."

I could kill Francine. Why would she keep something like that from her doctors and primary caregiver? This wasn't something to mess around with!

"This will be really important to watch out for when she goes back home," Jason warned.

Jackie nodded solemnly.

"Why don't you go call Mom and Dad?" I suggested gruffly to Jason.

He had no business being so harsh with Jackie. It was Francine who had kept information from all of us...not Jackie!

"Yeah, sure," he replied resignedly.

"I'm going to go for a walk," Ben said. "Call me if you hear anything more."

I nodded and watched my brothers walk through the emergency room doors, and then I turned my gaze to Jackie. Her face was red and blotchy from crying, but still beautiful.

"Kyle, I'm so sorry. I let you all down," she sniffed.

"What do you mean?" I asked, pulling a tissue from the box on the stand next to me and handing it to her.

"I should have known what was going on," she said, pausing to blow out gently before continuing, "instead I wrapped myself up in a file of bogus papers thinking it would clear my parents."

"Jackie, look at me," I ordered and waited for her red-rimmed brown eyes to meet mine. "This is not in any way, shape, or form your fault. Francine was hiding this from all of us. There was no way you would have known."

"But if I hadn't been so distracted, I would have been able to see that she was hiding something," she insisted.

Her words rang true for me too. If I hadn't been so distracted when I was at their house, I would have seen that my sister wasn't well too.

"She'll be fine," I said to reassure both of us, "and when she is, she is getting an earful from me!"

Jackie snorted out a tearful laugh and leaned back into my chest. I put my arm back around her and held her tight to me. We sat quietly, just holding each other as if we'd done it without pause, without an ounce of heartbreak. It felt so right having her in my arms. It calmed me and made me believe my own words a little more. Francine would be okay. She had to be.

Ben came back first and settled back into the chair he'd been sitting in earlier.

"Any word?" he asked.

"Nothing yet," I replied. "Why don't you try to find a chair you can sleep in? I'll wake you up when the doctor comes to talk to us."

"I could sleep standing up at this point," Ben laughed ruefully. "We had a call almost every hour on the hour last night."

I nodded in sympathy. I'd had similar shifts on the force. They left you feeling dog-tired but proud of your chosen profession.

Ben sank down a bit and put his feet up on the coffee table in front of him. I'd usually scold him for doing that in a place like this, but the man was wiped. The least I could do was let him catch a few z's if he could.

Jason came back in just as Ben had finally dozed off and sat down wordlessly so as not to wake his brother. We all settled into quiet anxiety as we waited for word on Francine. Each of us got up a time or two to pace around the waiting room before realizing it did no good and taking our seats again.

When I thought I couldn't take another minute of waiting, the surgeon came out and gave us an update. Francine had indeed torn the incision from her gastric bypass procedure. She'd been throwing up so consistently week after week that it had torn open, healed partially and torn open again, so it was a mess to repair and riddled with infection.

"We believe we have removed all the infected tissue and closed up her incision again. However, shortly after we brought her back around after surgery, she slipped into a coma called toxic-metabolic encephalopathy. We will continue to check her condition and fight the infection as needed. We hope that this brings her out of the coma," the doctor explained.

"Can we go see her?" I asked.

"Yes, the four of you can come back for a few minutes while we prepare a room for her. Once she's moved to the ICU, we ask that you limit it to two visitors at a time," the doctor advised. "Follow me."

We all walked in formation behind the doctor, like a group of baby ducks following their mother through the endless turns down sterile white hallway after sterile white hallway. It was almost dizzying. Finally, we stood at Francine's bedside. Countless machines and tubes were connected to her, with an IV with several bags of fluid flowing through it. She looked so small lying in the bed, motionless aside from the rise and fall of her chest. They had re-intubated her when she slipped into a coma.

I stared down at her, and all of my emotions bubbled into a hot brew of anger in my chest. I'd never been so angry with her before. How fucking stupid could she be?

"Excuse me," I said, leaving my family in the room in stunned silence as I marched back out through the waiting room and outside. I couldn't be in that building a minute longer looking at her like that. She didn't need to have had that surgery in the first place. She wouldn't be lying in that bed now if she had just opened her Goddamn mouth and told her doctor or Jackie...or Hell ME...what the Hell was going on with her.

"Kyle," Jackie called from behind me, "are you okay?"

"No, I'm not fucking okay," I bellowed, walking out to my car.

"Where are you going?" she asked, scurrying behind me to keep up with my long-legged strides.

"Where does it look like I'm going?" I asked, whirling around to her so quickly she nearly slammed into my chest.

"Kyle, you can't drive right now," she said so calmly it made my blood boil. "Give me your keys."

The logical side of me knew she was right. I should not get behind the wheel right now, but the fury I had boiling over within me wanted to ruffle the calm authority that had washed over her.

"No," I replied, crossing my arms over my chest.

"Kyle Anthony Carrollton," she scolded, mirroring my cross-armed pose, "give me your keys. I cannot handle it if I have to worry for the lives of two people I love today."

We held down a staring contest, neither of us flinched. She silently held out her hand for my keys.

"Fine," I seethed, putting the keys in her outstretched palm.

"Jason is going to stay with Francine so that the rest of us can go home and rest. Ben is on call tonight but he will go in the morning to relieve Jason after he gets off work and I will relieve him around noon tomorrow so that you can go to work if you want and come in when your shift ends," she explained the plan that was made for me.

I took a deep breath in and forced it out through my nose.

"Ben is going to call your parents and give them an update on what we just learned. They were already looking for different options to get up here when Jason called them earlier," Jackie continued, reciting the information she had gotten.

"Can we go now?" I asked, opening the driver's side door and inviting her to take the wheel with an exaggerated sweep of my hand.

She gave me a look that told me I should take my attitude down a peg. When she got in the car, she adjusted the seat forward so her legs could reach the pedals.

I closed the door for her and circled around to the passenger side and got in. I stared out the window as Jackie drove us back to Francine's house. Hurt and anger coursed through me.

Jackie reached over and took my hand and gave it a comforting squeeze. When she was about to let go, I gripped her hand tighter, wordlessly begging her not to let go. She glanced over, and our eyes held briefly in quiet understanding before she went back to watching the road, but her hand never left mine the rest of the ride to my sister's house.

At that moment, I realized how grateful I was that she was back and had insisted on driving me home. As much as I had been fighting it, that was the instant that I let myself admit I was still in love with her. With that knowledge, I wasn't sure I would ever let her go again.

CHAPTER 13

Home at Last

Jackie
September 11, 2017

When I offered a comforting squeeze of Kyle's hand, he held on, saying without words that he didn't want me to let go. I saw something shift in his eyes. The pulsing anger that had overwhelmed him at the hospital gave way to dread and fear the closer we got to Francine's house. Behind the dread and fear, there was something else too that was familiar, but I couldn't name it. Maybe I felt that way myself and just imagined it was what he was feeling too. He hid so much of what he was feeling behind anger, yet I had always been able to read the subtle nuances within him. If I weren't mistaken, the feeling peering out from his eyes was love. Love for me? Now that was wishful thinking on my part.

I parked the car outside Francine's house. Kyle sat stone silent, staring ahead of us. It seemed numbness settled over him. I opened the car door, got out and went around to his side. When I opened his door, he looked up at me, confused.

"Come inside," I urged, "at least for a little while."

He nodded and got out of the car, following me up the porch steps and to the door.

I unlocked the door and let us into the house. Kyle continued to follow me from the foyer into the living room, and then to the kitchen like a lost puppy.

"I need to clean the bathroom—we left so quickly to get her to the hospital, I didn't," I explained.

Kyle nodded and went to the tall cabinet where Francine stored her cleaning supplies and pulled out a roll of paper towels, the mop and bucket, a cleaning caddy with several tools and cleaners and the mop solution. He set the paper towels and caddy on the counter and put the bucket in the sink to add solution and water to it.

"Master bedroom?" he asked, his tone subdued.

"Yes," I replied.

Kyle led the way to the master bedroom, carrying the mop and bucket, and I followed him with the cleaning caddy and paper towels. When we came to the bathroom, he let out an astonished breath. A bit of blood was streaked on the corner of the sink, and a puddle of vomit had dried in the place where I had found her.

He looked back at me with compassion showing in the depths of his brown eyes as he set the mop bucket down and leaned the mop against the wall.

"I can do this by myself," he offered.

I shook my head. "I can help."

Together, we cleaned the mess that had been left behind, including various wrappers and swabs from the EMTs that had fallen to the floor. When we were done, we went back to the kitchen and put away the cleaning supplies.

I turned around to talk to Kyle, and he almost ran right into me. He'd been following so closely behind me. He stopped just in time but grabbed my arms as if we'd already banged into each other.

"Sorry," he said, making sure we were both steady on our feet before releasing me.

"It's okay," I replied.

I could see the haunted look in his eyes and couldn't help myself. I wrapped my arms around his waist in a hug. I felt him stiffen for a couple of seconds before he wrapped his muscular arms around me and hugged me the way I remembered...the way I had dreamed about for five long years.

His hand stroked my hair as he pushed the side of my face against his broad chest. The way he'd held me at the hospital was nice, but he had done it just for me because he knew it was what I needed. This hug right now was for both of us, and I never wanted to leave it. It felt like home, and I hadn't been home in so long.

"I gave her shit for asking me to bring her stuff from the store," he said, still holding me tightly, and added with a miserable laugh, "she called me a peasant."

I sniffled and squeezed him back with a laugh. "You called her Princess Francine first."

"Jacks, she just needed my help, and I treated her like a nuisance," he choked out between tears.

I'd only heard Kyle cry one other time…when he had left me a drunken voicemail after I'd moved to Chicago. Both times it tore up my insides. Kyle was such a strong man that it was unusual for him to shed tears. When he did, I felt his heartache as if it were my own.

"Most of the time she is a nuisance to you on purpose," I tried to tease. "Francine knows you love her."

Tears of sympathy for him fell down my cheeks too, and I added, "She knew you would always bring that stuff for her, even if you complained about it. That's why she called you and not one of her other two brothers."

His arms tightened, and he buried his face against my shoulder. I rubbed his back soothingly and then gripped his shirt to pull him tighter to me.

"What if she dies, and that's the last conversation we have?" he asked miserably.

"Kyle," I said, pulling back and forcing him to meet my eyes, "Francine will not die for a very long time."

I needed to hear the words as much as he did. The truth was, no one knew if she would recover yet, but negative thoughts put energy into the universe, and I couldn't let it seep out there.

Kyle nodded, and we let go of our tight grip on each other. Every nerve ending I had was hyperaware of the man in the room with me. Kyle went to the fridge and pulled out two bottles of water, offering one to me. We each took a sip from our respective bottles. The energy in the room was different somehow...nervous, excited, uneasy or some combination of the three.

"I need to ask you about something you said at the hospital earlier," he reminded me, "that you couldn't worry about the lives of two people you loved. Did you mean that?"

Our eyes held for a protracted moment. His brown eyes were red from tears. I reached up and wiped one from his cheek with my thumb. He covered my hand with his larger one, pulled it from his face and lifted it to his lips and kissed the inside of my wrist. The spike of his mustache sent excited sparks through my skin.

"Kyle," I breathed.

Kyle's phone rang, and he reached for it quickly, breaking the moment. My heart thudded in my chest from the thrill of feeling his lips on my skin.

"Hi Mom," he said after a second, "I came back to Francine's with Jackie to clean things up here. When are you getting in?"

My system was on overload, so I stepped away to give him a little privacy with his family. The stress of the day: my conversation with Uncle Masso, coming home to find Francine, the ride in the ambulance and now Kyle's lips touching my skin...it was all too much.

I went to the living room and huddled myself in my favorite spot on the couch and covered up with the lightweight blanket that Francine kept draped over the back of it. I only meant to close my eyes for a minute, but before long, the sound of Kyle's warm voice faded to a murmur as I drifted off into a catnap.

When my eyes opened again, the house was silent. I thought Kyle might have left, and I was angry with myself for dozing off. I hoped he wouldn't take it as my answer to his question of whether I still loved him?

I felt like an idiot for not taking my chance to tell him, but then I remembered his kiss to the inside of my wrist and my skin tingled once more. I rubbed the sleep from my eyes and stood up to head to the bathroom.

When I opened the door, there he was, standing in a pair of boxer briefs, hanging his towel on the rack to dry. I gasped in surprise, and he turned quickly at the unexpected sound.

"Sorry, I went straight from the gym to the hospital, and I needed a shower," he apologized.

My eyes, without my full permission, trailed his body from head to toe. When I had last seen him in any state of undress, he'd been rather soft and doughy, and I loved every inch of him. The grown man before me was still soft in the middle, but his arms and pecs, even his back and legs, had finely sculpted muscles and a smattering of tattoos. I wanted to touch it all.

"I guess I should apologize for not inviting you to join," he teased, noting my ravenous look at his form.

"Sorry," I gasped, "I didn't realize you were in here. I should go."

"Jacks, you don't need to go," he laughed. "I'm not fully naked or anything."

I did need to leave, though. He looked too good for words, and I wasn't sure what to do with myself.

"I'll use Francine's bathroom," I stuttered, running down the hall to Francine's freshly cleaned bathroom, closing and locking the door behind me.

I leaned against the door and let my heart slow down as I blew out cleansing breaths. When I finally calmed myself, I used the toilet and then looked at myself in the mirror as I washed my hands. I was horrified to find I had some mascara smudged under my eyes and my hair was a mess. Using a makeup wipe, I scrubbed it under my eye to clean it up. I smoothed my rumpled hair with my fingers and decided I was at least presentable. It wasn't fair that I looked like a mess, and he looked so good. So, so good...

When I opened the door, Kyle was waiting for me, sitting on the bench at the foot of Francine's bed. A startled gasp leapt from my lips, and he turned quickly to face me.

"We have to quit meeting this way," he teased. "I'm going to take it personally if you gasp every time you bump into me."

I let out an uneasy laugh. He patted the seat on the bench beside him, and after warring with myself for a few seconds, I finally sat down beside him, careful that I wasn't touching him, though there was nothing else in the world I wanted to do more. We sat quietly for a long time; me looking at my hands folded in my lap as I felt his eyes burning into the side of my face. He took my hand and wrapped it between his two bigger ones in his lap, stroking the back of my hand with his thumb. When I gathered my courage and met his gaze, I saw the emotion that had been trying to peek out on the car ride home.

"When you left, it nearly destroyed me. I looked for you for a long time, but every clue led to a dead end. The longer you were gone, I convinced myself that you never loved me. When you first got back to town, I didn't know how to feel," he admitted. "I had been so in love with you, and it really hurt when you left. I pretended I didn't know who you were just to hurt you back."

I flinched. Of course, I knew he recognized me that first day. All three of his siblings confirmed he knew who I was, but it hurt a bit to hear him admit it was meant to hurt me. 'Had been in love with you...' was it still a past tense?

"Then I saw you everywhere I went, and I thought it was some kind of prank," he added.

"It was entirely a coincidence," I reassured him.

"Is that what you believe?" he asked, our eyes locking.

My heart raced in my chest as he rubbed circles on the inside of my wrist with his thumb. There was no way he didn't feel my pulse dancing wildly under his touch.

"What do you believe?" I asked hopefully.

He broke our gaze and stared down at my hand in his for a moment before answering, "When I ran into you at Penny's Diner, I started to believe we were meant to find each other again. I believe we have both been living half-lives waiting for the other one to find us."

"Why did you stop looking for me?" I asked, hating myself for asking the question.

"Ego, mostly," he admitted sheepishly. "The longer you were gone, the longer I let our last argument feed into my ego, and I felt the need to show you I was more than just a broke baker. Eventually, I convinced myself you'd never come back to me, and I knew I had to move on."

And move on he did. One of the first times I bumped into him after coming back to Brooklyn was when I was buying tampons and found him picking up a pack of condoms. It almost destroyed me. I had to know.

"Are you still seeing other girls?" I asked, dreading his answer.

"No," he replied, "I had a date planned the week we ran into each other, but I canceled it. I haven't gone on any dates with anyone since."

I didn't realize I was holding my breath until it whooshed out with the end of his answer. A tear streaked down my cheek.

"Are you okay?" he asked, tenderly wiping the tears from my cheek.

I nodded and replied, "just relieved."

He flashed a smile and turned my face to his and kissed me gently. His hand wrapped around the back of my neck as he deepened the kiss, and I floated away to my own personal level of heaven.

When we broke apart to catch our breath, he rested his forehead against mine and said, "You're so beautiful."

"Please stay," I whispered against his lips, "I need you, please."

He nodded and replied, "I couldn't leave now if I wanted to."

With that admission, he pulled me back in for a kiss. Each kiss told a story:

You hurt me.

I'm sorry.

You came back.

I missed you.

Don't ever leave me again.

I'm here to stay.

Happiness flooded through my being, forcing tears down my cheeks. Kyle pulled back to look at me.

"Jacks?" he asked, worried.

"I'm just so happy," I laughed as I choked on a sob. "You wanted to know earlier if I meant what I said at the hospital. I did. I do. I always have."

"Then say it again," he challenged me, his eyes not wavering from mine.

"I love you, Kyle Carrollton. I love you," I insisted, "and I'm here to stay. I am yours."

With that, Kyle stood and scooped me up. I squealed in surprise but settled into his secure hold, trusting that he would not drop me.

"Where are we going?" I giggled.

"My room," he answered.

Kyle's old bedroom had been the scene of so many make-out sessions we had in our teens. I wasn't sure if it was nostalgia or if he was being respectful of his sister that he moved us to another room, but I didn't want whatever was happening to stop.

When we got to the hallway between Francine's room and his, he pressed me against the wall and kissed his way down my neck. I scratched lightly down his back, encouraging him to continue.

"You smell so good," he mumbled against my skin between kisses.

"So do you," I replied hazily.

My hands found the bottom of his shirt and made their way up it to feel the skin there. The defined areas of muscle were at odds with the memories I had of touching him in the past, but I loved his body both ways.

"Take it off," he whispered his encouragement into my ear.

With trembling hands, I pulled his shirt over his head and off.

"Now yours," he demanded, his eyes alight with desire.

A blush crept up my neck. I hadn't been undressed in front of anyone since we made love after prom. Seeing my unease, he caressed my cheek with his hand.

"You don't have to be shy with me," he insisted. "Your beautiful body is safe with me."

I felt my lips curve up into a smile. Kyle always made me feel beautiful, even when I didn't quite believe I was.

"Let me see you," he pleaded, kissing my ear. "Do you want me to help you?"

I nodded. It turned me on when he took my dress off that night. I wanted to feel that again.

Kyle stepped back just far enough to reach between us and pulled my shirt up over my head and dropped it on top of his on the floor.

"I knew it," he smiled, "gorgeous."

His hands caressed down my side, sending chills down my body. He grabbed my hips and pulled me against him and into a fiery kiss. I returned each one, knowing it would probably take me a lifetime to make up for the kisses we had missed in our years apart.

Kyle deftly unhooked my bra and tossed it toward the growing pile of garments in the hallway. His hands cupped my breasts, thumbs tracing circles around my nipples. They strained toward him, begging for his attention.

"Kyle," I pleaded or begged. I wasn't sure.

"Yes? What do you need?" he asked, playfully trailing kisses down to my breasts.

"I need...I need..." I stuttered, his ministrations wiping out my ability to speak coherently.

"Tell me," he prodded.

"You," I answered, "I need you."

"I'm right here, Sweetness," he smiled, holding us steady for a moment so that we could both catch our breaths. "I need you to tell me what you need me to do."

His eyes held steadily on mine, waiting for the words. How could he just stop everything? My breath raced in and out of me in frustration. Words? Who needs words right now? Why was he doing this?

"Jackie, I'll do what you ask," he encouraged. "All you have to do is tell me that's what you want."

I realized why he was asking. He spent the last five years worried that the reason I had left was that he had pushed me to do something I didn't want to. Even though I had reassured him that wasn't the case, he needed the words. I took a fortifying breath and met his eyes again. I knew exactly what I wanted...what I needed.

"I need you to make love to me," I admitted, "I need you inside me."

"Here in the hallway?" he asked, teasing me, stroking the back of his hand over my breast.

"Here, your bedroom, Time's Square," I replied, "I don't care, I just want you right now."

"Good answer," he grinned and reached down to unzip his pants, his hardness pushing his boxer briefs through the open fly.

He reached out and undid my pants and pulled them along with my panties down my legs, letting them pool at my feet and then did the same with his own. We were naked...gloriously naked together.

Cautiously, I took hold of his length and stroked from shaft to tip. His breath grew ragged as I repeated the action again and again.

"Are you ready for me?" he asked, slipping a finger between my folds and massaging my clit in a rhythm that set my knees knocking.

"I'm ready," I insisted.

Kyle cupped the backs of my legs and lifted me to straddle him. He pressed me against the wall.

"Guide me in," he said.

I lifted the head of his penis to my opening and pushed my hips forward to take him in. He thrust in the rest of the way, and we both let out a satisfied groan.

"You feel so good," he said, pulling back and then thrusting in once more.

His eyes grew wide, and he held himself inside me, not moving.

"Shit, condom," he said.

"Pill," I managed to say, "please."

"Are you sure?" he asked.

I nodded, desperate for him to keep going. He kissed me, and we made love against the wall in the hallway. The textured paint scratched against my back, adding a pleasant sensation to the experience. Kyle sucked my nipple into his mouth almost to the point of pain and then with a pop released it to repeat the process with the other nipple. He pulled out of me fully, and I gave him a look of confusion. Was he stopping?

"Hold on to me," he panted.

I wrapped my arms around his neck, and he carried me the final steps to his bedroom. Kyle put me down on the bed and covered me with his body. He reached between us and guided himself back to my opening. His hips rocked into me, and he set a delicious rhythm to drive us both toward orgasm.

"So good," he praised.

That ended me. My orgasm burst through me in circles, like a race car driving a widening track each lap. It started at our point of contact and wound up through my belly, and then the next circle stretched out to my breast and down to the tops of my thighs. The final round sent tingles out to my toes, through my arms, up my shoulders, my neck and out my mouth in loud moans of pleasure.

Kyle's body shook above me with his own orgasm coming over him. He grunted and thrust into me jerkily before going stone still, sending hot spurts of his pleasure inside me. It was messy and beautiful and everything I had been waiting for, which sent me into a second wave of orgasm, my cries louder than the first time. He covered my mouth with his in a kiss that quieted me.

After a minute, he pulled out of me and rolled over beside me on the bed, his chest rising and falling from the exertion. I turned to get a better look at him and rested my hand on his chest.

His eyes met mine, and a smile broke over his face. I leaned down and kissed him.

"My teenage dream came true," he chuckled, "My best girl naked in my bed."

"Worth the wait," I agreed with a smile and stroked a piece of sweat-damp hair from his forehead.

"But we're never waiting that long again, right?" he asked, tucking my long hair behind my shoulder.

"Never," I assured him.

CHAPTER 14

Tattoos and Momma Bears

Kyle
September 12, 2017

A beam of sunlight woke me up, leaving me feeling disoriented the next morning. Slowly, I realized where I was—I was in my childhood bedroom with my dream girl wrapped around me. Her long brown hair was covering her face, so I gently slipped the brown lock behind her ear and stroked my hand down her bare back. Her head dropped back sleepily, exposing her sweet throat to me. How was I to resist kissing every inch of that skin?

"Mmm, Kyle," she moaned.

"Sorry, baby, did I wake you?" I asked between kisses. I wasn't really sorry.

"I'll allow it," she purred, running her hands over my chest.

We kissed and explored with our hands a bit.

"Your body is incredible," she remarked. "How often do you go to the gym?"

"At least 3 times a week, sometimes more," I answered. "My partner Oscar comes with me, and we push each other. I just hit a new personal record—400 lbs."

"Wow," she said, dotting my chest with kisses, "You added more tattoos."

I nodded. I ran my hand over the one that she knew: the dragon with a tail made to look like a DNA helix with spades, hearts, diamonds, and clubs in it. The tattoo I'd gotten for her. I used to always call her Jacks, the Queen of my heart, so it was a reference to a deck of cards, and dragons were her favorite.

"I'm so glad you didn't cover that one," she smiled, covering my hand with hers. "I love that one."

"I couldn't," I replied. "Even as angry as I had been, it belonged there."

She nodded and then slipped her hand over my right arm. At the top were the four Teenage Mutant Ninja Turtles, just a strip of their eyes with masks. She smiled in understanding.

"For your siblings," she said, her eyes meeting mine.

I nodded. Our father was a huge fan of TMNT and had given us our nicknames based on the turtles. Francine was Leonardo, the oldest and our leader. Jason was Donatello, our science-loving, level-headed brother. Ben was Michaelangelo, the life of any party. I was Raphael, the one with the temper who always challenged our leader. I'm not sure if our father just knew us that well when we were first born or if it was in the way we were raised that we became more like our nicknames as we grew. Either way, it matched each of us completely. We were a unit through and through.

Jackie's hand traveled just below the tattoo to the next one, a blue band with my badge number 55228.

"Your badge number," she smiled again, running her finger reverently over the numbers.

"Are you sure you wanted me to tell you about my tattoos? It seems you know them all already," I laughed.

"Maybe I just wanted an excuse to explore your body," she teased.

"No excuses needed. Explore all you want," I invited.

There's nothing that makes you feel more awkward than being in bed with your girl and your parents finding you. I heard the front door open and my parents talking to each other.

"We have company," I warned, quickly getting out of bed and pulling on the pair of pants I had lying next to the bed.

Jackie's eyes went wide. "Kyle, none of my clothes are in here."

"Shit," I said, remembering the string of clothes we'd left between the master bedroom and my old one. I pulled an old shirt from my dresser and handed it to her.

"Here, put this on for now. I'll go distract them," I said.

She pulled the shirt over her head and covered her magnificent breasts, much to my disappointment. I rushed out into the hallway and grabbed the slew of clothes.

"Kyle!" my mother chirped.

"Mom!" I replied, hugging her with my free arm as I tried to hide the clothes I had picked up from the floor.

"I didn't know you'd still be here, but we saw your car parked out front," she said, her smile wilting as she noted the bra in my other arm, "you brought a date here?"

"Not exactly," I replied and cleared my throat. "Jackie is here."

My mother's eyes widened. She flushed and then pivoted and walked back to the living room without a word.

I closed my eyes and let out a breath I didn't realize I had been holding. I looked down again at the clothes that I was holding and felt no regret for last night. I went to the bedroom and handed the clothes out to Jackie, who was twisting the blanket in her hands.

"They know I'm here?" she squeaked.

"Was that supposed to be a secret?" I asked, a knot growing in my stomach.

"No, of course not," she replied, reaching out and squeezing my hand. "I just didn't think they'd learn this way."

I nodded in understanding. Jackie was always modest. She used to get embarrassed when I'd kiss her in front of my family.

"It'll be okay," I assured her, squeezing her hand back. "Why don't you get dressed and come out to say hello?"

She looked like she would rather die but nodded and got up to finish dressing. I left the room to meet up with my parents in the living room.

"Kyle, it's good to see you," my father boomed, wrapping me in a back-slapping hug.

Tattoos and Momma Bears | 147

"Good to see you too," I said, giving him a pat on the back as well.

"Kyle Anthony Carrollton," my mother scolded, "what on earth are you thinking! Sleeping with Jackie D'Marco in your sister's house while your sister is in a coma!"

My ears burned with embarrassment and anger. "Mother, I'm not a child. My sister being in a coma did not change the fact that I needed to sleep, and whether I chose to do that on my own or with someone is no one's business."

My mother's fair skin reddened in anger at my retort. She and I were much alike in that regard. Our feelings were often hidden behind anger. It was the dragon that guarded our hearts.

"Well, your father and I haven't slept at all since finding out," she shot back.

"Do you want a medal for that?" I asked incredulously. "Jackie was here and got Francine to the hospital. She made sure I got home safely, and she cleaned up the blood and puke from the floor. She helped me realize I wasn't a shit brother, and we comforted each other after a really long day."

"And what about five years ago? That girl tore your heart out. Let's be honest—all our hearts. Why would you let her back in?" my mother asked.

"Because I love her," I replied, "I always have."

It was then I could see Jackie out of the corner of my eye, listening from the doorway, wiping a tear that trickled down her cheek. I took a step forward and took her hand, pulling her into the room.

My mother's face washed with horror at having been heard.

"Jackie, I--" my mother stammered.

"It's okay, Mrs. C," Jackie said. "You're right, I made bad choices as a young woman. I abandoned your son and broke his heart. We've had so many conversations over the last few months, and last night, he made the choice to forgive me. I'm still working to forgive myself."

I pulled her to my side and squeezed her shoulder.

"Jackie, I'm sorry to hurt your feelings, but I don't know that I can forgive so easily. You didn't abandon only my son, you also abandoned our entire family without a word. We'd always been like family before everything happened," Mom reasoned.

"I know," Jackie replied, "and for what it is worth to you, I am sorry for leaving the way I did. I did what I thought was necessary to protect you."

"Mom, Dad, why don't you rest and clean up here? Jackie and I were just going to go to the hospital before my shift to relieve Jason," I said.

"Thanks Kyle, I think that's a good idea," my father said, taking my mother's hand and leading her back to the bedroom.

"Aren't you going to work?" Jackie asked once my parents had cleared the room.

"Oscar is going to pick me up from the hospital," I explained. "I need to check on my sister myself."

We went to the foyer and got our coats from the coat rack, which had Francine's fancy coats hanging from it. I pulled down the one I had seen Jackie wear yesterday and held it out to help her into it.

"Thank you," she smiled shyly at my gesture.

I leaned in and kissed her neck from behind, wrapping my arms around her waist to get one last cuddle in for the morning, and then I slipped into my coat and guided her out of the house.

"Why don't you drive?" I suggested.

"Really?" she asked. "I thought you didn't like it when other people drove your car."

"I'm trying to loosen up," I replied, getting into the passenger side.

She laughed, which is what I had hoped for. I knew that would help her get over the confrontation with my mother, plus I loved the sound.

"I wonder how Francine is doing," Jackie said, pulling out of the driveway and onto the street.

"Hopefully better than yesterday," I replied, resting my hand on her thigh.

She nodded and asked, "What time is Oscar picking you up?"

"He said he'd be there around eight, so I won't have too much time with Francine, but I'll call you later and see if you are still sitting with her. If you want to leave once my parents get there, I totally understand," I answered.

Tattoos and Momma Bears | 149

"No, I'd like to try to make amends," she said. "I love your parents, Kyle. I don't want things to be like this morning forever."

"Okay," I replied. "All the same, if things get to be too much today, you're welcome to take my keys and go rest at my place. Toby would probably love the company anyway."

"Thanks. Is Toby your roommate?" she asked.

"In a manner of speaking," I replied, "He's my cat."

"You have a cat?" she asked in surprise.

I nodded. Toby was supposed to be an engagement present for her. She loved cats, and we had seen this little yellow and white puff of fur on the humane society website a few weeks before she left. It was torture trying to hide him from her at the time to keep the surprise. I wondered if she would recognize him when she saw him all grown up.

It wasn't long before we pulled into the hospital. Dread sat heavy in my chest as we walked the corridors to the room number Jason had texted to me last night once they got Francine settled in the ICU ward.

We walked into the room hand-in-hand, and Jason stood to greet us.

"Hi, Sis," he said, greeting Jackie with a hug.

"Hi, Bro," he said, giving me a hug.

"Jason, how did she do last night?" Jackie asked, taking the seat closest to Francine and picking up her hand to hold it.

"She did well. Her vitals have been steady, but she hasn't regained consciousness yet," Jason said, his voice hoarse from exhaustion.

"She looks like she has a little more color," I noted, keeping my distance.

Jason nodded. "I couldn't be sure, but I thought so too when I woke up this morning."

I didn't believe telekinesis was real, but I tried to use it on Francine, begging her to wake up. Begging her to get better and come back to us. When she didn't stir, I turned back to my brother.

"Mom and Dad made it in," I said. "They'll come visit her later, but they need to clean up and rest first."

"Are they staying at Francine's house?" Jason asked.

"I think that's their plan," I replied.

"Jackie, you're still staying with her until Mom and Dad get here, right?" Jason asked.

"Yes, Kyle's going to work soon, but I'm here to stay," she replied.

Our eyes met, and I couldn't help but smile at the double meaning. She was here to stay with Francine, and this time I was sure she was here to stay with me.

"Speaking of which," I said, "I should head back down. Oscar should be here soon to pick me up, but I'll call you later."

I leaned down and gave Jackie a peck on the lips. Jason didn't let anything slip about how he felt about seeing that, but I wouldn't have cared what he thought. This was my life, my girl.

"I'm going to go now too, why don't we walk out together?" Jason suggested.

We walked together, and when we got into the otherwise empty elevator together, Jason's silence broke.

"Are you and Jackie back together?" he asked.

"Yes, and if you have a problem with it, keep it to yourself," I growled. "I already heard Mom's concerns about it this morning."

Jason nodded and stood silently for a moment as the elevator took us down another flight.

"When she left, it hurt us all," Jason said, "but I know that it hit you and Francine the hardest. I just hope she is back for good."

"She is," I grumbled.

"Good," Jason replied. "If there was anything good to come of this whole situation with Francine, it's that Jackie is back."

I nodded. As far as I was concerned, it was the only good thing that came out of Francine having that stupid surgery.

The elevator stopped at the lobby, and we left the hospital walking side by side, but Jason stopped me just outside of the doors.

"Be safe, Kyle," he said, and hugged me.

I clapped him on the back and replied, "I always am. Get some rest."

He nodded and went to his car. I found Oscar in the patrol car parked two rows over.

When I got into the car, he reached out and slapped my shoulder affectionately. "How is Francine?"

"Still unconscious," I replied, "but she had more color this morning."

"At least a sign of improvement," Oscar said, starting up the patrol car.

"Oscar, before we leave, can we say a prayer for her?" I asked.

Oscar looked my way and nodded. He knew I wasn't particularly religious and obliged me anyway.

"Yeah, of course," he said, pulling his crucifix from his shirt and holding it as we prayed for my sister's recovery.

CHAPTER 15

Get a Room

Jackie
September 15, 2017

I left Kyle in bed at 6:00 am to go see Francine. They'd removed her breathing tube, but she still wasn't conscious yet. They felt confident that she could wake up at any time, and I wanted to be there when she did.

My conversation with Uncle Masso was still weighing heavily on my mind and since I had read every magazine front to back at the hospital in the last few days, I took an accordion file of documents to look at from my parent's business to see if I could find anything else that didn't fit with what I had helped Nonni collect and turn into the police all those years ago.

I tucked the files under my arm as I walked to Francine's room. The nurse at the station waved to me as I walked by, recognizing me from visiting every day that week. I waved back and headed to Francine's room. When I got there, I found Ben and Francine's friend Shreya, deep in conversation about computers. When they heard me, they stopped abruptly and greeted me.

"Good morning, I'm sorry I didn't mean to interrupt your conversation," I apologized.

"Good morning?" Shreya croaked, "What time is it?"

"About 6:30," I replied, "I'm here early."

"Oh my goodness, I did not mean to stay here all night. I should go," Shreya stammered, picking up her things.

"Why don't you give me your phone number? I'll let you know if Frannie wakes up today," Ben suggested.

Shreya pulled a business card out of her wallet and handed one to Ben and one to me.

"Please, if either of you can give me an update on her, it would be a huge relief," she said. "I need to go home and get ready for work."

"Thanks for staying and keeping us company," Ben gave her his patented charming, crooked smile. "It was so nice to get to know you a bit."

Shreya nodded and escaped the room quickly, as if she had been caught doing something she shouldn't have.

"You've met Shreya before, right?" Ben asked casually after she had left.

I nodded. "Several times. She's very nice but quiet."

"She came by to sit with Francine, and we just started talking," Ben smiled. "She's a tech nerd like me."

"That's cool," I replied encouragingly.

It was adorable to see baby Ben with a crush on a girl, and Shreya was as sweet as could be. I didn't know how she would handle his boisterous nature, but who was to say? Maybe she would be the Yin to his Yang.

"No changes with Frannie yet," he said, looking down at his sister in loving concern. "I wish she would just wake up."

"Me too," I said. "How are you?"

"Worried," he smirked, "how is my brother?"

"Which one?" I asked.

He rolled his eyes and replied, "You know which one. Grizzly Adams."

I laughed, "He's doing alright. He's focusing on work, but I know he's worried too."

"You hear that, sis?" he said to his sister. "You've ruffled the great and powerful Kyle."

I smiled, but we all knew it was easy to ruffle Kyle. He cared too much about everyone and everything.

Ben turned back to me and said, "I'm going to go home and get some rest. Please let me know if anything changes."

"You know I will," I said, squeezing his shoulder.

"Mom and Dad said they were coming in around nine," he said.

I nodded and took my seat next to Francine and took her hand as I had done every morning. When Ben was gone from the room, I spoke aloud to my friend.

"Good morning, Frannie," I said. "It's September 15th...a great day to come back to us. We all miss you and want you to get better soon."

"I second that," Kyle said from the doorway, startling me.

"What are you doing here so early?" I asked.

"You left without something," he said.

"I did?" I replied, looking around at the few items I had brought, trying to remember what I left behind.

"Yep," he said, crossing over to me and leaning down, "this."

He tilted my chin up and kissed me soundly.

"Get a room," croaked a voice I hadn't heard in days.

We broke apart quickly and looked at Francine for a sign that it wasn't in our imagination.

"Frannie?" Kyle asked, touching her arm.

"Hmm?" she replied.

"You need to wake up now," he said.

"No," she muttered obstinately.

"I'm going to go get the nurse," Kyle said. "Don't let her fall back asleep."

I nodded as he raced out of the room.

"Frannie, don't go back to sleep; keep talking to me," I urged her.

She said something unintelligible but opened her eyes halfway as if the room was too bright.

"Hey gorgeous," I smiled, "welcome back."

"Water?" she asked, licking her lips, but her tongue was too dry to even wet them.

"Let's wait until the nurse checks you," I said.

The nurse rushed in, adjusted the bed to a more upright position, and began checking Francine over.

"She asked for water. Is she able to have some?" I asked.

"Until the doctor makes his rounds, all we can do is give her a little glass of water with a sponge to wet her mouth. We don't want her to take in too much until the doctor releases her for more," the nurse explained. "I'll be right back with that."

Kyle stood behind me and wrapped his arms around me, his head resting on my shoulder. The nurse came back in with the cup of water and the sponge on a stick for Francine to use to wet her mouth. Once she made a few swipes over her lips and inside her mouth, she looked over at Kyle and me and smiled.

"You look good, sis," Kyle said.

"So do both of you," she replied, smiling up at us weakly. "Happy."

Kyle squeezed me closer in agreement.

"We are," I replied.

"Good, my work here is done," she smirked, her eyes closing a little longer than a blink.

"How are you still tired when you've been asleep for days?" Kyle asked.

"I don't know," she muttered, "I just am."

"Well listen, I need to take off, but I will come back and see you this evening," he said, giving her hand a squeeze.

"I'm sure I'll still be here," she muttered.

He smiled and bent down and kissed the top of her head and said, "I love you."

"I love you too," she replied, surprised by his unprompted show of affection toward her.

"I'm going to call Mom and Dad. Jackie, can you call everyone else?" he asked, touching my shoulder.

His touch still felt surprising to my skin after years without physical touch from anyone. Surprising, but wonderful.

"Of course," I replied. He leaned forward and pecked a kiss on my cheek before leaving.

Shortly after Kyle left, the doctor came in to look at Francine and asked me to step out into the waiting room. I called out to Ben first, hoping to catch him before he went to bed.

"Is everything okay?" Ben asked, out of breath as though he had run to catch his phone.

"Ben, she's awake," I smiled, glad to be sharing some good news for a change.

"She is?" he replied, relieved.

"Yeah, the doctor is with her now, looking her over. I'm going to call Jason next and let him know," I said.

"Good, I'll call Shreya and let her know too," he offered eagerly.

"Thanks Ben, get some rest and come see her when you can," I replied.

"I'll definitely sleep better!" Ben replied. "I'll see you in a few hours."

"See you later," I said, hanging up with him.

I dialed Jason next, and he answered, "Hello?"

"Jason, it's Jackie," I said. "Francine is awake."

"Thank God!" Jason sighed. "Has the doctor been in?"

"He's with her right now. They asked me to step out," I replied.

"Thanks, I'll be there soon. I wanted to see her anyway before the start of my shift," he replied.

"I'll see you soon," I replied.

We hung up, and the nurse who had checked Francine out earlier came to get me in the waiting room and bring me back to see Francine again. When I walked into the room, I caught the tail end of the lecture the doctor was giving Francine about being secretive when she was sick post-surgery.

"It's very important that you mention all the side effects that you have going forward. Your body underwent some major changes with surgery and in the way it metabolizes things. We need to know about instances of vomiting so that we can understand why and treat it right away," the doctor said.

Francine nodded as though she were receiving a lecture from a parent.

"Miss Carrollton, I am also going to recommend that you see one of the therapists in our network to help you work through this," he continued.

"But she's going to be ok?" I asked.

"You are her caregiver at home, yes?" he asked.

I nodded.

"Miss Carrollton was very sick and neglected to tell her primary care physician. We need to make sure this doesn't happen again. As long as it doesn't, I expect she will make a full recovery," he replied.

I released my breath in relief.

"We're going to keep you overnight," he said to Francine, "but if no new concerns arise and you're able to hold down a few meals, we should be able to release you tomorrow evening."

Francine nodded and thanked the doctor. I went and settled back in the seat beside her bed.

"Well, that's good news," I said cheerfully. "Sounds like you should be on your way back home tomorrow."

"I hope it is that easy," she replied nervously. "It's been hard for me to keep food down for a while now. That's why I got so sick."

"I know, but they should be able to help you with that too," I encouraged her, squeezing her hand.

"Can you help me brush my hair before my family gets here?" she asked.

"Of course," I replied.

I got up and found the bag of toiletries I'd brought from home and dug out her hairbrush. I took half of her long blond hair and, starting from the bottom, worked my way up to her scalp in gentle strokes, working out the tangles she'd accumulated over the past few days in bed. When I was done, I went to the other side of the bed and combed the other half of her head in the same manner.

"I'm going to put it into a braid, so it doesn't tangle so much for you," I said, pulling both sides of her hair over her shoulder and braiding it neatly before tying it off at the end.

"Thanks," she smiled tiredly.

We sat quietly, me just observing my friend and being thrilled that she was with us once more. When she caught me watching her eyes locked on mine.

"Is Kyle still mad at me?" she asked, tears welling along her bottom lashes.

"What?" I asked.

"When I came out of surgery, I couldn't respond, but I could hear everything going on around me," she explained. "I heard Kyle leave in a huff when he heard how sick I had been."

"He was never mad, Francine, he was just worried that he was going to lose you," I assured her.

I pulled a tissue from the small box on the table tray and handed it to her. She sniffled, laughed, and dabbed at her face.

"He and I made a pact when my dad had his heart attack that we would always tell each other the truth about any illness we were experiencing. I didn't do that," she sighed regretfully.

I nodded. Kyle hadn't told me that part, but that made a lot of sense when I thought about what he had been spouting off that day.

"Francine, why did you keep it a secret from everyone?" I asked gently.

"I don't know," she replied. "I thought I had it under control. I didn't realize how sick I was until it was too late."

Francine's parents and Jason came into the room and smothered her in kisses and hugs. I took my files and stepped out of the room to give them space as a family to visit. I sat out in the waiting room and sorted through page after page, pouring over every detail to see if I found any anomalies in the paperwork, growing more frustrated by the minute with the lack of results.

I saw someone out of the corner of my eye, and when I looked up, I was surprised to see that it was Mrs. Carrollton.

"Can I sit with you?" she asked.

I nodded, and she took the seat next to me.

"I'm sorry for the way I reacted when I saw you and Kyle together again," she said quietly.

"You were going through a lot," I reasoned.

"Yes dear, but so were you," she replied, "and from what I've heard, you've gone through a lot since we last saw you. I'm sorry about your Nonni."

"Thank you," I nodded.

"I grieved losing you alongside my children," Mrs. C. said. "You were at my house so often, I forgot you weren't one of my children."

We both chuckled, and I replied, "I loved having other kids around. Growing up as an only child was lonely."

"Jackie, please swear to me you won't leave us like that again," she pleaded. "We can't take it again."

When she said we, I knew she genuinely included herself in that and wasn't speaking just for Kyle and Francine this time. I had voicemails and messages from her as well when I moved to Chicago.

"I'm not going anywhere," I replied, giving her a hug.

CHAPTER 16

What Should Have Been

Kyle
September 17, 2017

Ith Francine home from the hospital, life was finally getting back to normal. Well, a new normal: Jackie had agreed to come stay with me so that my parents could dote on their one and only daughter. Francine was thrilled with the attention and time with our parents. Jackie and I were both excited for some privacy.

Jackie and I brought several bags and suitcases of her things over to my place so that she would be comfortable. We left her furniture behind at Francines for the time being. There was space to set it up in the second bedroom for guests if we wanted to later.

Toby heard the door open and came running to me, the bell on his collar jingling. When he saw all the bags and the extra person, he scurried away to hide.

"Oh, poor baby!" Jackie sympathized. "We must have startled him with all this extra stuff."

"Don't worry, he'll be fine," I reasoned, adjusting the bags in my grip to close the door behind her.

"This is beautiful," she smiled at me, following me further into the apartment.

"Even more beautiful with you here," I replied. "Let's take your clothes back to the bedroom. I made some space for you in the closet and dresser."

Jackie followed me to my bedroom and put her bags on the bed. She was a very organized person. Even when she went through the files from her family's business, she liked to go through them in chronological order and put flags on things that she wanted to look at more closely rather than just pulling the paper out and re-filing it later. I just worried that she'd be crushed if she didn't find something soon. The document that she'd found weeks ago really got her convinced she would find something. Well, that and her Uncle Masso's behavior when she asked him about it.

I had to admit; the answer seemed too simple. It just felt like there had to be more to it. Her parents, Davide and Susan, were two of the kindest people I had ever met. Davide got me a huge discount on my tux for prom because he was good friends with the tailor. Susan would make a special meal for me anytime they knew I was coming over. It just never made sense to me that they would have conspired to steal millions of dollars from their clients and let their business go up in flames while they hid out around the world.

But I believed in justice with sufficient evidence, and there was certainly enough evidence that they had been involved in the scheme, so justice prevailed. Still, I wished they were innocent for Jackie's sake.

As we finished putting her clothes away, Toby came out of his hiding place and jumped up on the bed. Jackie was the first to notice and cooed over him.

"What a handsome boy!" she praised, scratching his ears.

She picked him up and cuddled him against her shoulder. He used his nose to nuzzle her chin. I could hear him purring from where I stood.

"Wait..." she gasped, looking over at me, "is this the little fluffy kitten we saw on the humane society website before graduation?"

I nodded. Her jaw went slack, and she looked Toby over again.

"I can't believe you got him!" she sniffled. "You've taken such good care of him."

For her. I had gotten him for her. Selfishly, I had thought of returning him to the shelter when she left, but I couldn't bring myself to do it. It wasn't his fault what happened. Over the years he'd become my buddy, and I was glad I hadn't let my impulse get in the way of keeping him.

Toby let out a familiar cry that meant he was ready for dinner. Jackie put him down on the ground, and he raced off to his food dish in the kitchen. That reminded me of the plans I had made for us. I was going to take Jackie out for a special evening. A smile crossed my face as I hung the last of her clothes in the closet.

"Could I persuade you to wear something special for me tonight?" I asked, shuffling through the clothes I had just hung for her.

She crossed to the room and shifted through to the other side where my clothes hung and replied, "That depends...can I persuade you to wear something special for me?"

We grinned like idiots at each other and pulled out the special outfits we wanted the other to wear.

I found a sweet, taupe-colored dress with small red flowers on it. When I looked to see what she had pulled, we both burst out laughing. It was a green T-shirt I had worn for Saint Patty's Day last year that said, 'Let me borrow a kiss, I promise I'll kiss you back.'

"Is that a request?" I asked, pointing to the shirt.

She shrugged playfully and tossed the shirt at my face. I caught it in my hand before it made contact. She rushed me and tackled me onto the bed, covering my face in kisses.

"You're falling behind," she complained and looked lovingly into my eyes.

"Here I was trying to be romantic and take you on a date," I smiled, pulling her into a long kiss.

When her brain caught up with what I had said, she pulled back again.

"A date?" she grinned excitedly.

"Yeah, to a nice place I haven't tried yet," I answered, running my hands up and down her arms. "Do you want to go?"

She nodded.

"Will you wear the dress I picked out?" I asked.

She nodded again with more enthusiasm and then nuzzled her face into my chest. Her hand slipped over my chest, up my neck and caressed my cheek.

"What are you doing?" I laughed.

"Just enjoying this perfect moment," she sighed dreamily.

I wrapped my arms around her and ran my hand up and down her back, eventually making my way to her ass and giving it a squeeze. I could appreciate a perfect moment, but if we were going to make it to dinner, we needed to get up.

"Let me give you a perfect evening," I whispered against the top of her head.

"Please let me pick an appropriate shirt for you," she insisted.

I nodded, and she gave me a kiss before getting off of me. The cool air of the room replaced the heat of her body, and I immediately wanted to pull her down with me once more.

Instead, I got up to run my errand, promising her I would be back soon. I had called the florist and asked them to put together a bouquet of dark red ranunculus flowers. They looked like roses to me, but Jackie insisted they were different, and they were her favorite, so I was happy to get them for her if it made her smile.

Our reservation was for 7:30 at the newest restaurant in town that we passed a zillion times over the last week while Francine was in the hospital, The Appleton. It was supposed to have the best dinner menu in town, with a live band and dance floor. I wasn't much of a dancer, but I knew Jackie would pull me out there at least for one song. I would do it just for the chance to hold her close and sway to the music. It would be a nice cap to the evening.

I rushed off to pick up the bouquet from the florist before picking up Jackie. The florist paired the deep red flowers with a stalky kind of flower with little light blue buds and tucked them into a clear vase. They wrapped a simple twine around the center a few times before ending in a bow. She would love this. Hell, I loved it, and flowers weren't really my thing.

The girl at the shop was kind enough to put the vase down in a box so that I could put it in the car and it wouldn't roll around all over the place while I went back home.

It was 6:30 when I got back with the flowers. Being funny, I rang the doorbell and waited for her to come to the door. When she opened it, my heart jumped in my chest. She was in her bathrobe with her hair pinned up, and I was almost certain nothing was underneath.

"Flower delivery, ma'am," I replied businesslike.

"Oh, sorry, I thought you were my blind date for the evening," she replied, playing along with my game.

"No, ma'am, I'm not blind. I have to have good vision to make the deliveries. I am just here to deliver the flowers, but I was told I may still get a tip," I continued.

Jackie smiled mischievously and quickly flashed what was underneath her robe at me, shocking me into silence, before taking the flowers from my stunned grasp and closing the door in my face. She laughed hysterically on the other side of the door. When I heard that she had moved away from the door, I came in and followed her to the kitchen, where she set the bouquet on our small kitchen table.

"Do you give that kind of tip to all the delivery guys?" I asked, wrapping my arms around her from behind.

"Nah, just the really handsome ones," she giggled. "These flowers are beautiful. I can't believe you remembered I love ranunculus."

She turned in my arms and gave me a quick kiss on the lips.

"I'm glad you like them," I replied, hugging her against me.

"It's not time to go yet, is it?" she asked. "You told me we needed to leave at 7:00."

"I figured I'd clean up a little too," I replied, "maybe change into my special shirt you picked?"

"Can I watch?" she teased.

"You can help if you like," I replied wolfishly.

"If I help, we definitely won't be ready on time," she laughed.

"And we do have a reservation," I sighed, pecking a kiss to her lips before releasing her from my embrace, "Another time, perhaps."

"We have a reservation?" She squealed in delight, "Where are we going?"

"You'll see," I answered coyly.

She sighed in exasperation but went back to our bedroom to continue getting ready. I took a quick shower and changed into the navy-blue shirt she picked from my closet and paired it with gray slacks and brown shoes and belt. I wasn't much for getting dressed up, but for her I would wear a monkey suit every day if she asked me to.

"Kyle, can you come zip me up, please?" Jackie called from the bedroom.

"Be right there," I called back, settling my tie in place and giving myself one last look over.

I made my way to our bedroom and found her standing in front of the mirrored closet door trying to do up the zipper herself.

"I've got it," I said, taking over zipper duty.

She took a deep breath in to give the dress a little more room to come together, and I could slide it all the way up with minimal effort. When I was done, she released her breath, and I finally looked at her. She styled her silky brown hair in waves, pulling the sides back with a sparkling clip. She had a pair of dangling silver earrings and a matching silver necklace with a red gemstone that rested at the top of the valley between her breasts. While I loved seeing her in heels, I was grateful to see that she'd chosen to wear flats so that she was comfortable walking around.

We went out to my car, and I helped her into the passenger seat before getting in on the driver's side. I started it up and drove us to The Appleton.

"Oh, Kyle, The Appleton?" she sighed happily as I held open her door. "I've been dying to try this place!"

"Me too, Jacks," I smiled, taking her hand as we walked up to the front door together.

The host seated us near the window that faced out to a little garden on the west side of the building. I admired the scene with the sun setting in the background. Francine would love it. Maybe we could take her once she was feeling better and eating normal foods again.

"The garden is just beautiful," Jackie remarked, "we got so lucky with our table!"

"We did," I smiled, "have you looked at the menu yet?"

"No, I was too busy taking everything in. This place is just gorgeous," she said, looking at every corner of the room.

"I've heard the food is even better," I replied, picking up my menu.

"Oh? Anything specific?" she asked, finally picking up her menu too.

"Truffle fries," I said, "I've heard the truffle fries are heaven."

"So besides that, what are you getting?" she asked.

"I was thinking about the duck," I replied, "I've never had it."

She nodded and continued perusing the menu, her forehead crinkled in concentration.

"You're looking damn good tonight, Jacks," I commented.

I startled her from thought, and she smiled at the compliment.

"You do too, Babe," she winked.

When Jackie saw the server coming, her eyes went wide. She felt the pressure to decide before he made it to us.

"We can have him come back if you're not ready to order," I laughed.

"No, you just order first, and I'll make my choice," she insisted.

"Welcome to the Appleton," the server said. "Have you been here before, or do you have questions about the menu?"

"This is our first time here, and the place is just beautiful," I remarked kindly.

"Thank you. Do you know what you'd like to order, sir, or would you just like to start off with some drinks?" the server asked.

"I'd like the duck with a side of truffle fries," I replied, "with a house-brewed beer."

"Of course, and you, ma'am?" he replied, turning the question to Jackie.

"Can I get the Creole Chicken with bacon asparagus?" Jackie asked.

"Excellent choice," the server remarked. "Would you like a glass of wine or something from the bar?"

"No, I'll just have water, thank you," she smiled, closing her menu and holding it out to the man.

What Should Have Been | 171

The server took our menus and went back to the kitchen to place our orders.

"I'm glad your parents decided to stay in town until after the holidays," she smiled. "I think Francine really enjoys being doted on."

If you'd have asked me about a week ago if Jackie would express happiness at the idea of my parents staying in town, I'd have said you were crazy. I'm glad that she and my mom worked things out and are on speaking terms again. She'd always felt close to my mom, and I knew my mom felt the same way.

"We're all glad they're in town for a little while," I replied. "I don't know if I could take the constant interruption from my dear sister to fluff her pillow or fetch her slippers."

Jackie playfully kicked my shin under the table and feigned indignation. "Kyle, your sister is not so needy that she would ask you to fluff her pillow. She'd be afraid you'd try to smother her with it."

We both laughed. Truth was, I would do anything Francine asked and probably offer to take out her trash too. I was relieved that she was recovering well, but I still felt guilty about giving her such a hard time before she went to the hospital.

"Still, I'm sure she appreciates being cared for by our mother more than she does being cared for by any of her brothers. I think Mom loves it just as much," I replied.

"She does," Jackie replied. "I stopped by while you were at work, and Mrs. C was making a grocery list with Francine so that she could make things she could eat post-surgery. She had read a bunch of stuff about what was good to eat to get the most nutrients with the smallest serving sizes."

"Good, maybe that will help Frannie with planning out her meals once Mom and Dad go back to Florida," I replied.

Jackie nodded.

"I'm glad you and Mom are talking again," I added.

"Me too. She and I talked about it, and she was very worried that I would leave again," Jackie sighed. "The only way I can prove I'm staying is to do just that."

There was a tug at my heart from hearing that. Jackie had been so sincere about staying, but my whole family worried that one false move and she would be on the run again. It had to be hard for her.

"I'd be lying to you if I said I didn't worry about it too. Not because you left before, you've explained your thoughts behind those decisions. While I may not fully understand it, I do respect it and understand that you were in a tough place," I explained. "What I worry about now is the challenges that come with being the partner of someone on the police force. Oscar's wife tells me all the time that it is hard on her and the kids knowing he could be in danger at any time during his shift."

Jackie held my hand on top of the table and looked deeply into my eyes.

"Kyle, even before we got back together, probably even before you ever decided to become a police officer, I worried about you every day. I can't say that there won't come a day where being the partner of a police officer nearly breaks my heart in two, but in the time you've been helping me look through my parents' files, it is so clear to me you love what you do. It's what you were made to do, and I can't imagine asking you to give that up unless you physically couldn't do it anymore," she said, squeezing my hand affectionately.

"Still, I would feel better if I introduced you to Oscar's wife, Maria. They've been together since before he joined the force," I insisted.

"Kyle, I'd love to meet your friends, and I can only imagine having someone that knows what it's like to be with a police officer would be good for both of us." She smiled reassuringly.

"Thank you, that makes me feel better," I replied with a sigh as the tension left my shoulders.

I didn't know how much relief it would bring me to hear her agree to meet Oscar and Maria. The thought that she could walk away again because of my job ate at me every day, but giving her someone to lean on put me at ease.

The server swept through to bring my beer and refill Jackie's water goblet. We each took a sip of our drinks and let the conversation fade for now.

"I applied to Brooklyn College and got my acceptance letter," she smiled widely.

"That's amazing, Jacks!" I beamed with pride. "When do you start?"

"Well, I decided to start in the spring, so just after the holidays," she replied excitedly. "Registration starts in a few weeks. I'm so excited!"

"I'm excited for you too, Babe. You've wanted to be a teacher for so long. You're finally on your way to making that dream a reality," I said.

She nodded enthusiastically. "Now I just need to get a flexible job and figure out where I'm going to live."

"What do you mean, where are you going to live? Am I kicking you out at the end of the year?" I asked.

"Well, no, but we didn't talk about me staying there on a permanent basis, and the original agreement with Francine was that I would find a job and a place to live by the end of the year," she replied sheepishly.

"Well, consider the place to live checked off your list," I grumbled, "I don't know how many other languages I have to ask you to stay in but give me a week or so and I'll learn that phrase in each of them."

She burst out laughing because she knew I was serious. I might just do it for the hell of it and say it to her every day until she finally gets it through her thick skull that I want her with me always.

I reached across the table and took her hand in mine. With every ounce of sincerity, I looked deeply into her eyes and asked her for the one thing I wanted most in the little Italian I had learned, "Per favore resta con me. Stay with me."

"I'd love to," she replied earnestly, squeezing my hand.

My heart filled with the promise that she was staying. With the weight of worry lightened, we enjoyed a beautiful evening of dinner and dancing.

PS. Word on the street was correct; the truffle fries were awesome!

CHAPTER 17

Suspicions at the Storage Unit

Jackie
September 25, 2017

My duties as Francine's caregiver were essentially over since the Carrolltons were staying through the holidays. This left way too much room in my mind to think and overthink about how lunch with Uncle Masso had gone. Kyle mentioned the police had investigated him back when my parents were arrested, but they had nothing to go on. Still, I felt in my gut that he knew something and wasn't telling. Seeing my parents in prison was just more than I could bear. I just couldn't face them when I felt like I had betrayed them.

The only possible clues were in boxes at the family storage unit. Before Francine went to the hospital, I'd gone through the last of the files I had picked up. Nothing stood out as I made copies of a few things before re-filing. Some of the documents had transactions transferring funds to the accounts that incriminated my parents. I was determined to find out when it all began. The amounts moved over to the two accounts in 2012 were not huge on their own, but the frequency made it add up quickly–especially in the last few months leading up to their arrest.

I drove my car out to the storage facility and parked. The facility was enclosed, so I made my way into the building and went to unit #34. The door opened easily to a unit filled with banker's boxes containing files from the beginning of my parent's business in 2000 to its closure in 2012. There was a walking path and then a similar stack of boxes from 2007 to 2017 in the center of the unit for Uncle Masso's reign as the owner and operator of D'Marco Italiano and then another walking path and against the far wall was the boxes from Nonno's reign as owner of D'Marco Italiano from 2000 to 2007. Why had my family kept records back this far, I did not know, but it made them feel better, so I didn't question it.

I walked down the aisle facing my parents' business and replaced the box I had taken the last time I was in. I pulled a couple of boxes from the top of the stack for 2011 to get to the summer months of that year. That was around the time the restaurant was starting to struggle and Mr. Clearwater first offered to partner with Uncle Masso. Maybe my parents were trying to help save the restaurant? If that was their intention, surely there would have been better ways to go about it!

Lost in my thoughts, I didn't hear the dangerous-looking Latino man come up behind me.

"What are you doing here? Are you a reporter?" the man demanded as he staggered menacingly toward me.

I dropped the box I was pulling out, completely startled by his hateful gaze. I backed up further into the unit—he'd blocked my only other way out with his broad body. Dread consumed me as I looked past the man and found no way to escape him.

"What? I'm no reporter," I explained. "I-I think you have the wrong unit. This is my family's unit for our business files."

I stepped backward until I found myself pressed against the wall of boxes lining the back of the unit. He stalked closer to me.

"I've never seen you before. Why should I believe you?" he asked.

"I've never seen you before either, and-and I'm the one that entered this place with a key," I stuttered nervously. "I think you're the one in the wrong p-place. You need to l-leave."

"I'm not leaving," he persisted.

"Jackie?" a familiar voice called out from the open doorway.

"Stay back Drew, this guy is crazy," I warned.

"Luis isn't crazy," Drew said, walking up behind the towering man and putting his hand on the other man's shoulder. "He's my boyfriend."

I felt my mind race and my eyes blink rapidly in surprise. I had no idea that Drew was gay. Thinking back, he never really dated anyone while we were in school. At least not that I knew of...I guess I never really thought about it. I felt the tension released from my body, and I steadied myself against the boxes.

"Oh, I'm so embarrassed," I laughed in relief. "I didn't know you were seeing anyone!"

"Luis Vazquez, this is my cousin, Jackie D'Marco," Drew explained. "She's one of the few people allowed in here."

Luis took a step back from me, but the tension didn't fully leave his body.

"Sorry he scared you. We came to bring some files out from the restaurant, and I think you just surprised him," Drew whispered conspiratorially. "What are you doing here, anyway?"

"I was just going back through some files from my parent's business. Some things just don't make sense to me still," I explained.

Drew gave me a concerned look.

"Jackie, you and Nonni were the ones who found the original evidence that convicted your parents. I'm not sure what you still expect to find," Drew sighed sympathetically.

"I don't know yet either, but I have to check it out so that I can let it go," I rationalized.

"Suit yourself," Drew shrugged.

He turned toward his giant boyfriend and said, "Luis, Jackie's going to take a few boxes from her parent's business. She shouldn't be in our way when we bring in the rest of the boxes from the restaurant, but she may need some help taking what she needs out to her car."

Luis nodded and went on stacking boxes in the next aisle over.

"Hey Jackie," Drew called back out to me as I started pulling out another box for myself, "Please don't mention Luis to my dad. He's not quite comfortable with finding out that I'm gay yet...I'm just trying not to rub his face in it."

"No problem," I smiled reassuringly.

Suspicions at the Storage Unit | 179

In record time, Drew and Luis brought in about half a dozen boxes between the two of them. I had two boxes I wanted to take out to my car sitting by the door.

"Jackie, let us help you carry your boxes out," Drew offered.

"If you guys don't mind, that would be great," I smiled at my sweet cousin.

Drew took the box at the top of the stack as I pulled one more box to take with me. Luis took the box from me and sat it on top of the other box before picking it up too.

"Oh wow, thank you," I said appreciatively. "Now I'll have free hands to lock up."

Luis acknowledged me with a nod and a grunt and stood outside the door as I lowered and locked it. Before I could step away, he used the boxes to hold me against the door. I let out a startled gasp.

"Drew may be okay with you taking this stuff, but I'm still suspicious of your motives. I know the police had investigated his dad back then. Are you trying to frame Masso?" he asked.

"No," I squeaked, "I'm just trying to see if someone framed my parents."

"From now on, keep your distance from here," Luis warned. "As far as I'm concerned, this is the last set of boxes you are getting from here. Right?"

Who was he to tell me I couldn't come for more boxes? This was *my* family's storage unit. I was welcome to go through anything I wanted to.

"It's really none of your business," I replied. "I'm not out for Masso or anyone else. I'm just looking for the truth."

He glared at me for several thuds of my heart against my rib cage before setting me free and walking off ahead of me. My legs were like jelly after the strange encounter. What is Luis trying to protect in storage? He has no real stake in the situation other than his relationship with Drew, so I didn't understand his reaction to me and my boxes.

I made my way out to my car and unlocked the door for Drew and Luis to put the boxes in. Drew gave me a tight hug.

"I'm glad you know about us now," he said, jerking his head toward Luis.

While I wasn't sure what to think of Luis, I was glad my cousin felt safe enough to come out to me. I felt bad I hadn't been around sooner to support him when he came out to his father.

"Me too," I replied. "I'm sure your dad will come around soon."

He nodded, though I could see in his eyes he wasn't sure that would ever be true, and called out, "See you again soon!"

"See you soon," I replied, promising myself I would make another lunch date with what remained of my family.

I could see Luis and Drew talking somewhat heatedly as I pulled away from the storage facility. If I gave time for the dust from today to settle, maybe I could ask Drew some questions about his boyfriend without making him defensive.

Luis' reaction was still rather unexpected. Why did he think I was a reporter? Had reporters been asking questions about my parent's case recently? The storage facility itself wasn't in the greatest part of town. I would have assumed someone was trying to steal from the unit before I would have suspected a reporter.

I also worried about my cousin being with someone who had such a dangerous demeanor. Did Luis intimidate Drew when he didn't get his way? Drew was so mild-mannered, I couldn't imagine him being comfortable with someone capable of such menace. Perhaps I could have Kyle run a background check on him. I wondered what Kyle might find about Luis Vazquez and hoped that it would be nothing, for Drew's sake.

CHAPTER 18

Poor Penmanship and Punks

Kyle
September 25, 2017

I sat at my desk grumbling as I tried to read Oscar's horrendous handwriting. Hating myself for each report I had to fill out after my stupid bet with him, my cell phone started ringing. Jackie's sweet face lit up my phone screen, and that made me smile for the first time that day. I picked up the phone and answered.

"Hey, Sweetness," I said, leaning my head to the side to hold the phone between my ear and shoulder so that I could continue working on my reports.

"Hey," she said hesitantly.

"Is everything okay?" I asked, my skin prickling with dread.

"Yeah, um…I just had a weird afternoon," she answered mysteriously.

"Well, I should be home in about an hour or so," I offered. "Do you want to just wait and tell me about it then?"

"Actually, I was wondering if you could look into someone for me," she said in a rush.

"Why-y-y?" I asked, dragging out the word for effect.

"Well, I was out at the storage facility today and–"

"What the hell were you doing out there by yourself?" I demanded, cutting her off, "I've told you it's not safe for you to go there by yourself."

"I'm a grown woman who lived in Chicago for five years," she reasoned with me.

"I know. I'd rather you waited and let me go with you," I insisted.

"Fine, I'll ask you to go with me next time," she sighed with what I could tell through the phone was a dramatic eye roll.

I could understand why people had spanking fetishes. I could have put her over my knee right then and there. Perhaps something to try out later.

"So, what happened when you were there?" I asked, bringing us back to the topic.

"Well, I was pulling boxes to take home, and this guy was there and accused me of being a reporter. It turns out the guy is my cousin Drew's boyfriend," she explained.

"Drew's boyfriend?" I asked, making notes for myself as she spoke.

"Yeah, I didn't know he was seeing anyone. Anyway, um, his boyfriend sort of threatened me before Drew got there to clear up the confusion. I thought we were good, but then he threatened me again when we were getting ready to leave," she confessed.

"This is exactly why I don't like you going over there by yourself," I chided. "What did he threaten to do?"

"Well, he didn't really threaten to do anything, per se. He just kinda backed me into the wall and told me I wasn't to come back for any more boxes," she clarified.

"That's odd. What's it to him if you take more boxes home to go through?" I remarked.

"That's what I thought too," she agreed. "I'm just worried about the way he overreacted to the whole situation. I wanna make sure Drew is safe being around this guy."

"What's his name?" I asked, pen at the ready.

"Luis Vazquez," she said, "first name: L-U-I-S. Last name: V-A-Z-Q-U-E-Z."

I blew out a puff of air and replied, "It's a pretty common name, Babe, but I'll see what I can find. Chances are it's probably not going to lead us anywhere."

I pulled up my database and typed in the name and, as I suspected, there were pages of hits.

186 | Speak of the Devil

"I found his social media, so I could forward you a picture of him if that would help," she offered.

"It'd at least narrow it down," I admitted.

She texted a picture of the guy.

"You'll probably uncover just as much digging through his social media as I will through police records," I teased.

"Detective Jackie on the case," she sparred back.

"Alright, Detective, I have to go," I said. "I love you; see you soon."

"I love you too," she said and hung up.

I took a good look at Luis Vazquez's face.

"You are on my shit list, pal," I said to his picture. "You don't threaten my girl."

I started the search for any records pertaining to Luis Vasquez and the birth date that Jackie had found on social media and let it run while I continued filing the reports Oscar and I had taken for the day.

I went back to Oscar's notes from the day and continued typing, squinting to make out his horrible chicken scratch until I saw that my search had completed.

I pulled the record that looked like it best matched the Luis Vasquez that Jackie had encountered. The picture looked like the same guy, so I read through a laundry list of speeding tickets he'd gotten over the last few years, a drunk and disorderly back in 2012 and a sealed juvenile record. Interesting, but nothing that added up to the behavior Jackie had seen today. Luis Vazquez's only offense of note was being a bit too old for Jackie's 23-year-old cousin—he was nearly 33.

I sent a text to Jackie to let her know what I had found out about Luis Vazquez. I knew she'd be disappointed, but I was just glad it wasn't a rap sheet a mile long. It sounded to me like Vazquez was just trying to protect Drew.

After another 10 minutes of trying to read Oscar's notes, I let out a frustrated huff and called him.

"Romero, what the hell does this say?" I asked when he answered the phone.

"Kyle, is that you?" Maria asked.

I didn't normally curse around Maria out of respect for her, so I felt bad she had heard it from me.

"Yes, sorry Maria, it's me," I sighed.

"How are you? We haven't seen much of you lately," she made a tsk noise at the end of her accusation.

"I figured Oscar would have told you," I said by way of apology. "I've reconnected with my high school girlfriend, Jackie."

"Ha! I knew he was lying to me!" she cried out and then began cursing at Oscar in Spanish.

I caught something about him being a lying cheater who owed her 50 dollars. I guess I didn't need to feel so bad about cursing in front of her. She was giving him a good-natured earful!

"Were you two betting on me?" I sighed.

"Always," she laughed, "it's what keeps our marriage going."

"Well, that's just sad," I quipped.

"I didn't say it was the only thing that kept our marriage going," she volleyed back. "A girl doesn't get pregnant 4 times by herself."

"Ah, come on, Maria! You promised me you'd stop talking about that stuff to me," I whined.

"I made no such promise," she said, "but I do want YOU to promise me you will bring Jackie to meet me soon."

"I promise," I replied. "I already talked to her about it. Would you talk to her about what it's like being the partner of a police officer?"

"You sure you want her to hear it from me?" she teased.

"I can't think of anyone else I'd rather she hears it from," I replied sincerely.

"Fine, fine. Well, I know you didn't call just to chat me up," she laughed.

"How do you know?" I bantered back.

"Because you were asking what something says. I assume you got stuck filing reports again?" she said.

"Yep. How the hell do you read his writing?" I asked.

"Years of practice, plus you forget I was a nurse before I quit to stay at home with the children," she replied. "Here's Oscar."

I heard the phone shuffling from one Romero to the other. I was pretty sure Maria scolded him for his bad handwriting too.

"Hey buddy, how are the reports going?" Oscar snickered into the phone.

"I'm going to sign you up for calligraphy classes for Christmas or send you to a Catholic boarding school until they smack your knuckles with a ruler enough for this shit penmanship you have," I complained.

"I went to Catholic school; that's the best they could do. Besides, it's better than it used to be," he replied.

"I don't think that's possible," I insisted.

"Alright, what are you stuck on?" he asked.

We ran through about 10 or so different phrases that I couldn't make out at first. That helped clear it up enough that I could remember the stop and could fill in from my notes and memory.

"Seriously, man, penmanship!" I cried out when we were done.

"What? I can read it...mostly," he laughed.

I heard a bit of commotion at Oscar's end.

"What's going on?" I asked.

"Maria thinks she's in active labor. Her mother came to town to be with her and help until we can bring the baby home. I think we need to go now," Oscar replied, an old pro at getting Maria to the hospital.

"Shit, is it time already? I thought she still had a few more weeks," I replied.

"We thought so too. Guess this one wants to be born in September instead of October. I need to pull the car around so we can leave. We don't want Maria to have the baby in the car like last time," Oscar said.

"Of course, keep me posted," I said.

"You got it," Oscar replied and hung up.

It was hard to think of what life would be like with one child, let alone child number four soon to make his entrance into the world. Maria and

Oscar made it all look so easy, but I knew better. Sleepless nights with sick kids and keeping the peace so that they don't kill each other.

Growing up in a big family was fun, but I think it might be nice just to have 2 kids and be able to spoil them while they still have a playmate. I hadn't thought much about kids in the past. When Jacks and I were together in high school, that stuff seemed so far away. It was probably too soon to have the conversation at this stage in our new relationship, but maybe it wasn't? We were having sex damn near every day. She was on the pill, but it wasn't 100% effective.

We weren't ready for kids yet. She wanted to go back to school to get her teaching degree, and I wanted to get married before we started a family. We had plenty of time to think about having kids. Why rush this time with each other? Still, I couldn't help but wonder what a child we made together would look like.

CHAPTER 19

Too Close for Comfort

Jackie
October 2, 2017

Francine was itching to get back to work. She hadn't been home long, but I could see the restlessness in her as I sat across from her in her living room. She loved working at Charmed CRM Solutions. I couldn't blame her! Being able to afford her parents' home at 24 was quite a feat. Granted, they sold it to her well under market value, but it was still something that was years away for me and Kyle.

"How have you been, Frannie?" I asked.

I hadn't seen her much since she came home from the hospital and I moved into the apartment with Kyle. I felt terrible for not having checked in sooner.

"Better," she smiled. "The vomiting has stopped completely. I started seeing the therapist my doctor referred me to. I'm not sure I need it, but I want the surgery to be successful, so I'm going to keep going."

Kyle and I had many conversations about her choice to have surgery. Before her complications, it was something I was considering myself. I knew Kyle loved me exactly as I was, but I wanted to have the kind of beautiful figure every man dreamed of. Not to chase other men or to make Kyle jealous...I just wanted to feel beautiful in my skin.

"Can I ask you something?" I asked and hesitated.

"Yes?" she replied wearily.

"Why did you decide to have the surgery?" I asked. "You'd lost a lot of weight before the surgery on your own."

"I did," she conceded, "but I was still dangerously close to developing type 2 diabetes, and my blood pressure was higher than they wanted. The doctors felt that having the surgery would likely improve both. At 24, I didn't want to depend on medications for both things, so I moved forward with it."

I nodded.

"Are you thinking about it?" she asked curiously.

"No, well, I don't know. I was just surprised that you had decided to do it. You always loved the way you looked, and you're beautiful at all sizes. I just wondered why you made the decision," I replied.

"Honestly, it was Kyle. He and I made a pact to encourage healthier behavior within our family after Dad's heart attack. The boys all have jobs that require some level of physical fitness. Even though they are still big guys, they're probably in the best shape they've ever been in. It was time for me to do the same so that I could be there for them and have a long, healthy life," she replied simply.

"Good for you, Frannie," I smiled encouragingly, "I'm so proud of you."

"Enough about me," she smiled conspiratorially. "How are things with Kyle? No dirty details, please."

My heart raced at the thought of him. He made me so happy.

"Really wonderful," I smiled dreamily. "He took me to the Appleton about a week ago and bought me my favorite flowers. It was such a perfect night."

"Aw, I'm glad he's finally stopped keeping you at arm's length. That was hard to watch," she admitted sympathetically.

It was hard to live through, so I could only imagine how hard it was to watch. Kyle didn't make it easy for me to win his heart again, but it had been worth every ounce of effort.

"There are times he still seems guarded with me. Then we have a night like we did at the Appleton, and I know we can get through it. Unfortunately, I have to put in the work to break down the walls," I sighed.

"He's worth the work," she replied.

"I know," I smiled.

"So, are you going to come back and stay with me a little after the holidays when my parents go back to Florida?" she asked casually.

"Do you think you'll still need extra care for that long?" I asked, hoping she would say no.

I was so content at Kyle's apartment, but if my best friend needed me, I would of course go.

"No, I was just wondering what your plans were," she replied coyly.

"Oh," I laughed, seeing the neon lights of what she was asking without asking, "Kyle asked me to continue living with him as long as I want."

Francine squealed and clapped and laughed excitedly. "I'm so happy for you!"

"You have no idea how happy I am too," I replied, sunlight practically beaming from my face.

"How is it going, living with him?" she asked curiously.

"He's surprisingly tidy," I admitted. "Everything has a place, and everything goes back to its place when he's done using it. You'd never know Toby lived there too. He keeps the floors and furniture swept multiple times a week, if not every day."

"You hadn't noticed that about him when you guys were dating as kids?" she laughed. "Kyle has a bit of OCD. He always has been when it comes to the spaces he lives in. If it doesn't have a place, he gets rid of it."

For the smallest of seconds, I wondered if that habit extended to people. We were so new in knowing the adult versions of each other...surely I had a permanent space in his heart?

"You look worried," Francine noted. "What is it?"

I shook my head and laughed. "Nothing...I just got lost in thought for a minute there."

She nodded, but the look she gave me betrayed the fact that she didn't fully believe me.

"It's taken some getting used to having the police radio squawking all day and night," I admitted, changing the subject.

"Oh yeah! I nearly murdered him in the two weeks I stayed there when I was doing some work in the house. Never again!" she vowed.

"It mostly fades into the background for me now, but anytime I hear his patrol car number respond to a call I can't help but listen," I admitted.

"I would too," she agreed. "It's interesting to listen to his day as it's happening. It just grated on my nerves after a while. Too many 'code this' and '1 Alpha' that's."

"Kyle's been helping me learn the codes, so I am getting familiar with what some of the more common ones mean," I said. "It's fun! It feels like he's letting me into his secret clubhouse."

"Aww, that's great, Jackie!" Francine grinned.

I saw the time on the clock hanging behind Francine and realized it was time for me to go.

"I'm sorry to cut our visit so short, but I need to go over to Brooklyn College and sign up for my classes," I said, standing up from my spot on the couch.

"I'm so happy that you got accepted," she said, standing and wrapping me in a hug. "You'll be the best teacher there is!"

"Thanks, I'm so excited to get started," I replied, hugging her gently in return.

"We'll have family dinner on Sunday this week," Francine said. "Can you please let Kyle know? Seven o'clock."

"Of course, we'll be here," I said. "Take care and call me if you need anything at all."

"I will," she said, as we walked out onto the front porch.

Francine watched as I got into my car and pulled out, waving from the top step of the porch.

As I made my way to the college, I heard my phone ringing in the pocket of my purse. I pulled it out and answered, "Hello?"

"Hey Jackie, it's Drew," my cousin greeted me amicably.

"Oh, hey! How are you?" I asked.

"Great! I was just wondering if you might be able to hang out with Robbie for a day for me," he asked.

"I'm sure I could," I replied. "I am job hunting right now for something that will work around my college classes, but it'll probably be a restaurant job or something, so there should be some flexibility."

"You're the best!" he said. "I'll text you the details; it sounds like you're driving."

"Yeah, I'm headed over to Brooklyn College to sign up for spring semester classes now," I admitted. "I'll watch for the text about Robbie."

"Thanks again, I'll let you go," Drew said.

"Bye," I replied and hung up.

Soon, I parked at Brooklyn College and made my way to the admissions office. The campus already felt welcoming, like it was just waiting for me. The admissions office was buzzing with students trying to resolve financial aid inquiries and new students coming to sign up for classes, like me. I joined the line for the class registry and waited my turn.

"Next please," a middle-aged woman called out, waving me toward her window at the long desk shared by four people.

"Hi," I said in greeting, "I've filled out my registration for spring semester, and I just wanted to turn it in."

I handed her my form and my student ID that I got when I came in last week to pick up the paperwork.

"Ok Ms. D'Marco," the woman said, "let me just enter these in the system for you so that I can print your official class schedule."

She punched loudly on the keyboard in front of her, filling in my class schedule on the computer system. I was excited to get back to school. I loved the atmosphere and the way each teacher had their own style.

"This is a pretty ambitious course load," she explained. "Are you sure you don't want to move one of these courses to the summer or fall semester?"

"I'd like to at least give it a try before the drop period," I replied. "I graduated in the top five of my class in high school. I think I can manage it."

She nodded and finished inputting my registration. She printed a copy of the class schedule and handed it to me, the paper still warm and smelling of toner.

"Here you go. Payment for classes is due by November 15th," she said. "If you need to speak with financial aid, it is just down on the left."

She gestured toward the line on her left.

"Thank you," I replied and jumped over to the end of the line for financial aid.

I felt a tightening in my chest. My parents had established a trust fund for my education, but the authorities seized and used it to repay the millions of dollars they were accused of stealing. I had a little money I had set aside for living expenses, but it wasn't nearly enough to pay for my courses outright.

Lost in thought, I didn't realize I was next in line until the girl from behind the counter called out, "Can I help you?" in an irritated tone.

I approached the desk and handed her my forms.

"No parental co-signer?" she asked dispassionately.

"No," I replied, "they are unable to co-sign."

She nodded and punched my information into her system.

"You're all set," she said. "They'll issue payment to the school about a week after the dropout period, and any leftover amount will be mailed to you on a check."

"Thanks," I replied, taking the stack of documents and leaving the school for the day, a little more melancholy than I had come in. Realizing how my parents' actions had once again messed with me and my future was just upsetting and infuriating.

As I got closer to my car, I saw a flyer on the window and smiled once again, excited for the college student experience. Though I would not be attending as a traditional 18-year-old student who stayed on campus, I still wanted to attend events that were important to me and enriching to my experience.

When I lifted the paper from under my wiper blade, I nearly dropped everything I was holding as I read the type-written note.

Jackie,

Your parents are guilty! You'll never find evidence to free them. Stop searching.

You'll be sorry if you don't!

My hands shook. Who could have left this note? How did they know I would be here today? The only person who knew I was here was Francine, and she had been supportive of me seeking information on my parents. Not to mention she was my best friend.

I sat down in my car and hit the speed dial for Kyle's phone.

"Kyle," I croaked when he answered the phone.

"Jackie? Are you okay?" he asked.

"I think someone is following me," I sniffled on a shuddering breath. "I went to the college today to register for classes, and someone left a note under my wiper."

"What does it say?" he asked, his tone darkening.

"That my parents are guilty. Stop searching for evidence, and if I don't, I'll be sorry," I replied, ending in a horrified sob.

"Are you still at the college?" he asked.

"Yes," I answered, choking back tears.

"Stay right where you are. Lock yourself in the car and wait for me. I'm going to come out and take down a report," he said. "I'm only a few minutes out from the college."

I cried into the phone, scared for my life and his. At the same time, I was relieved he was the one that would be coming.

"You're safe, Jackie. I'll make sure of it," he insisted. "I'm pulling up to the college now. Are you parked in the admissions lot?"

"Yes," I replied raggedly.

"I see you," he said. "I'm going to hang up now and find a parking space."

We hung up, and I stayed seated in my car, not certain that my legs would hold me. When he parked, he got out and came up to the passenger side of the car and carefully picked up the note and my stack of school papers with gloved hands.

"Are you okay?" he asked, settling in the seat beside me.

"I'm freaked out," I admitted quietly.

He nodded. "Did you see any suspicious vehicles that looked like they might be following you as you were driving today?"

"No," I replied.

He picked up the note and read it, his ears reddening with anger that someone would dare threaten me.

"We'll need to eliminate your fingerprints since you would have touched this with your bare hands," he said.

I nodded.

"You can come down to the precinct another day to do that. I'm sure you'd just like to go home," he replied compassionately.

I nodded again. Words escaping me.

"Who knew you would be here today?" he asked.

"Just Francine," I replied. "I went to visit her before I came here."

"You didn't mention it in passing to anyone else?" he asked.

"No, I went to Francine's and then straight here..." I said, but then I remembered Drew's phone call, "oh wait, I spoke to my cousin Drew on the phone!"

"And you told him where you were going?" he asked, making notes in his notepad.

"I did, yeah," I replied, recalling our conversation, "but Drew's a sweet person; he wouldn't do this."

I would bet my life on that. Drew was one of the best people I knew. He wouldn't go to these kinds of lengths to scare me off.

"Weren't you just very suspicious of his boyfriend's behavior the other day?" Kyle reminded me.

"Do you think he could have done it?" I gasped.

"Anything is possible, Jacks," he said. "I can't even rule out Francine until I corroborate her whereabouts at the time."

I was horrified that Francine would be dragged into this. She was recovering from major surgery.

"She's your sister!" I replied outraged, "You know she didn't do it."

"Yes, I do, but I still have to present evidence to prove who did without a shadow of a doubt. My word on the matter only goes so far," he replied in an irritatingly calm but authoritative voice...his cop voice.

"I can't believe this is happening," I sighed, rubbing my forehead with the heel of my hand.

"Don't worry, we'll get to the bottom of it," he assured me.

I vowed to myself that I would work equally hard to figure it out. Surely, this note was a sign that my parents were innocent if it was worth threatening me. Whoever left it must have a lot to lose if the truth were to come out.

CHAPTER 20

Mackenzie Mayhem

Kyle
October 23, 2017

I would never admit it to him, but I had missed Oscar Romero while he had been on parental leave for the last few weeks. He had a way of making the days go by faster with his stupid dad jokes and ever-present smile.

I was grateful to have him back on patrol with me again.

"Hey Carrollton, can we stop and say a quick prayer?" he asked. "I got an extra little one to make sure I come back home to, and you've got a girl waiting for you at home now too."

I nodded and pulled off into the parking lot of a shopping plaza. Oscar pulled out his crucifix and held it in his hand as he bowed his head and recited his police officer's prayer.

"Dear Lord, we ask for courage to face our fears and courage to take us where others will not go. We ask for strength of body and spirit. We ask for dedication in doing our jobs well. Give us compassion for those who need us. And please, Lord, through it all be at our side. Amen."

"Amen," I said in reply.

I didn't usually feel anything one way or another when Oscar recited this prayer, but it hit me a little differently that day, like someone had joined us in the car. A protective force for good.

We got back on the road a minute or two after navigating the exit of the parking lot.

"So how is Kyle Jr." I teased him.

"You mean Emilio?" he smiled, unfazed by my antics.

"If that helps you sleep at night," I continued.

"At this point something has to," he chuckled. "Little Emilio has not figured out day from night yet. He's got a touch of colic."

I recalled one of the girls had that too. Maria looked like a zombie for months until the illness settled down.

"Didn't Rosalie have that too?" I asked.

"No, it was uh...Carmen, the third baby," Oscar replied.

I nodded.

"Are you taking notes for your own little brood of Carrollton children?" Oscar asked coyly.

"No," I answered plainly, "we're not ready for kids just yet."

"Ah, just at the stage where you're having lots of fun practicing, eh?" he laughed.

"Something like that," I replied, with a cocky smirk escaping my lips.

"How is it going with her?" Oscar asked, his tone serious but light.

"Really good, man," I replied. "My life feels different with her in it. Better."

"Of course it does," he teased. "You were a miserable son of a bitch when she wasn't."

"Thanks, partner," I chuckled.

"You know what I'm talking about, man," Oscar said.

"Yeah, I do," I acknowledged.

It was true. Jackie D'Marco had chased the black clouds that had been hanging over my head, for as long as Oscar had known me at least. It felt so good to have her light in my life again.

"So, Maria wanted me to ask if you guys wanted to come over on Halloween," Oscar said, "she thought she and Jackie could stay home and chat while passing out candy and taking care of Emilio so that you and I could take the older kids around the neighborhood."

I was anxious for Maria to meet Jackie, but if I had to look like an idiot, I was going to pass on behalf of both of us.

"Seriously man? Do I have to wear a costume?" I grumbled.

"Nah, just your sterling personality will be enough," he laughed.

I was relieved to hear that. My brother, Ben, was the Halloween nut, not me. Even Francine enjoyed a good costume party. I knew when it was time to have kids, Jackie would want to do a family costume, and I would do it with gusto for them. For now, I am keeping my dignity.

"I'll check with Jacks, but I'm sure she'd love that," I replied.

"Good, ever since Maria heard you two were together, she's been dying to meet Jackie," Oscar said.

"I'm glad to hear that. I think they'll be fast friends," I replied. "Jackie needs to have someone to hang out with other than my sister. Francine is so busy with work most of the time."

"All units, all units, shots fired. There's a standoff in progress at 1616 Caldwell Avenue. Requested backup, again, all units," the dispatcher's voice called through our radio.

Oscar picked up and radioed back to dispatch our location and ETA as I turned on the lights and sirens.

"This can't be good," he said grimly. "It's the Mackenzie house again."

Shit, I hadn't realized until he said that, but he was absolutely right. Timothy Mackenzie had a habit of beating his wife and six small children when he was on an alcohol-filled bender. Unfortunately, his wife, Lorna, had a habit of calling the police out only to drop the charges and let him back into her home. We saw it all the time, but none that matched their frequency.

Lorna refused to believe that she and the kids could make it without Timothy. He'd so thoroughly convinced her she couldn't, that she truly believed the son of a bitch. The last time we took the call, I "accidentally" cracked his head against the top of the police car when I was shoving him into the back seat. It was totally worth the two-day suspension. Apparently, it doesn't seem so accidental when the person's head hits the top of the car more than once. Who knew?

I pulled up to the scene and used my patrol car to block off the street from all regular traffic to minimize the risk of casualties. As we got out of the car, I could hear Timothy yelling at Lorna to shut up, and Lorna was screaming and crying.

Oscar and I drew our weapons and aimed them at Timothy, cautiously crossing over to join our fellow officers, who were using their car doors to give themselves an added layer of protection from any shots that might be fired next. Timothy was standing in the doorway, holding a handgun, and waving it around as he continued to yell at Lorna to shut up.

"What's happened?" I asked the officer closest to me.

"Mackenzie fired one shot inside the house and then one shot out toward us—it hit the hood of the cruiser. We believe it's the missus that was hit by the shot fired inside. Paramedics are on standby to take the injured party once we can secure the place."

"Carrollton," Oscar whispered to me from the other side of the car.

I crossed behind the car and squatted down beside my partner.

"They have a back door to this house," he whispered. "Maybe we could at least get some of the kids out through the back door. They should remember us from the last time."

I nodded; the other officers on the scene clearly had not been here as often as we had. It seemed as good an idea as anyone had at the moment.

"We're going to try to go around back and get the kids out of the house," Oscar whispered to the other officer, "you keep Mac distracted."

The officer and his partner nodded as Oscar and I sneaked down to the corner and followed the alleyway around to the back of the Mackenzie house. Four of the six children were outside by themselves, probably numbers five and six were in school, these looked like they were the younger four.

"Hi kids," Oscar said, "do you remember us?"

The oldest one in the bunch, a little blond girl with dirty clothes, nodded, which prompted the other three to nod as well.

"We're going to get your mommy out of the house, but first she wanted to make sure you guys were safe with us," Oscar continued. "Can you two go with my friend Officer Kyle?"

The older two children ran to my side, and I took their little hands in mine, and we turned back down the sidewalk. Oscar hefted the two smaller children into his arms and began to follow.

"What the fuck do you think you're doing? Those are my fucking kids!" Timothy Mackenzie shouted as he raced out the back door of his house.

"Keep going, Carrollton," Oscar ordered me before speaking to Timothy. "We're just making sure your kids are safe until we get everything sorted out."

"Like hell you are!" Timothy shouted, holding his gun out and firing off a shot.

I looked back and saw Oscar crumble to the ground, and the two smaller Mackenzie children ran toward me and their older siblings to get away from the danger. Their little faces were full of fear and unshed tears. The kind of terror no grown adult should face, let alone ones so small. A father was supposed to protect their children from monsters, not be the monster.

Shots continued as we ran around the corner to the safety of my patrol car. We passed the other two officers as they rounded the building to try to subdue Timothy and take control of the situation.

I placed all the kids in the back of my patrol car and handed them the bottle of water I hadn't opened yet this morning and the lunch box that Jackie had packed for me so that they could snack on it if they were hungry.

"You all need to stay here," I ordered before closing the door and running back toward the danger. Their four sweet faces contorted in looks of absolute terror.

When I got back to the back side of the house, more units were arriving and surrounded Timothy as he fired off yet another shot, barely missing one of the first responders to the scene. He backed himself to the back doorway of his home and pointed his gun from officer to officer, working out which one to take out first in this showdown.

I looked for Oscar and was grateful to see another officer putting pressure on the wound he'd sustained to his leg. He appeared to be in pain but responsive.

"Stop firing, Mackenzie," I ordered. "It doesn't have to go down like this. Let us take you in and get help for you and Lorna and the kids."

"You can't help me," Timothy said, tears running down his face. "You can't help Lorna. I'm pretty sure she's dead."

"What about your kids, man?" Officer Brady asked. He'd been to this house as many times as we had. "They'll need their dad."

"And their dad will be rotting in jail for killing their mother," Timothy shouted in agony.

He was right. If Lorna really was dead, he would be prosecuted for her murder.

"She should've left me when she had the chance," he sobbed and lowered to his knees, gun still in hand.

I saw an opportunity to disarm him and approached him slowly.

"Timothy, let us help you," I urged as I slowly got closer to him.

Just as I made it close enough to him to take the gun from him, he looked me in the eye with an expression of pure malice and said, "I told you. You can't help me," and fired his gun.

My life flashed before my eyes in the seconds that followed as his body slumped back, and blood sprayed in all directions. Timothy Mackenzie had shot himself in the head. Right in front of me. I fell backward onto the ground too, my weight suddenly too much for my legs to hold.

Officer Brady ran up to me and squatted beside me to see if I had been wounded too.

"I'm fine," I said, sitting up in the grass.

"Carrollton, what were you thinking?" he scolded. "That fucker could have killed you."

"I thought he was submitting and I could disarm him," I admitted.

"You're very lucky," Brady remarked as a flurry of ambulances came onto the scene to help with the injured.

"Trust me, I know," I replied. "Please go check on Lorna. I'm fine."

"Kyle! Oh my God, are you hurt?" Jason called as he ran up to me, noting I was covered in blood.

"I'm fine—it's the shooter's blood," I replied. "Oscar got hit in the leg. He's over there."

"I've got him," Jason assured me. "If you want to ride along, get in the ambulance."

I found one of the officers who were first on the scene. He was a rookie and looked like he was about to cry or puke or both. Officer Matthew James stood perfectly still, like a statue, still in shock at the events that had unfolded.

"James," I called out to him, and he shook himself from his trance.

I tossed my cruiser keys his way, and he gave me a look of pure confusion.

"The Mackenzie kids are in the back of my patrol car. Go stay with them until CPS gets here," I ordered. "I'm going to ride along to the hospital with my partner."

He nodded and rushed around the other side of the house, grateful for the task I had given him. The task that got him away from the spot he most likely pissed himself in near his colleagues for the first time.

I caught up with Jason and his partner and helped them heft the gurney with Oscar on it into the back of the ambulance before getting in.

"This one was too close, man," Oscar said as a way of apology.

"Yeah, it was," I agreed.

"Can I borrow a phone to call home?" Oscar asked.

I patted my pockets and remembered that mine was still sitting in my patrol car set on silent mode.

"Sorry, I left mine in the patrol car," I said.

Jason pulled his phone from his pocket and let Oscar call his wife.

"I texted Francine and told her you were okay," Jason said.

"Good," I said. "She'll let Jackie know. I'll call her once we get Oscar to the hospital."

Oscar let Maria know we were on the way to Brooklyn Memorial and asked her to bring me a clean shirt. Oscar was about the same size as me, so that would work.

"Thanks, man," I said as he hung up with her. "I'm sure she's got better things to worry about than to bring me a clean shirt, though."

"It's the way she copes with stuff like this," Oscar explained. "She needs something to do, so she feels like she can help."

I nodded. I wondered what Jackie would need to feel better in these situations. Definitely a long night of hugging and cuddling, but in the heat of the moment, what did she need? I instantly regretted that I had left my phone behind because I wanted to ask her.

As we pulled up to the hospital, I turned to my brother, "Jay, can I borrow your phone?"

He pulled it from his pocket and handed it to me and said, "Just put it on the passenger seat up front when you're done."

I nodded, and when the ambulance stopped, I got out and helped him lower the gurney with Oscar, popping the wheels into place. His partner nudged me out of the way and finished the task so that they could rush Oscar in.

I dialed Jackie's number, one of the few I knew by heart, and it rang several times before going to voicemail.

"Hey Jacks, it's me calling from Jason's phone. I left mine in the patrol car. I'm fine, but I rode along to the hospital with Oscar. Can you come pick me up at Brooklyn Memorial in an hour or so? I am going to hang around until he is done with surgery. I'll explain everything when you get here. I love you," I relayed to her voicemail.

As I hung up the phone and put it on the seat as Jason had asked, I heard a commotion in the waiting room that was just on the other side of the ambulance entrance doors. I rushed in to help, not considering my present condition, and was stunned to find that it was Jackie causing the uproar.

"You need to tell me where Kyle Carrollton is now!" she demanded of the receptionist.

"Ma'am, we don't have a patient here by that name!" the woman shouted back.

"His police scanner said he was on his way to this hospital," she said, "why don't you get off your ass and ask someone if he's just come in?"

"Why don't you take a seat?" the receptionist bellowed back.

Jackie dove over the desk for the woman. I rushed forward and pulled her back.

"Let me go!" she yelled, not realizing yet that it was me.

"Sweetheart, I'm right here," I said, holding her tighter as she thrashed around trying to escape my hold.

When she let her brain catch up with my words, she stopped thrashing, and her brown, red-rimmed eyes looked up at me, pooled with tears, and she screamed in horror.

"Help him!' she cried. "Please help him; he's hurt! He's covered in blood!"

"Jacks, Jacks, it's not mine!" I assured her, quieting her down.

She sighed and crumpled into me. I caught her weight against my blood-soaked shirt and dragged her lifeless form to the closest bench. When she was sitting next to me, I slapped her cheeks until she came back around.

"Jacks, I'm fine," I assured her as she came back around. "I swear."

"I thought I lost you!" she sobbed.

I shook my head. "Just a close call, that's all."

CHAPTER 21

Trick or Treat!

Jackie
October 31, 2017

I seethed from the passenger seat as Kyle and I drove to the Romero house for dinner on Halloween night. We had an argument at the apartment about his picking me up late to leave. He had been late every night for dinner over the last week. While I understood his job wasn't a 9-to-5, I felt at the very least he could let me know when he was on his way home. Couldn't he understand his close call recently had done more than rattle me? He hadn't been hurt at that time, but Oscar hadn't been so lucky. What if it were Kyle next time? My stomach clenched at the thought.

When we arrived, Kyle shut off the car and turned to me.

"Jacks, I know you're upset with me, but can we please put it aside for the evening? I want Maria and Oscar to meet the girl I fell in love with," he said and cupped my cheek with his large hand.

His admission of love melted me every time. While I still wanted to be angry, I knew this dinner was important. Oscar spent just as much time with Kyle as I did, if not more. Being in his good graces would only expand my relationship with Kyle.

"Okay," I replied.

He leaned forward and kissed me. He whispered a promise over my lips, "I'm sorry. I'll call next time."

"Thank you," I replied and kissed him back.

We took the dessert I made and rang the doorbell. Oscar opened the door for us.

"Hola, welcome to my home," he smiled and reached out his hand for me to shake, which I did and then leaned forward and kissed his cheek.

"Thank you for inviting us. I'm so glad to see you out of the hospital, Oscar," I said.

"Carrollton, is your girl hitting on me? I think she's hitting on me," he teased Kyle.

"You wish," Kyle replied good-naturedly, following Oscar into the house.

It was incredible to me that someone could be shot in the leg a week ago and be home in time to take his children out for Trick or Treat. Granted, he would do it in a wheelchair, but Oscar was every bit as happy-go-lucky as Kyle had always described him.

"Oh, Carrollton, when I was at the hospital for my rehab today, I checked in on Lorna Mackenzie. She's going to be in the hospital a while longer, but it looks like she is recovering well," Oscar mentioned. "She was able to speak to me a little today."

"That's incredible," Kyle remarked. "She was shot in the head. She's lucky to be alive."

"Her kids are split up in foster care. No one in the family could take them all," Oscar said, checking in on his new baby in the bassinet with a haunted look.

"At least they never have to worry about Timothy ever again," Kyle reasoned.

Kyle had told me there were six children in the Mackenzie family. I couldn't imagine fighting for your life while worrying about all your children. And those poor children! Some of them had witnessed their mother being shot by their father. Did they even know he was dead and that their mother had survived? And then to be separated from one another... what a horrible thing to happen to innocent children!

I tried to clear my thoughts of my earlier hurt and the sadness of the news about the Mackenzies by taking in my new surroundings. The

Romero house was small for such a large family, but you could feel the love and warmth it held. Family pictures and religious pieces covered the living room wall. The room was tidy but clearly lived in—a basket of toys in the corner, a bassinet with a sleeping baby in another corner, a stack of magazines and papers on one of the end tables, a half empty baby bottle and a clean diaper and pack of wipes on the coffee table.

"Your house is lovely," I praised, changing the subject as I took off my jacket and hung it on the coat rack inside the doorway.

"Thank you, but I can't take credit," he said. "Maria keeps this place running. I just work and play with the kids. Right, mi amor?"

"That's right," she agreed, coming into the room from what I assumed was the kitchen. "Jackie, your dress is beautiful!"

"Thank you," I replied, "you look great too. Are you sure you had a baby just a month ago?"

"He's sleeping just over there if you need proof," she laughed. "He's kept me running day and night; I am thinner than I was before I got pregnant with him."

"You poor thing!" I commiserated.

"I love it though. New life in this house is always a welcome blessing," she smiled. "Kyle, I know you didn't bring whatever that heavenly smelling dish that you're holding. What did you make, Jackie?"

"Oh," I laughed, "I hope it's okay, I brought caramel apple crumble for dessert. There's vanilla ice cream in the bag if you want to make it a la mode."

"I'm keeping her Kyle, your decision doesn't matter anymore," Maria said, hugging me tightly. "She can come live with us if you get tired of her."

"I don't think so," he said, playfully pulling me from Maria to give me a possessive squeeze, and added, "I'm going to put this down in the kitchen."

"Be careful not to knock over my milk in the freezer; I just pumped." She called after him.

I heard Kyle let out a theatrical shudder, which made me smile. Kyle was always a bit squeamish about bodily fluids, though blood never bothered him much. I never understood the distinction in his mind, but I guess not all phobias make sense.

Oscar and Maria exchanged a knowing glance and laughed. It seemed they were aware of his disdain as well.

"Maria, there's no milk in here. Did you leave it attached to the pump again?" Kyle asked.

"Nah, I just wanted to make sure Jackie knew what she was getting into," Maria smiled and gave me a conspiratorial wink.

Maria may have decided to keep me, but I was keeping her too! She was so much fun, knew which buttons to push with Kyle, and I could just feel goodness radiating off her.

"Jackie already knows all my embarrassing secrets," he said, coming back into the living room and giving Maria a peck on the cheek. "Don't forget, she knew me before puberty after all."

Oscar's eyes lit up.

"Ooh, maybe I should stay for girl talk and send you out alone with the kids, Carrollton," Oscar grinned, rubbing his hands together mischievously.

"Forget it! You are getting out of this house," Maria ordered. "I love you, but if you don't leave me for an hour or two, I might strangle you."

"Alright, but take notes, eh?" Oscar said, giving Maria an affectionate pat on her butt.

"You know I have a mind like a steel trap," she replied. "I don't need notes."

"But I do!" Oscar complained.

"And his handwriting is terrible," Kyle reminded Maria.

The three older Romero children zoomed into the room dressed in their costumes. The two little girls were dressed as Elsa and Anna from Frozen, and the little boy was dressed like a police officer. My heart squeezed at the sight of their sweet, excited little faces.

"Papa, Papa, is it time to go yet?" the little boy asked excitedly.

"No, Raul, we are eating dinner first, remember?" Oscar reminded his son patiently.

"But what if all the good candy is gone by the time we go?" the little girl dressed as Anna asked in concern.

"I promise there will be plenty of good candy, Carmen," Oscar assured her, sitting her on his lap to fix her auburn wig so that the braids were even on both sides.

"Mama, will you go with us?" the other little girl asked.

"No, mi hija, I have to stay home with baby Emilio," Maria reminded her. "He's still sick."

"Babies are stupid," the little girl huffed, crossing her arms over her chest.

"I thought so too, Rosalie," Kyle said, squatting down in front of the little girl and taking her little hand in his, "but eventually they grow up and become fun playmates."

"I don't think so," Rosalie replied, eying him suspiciously.

"Scout's honor," Kyle promised her, "My brothers were both babies when I first met them, and now they're all grown up, and they're my best friends."

"Hey!" Oscar cried out, feigning hurt.

"Besides your dad, I guess," Kyle added.

"Papa, were you a baby when you met Uncle Kyle?" Rosalie asked wide-eyed.

Kyle laughed at her naïve question and replied, "I still think he's a baby now."

Rosalie threw her head back in laughter, and the rest of us joined in.

The moment melted all my insides like chocolate in a fondue pot. I had no idea how sweet Kyle could be around small children!

"Dinner should be ready now, if everyone wants to take a seat in the dining room," Maria said, making her way to the kitchen.

"Can I give you a hand with anything?" I asked.

"Sure, come with me," Maria replied, waving for me to follow her.

"Uncle Kyle, sit with me!" I heard the children plead in turn.

"Uncle Kyle is going to sit with Miss Jackie," Oscar announced. "She's our new friend, and she already asked to sit beside Uncle Kyle."

"Awww..." they all cried out in unison from the other room.

"I don't have to sit beside Kyle," I offered to Maria in the kitchen.

There was no need to upset the children over seating arrangements.

"Of course you do," she insisted. "My children have heard no before. They just don't always accept it the first time they hear it."

"Your children are just the sweetest," I cooed. "I can't believe little Emilio is still asleep with all the commotion!"

"If he didn't learn to sleep in the midst of commotion, the poor boy would never sleep at all," Maria sighed and gave me a tired smile. "Four kids under the age of seven are nothing but commotion all the time."

Maria and I carried the tray of pot roast with carrots and potatoes and a colorful salad and tray of fruit cut in fun shapes for the children.

"The meal looks beautiful, mi amor," Oscar praised his wife as she took her seat.

"Thank you," she beamed.

Kyle smiled at me as I took my seat next to him. I felt a tug on my sleeve from my other side, and it was Raul, the miniature police officer.

"Are you Miss Jackie?" he asked.

"Yes, you must be Raul," I replied, holding out my hand.

He shook it with the firmness of an older man.

I wanted to ask Maria and Oscar if they would mind terribly if I adopted one of their children. Raul was tugging at my heartstrings, behaving like a gentleman. I could almost envision what a son with Kyle would be like, and I wanted that with him as much as I wanted to take my next breath. Was it too soon to think about children with him?

"Raul, please tuck your napkin into your shirt collar," Maria asked, helping her daughter to tuck their napkins into the tops of their dresses to keep them clean.

He dutifully tucked his napkin into shirt collar.

"Miss Jackie," Raul turned to me, "tuck your napkin into your collar."

Kyle laughed. "She needs help like Rosalie and Carmen."

He picked up my napkin from my lap and tucked it into the top of my dress.

"Kyle, stop," I elbowed him playfully, a blush creeping up my cheeks.

"You don't want to get your dinner all over that beautiful dress," he insisted with a laugh.

I looked up at our hosts, and they were sharing a bemused smile. I mouthed an apology to them, and they both waved off my concerns.

We bowed our heads and prayed before the trays were passed around. I held each tray to Raul, but he served himself each time with great dexterity. Had he been just a little bigger, I probably would have passed the tray to him like another adult at the table, but they were still a little too heavy for him to manage on his own. It was clear that Maria and Oscar spent a lot of time with their children, ingraining manners and family values into them.

We dug into our dinner, and it was amazing! The pot roast wasn't seasoned with traditional herbs, and the tastes just exploded one by one in a delicious burst of flavors.

"Maria, this is amazing," I sighed in pleasure. "Can you please write down your recipes for me?"

"Thank you, but I have no recipe. I just measure with my heart," she smiled.

"Can you at least write down how you season everything?" I asked.

"Of course, I'll do that once the kids go trick-or-treating," she replied.

"Mama, I don't like carrots," Carmen complained, crossing her little arms over her chest.

"How do you know, you haven't tried them?" Maria asked.

"They're brown," she scrunched her little face.

The little girl didn't know what she was missing! They were so beautifully glazed and delicious.

"Close your eyes and try them that way," Oscar suggested amicably, "then you can imagine they're whatever color you want them to be."

She looked at him disbelievingly.

"Watch, this one is purple," Oscar said.

Oscar made a production of closing his eyes as he held up one carrot on his fork before sticking it in his mouth. "Mmmm, so purple!"

"Papa, no! Carrots are orange," she giggled.

"In my imagination, they are purple. Come on, sweetheart, you try it; just imagine the carrots are orange," he encouraged.

She pinched her little lips together as she eyed the carrot on her plate suspiciously. She picked it up with her fork, holding it up the way Oscar had. She pinched her eyes closed, and said, "My carrot is orange."

She stuck the carrot in her mouth as we all held our breaths, waiting for her reaction. Her eyes opened, and she giggled. We released our collective breath, and the adults shared a smile. I couldn't help but smile at this little family. I barely knew them, and already I loved them so much.

"Papa, it tastes orange," she squealed as she chewed and scooped up another.

"See, I told you it works," he winked at her. "Let's eat up so we can go trick or treating soon."

All was well again as we finished the meal. I didn't know how anyone could possibly have room for the dessert I made, but Oscar insisted he was not leaving the house until we all at least tried it. Kyle served it to each person with a small scoop of ice cream on the side.

"What is this, Uncle Kyle?" Rosalie asked.

"It's a caramel apple crumble that Miss Jackie made," he answered.

"Carmen apples?" little Carmen asked, her eyes wide.

"No sweetness, caramel," Kyle corrected, sitting a little bit in front of her.

"It's a dessert; you'll like it," Maria smiled at her young daughter.

"Yum!" Carmen said, eyeing the dessert with newfound desire.

Once everyone was served, we all dug in.

"Miss Jackie, this is my favorite dessert ever," Raul marveled from beside me.

"It's mine too," I replied, giving him a conspiratorial smile.

"I can see why, it's delicious," Maria smiled at me. "I'll exchange my pot roast recipe for your recipe for this."

"Deal," I agreed.

"It's a good thing I wasn't planning on walking this evening," Oscar said. "I don't know if I can even wheel myself. You think you can push me, Carrollton?"

"I was thinking of hitching a ride on the back of your chair," Kyle replied, patting his belly.

"No way," Oscar replied.

"Alright, Ethel and Lucy," Maria chided, "you need to take these kids out."

"Yay!" The three little ones cheered as they pulled their napkins from their clothes and ran off to their rooms to get their pillowcases for their candy haul.

Kyle and Oscar held the door for the little ones while Maria and I waved them off as they left for their adventure.

"I love them all, but it is such a relief to be in the house with another grown-up and only one baby that needs me," Maria admitted with a laugh. "Do you want a cup of coffee? It's decaf."

"No, thank you, I don't think I could eat or drink another thing," I sighed, helping her take the empty trays of food and dishes to the kitchen.

"Just put that on the counter. I'll scrape them off into the garbage disposal and throw them in the dishwasher. Would you mind checking on Emilio for me?" she asked.

"No problem," I replied, heading out to the living room to peek in on little Emilio. He was still sound asleep in his bassinet, his little body stretched out like a starfish.

"He's still sleeping," I said loud enough for Maria to hear in the other room.

"Good," Maria said, wiping her hands with a dish towel before joining me in the living room.

The doorbell rang with the first group of kids there for candy. Maria took the bowl of candy from the entry table and opened the door.

"Trick or treat!" came a chorus of children's voices.

"Look at all of you!" Maria cooed, putting candy in each child's bucket. "Happy Halloween!"

It went on like this for a good half hour; just as Maria would get ready to sit, another group of children would ring the doorbell.

I heard noises from the bassinet, the warning sounds of an upcoming big cry from the little boy.

"Let me get them for a while," I offered. "I think Emilio is waking up."

She nodded and handed off the candy bowl to me while she tended to Emilio.

"Do you mind if I feed him out here?" she asked.

"Not at all," I replied.

She got him latched on and then covered herself with a lightweight sheet so that parents didn't complain as their children came to the door.

"It usually slows down a little about this time," she said. "Why don't you sit with me for a little before they come back."

I smiled and set the bowl of candy down on the table next to the door.

"Wait, bring me a Snickers bar," she called.

I smiled and took a Snickers bar for her and one for me. I didn't know where I was going to fit it, but it was a fun-size one, so I figured it would find space when it hit my stomach.

"It has been so nice getting to meet you this evening," Maria remarked. "Well, I suppose we met in the hospital last week, but I wasn't exactly myself."

The sterile smell of the hospital and the metallic smell of blood on Kyle's shirt that day hit my nose, and my stomach flopped. The fear and frustration I felt at the hospital were overwhelming, and he hadn't been hurt. I couldn't imagine how that memory would hit me if he had been.

"It's understandable. Hearing that your husband is shot...I can't imagine getting that call," I said with a shudder.

"It's the stuff of nightmares, that's for sure," she sighed, "but Oscar has made sure that we will be well taken care of."

"That's good," I replied, not sure what else to say.

"Are you having any second thoughts about being with Kyle?" Maria asked. "It's understandable if you do."

"I—uh," I stammered, surprised by the bluntness of her question, "None so far. I love him."

"I don't mean to imply that I doubt your feelings for him. It's just that calls like that can happen any day, sometimes every day. They need to know we are all in. If they are worried about their relationship at home, they cannot be safe on their patrol," she warned. "Lives depend on it."

Maria knew what she was talking about. From what Kyle had told me, she had been a police officer's wife for ten years. Kyle had been more nervous about me meeting Maria than I had been. I knew the point of meeting Maria was to hear about her experience and make sure I knew what I was signing up for.

"I'd be lying to you if I said I wasn't worried about his job, but I'd never ask him to give it up. I see the light in his eyes every morning when he puts on his uniform," I admitted. "But the idea that he might not come home one day...how do you deal with that?"

Maria sat quietly, mulling over my question as she burped little Emilio.

"Every day I remind myself that none of us are guaranteed to come home," she reasoned. "I could go to the grocery store and get hit by a drunk driver. None of us knows when it will be our time."

I thought of Nonni, stuck in bed for a year. Toward the end of her life, I heard her speaking to Nonno, and for a long time, I found comfort in thinking he had come to prepare her for what came next and to walk her to their eternal home. I never gave much thought to who helped Nonno with the transition. He went so quickly I just figured he didn't have time to be scared. Besides, Nonno was one of the bravest men I'd ever known, next to Kyle.

"I suppose that is true," I replied, absorbing her advice.

If my experiences had taught me anything, it was that life was unpredictable.

"Being the wife of a police officer is just as much a duty to the public as their job is," she explained. "Little arguments must be let go of so that they can focus on keeping themselves and the community safe. It's a commitment beyond just loving him."

I felt naked in front of this woman. Did Kyle tell her about our argument on the way here? I don't remember a time when the two of them were alone since we arrived. Maybe she just knew that small fights were inevitable, and I was the type of person that held onto too much. Either way, I felt seen in a way that I hadn't been in a long time.

"You and Oscar seem like you wouldn't have many arguments. You're both such amiable people," I commented.

"Every couple has their squabbles," she smiled. "We're no strangers to make-up sex."

She jerked her head toward Emilio, implying he was a product of such. I laughed, surprised by her candor.

"Jackie, we all want Kyle to be happy and loved. He's been both since you came back into his life. I can see a light in him I haven't seen since I met him. I also know that being the life partner of a police officer is one of the hardest jobs there is. We are cut from another cloth compared to other wives. We're abundantly aware of the preciousness of life. I think you have what it takes to join our ranks, but at the end of the day, it is up to you. Just make sure you consider both of you when you make the decision."

"I will," I agreed somberly. "I love him with all my heart. I hope you see that."

"I do," she smiled kindly, "and it is evident to me he feels the same about you."

Her ability to see that allowed me to release the breath I had been holding. I knew Kyle loved me...it was just nice to hear it from other people too.

The front door opened, and the two little girls raced in to tell their mother all about their candy. Raul came and sat on the couch beside me.

"Miss Jackie!" he cried out to me, "Uncle Kyle said this was your favorite."

Raul handed me a Hershey bar with almonds, and I smiled.

"Ooh, these are my favorite!" I confirmed and handed the bar back to him.

"It's for you!" he insisted, handing it back to me.

"Raul, don't you want it?" I asked, touched by the little boy's sweet gesture.

"I want you to have it," he smiled up at me.

I pulled his little body into a hug as thanks for the candy.

"Raul, my man, are you trying to steal my girl away with your chocolate?" Kyle asked, giving the little boy a suspicious look.

"Maybe," Raul flashed a smile up at me. It was so much like the flirty one his father flashed me when I kissed his cheek earlier that night, I almost did a double take.

"Oh my goodness, Maria, you are going to have your hands full with this one," I laughed. "He is far too charming for his own good."

"Don't I know it," she laughed.

Kyle smiled at me, and I could see something that looked like relief and love.

"Alright, kiddos," he called. "It's time for me to take Miss Jackie home."

"And it is bedtime," Maria announced.

The three little Romeros let out a groan at the two announcements. Rosalie sniffled, and tears streaked down her cheeks.

"Uncle Kyle, I don't want you to go," she sobbed and wrapped her little body around his leg.

Kyle bent down and lifted the little girl up to cuddle her and wipe her tears.

"Don't be sad, Rosalie," he pleaded. "You had fun tonight, didn't you?"

She nodded, hiccupping back her tears.

"And you got lots of candy, right?" he asked.

She nodded again.

"And you met your new friend Miss Jackie," Kyle prodded.

She nodded, her tears done, and a small smile lit up her face.

"It's been an exciting day! When you lie down in your bed, you're going to realize how tired you are, and you're going to fall asleep so fast," he said and tickled the little girl's neck by snorting against the skin there. She squealed and wriggled as he alternated from one side of her neck to the other.

"Am I that tired, too, Uncle Kyle?" Carmen asked, pulling on his pants leg.

Kyle bent down, putting Rosalie back on her feet next to her sister, and he looked Carmen in the eyes, assessing.

"No, I think you're so tired you'll be blowing raspberries," he said and did just that against Carmen's neck.

Carmen giggled and slapped his shoulders.

"I don't do that!" she declared.

"No, you just stick your feet in my face when you sleep," he accused.

Carmen giggled again.

This man...this man, this man, this man! Did he have any idea what he was doing to me? I'd never seen him like this, and it was about the sexiest thing I'd ever seen. As if he heard my thoughts, he made eye contact with me across the room and his lips curved up in a sexy smile.

"Say goodnight to Uncle Kyle and Miss Jackie," Maria ordered kindly.

Dutifully, the two little girls wrapped their arms around Kyle's neck and pecked a kiss on his cheeks.

"Goodnight," he smiled and hugged them into his chest before letting them scurry off down the hallway.

"Goodnight, Miss Jackie," Raul said softly from beside me.

He leaned forward and pecked a kiss on my cheek.

"Goodnight Raul. Sweet dreams," I said, giving the boy a hug.

"Bye, Uncle Kyle!" he called, running out of the room toward his bedroom.

"Bye little man," Kyle called after him.

I stood up from the sofa.

"Don't forget your dessert," Maria reminded me.

"Would you like to keep the dish and finish it?" I asked, "It's more than Kyle and I would eat."

"Speak for yourself," Kyle teased under his breath.

"Are you sure?" Maria asked.

"Of course, I don't need the dish back right away. Just send it back with Oscar when you are done with it."

"Gladly! I will probably have some with my coffee in the morning," she grinned.

"Absolutely, enjoy it," I encouraged. "Thank you so much for dinner; it really was lovely."

"I'm glad and I hope you will come back to see us again soon," Maria said, standing to give me a hug.

Kyle smiled down at Maria and asked, "Does that invitation extend to me too?"

"You know it does," she smiled back and wrapped him in a sisterly hug.

"Thanks for taking the kids out with me, man," Oscar said. "I'll see you in the morning."

"See you in the morning," Kyle replied, giving Oscar a special handshake they had invented: grip of the forearms to shake twice, fist bump, fist bump, then opening their hands in a "pow."

"Goodnight, Oscar," I said, kissing his cheek again before letting Kyle help me into my coat.

"Goodnight, Jackie. Don't keep my boy up too late," he teased, "I saw those looks you had."

I went red with embarrassment and giggled.

"I'll try not to," I choked out.

Kyle's head turned quickly in my direction at that. I'm sure he thought that it was off the table when we were on our way here. Suddenly he was in a hurry to go home.

"Okay bye!" he said, ushering me out the door to a chorus of laughter from the Romeros

When we got settled in the car, he looked my way and grinned widely.

"They love you," he gushed.

"The feeling is mutual; I love them. What great people!" I replied.

Kyle ran his hand up and down my thigh, as he always did when he was happy and we were driving home. I was happy too and considering our future. We had a plan years ago of what our life would look like, but since we had got back together, we really hadn't planned a future much beyond my staying with him indefinitely and me going back to school and getting a job to help with the bills.

Was he afraid to make plans with me this time because of what happened before? Was he just taking it slow? I had to remind myself we'd only been back together for a little over a month. We were still getting to know this version of each other.

"You're quiet," Kyle remarked, giving my knee a squeeze.

"Sorry, I just got lost in thought," I apologized. "I've never seen you around children. They love you."

"It took some time for Raul and Rosalie to warm up to me," he admitted. "They remind me so much of Francine and me because they are right about a year apart."

I could see that. There was a closeness between them that brought out antagonism sometimes.

"I actually was there when Carmen was born," he added. "She didn't wait to get to the hospital, so Oscar helped Maria deliver her on the side of the road while I finished driving to the hospital. Luckily, we had the forethought to grab one of the waterproof sheets they had for the kids for potty training. It left very little to clean up."

What an experience! When I have a baby one day, I want to be surrounded by medical professionals and loaded with good painkillers. I wanted to know if that was the future he saw too.

"I know this question is way too soon, but–"

"Of course I want to have kids with you," he answered without me asking, "if that's what you want."

"You do?" I asked, my heart sprinting in my chest.

"Yes, I do," he stated simply.

My head was spinning. I have wanted to be a mom since I was a little girl trying to play with dolls with Francine. She always wanted to play boss babes and had no interest in pretending to care for babies.

I also wanted to be a teacher. At least I thought I did. How would I juggle both?

"We don't have to have a baby tomorrow," Kyle laughed, noting my expression.

"I know," I said stiffly, though relief was flooding my system.

"I just mean someday, but if you don't want kids, that's okay too," he explained. "The vision I have of the future includes you no matter what path we take."

I linked my fingers with his and gave a gentle squeeze. The future was wide open, and he wanted to face whatever that looked like together. Just as much as you couldn't predict death, you couldn't predict the course your life would take. It wasn't "the plan" talk I was hoping for, but in many ways it was better.

Maria's words about letting go of little hurts came back to me, and I knew I needed to address what I had really been feeling with Kyle.

"I'm sorry I was upset with you earlier," I began. "I know your job doesn't have a set schedule."

I squeezed his hand for strength to say the next words without crying.

"It's just so soon after Oscar got shot and you almost..." I sniffled back the emotions threatening to overwhelm me, "With every minute you're late, my worry grows that it will be the day that you don't come home."

Kyle looked over at me with a softness in his eyes before looking back to the road.

"I'm sorry too," he said. "I know I have someone waiting at home for me, and she deserves to know I'm okay."

We sat quietly for a few blocks, letting our conversation soak in. I was grateful that he understood where I was coming from and would try to reach out when he was running late. We pulled into a parking spot near the front of our apartment.

Kyle turned to me and leaned forward to kiss me. It was soft and sweet and slow.

"Can you promise me something?" he asked, meeting my eyes.

"What?" I whispered.

"Please don't go to the storage facility again without me," he pleaded. "I worry about your safety there. I need to know you're safe."

Maria's words rang in my ears about putting aside feelings for our partner so that they could stay safe at work. I couldn't stand the idea that I could distract Kyle to the point that he or someone else would be hurt. I didn't understand why he felt the storage facility was unsafe, apart from the mix-up with Luis, but if it meant Kyle was safer at his job for it, I would concede...at least for now. Maybe after he went with me a few times, he would see his worry was unfounded.

"Okay," I replied.

His smile lit up his face, and I knew I had said the right thing.

"Can we go upstairs now? I missed you today," I admitted, giving him my puppy dog eyes.

He leaned in and kissed me. "I missed you too. Race you to the bedroom!"

His eyes lit with mischief as we grinned at each other like idiots. We each burst out of the car and raced each other to our apartment door. We laughed and playfully shoved at each other as we made it to the door, but I managed to slip past him and unlock the front door. As soon as I opened it, he scooped me up off my feet and tossed me over his shoulder, and I squealed in protest. I saw Toby from my upside-down position for only a moment before he ran away from his crazy humans.

"Poor Toby!" I laughed.

"He'll be fine," Kyle insisted, kicking the door shut behind him and carrying me back to the bedroom.

He flopped me down on the bed and parted my legs so that he could stand between them. Smiling down at me, he stripped off his shirt and tossed it to the floor.

"I thought this was supposed to be a race?" I asked breathily. "Does this mean I won?"

"Sure, but I'd like to think we both won," he said, unzipping his pants.

I nodded and curled my finger, beckoning him to join me on the bed.

CHAPTER 22

Robbie's Got Your Number

Kyle
November 1, 2017

I looked across the desk for the 1,000th time that day at Oscar. Every time he moved it caught my attention, and I was so bored I couldn't help but watch what he was up to. This time he was picking dirt out from under his fingernails. And this was my entertainment for the day!

"I know it's heartbreaking for you, Carrollton, but I'm taken," he said, not looking up at all.

"What?" I asked, shaking myself out of my trance.

"I'm just so beautiful you can't help but stare at me," he replied, "but really, fella, it's getting awkward. The other guys are starting to talk."

"You're an asshole," I laughed. "I wasn't staring at you; I just spaced out, and your movement caught what little attention I had."

"It's been all day," Oscar continued chiding me, "me thinks thou dost protest too much."

I shook my head and threw a paper clip at him.

"I'm bored out of my mind," I complained. "I hate being stuck inside."

"So go walk around," he recommended.

"We're supposed to be filing this paperwork," I reasoned.

"You know it's just bullshit busy work they give us so that they don't have to lay us off until I'm well enough to patrol again," he said under his breath, "it'll be here when you get back from your walk, I swear."

"What's this above your head?" I asked, "Is it a little black rain cloud forming? Did someone stay up too late eating candy last night?"

"Don't say that word to me again," he groaned, patting his mostly flat stomach.

"Ah, we've found the source!" I declared. "Why don't I bring you some water and grab a coffee."

"Fine," he said, "Officer Gimpy will carry on duty without you."

"I'll be back soon," I promised.

Oscar had been right; I needed to get up and walk around. My body creaked as I stood from sitting in the office chair that was probably as old as me. I went to the break room and put money into the vending machine for bottled water for my partner. I set it down on the counter and stretched out my arms before grabbing a disposable cup from the dispenser and filling it with coffee, leaving just enough space for a couple of scoops of sugar. Once I got my coffee situated, I took a moment to text my girl.

Kyle: I should be done with work around 5, can you pick me up?

Jackie: I'll be there. Any requests for dinner?

Kyle: You...on a silver platter.

Jackie: You can't have dessert for dinner! Besides, we have company.

Kyle: We will?

Jackie: My cousin Robbie. It's the reason you loaned me your car.

Kyle: Right. Sorry, forgot.

Jackie: It's OK. See you at 5.

Kyle: Let Robbie pick our dinner. See you at 5. Love you.

Jackie: Love you too.

I picked up the drinks and went back out to the bullpen, handing Oscar the bottle of water and taking a big slug of coffee. It was terrible but serviceable.

I sat back down and got back to work filing. I found a bit of a rhythm with it for a while. Caffeine helps so much. I started to hum a tune to myself as I worked.

"God, is that how annoying I am when I whistle?" Oscar laughed ruefully.

"You're worse," I replied.

"I guess I owe you a week of reports when we get back out on the road," he replied, shaking his head.

"What's up with you, man?" I asked, genuinely concerned by his shift in mood.

"I'm just having a lot of pain today. The girls climbed into bed with us last night and kicked me right where my wound is on my leg," he admitted.

I winced in sympathy. "Shit, man! I probably would have pissed the bed, wrapped them in the sheets, and tossed them back into their bed until morning."

"It was tempting," Oscar replied.

"Why don't you call Maria and see if she can bring some medicine over?" I asked.

"I have what I need," he said, holding up a bottle of Advil from his desk.

Surely that wasn't strong enough, but I knew better than to question someone's medicine choices. Oscar didn't like using heavy pain killers and I couldn't blame him. We'd seen way too many instances of drug abuse during our partnership. The Mackenzies were a prime example. You do what you can to avoid becoming a statistic.

Officer Brady stopped at our desks and set a test result sheet on my desk.

"We found a couple of partial prints on the note from your girlfriend's car, but nothing came back. Whoever did this is probably not in the system," he said.

"And you ruled out the prints as being hers, right?" I asked.

"Of course. Miss D'Marco had prints on file already, but she also gave us fresh prints to work with too," Brady said.

"Oh yeah, she got printed for school. I forgot," I said, wishing the sheet had some conclusive evidence of who threatened her.

"I didn't realize your girl was the same Jackie D'Marco that put her parents in jail for stealing from their own company. That's pretty badass," Brady commented.

A flood of pride washed over me. I knew how much she struggled with what she had done, but I couldn't argue about how brave it was.

"It wasn't easy for her," I explained. "She still wrestles with it and thinks it might have been a mistake."

"I can imagine," Brady sympathized. "You think you can trust your parents, and they let you down in such a big way. It's gotta be tough."

I nodded.

"Well, if you need anything else, let me know," Brady said before taking off.

"Too bad there aren't better clues to go on," Oscar offered.

"Yeah, it just makes me worry it might be her cousin and not the boyfriend as I originally thought," I sighed.

"Why would you think that?" Oscar asked.

"Her cousin doesn't have a police record, but his boyfriend does. The boyfriend would have prints in the system, but her cousin doesn't," I explained. "I suppose they could be working together on it?"

"But why would her cousin try to chase her off of looking into her parents?" Oscar asked.

"Maybe he's afraid that she'll uncover something she shouldn't," I reasoned. "Who knows. It's clear from the note, though, that whoever did it doesn't want her digging into her parent's business anymore. That just makes us both want to dig into it even more."

"I know you're a stubborn ass. I didn't realize she was too," Oscar chuckled.

"She's probably worse than I am," I laughed.

"God help us all," Oscar said, making the sign of the cross over himself.

I just shook my head and got back to filing. I needed to warn her that her cousin might be involved. Maybe I should ask Francine to bring up the topic. She usually had a much kinder way of bringing up tough topics and talking them out with people than I did. She always played good cop to my bad cop when we were kids.

As the day came to an end, I felt a tap on my shoulder. When I turned, there she was, beautiful as ever, with a stocky young man with the telltale face of someone born with Down's Syndrome.

I smiled at them both and stood to hug her.

"You're here a little early," I gave her a quick kiss on the cheek.

"I know," she smiled, "Robbie just wanted to come over and see the precinct. I hope that's okay."

"Sure," I replied, "there's not much to the place, but I can show you around."

"Hi Jackie," Oscar greeted her, and she bent down and kissed his cheek again.

"This must be your cousin, Robbie," Oscar greeted Robbie with a handshake.

"I'm Robbie," Robbie confirmed, shaking Oscar's hand. "Cousin Jackie said you got shot last week."

"Yes, I did. I was lucky; I only had to have 12 stitches. In a few weeks, I'll be good as new," Oscar assured.

"Twelve stitches," Robbie marveled and then asked brightly, "Did you know this is the 73rd precinct?"

"Yes, we did," Oscar smiled indulgently. "You know our squad car is number 111?"

"Wow, 111!" Robbie gasped. "Can I ride in it sometime?"

We had done a citizen ride-along before. Though Robbie was an adult by age, I was sure the department would require a guardian to sign off on it as well.

"Maybe," I said. "We'll have to see if your dad will let us have you on a ride along."

Robbie slumped dramatically. "Never mind, he'll just say no."

"Sorry, buddy," I replied, giving him a consoling pat on the shoulder.

"It's okay," he said back to his smiling self almost instantly. "Can we go now? I'm hungry."

"Sure, let's go," I said. "Oscar, see you tomorrow."

"Don't tease me," Oscar quipped.

"Make sure you take care of that leg," I warned him. "The second you can be released; I want to be back on the streets."

"Me too, brother, me too," Oscar smiled.

As we walked out of the precinct, I could hear Robbie muttering something under his breath as he looked around the precinct, taking everything in one more time before we left.

He got into the back seat, clearly out of habit, which allowed me to take the front passenger seat next to Jackie. As we drove toward home, Robbie's muttering got a little louder, and I could finally make out some of what he was saying.

"Call 9-1-1 when you're in trouble, ask for car 111 from precinct 73 but not until the 12 stitches are gone," he chanted like a mantra over and over again.

"Is he okay?" I asked Jackie quietly, concerned.

"Oh yeah, he just likes to remember his day in numbers with little stories like that," she explained quietly before speaking louder, "Robbie, why don't you tell Kyle about the cookies we made earlier."

"Yeah," he brightened and recited a new mantra, "One cup of butter seems like a lot but not! When it's soft, mix it with one cup of sugar and one cup of brown sugar. Stir, stir, stir! Two teaspoons of vanilla, two large eggs and three cups of flour. One teaspoon baking soda but only half of the powder. Stir, stir, stir! Then two cups of chips and stir again, that my friend is how you make 'em; you just gotta bake 'em."

"Wow! I said, amazed at his memory, "Did Cousin Jackie teach you that?"

"No, I taught HER that!" Robbie replied smugly.

"He did," she admitted. "I had to pull out Nonni's old recipe card, but he had it exactly right. He loves numbers. It's like when he sees them, they are just ingrained in his brain forever."

"That's really cool, Robbie," I replied.

"I know!" He exclaimed.

We all laughed and settled into an amiable silence until I heard the 867-5309 song playing at low volume.

"Do you know this one, Robbie?" I asked, cranking up the volume.

"Jenny!" he cackled and began singing along, getting louder each time the number part was repeated.

I joined in with him, and I think Jackie was ready to kill us both by the time we got back to our apartment.

"Hey, Rob," I said, as we walked into the building, "Christmas will be coming up soon, do you know the 12 days of Christmas?"

"That. Is. My. Favorite!" he stated emphatically.

"Mine too, man," I replied, giving him a high five.

"God help me," Jackie muttered under her breath as we entered the building.

"We're going to Apartment 12A, right, Cousin Jackie?" Robbie asked, ambling off ahead of us to lead the way.

"Yes, 12A," she smiled.

He hustled down the hallway, and I marveled at him once more.

"That's incredible," I murmured to her. "His memory for numbers is astonishing."

"He's been that way our whole lives. It's his superpower," she smiled proudly.

"He should come hang out with us more," I said to her as we entered the apartment together.

"Yes! Cousin Jackie, please say yes," Robbie urged her excitedly, taking her hand and swinging it back and forth between them. "I can help you make dinner, and we can have fun days!"

"I'd love that, Robbie, but it's up to your dad and your brother. We don't live too far away, but they may want to keep you closer to home." She reasoned with him.

"It'll be fine," he assured her.

"Then I'm happy to have you come over anytime, Robbie," she smiled at him.

He laughed excitedly and went off to the living room to pick up his massive headphones and tablet from the coffee table.

"We should be ready to eat in just a few minutes," Jackie said to me, the light in her eyes dimming a bit.

"How was your day, Babe?" I asked, concerned by her expression.

"It really was great," she replied, melancholy, "I just get a little blue when a visit with Robbie ends. He was my best friend before I started school, and we've always been close. I guess I just didn't realize how much I missed being away from him for so long."

"Why don't you visit him more often?" I asked, "He's welcome here anytime you want. Hell, he's welcome to spend the night when he comes over."

"Really?" she asked, her eyebrows wrinkling.

"Yes, really," I replied. "I haven't set up anything in the second bedroom yet. We can let him pick out the bedding that goes in there and everything.

We can bring over the bedroom set you have at Francine's; it should fit in there just fine."

She put her hand to her heart and pouted her lips as though she were about to tear up.

"I just love you," she said, wrapping me in a hug.

"I love you too," I replied, running my hand down her hair as I pecked a kiss to the crown of her head.

We held each other for a little longer before we stepped back and resumed our normal activities. I went to the bedroom and changed out of my uniform and put on my gym clothes. I would probably go for a little bit after Drew came to pick up Robbie. I was sure I would need to release some tension after warning him that if he was involved in the threat left on Jackie's window, he'd have me to deal with.

When I came back out, Jackie was pulling a tray of baked pasta from the oven followed by some garlic bread. She was an amazing cook, but her pasta dishes were always exceptional. She learned a lot of tips and tricks from Nonni, and she often made the pasta from scratch. Dried pasta from the store was okay, but the pasta she made from scratch made a mess in the kitchen and tasted like heaven.

I looked over at Robbie, who was having his own private little dance party in the living room, listening to what must have been an excellent jam in his headphones. Jackie and I smiled at each other and started dancing along with him, even though we had no music going. It was a minute or two before Robbie noticed he wasn't dancing alone, and he gave us a look of confusion as he pulled his headphones from his ears.

"You're dancing but there's no music," he laughed.

"We make our own music," Jackie smiled.

"Is dinner ready now?" Robbie asked, "I'm hungry."

"Yes, go ahead and take a seat at the table," she replied with a laugh.

Robbie took a seat at the table, and I helped Jackie bring the pasta over to the table as she carried the basket of garlic bread and serving utensils.

We spent the meal laughing and talking about their day. Jackie had taken Robbie to Coney Island for a few hours before they came home to start dinner and then came to pick me up.

"Sounds like you guys had a busy day!" I remarked, "I should have come with you instead of going to work."

"Next time! Next time!" Robbie chanted in his way of asking me to promise.

"Next time," I agreed.

The doorbell rang, and Robbie jumped up from his seat. "I'll get it!"

He walked over to the door and opened it. On the other side was his brother Drew.

"Drew, Drew! I had the best day; wanna hear about it?" Robbie asked, letting his brother in.

"How about on the way back home? It is an hour drive after all," Drew smiled, tiredly.

"Right, okay," Robbie replied, unfazed by his brother's brush-off.

"There's plenty of food left if you're hungry, Drew," Jackie offered, "Nonni's chocolate chip cookies too."

"Thanks," Drew replied. "I had dinner already, but I will take a cookie."

He took one from the tray and nibbled it.

"We'd love to have you and Robbie both over again soon," Jackie said, packing up Robbie's backpack with the things that he had scattered around in the little time that he was with us, "or even just Robbie if you need a night off."

"I may take you up on that," Drew smiled. "Actually, I wanted to invite you to Thanksgiving at the restaurant if you can make it. You too, Kyle."

I was glad to hear that Jackie had been invited to her family's gathering. Family meant so much to her, and I knew she wanted to ask, but had been afraid to.

"Oh, when are you having it?" Jackie asked.

"Usually, we do lunchtime on Thanksgiving Day," Drew replied. "Dad always makes enough food for an army. It might be nice to have a few less days of leftovers this year."

"Okay, I'll text you next week and let you know if we can make it," Jackie replied brightly.

"We can make it," I assured her.

She smiled and nodded her thanks to me.

"Great! Come on Robbie, it's time to go," Drew called to his brother.

"Okay," Robbie sighed and let Jackie help him put his backpack over his shoulders.

"Come by and see us again soon, Robbie," I said, wrapping him in a hug.

"Bye, Jackie," he said and then turned, giving me a high five as he walked by. "Bye, Kyle!"

"I'm going to go down with them," she said, following Robbie out the door.

"Drew, hold up one second," I called to him.

"Yeah?" he replied.

"Where were you on October 2nd between one and three pm?" I asked.

"What?" he laughed nervously. "How should I know? I don't even remember what day of the week that was."

I didn't give two shits. He'd better have a solid alibi for where he was that day.

"It was the day that you called Jackie to see if she could take Robbie today. Where were you?" I persisted.

"Oh. I went to work that day, my boyfriend called me and asked about doing a special date night tonight, and then I called Jackie to see if she could watch Robbie," he said.

"Did you tell your boyfriend where Jackie would be that day?" I asked.

"I didn't know where she would be that day at the time I spoke to Luis. Besides, why would he care?" Drew asked, puzzled, "Did something happen to her?"

"Yes," I replied. "Someone left a threat on the windshield of her car while she was out signing up for college classes that day. The only two people who knew she was going there were my sister, who couldn't drive at the time, and you."

"I don't know what to tell you; I was at work all day. I didn't even take a lunch break that day. I didn't tell my boyfriend where she would be. Even if I did, I don't think he'd threaten her," he guffawed.

"He already has," I stated. "Did he mention that to you?"

"He did what?" Drew asked, alarmed.

"He told her not to come back to the storage to get any more boxes. Any idea why?" I asked.

"No, that makes no sense," he replied nervously.

"She said he thought she was a reporter at first," I reminded him.

"Oh, yeah, he told me about that," Drew laughed sheepishly. "There have been a handful of reporters over the years that have tried to break in and find exclusive unpublished documents regarding the case against Davide and Susan. He was just being protective of our family, but he had his wires crossed."

"That better be all it is," I warned. "Do you know who else would have threatened her?"

"No clue, I swear," Drew replied earnestly, raising his hands in surrender.

"Okay," I replied, "if you think of anything, please call the precinct. Your brother has the number."

Drew smirked, getting my meaning.

"See you later, Kyle," he replied and left my apartment quickly.

When it came to uncovering who threatened Jackie at the college, it seemed like I was right back at square one. I hated that. I had to admit, maybe someone really was tailing her. But who?

CHAPTER 23

DiMarco Family Thanksgiving

Jackie
November 23, 2017

Kyle looked so sexy in his gray sweater and blue jeans, and dear Lord, he smelled good! I almost asked him to pull over several times on our way to D'Marco Italiano on Thanksgiving Day. We had a long day of family gatherings ahead, and everything about him that day made me want to ask him to turn around and go back home so that we could spend the day snuggling in bed together.

My family Thanksgiving was bound to be a little awkward without my parents there; however, it had been way too long since I had Thanksgiving with my family. I wasn't about to miss out on a traditional Thanksgiving meal with his family, either. Snuggling would have to wait.

We made green bean casserole for my family meal. Uncle Masso was making everything else, which was fine with me! It'd been years since I had Thanksgiving with my family, and I was going to enjoy every bit. My last two Thanksgiving meals had consisted of a cheap deli meat turkey sandwich and a single-serving instant mashed potato bowl. Sad really.

"What's on your mind, Gorgeous? You've been quiet," Kyle asked.

"I was just thinking how sexy you look," I smiled over his way, wrapping both of my hands over his firm biceps in a flirty hug.

"Yeah?" he asked, his smile bordering on the cocky side as his right hand rubbed up and down my thigh. My skin pebbled in the wake of his touch. What this man does to me!

"Yeah," I replied, running my hand over his muscled forearm before planting a kiss on his shoulder.

"That's not something to keep quiet about," he chided. "Tell me all the dirty thoughts running through that beautiful head of yours."

"I can't...it's Thanksgiving," I laughed, resting my cheek on his shoulder as I felt a blush creep up my neck.

"And the thing I'm most grateful for is the way your mind works," he replied, "especially when it comes to the things we do together."

"You'll have to keep it in your pants, Carrollton!" I giggled, "At least until we get home tonight."

"I can turn around right now," he insisted, rubbing his thumb in a circle over the sensitive spot just on the inner side of my knee he knew all too well.

"Don't you dare," I squealed, "this is our exit ahead. We are having dinner with both of our families today."

"Quickie in the back room at the restaurant?" he asked playfully.

"No!" I cackled.

"Fine, but we're not staying for dessert at Francine's," he said, taking his hand from my thigh.

"We're staying for dessert too," I insisted. "It's the best part! I am not missing your mom's pumpkin pie."

"Do you suppose she will let us take it home instead?" he asked hopefully.

"No, and you're not going to ask her to," I warned, pointing a finger at him.

"Jacks," he complained.

"I promise it will be worth the wait," I assured him.

"It always is," he smiled.

We pulled into D'Marco Italiano, and Kyle took the carrying case with our green bean casserole in one hand and took my hand with the other as we walked to the back entrance and let ourselves in.

"Hello!" I called out to announce our presence.

"In the kitchen!" Uncle Masso called back.

Kyle and I made our way to the kitchen, where Masso was systematically stirring several pots to keep anything from burning.

Robbie was loading the industrial dishwasher with the prep bowls and other utensils Uncle Masso had used to get things going.

"Happy Thanksgiving!" I gushed, "Everything smells so good!"

"Happy Thanksgiving," Masso replied. "Jackie, can you stir this?"

I took over stirring the gravy for the mashed potatoes without hesitation.

"This is my boyfriend, Kyle Carrollton," I said, jerking my head behind me to indicate the man...my man. "Kyle, this is my Uncle Masso, and you've met Robbie."

Masso stuck out a hand to shake Kyle's but didn't stop stirring with the other.

"Welcome, it's so nice to meet you," Masso said.

The words seemed welcoming, but his tone didn't. I wasn't sure if that was a sign that Masso was still upset with me, or that he disliked Kyle on sight. Either way was disappointing to me. I wanted to have a nice day with my family, not a repeat of the lunch we had the last time I was here.

"Likewise," Kyle replied, shaking his hand quickly, "I have the green bean casserole. We wrapped it up well, so it should still be hot. Is there somewhere you'd like me to put it down?"

"If you want to take it straight out to the table, we'll be eating soon," Masso replied. "Robbie, show him the way."

"Hi Kyle!" Robbie greeted Kyle with a hug, forgetting his apron was wet from the dishes.

Kyle didn't flinch or recoil; he simply patted the other man on the back and replied, "Hi Robbie, what's new with you?"

I couldn't have loved the two of them more.

"I have a girlfriend, but she couldn't come today," I heard Robbie say as they made their way out to the party room.

I smiled at that. When we were young, Robbie always had a girlfriend, and it never seemed to be the same one.

"He looks familiar," Masso commented when we were alone in the kitchen.

"Who?" I asked, continuing to stir the gravy.

"Your boyfriend. How did you meet?" he asked.

"Oh, we dated in high school and reconnected when I came back to Brooklyn," I explained. "I think you met him at my graduation."

"What does he do for a living?" Masso asked, taking large oven mitts to pour the hot pan of mashed potatoes into a serving bowl.

"He's a police officer," I replied.

In response, Masso nearly dropped the empty pan on the floor, but quickly recovered.

"And he knows what your parents have done?" he asked, his eyes flaring with something I couldn't quite name. Anger? Fear?

"Yes, of course," I replied. "I'm pretty sure there's very few people from Brooklyn that wouldn't at least know the headline version of the story."

Masso nodded, grumbling under his breath, and took the pan back to the counter beside the industrial washing machine for cleaning.

"Is something wrong, Masso?" I asked, "Kyle and I have known each other since we were children. His sister is my best friend. They are from a good family."

"It's nothing," he replied. "Why don't you take the potatoes out to the table? I'll finish up here and be out there soon."

He held out the bowl to me, and after a beat, I took it from him and walked from the kitchen out to the dining area where Kyle and Robbie were setting the table. Kyle looked up and smiled, but I watched his smile fall when he caught my expression.

He crossed to me and took the bowl of potatoes from me.

"What's wrong, sweetheart?" he asked quietly.

"It's probably nothing," I replied quietly.

"Tell me anyway," he urged.

"Not right now," I said, with a reassuring pat to his forearm.

He nodded and took the bowl of potatoes to the table.

"Mr. Clearwater!" Robbie called out, rushing to the man coming through the patron doors of the restaurant.

"Hello Robbie," Mr. Clearwater replied, giving Robbie a hug as though he were family.

"Robbie, what about me?" The young woman on the arm of Mr. Clearwater pouted.

"Hi Candi," Robbie blushed and hugged the busty woman as well.

Candi kissed his cheek, leaving a pink kiss mark on him before she giggled and wiped it away for him.

"My cousin is here," Robbie announced excitedly to the two newcomers.

"Jackie D'Marco," Mr. Clearwater stated, meeting my eyes.

"I'm sorry, have we met before?" I asked, stunned that he knew who I was.

"A long time ago," he smiled, "I used to invest with your parents when you were a little girl. I saw you a few times when you were there at the office with them."

"Oh," I replied, my stomach roiling. It was rarely a good experience to meet someone who knew me through my parents.

"Yes, luckily for me, I moved to another firm before word of the scandal broke out," he said with a laugh.

I felt Kyle's arm wrap around me protectively as though he sensed the same potential for venom from this man.

"I'm Jackie's boyfriend, Kyle Carrollton," he said, extending a hand to Mr. Clearwater.

Mr. Clearwater's gaze finally left me and gave an assessing stare at Kyle's hand, as though it might be poisonous, and trailed his eyes similarly up to his face.

"Reese Clearwater," he finally replied, taking Kyle's hand and giving it a single shake before releasing it.

"You're Masso's business partner?" Kyle asked, but it sounded almost like a statement.

"Yes, Masso and I go way back. We met when he worked for Jackie's parents. When he took over the restaurant, he needed a partner to help upgrade the business. The arrangement worked advantageously for us both, and we continued past our original arrangement."

"I'm Candi," the woman with Mr. Clearwater piped up in an overly perky tone, holding out her hand to Kyle.

"Nice to meet you," he replied kindly, giving her hand a shake.

"I'm Reese's wife," she giggled, holding up her left hand to display the huge diamond on her slender, manicured fingers.

"Candi, dear, why don't you go see if Masso needs help in the kitchen," Mr. Clearwater suggested, ushering his wife toward the kitchen with a few pats to her butt.

"Of course," she replied, not at all indignant at his dismissal.

Kyle and I exchanged an uncomfortable glance before looking back at Mr. Clearwater.

"I heard about your grandmother's passing a while back. Candi and I were out of the country and couldn't attend the funeral. I am so sorry for your loss." Mr. Clearwater offered.

"Thank you," I replied politely.

An awkward silence fell between us all.

"Shall we sit?" Kyle asked when he could no longer stand the silence.

"Of course," Mr. Clearwater said, smoothly gesturing for Kyle and me to go ahead of him.

Kyle took my hand. Even though Mr. Clearwater made me uncomfortable, I felt a wave of calmness sweep over me just from Kyle's presence. He'd always been able to do that for me, and I missed it so much in the years that I was away. I had lost track of the number of times I wished for him just to be in the same room as me.

I squeezed his hand in gratitude as we made our way to the table. He looked over his shoulder and gave me a reassuring smile. I smiled back and mouthed the words, "I love you" to him.

His smile grew wider at that, and I felt like the sexiest woman who had ever walked the earth. He helped me into my seat, and when I was settled, I felt his warm breath against my ear as he whispered, "I love you too."

He pecked a kiss on my cheek and took the seat to my right. Mr. Clearwater settled into the seat across from us and gave us an indulgent smile.

The patron door opened again, and I heard the call from my cousin Drew greeting us as he and Luis entered the restaurant.

"Happy Thanksgiving, everyone," Drew called out, hanging his coat on the coat tree by the door. "Sorry we were running late, but I think you'll forgive us."

Drew took a casserole dish from the silent Luis and carried it to the table and put it down in the middle. Drew made sweet potato casserole, but not just any sweet potato casserole: it was Nonni's recipe with walnuts and brown sugar glaze. I could kiss him.

"You beautiful man!" I smiled and stood to pull him into a hug and kissed his cheek.

"I made this especially for you," he said, hugging me back. "It was always your favorite. Besides, having you back to celebrate Thanksgiving with us is more than worth the extra effort."

A tear trickled down my cheek at his sweetness.

"Hey now, none of those," Drew admonished, wiping one of the stray tears with his thumb.

I laughed and swiped tears from my other cheek. "Sorry, I just missed you all so much."

"We missed you too," he replied, squeezing my hand.

Luis stood silently like a tower behind Drew. He didn't feel as menacing as he had when I had met him in the storage building, but he still felt dangerous. I decided to re-evaluate him. There was something a bit like Kyle about him. Very protective of Drew, which was beautiful.

"Hello Luis," I said, giving him a small nervous smile. "I'm glad you could join us."

"I'm glad to be here with you all," he said, no smile but the tension visibly ebbing from his shoulders, so I took that as a win.

"This is my boyfriend, Kyle Carrollton," I introduced the two men.

Kyle gave him a stony look but politely shook Luis's hand, and we all settled into seats at the table just as Masso, Candi and Robbie brought out the last of the dishes, including a platter of carved turkey. You'd think I had been in prison alongside my parents for the last five years, by the way my eyes stared longingly at each dish on the table before reluctantly moving to the next and starting the process all over again as everyone else at the table happily chattered with each other.

Masso cleared his throat, and everyone grew silent as they turned to look at him.

"Every year we come together, we are reminded of how we all got here. Mama and Papa brought me here when I was three and my brother was five. None of us spoke a word of English, but my parents wanted a better life for their sons and future generations," Masso said, gesturing between me and my cousins. "A kind guard met them at immigration, taught them English, and helped them find temporary jobs before they could open this restaurant that we all love. They worked hard every day to make sure their family would have the things they grew up without. Education, opportunities, beautiful homes. What they made abundantly clear to us was that no matter what, the love of your family could get you through even the darkest of storms, and here we are on the other side, enjoying the sunlight."

I couldn't help but feel guilty that my parents' actions nearly took that away from all of us. As much as I hoped to find evidence of their innocence, so far, my efforts have been fruitless. I would feel equally responsible if any of the people around me felt the effects of the darkest storm our family had weathered together again.

"Let's eat!" Masso declared as he wrapped up his speech.

Everyone chatted as dishes were passed around, and plates were filled. When everyone settled into eating, I felt Kyle's hand squeeze my thigh under the table. I turned to look at him, and the compassion in his eyes nearly broke me. He knew how hard today was for me.

My father (Davide), his brother (Masso) and their parents had landed in the United States after a horrendously long boat ride from Italy on Thanksgiving Day. My father nearly died from a terrible infection he had gotten when he and Masso were playing on the ship, and he cut himself on some of the rigging. The ship's physician worked tirelessly to ensure his survival. When they arrived at shore, he was not much more than skin and bones, and the guard that Masso had mentioned had asked my family to come home with him for Thanksgiving dinner. That's where he met and fell in love with my mother, Susan. She was the daughter of that guard. My father said she was the most beautiful girl he'd ever seen in his life.

My father worked so hard to learn English so that he could speak to her the next time he saw her, and by the time he saw her again the following Thanksgiving, he was nearly fluent. For years they would only see each other on Thanksgiving, but they grew to love each other despite the distance and time apart.

Needless to say, Thanksgiving growing up was the most special holiday in my home. We cherished the time we had with Nonno and Nonni and my cousins, but in the days leading up to Thanksgiving, my father would leave sweet surprises every day for my mother and me as though it was his own personal Valentine's month.

The food on my plate turned to sand in my mouth as I tried to enjoy it despite the emotions welling in my chest. Next to me, Robbie began muttering the words my father used to say, and I nearly lost it.

"One can never be thankful enough for two parents who had enough love to stretch three generations and beyond," Robbie muttered repeatedly. He loved the numbers in it.

"Enough, Robbie," Masso growled, slamming his hand against the table, rattling several dishes together. He ordered him, "Eat your dinner."

Robbie did quiet and went back to eating, but the table all grew silent as well. Masso usually didn't mind when Robbie rattled on about his number stories, but this one had clearly distressed him. Kyle and I exchanged looks and then went back to our plates for a very awkward dinner with my family. Was it too much to ask for a normal family dinner?

CHAPTER 24

Carrollton Thanksgiving Fun

Kyle
November 23, 2017

I could feel the sadness and anxiety radiating from Jackie. Her first Thanksgiving with her family in five years had not gone well. Masso was behaving strangely. Mr. Clearwater is a rich douche pretending to be a family man with his Playboy bunny bride who's clearly half his age, and I don't like the look of Drew's boyfriend, Luis. His criminal profile seemed relatively harmless, but he had a very hardened look about him that, as a police officer, I was all too familiar with.

Masso quickly shut down any talk that came close to mentioning Jackie's parents. It was worse than if they had died—their own family shunned them. I saw the light in Jackie's eyes dim as though they were shunning her as well. Sure, what her parents did was wrong, but it wasn't Jackie's fault.

"Baby, are you okay?" I asked when I couldn't stand the silence in the car any longer.

"I'm fine," she replied softly, but I could see her wipe a tear from her cheek in my periphery.

I grabbed the hand she had wiped the tear with and pulled it to my lips and kissed it gently, tasting the salty tear it had caught.

"I'm sorry dinner was so rough, sweetheart," I said, holding the hand to my chest, stroking the palm with my thumb as I continued driving with the other.

"It's okay," she replied. "I don't know why I expected it to be any different."

"Despite what they did, Davide and Susan are your parents, and you love them," I said. "There's no shame in that."

"Maybe there should be," she sniffled, "they hurt so many people. Your family included."

"Does this mean you think they did it?" I asked suddenly, feeling a panic rise in me.

It was strange, that feeling...we had yet to find anything that would prove them innocent in the sea of documents we had gone through over the last months. Yet, the people I knew, the people that were going to be my in-laws if life had gone my way, just couldn't have been guilty of this. I knew it in my gut, and until now I thought Jackie did too.

"The evidence certainly points to them, doesn't it?" she huffed.

"Jackie," I sighed, pressing her hand flat against my chest, "we're missing something."

"I hoped so too, but we've been through nearly every document," she sniffled. "I just don't think we're going to find anything."

"Well, if it is alright with you, I'm going to hold on to enough hope for both of us," I said, rubbing my thumb over her palm that I had pinned to my chest.

"Thank you," she said, squeezing the thumb I had been smoothing over her palm.

We sat quietly for the rest of the car ride, but it was a lighter silence that fell between us, one of companionship that came with knowing and loving someone for as long as we have.

When we pulled up to the curb outside of Francine's house, I released her hand, and we both got out. We had a spare green bean casserole that we had in the cooler in the back. It needed to be put in the oven, so I grabbed the cooler, and as I came around to Jackie's side, I took her hand, and we walked up to the porch. We came right in and put our coats on the hooks in the foyer. I could hear my family chattering animatedly in the living room.

To my relief, I saw the color come back to Jackie's face and the light shine from her eyes. It was hard to be gloomy at a Carrollton family gathering.

"Happy Thanksgiving, everyone," I called as we came into the living room where my dad and brothers were watching football. On the couch next to Ben was Francine's colleague Shreya. On the other side of Ben was a guy I'd never seen before.

My dad stood and gave me a huge bear hug.

"Glad to see you, son," he said, giving me his customary double thump on the back.

He released me and embraced Jackie. "Hello beautiful girl, so good to see you."

"It's good to see you too, Mr. C," she smiled and hugged my dad back.

"I'm going to take this out to the kitchen," Jackie said, grabbing the casserole dish from me.

"Will you bring me a beer when you come back, Baby?" I called after her.

"Yes, dear," she called back to me.

"Baby, huh?" Ben teased. "I guess that means things are going well?"

"Things are going great," I replied. "Happy Thanksgiving."

Ben and I hugged briefly, each mimicking our father's two-thump hugs.

"Shreya, good to see you again." I offered my hand to her.

"And you," she replied, shaking my hand.

"Is this your date for the evening?" I asked, referring to the man I didn't know.

"No, this is your sister's date," she replied with a small laugh and a quick glance toward Ben that probably would have been imperceptible to anyone but me.

The man stood and shook my hand. "Seth Easton. Francine invited me over. We met at the gym a couple of weeks ago, and I didn't have any other Thanksgiving plans."

"Welcome to our home then, Seth. I'm Francine's oldest brother, Kyle," I replied.

"Nice to meet you," Seth said.

"Likewise," I replied, taking a seat on the empty couch. "What do you do for a living?"

"I'm a fitness trainer at the gym. I just got my certification, and I'm trying to build up my clientele. Francine has a lot of great ideas to promote my services," Seth smiled.

"Frannie is great at that stuff," I agreed, smiling as Jackie came around the corner from the kitchen with my beer in hand.

"Thanks, sweetness," I said, taking the beer from her and taking a long draw from the neck of the bottle.

Jackie settled into the seat beside me, and I wrapped my arm around her and pulled her closer.

"Jacks, this is Seth," I said, pointing at the other man with the head of my beer bottle.

"Of course," she smiled, "Francine has told me so much about you."

"She has?" I muttered so that only she could hear me.

"Yes," she muttered back.

"Francine is a great girl," Seth smiled.

"We think so," our father said.

"Where's Jason?" I asked.

"He'll be here in a little bit," my dad answered. "He went to pick up a friend to bring with him."

I nodded and sat on the couch with Jackie to watch the game. She gently took my beer from the hand I had it in, resting on my knee, and took a long sip of it.

"Do you want me to get you one?" I asked when she handed it back to me, noticeably emptier than when she took it.

"No, I just wanted a sip of yours," she smiled playfully.

"Mi cerveza es tu cerveza," I volleyed back.

"Muy bien," she giggled, clearly elated that I had remembered something at all from all the tutoring she had done with me in Spanish.

"You guys are gross," Ben mocked.

It held no venom. Yet, I knew how to torture my baby brother. It was my right and duty as his oldest brother to do so.

"Damn, I guess we're going to have to go make out on the hood of Benny's new truck later so that we don't gross him out here in the house," I conspired with Jackie.

"We just might have to," Jackie's smile widened, her eyes dancing with equal delight at my brother's torment.

God, I loved this girl!

"You wouldn't!" Ben sat forward a bit.

"We have a bit of time before dinner will be ready, maybe we should go out there now," I continued, torturing my baby brother just a little more.

"Don't you dare," Ben warned. "I just got it cleaned and waxed."

"Then our butt prints shouldn't stick," Jackie giggled.

"Aw, not you too, Jackie!" Ben complained. "I thought you were my friend."

"I am, but I very much like making out with your brother," she laughed.

"So, no matter what I win," I crowed, "remember this, dear brother, before you tease me about being gross."

Ben sat back in his seat, relieved that we weren't going to go out there and defile his truck...at least not yet. He'd better keep on his best behavior though if he wants to keep it that way.

We all settled into watching the game, and I could hear Ben explaining some of the plays to Shreya next to him. She watched him as though he were explaining how to defuse a bomb, with such attention to detail.

"Happy Thanksgiving!" Jason called from the foyer.

"Happy Thanksgiving!" We all called back.

Jason came into the living room with a woman who had bright pink and purple hair, a sleeve of tattoos down her right arm and a variety of piercings in her nose and ears. After a moment of shock at her appearance, I recognized she was Jason's partner that he rode along with when he was on call.

"Officer Carrollton, nice to see you are not covered in blood this time," she smiled.

"Kyle," I said, standing to shake her hand, "I'm so sorry; that day was crazy, and I didn't catch your name."

Carrollton Thanksgiving Fun | 267

"It's cool; my name is Layla," she replied.

"Nice to see you again, Layla," I smiled and sat back down with Jackie.

"You too, thanks everyone for having me," she said politely.

"Can I get you anything to drink?" Jason asked.

"I'd love a beer," she smiled and took the seat on the edge of the couch Jackie and I were sitting on, leaving a space for Jason when he came back.

"One beer coming up," he replied and went to the kitchen to retrieve it.

"Jay, can you grab one for Jacks too, please?" I called after him.

"You've got it," he called back over his shoulder.

"What you don't like sharing with me?" she asked, feigning offense.

"We can share yours too," I replied.

"No way!" she cried in faux outrage. "Don't you know, what's yours is mine and what's mine is mine?"

"Good thing I brought one for Kyle too," Jason chuckled amiably as he passed out beers to me, Jackie, and Layla before taking the seat between Jackie and Layla.

"Good thing, I guess," I chuckled.

Although it may seem that Jackie had turned against me, it was a relief to see her playful side coming through. After the dinner with her family turned to shit a few hours ago, I wasn't sure that she could survive another dinner, even with this lively bunch...especially with this lively bunch! However, it seems it gave her license to tease me and have fun, and I couldn't be more grateful for this group of wackos I call my family.

"Dad, would you like to come carve the turkey?" Francine called from the doorway of the kitchen.

"Be right there," he called back, watching the current play as he slowly stood from his seat and made his way to the kitchen.

An hour later, dinner had been eaten and cleared up, my parents were ready to go back to their camper for the night so we could enjoy some time together, just us "kids." We tended to get rowdier with food (and alcohol) in us rather than more lethargic, so that was probably for the best.

"Is it time to play the Devil's hand?" I asked the room at large.

"Oh my God, you still play that?" Jackie asked with a laugh.

"Of course we do. It's a family tradition," Francine answered with a smile, "and based on that, I traditionally win."

"You traditionally cheat," Ben retorted.

"I would never!" Francine insisted indignantly.

"Frannie, you are a cheat and an even worse liar," I joined in on the teasing.

"Just to prove I do not cheat, we can play teams this time! We have enough people," Francine replied.

"So, you've been training Seth on this game, and you can both cheat effectively?" Jackie mused.

"Hey! You're supposed to be my friend!" Francine laughed at that jab.

"I am but when we play teams, I am your opponent and I know how dirty you play," Jackie smiled.

"I'm not very good at card games," Shreya admitted bashfully.

"It's okay. It's just for fun anyway," Ben assured her. "You can be on my team, and I'll show you how it works."

Shreya seemed pleased and smiled at him gratefully.

"Layla, buddy, you're with me," Jason said, bumping the side of her knee with the side of his fist.

"Nothing like being picked last," Layla teased him, jabbing her fist into his biceps.

"There's no such thing as being picked last; you partner with the person you brought to dinner," Jason explained, wrapping his arm around her and squeezing her into his side.

We all made our way over to the table.

"Partners sit across from one another," Francine said, ensuring everyone took their correct seat. "The goal of the game is that you and your partner must complete your assigned suit before any other team. Jokers are wild, so you can use any of the joker cards to substitute for a missing card that one of your opponents still has in hand as long as you do not use it for two missing cards in a row in one run."

"Normally, we play with one deck when we're playing as individuals, but since we are playing partners, we use two decks," Jason explained to our newcomers.

"We Carrollton siblings have our assigned suit that never changes. I have hearts because Jackie and I were a couple for nearly as long as this ridiculous game existed," I chuckled, giving Jackie a smile. "Francine loves plants, so we assigned her spades. When our brilliant brother Jason would study, he put so much pressure on himself to excel that we used to tease him he would turn into a diamond, so he got diamonds, of course. Ben has been the life of the party since he could move, so he got clubs."

"I'm not sure why we called it the Devil's Hand. We were just dumb kids, and it sounded more adventurous than Go Fish, and the name stuck," Ben smiled at Shreya as if to assure her we weren't summoning demons with this game.

"Let's play!" Francine declared and began dealing out the cards she had painstakingly shuffled as we explained the game to the others.

My eyes locked with Jackie's across the table from me, and I saw the girl I had been in love with since I could remember. She'd only grown more beautiful with time, and I decided I was most thankful for whatever destiny, or fate, or serendipity had brought her to me. I would always be thankful for that.

She always had a place with this family, and I wanted her to know that. I knew what I wanted to get her for Christmas.

"So, boys," I addressed my brothers, "when are you free to do some Christmas shopping?"

Jason pulled out his phone to look at his calendar.

"December 9th?" Jason suggested.

"I'll request it off," Ben replied.

"Good," I grinned and caught Jackie's suspicious gaze out of the corner of my eye.

"That means I get a girls' shopping trip with Jackie!" Francine declared; her competitive nature was shining through.

"Who's stopping you?" I asked calmly just to ruffle her feathers.

"I'm free pretty much all the time right now," Jackie admitted. "I don't start working at Holy Cannoli until the school year starts up."

"Janice is going to let you work for her?" I asked, excited by her news.

Jackie nodded and smiled.

Janice was a great boss to work for. She valued education and wanted the best for her employees, past and present, whether they stuck around to work for her or moved onto their dream job like I had. I was thrilled to hear Janice had a spot for her.

It really felt like things were coming together, and this life we were trying to build just might work out this time.

CHAPTER 25

You've Got Some Explaining to Do

Jackie
December 6, 2017

Kyle's alarm went off at five every morning that week since he was back out on patrol. He turned it off as usual, but instead of getting out of bed, he rolled back toward me and nuzzled his bearded face into my neck and started kissing.

"You look so beautiful," he said between kisses.

"I am certain I don't," I laughed, rubbing the sleep out of my left eye.

"Stunning," he tried again, pulling me closer to him as he continued with his barrage of kisses trailing their way down my chest.

"Probably not that either," I replied, running my hand through his messy hair.

Kyle pulled the cups of my camisole down, exposing my breasts to him. He cupped and squeezed them reverently, before planting a kiss on each one in turn.

"Captivating," he insisted, his eyes hungrily staring into mine before he took my mouth in a passionate kiss.

A moan escaped me when he began caressing his hands down my hips. His touch was a magical thing that made me feel feminine and desired. Like I was everything a man should want in a woman.

He rolled us over so that he was on top of me, nestled between my legs. My hands roamed his back as I kissed the skin of the dragon tattoo on his chest. The one he'd got for me. The one that meant I was the queen of his heart forever.

"I love you," he breathed into my ear as he rubbed the head of his cock along my slit, exciting every nerve ending there.

"Kyle," I sighed, "I am yours, only yours."

He thrust into me to the hilt and held himself there.

"Say it again, baby," he ordered huskily, "who do you belong to?"

"You," I replied breathlessly, "all that I am is yours."

He rewarded my answer by making love to me. He set a sweet, slow rhythm of his hips into mine as he explored my body with his hands and lips, stroking and loving every inch of me. His beard left scuff marks in its wake over the skin that he kissed and lathed with his tongue.

My orgasm came over me in gentle waves and stretched out in long contractions of my inner walls as he kept the easy pace he had set.

"Something tells me you have another one of those in you this morning," he smiled as the first orgasm ebbed.

"I don't know," I replied, panting.

"I know," he insisted, and increased his pace.

His hand reached down between us, and his thumb began drawing maddening circles around my clit. With the increased speed of his thrusts and the stimulation from his thumb, I was back up at my peak in no time. Loud cries of pleasure burst out of me involuntarily.

"You're going to wake the neighbors," he teased and covered my mouth with his in a kiss.

As my walls contracted again, this time more frantically, it was enough to pull him over the edge as well, and he let out a series of grunts as came inside of me. When he was done, he pulled out of me carefully and rolled over to his side of the bed.

"I told you, you had another one in there," he smiled at me, huffing with exertion.

"And you pulled it out of me," I smiled back, kissing him once more.

"If I could, I would stay here with you all day," he said, pulling me tighter to his side.

"I'd love that," I replied, burying my face in his chest.

"You know I can't though," he sighed, "I really need to get in the shower so I can go pick up Romero."

I groaned and buried my face deeper into his chest, which produced the laugh I was hoping to elicit from him.

"I'm sorry, Baby," he said, lifting my face from his chest gently and placing a sweet kiss on my forehead.

I gave his torso a squeeze and then let him go get ready.

"Can I make you something to eat?" I asked, watching his firm butt flex with each step he took to go from our bed to the dresser.

I was going to make him something to eat even if he said no, so I tossed back the covers and swung my legs out over the edge of the bed.

"Would you make me a couple of eggs and toast and just put it together like a sandwich so I can eat it on the road?" he asked.

"Of course," I replied, slipping into my fuzzy robe and slippers. I had fully planned to go back to bed after Kyle left.

"Thanks," he said, "I'll be out in a minute."

I nodded and padded my way out to the kitchen. I had some Italian sausage I had browned the day before and reserved some for breakfast, so I pulled that out along with the two eggs, some provolone cheese, mushrooms, diced tomatoes and arugula from the fridge and his favorite homemade bread from the bread box.

I pulled out the omelet skillet and put a tiny bit of oil in the bottom so that nothing would stick, and then I set to work on the scrambled eggs. I stirred in the diced tomatoes, sausage, salt, and pepper and poured it into the hot pan on the stove. I let the eggs set while I popped the bread into the toaster.

Sweet Toby must have heard me in the kitchen and let out a meow before circling around my feet in a near-perfect figure eight. I plucked the corner from a piece of cheese and tossed it down to him. With the cheese tax paid, I flipped the omelet, added the mushrooms, arugula, and provolone on top and let the underside cook until the cheese melted. I folded the omelet in half, concealing the ingredients between the two halves of the egg. I turned off the burner and caught the toast just as it popped up. On a paper towel, I began assembling the sandwich: bread, a little kick of hot sauce, the omelet, a bit of mayo and the other slice of bread. It was about that time I heard the door to our bedroom and Kyle's footfall crossing the room over to me.

"I don't know how you had time to do that, but that smells amazing," he said, wrapping his arms around my waist in a hug.

"Eggs are pretty easy," I smiled, taking a paper towel and a piece of foil stacked together and wrapping the paper towel side in against the bottom of the sandwich to keep it warm and stop any of the condiments from dripping out onto his uniform and handing it to him.

"I appreciate this so much," he said, kissing my lips. "I love you and I'll see you tonight."

"I love you, be safe," I called after him as he walked out of our apartment.

"Always," he smiled back at me and closed the door.

My heart ached every time he left for work. It was still hard saying goodbye to him each morning, knowing his partner had been shot a couple of months ago. It was especially hard now that they were off desk duty and back working in the field. I couldn't bear the idea of losing him ever again. The first time nearly destroyed me.

I double-checked that I had turned off the stove and put the few dishes I had made in the sink to wash later. My not-so-guilty pleasure was going back to bed after Kyle left for work. I would take the shirt he had worn that night and put it over his pillow and then snuggle his pillow so that I could enjoy his scent a little while longer. That way I didn't miss him more than I had to until he came back to me. Usually, it meant Toby would join me, and we would fall back to sleep for another hour or so.

I picked up Toby, and he rested, perched on my shoulder, and butted his nose against the curve of my jaw. I still couldn't believe Kyle had bought him for me as a graduation present and kept him for me all this time. Toby loved him as much as I did, so when I set him down on the bed, he cried out eagerly for me to pull the t-shirt out of the hamper and pull it over the pillow. Once I got it situated, Toby curled up along the bottom, and I wrapped my arms around it as though Kyle was still in bed with me.

When I got snuggled in with "Pillow Kyle" and comfortable, I closed my eyes and drifted to sleep almost immediately. I had no sooner felt myself slip away into a dream when my phone began ringing on the night table.

Francine's smiling face covered my screen, and while I loved her dearly, I didn't so much love her calling this early.

"Hello?" I grumbled into the phone.

"Good morning, Buttercup," she replied, entirely too perky for this time of day.

"Hey Frannie, what's up?" I asked, trying not to sound as grumpy as I felt.

"Well, I was wondering if you wanted to meet me for lunch at my office and then go do some Christmas shopping this afternoon," she explained.

"Um...sure," I said, "I was thinking of running by the storage unit again this morning to pull a few more boxes so I can go through them over the weekend, but that should leave me plenty of time to come meet you for lunch and go shopping."

"Great! I'm so excited. We haven't been shopping together in ages. Tell that brother of mine he's hogging you," she pouted. "I demand equal Jackie time, dammit!"

"I would, but he already left for work," I replied, pouting a little myself.

"Good, then I get you all to myself," she replied triumphantly.

"Yes, you do," I smiled. "So lunch at noon?"

"Yes, just come to my office and I'll meet you down in the lobby and we can figure out where we want to eat then," she said.

"Okay see you then," I replied.

"Jackie?" she called out, keeping me from hanging up with her.

"Yeah?" I replied.

"Kyle's going to be pissed if he knows you went to the storage unit without him after what happened the last time you were there," she said, a note of concern tinging her tone.

"He really doesn't need to worry about it. It was all just a misunderstanding with Luis. He thought I was a reporter trying to get a scoop on my family again," I replied, dismissing her concerns. "He was just protecting Drew. Kyle would have done the same for me."

I felt a little guilty that I had promised to wait for him, but Kyle couldn't come with me again until Monday evening. He was doing a weekend boys' trip with his brothers, so I would be home with nothing to do but wait.

"Still, he worries," she said gently, "and I do too. That place isn't as nice as it once was. There's been a lot of vandalism and chop shops stealing entire cars or parts off cars while the person is going through their things inside the building."

"I was assured by the owner that they've gotten new security measures in place and that it would be perfectly safe for me to go by myself. Please don't say anything to Kyle; he has enough to worry about with his job. He'll never notice that the boxes I'm going through are different from the ones that I have at the apartment now," I pleaded with her.

Francine let out a long-suffering sigh and replied, "I won't tell him, but I still wish you'd just wait and have him go with you."

"I promise I'll be careful. I'll bring my mace and taser with me. If anyone tries to mess with me, they'll be sorry," I assured her.

I've lived in major cities all my life. I know how to protect myself.

"Fine, but if anything looks even remotely shady there, just drive away. Promise me!" Francine insisted.

"I promise," I replied.

And I would. I didn't have a death wish; I just wanted to have something to keep me occupied over the weekend.

"I love you madly, you know," she said. "You can't leave me again."

"You couldn't get that lucky," I teased. "You're stuck with me forever."

"Good, I've gotta run, but I'll see you at my office this afternoon," she said.

"See you then," I replied, hanging up with her.

As glorious as going back to sleep sounded in my head, I knew, now that I had spoken to Francine, sleep would elude me.

Mentally, I knew Christmas was coming up, but it had been so long since I had bought gifts for anyone, and then last year I didn't even celebrate it at all since I was on my own. I had no clue what to get anyone. I hoped Francine had some good ideas she would be willing to share with me.

However, the nervous energy that filled me required some kind of action to displace it, so I got up, took the shirt off Pillow Kyle, much to Toby's dismay, and returned it to the hamper before I went to take a shower and get my day started.

Francine and Kyle were both being ridiculous about the storage building. It was still in a decent area of town with virtually no graffiti on any of the blocks surrounding it. The cars in the neighborhood were older, but appeared to be well maintained, so it was a working-class area but didn't have any of the usual telltale signs of trouble.

I stood in the shower considering Kyle and Francine's warnings about the place, but I just didn't feel that it would be dangerous enough to wait for him. He had enough things to worry about and take care of. It would just be a quick trip to swap out the four boxes I had for four new ones. I should be in and out in less than 10 minutes. Not worth the extra time out of someone else's day to make them come with me.

After my shower, I got dressed and loaded the four boxes I wanted to return into the trunk of my car and drove over to the storage unit. When I arrived, there was only one other vehicle there. I carried one box into the building with me and made my way to the unit.

When I got to the unit, I set the box down and unlocked the door. I opened the door and stuck the padlock in my pants pocket before picking up the box I was returning and putting it back in its place. I followed the row of stacked boxes and found the next one in chronological order that I wanted to look through and picked it up to take it back to my car.

I made the trip back and forth again, returning a box and collecting a new one. When I was going on my third trip, I heard several men talking to one another, but their voices were far enough away that I couldn't make out any words. I figured it was the people from the other car that were still there, but I hadn't passed the whole time I had been there. That soon changed when I nearly ran headlong into a familiar man with fading auburn hair.

You've Got Some Explaining to Do | 281

"Excuse me," the man said, his head barely peeking above the large box in his hands.

"Mr. Herrington?" I asked.

"Ms. D'Marco, what are you doing here?" he asked, just as surprised to see me as I was to see him.

"I was taking some things to my storage unit," I replied. "I thought you were living in Manhattan now?"

"I do, but my mother still lives here and asked me to pick up a few things for her," he explained, gesturing to the box full of Christmas decorations in his hands.

"Oh, that's nice," I replied, not sure what else to say.

"Well, it was good running into you again. I hope you found peace with your parents' situation," he said.

"Peace, no, but I found my way back to something good for myself." I smiled, "Take care, Mr. Herrington. I hope you have a good Christmas with your family."

"Thank you," he replied, and we slipped past one another to continue in the direction we each were headed.

When I got back to my unit, the fourth box I had wanted to take was not in the spot it should have been. I walked around a bit searching for it. My stomach tightened when an idea occurred to me. The file boxes were big, but they would have been small enough to fit in the box Mr. Herrington was carrying.

I tried to shake off the idea, but the longer I searched, the more the idea niggled at me. I heard his car start up, and I ran out and tried to catch him. By the time I got to the door, his car was further than I thought I could reasonably catch up with, so I returned to the unit to check for the box one more time. He couldn't possibly have been able to find that specific box in the time I had run one box out and come back with another. I was being ridiculous.

After a few minutes, I did finally find the box, mixed in with the records of D'Marco Italiano from the year after. This box is probably the one that was made with copies of the documents that the police took for evidence in the case against my parents. I hadn't been eager to go through these again, because when I did five years ago the evidence seemed so damning. It felt like going through this box again would be the last chance to find something that would prove my parents' innocence. If I couldn't, then that would only leave the truth I dreaded: they were guilty as I had believed all those years ago. I wasn't sure I was ready to face that truth.

I carried the box out to the hallway and pulled the door shut and secured it with the padlock once more. Lost in thought, I carried my box until I turned the corner and found that someone had vandalized my car and slashed the back tire.

My heart sank. I knew I needed to report this, whether I wanted Kyle to know about it or not. I pulled out my phone and called the non-emergency police line.

CHAPTER 26

The Fight No One Wins

Kyle
December 6, 2017

“What the fuck was she doing there?” I growled, my fingers digging into my thighs, wishing I were the one driving so I had something to do.

Was smoke coming out of your ears a real thing or did that just happen in the cartoons? If it were, the car would have been filled with smoke so thick you couldn't see.

“Apparently picking up some things from storage,” Romero volleyed back all too calmly.

I seethed. I have told her more times than I have breathed in the last week not to go there without me. What does she fucking do? She goes there without me after she promised me she wouldn't.

“You need to calm down,” Romero stated. “She's probably scared, and you being pissed off will not help.”

I heard what he was saying, I really did, but my blood was boiling too hot to calm down just yet. We talked about this. I would take her to storage when I got off work on Monday. My brothers and I had a plan to go do some Christmas shopping this weekend, and I couldn't go until Monday. It wasn't like I was asking her to wait until after the New Year, for God's sake!

As Oscar pulled the cruiser into the parking lot of the storage building, I saw her car and my anger flooded through me anew. Her back passenger window had been busted out. On the same side, the back tire was slashed. The hood was spray painted “Merry Xmas Bitch,” and the trunk lid had what looked like a penis. There was a set of boobs on the passenger side, and the driver's side mirror had been bashed with something. It was cracked but still attached to the car.

She could use my car to get back and forth from school and work until we could afford to fix this or get her something else. Hell, she could take an Uber. The car didn't matter. I was pissed that once again she had put herself in harm's way for some stupid boxes.

"Jackie, would you like to sit in the cruiser so you can stay warm while we take your statement?" Romero asked her.

She nodded and walked toward us.

"I'll take pictures of the scene," I said, afraid that if I tried to say anything else I would come unglued.

I brushed past her. Our shoulders touched ever so slightly, but somehow it made me feel the tiniest bit better she was unharmed. I was still too mad to comfort her or say the right words. Instead, I pulled out my phone and started documenting the scene and bagging what little evidence was left behind. A cap from one of the spray cans and an old bandana.

After Romero finished taking her statement, they both got out of the car, and he hugged her. I should be the one holding her. Instead, when I heard her sniffle, even though it tore me up, it sent my anger spiraling all over again.

"Jackie gave us a lead to follow up on. Mr. Herrington was here just before this happened," Romero stated.

"Herrington?" I asked, looking at Jackie. "What the Hell was he doing here?"

"He said he was picking up some things for his mother. I saw him pull away before this happened, but as Oscar said, he could have pulled back in when I went back inside to get one more box," she mused.

Herrington didn't seem the sort to do a petty crime like vandalism, but if he were trying to rattle her...maybe. Especially if he was trying to cover up an even bigger crime.

"Let's go talk to him," I said to Romero.

"Why don't you change out Jackie's tire and find something to cover that broken window. I've got the station trying to reach Herrington to find his current whereabouts. As soon as they track him down, I'll go talk with him," Romero ordered.

Part of me wanted to put her in the back of our patrol car and not let her out of my sight for the rest of the day, but I knew I couldn't. Oscar was right; I should change out her tire so that she could at least go back home.

"Right," I agreed. "Jackie, come pop the trunk so I can get to your spare."

Jackie came closer and did as I asked. When she opened the trunk, three more boxes filled it. She scurried to grab one, like I had found a dirty little secret. I suppose I had. I held up my hand to stop her.

"I've got it," I said, pulling them out one by one. "Is there anything we can use to cover this back window so you can at least drive it home?"

She stood for a moment, tapping her foot in thought and then got into her glove box and pulled out one of those thin silver blankets like when they rescue people on tv and then took the packing tape she had with her and held it up like she'd found treasure.

"Good," I replied. "Why don't you put that over the window, and I'll take care of the tire."

She nodded and set to work covering the window as I instructed. While she did that, I shuffled her precious boxes into the back seat and pulled out the jack and spare tire.

"Carrollton," Romero called to me.

I met his gaze and replied, "Yeah?"

"They've tracked down Herrington about two blocks from here. Why don't you finish up here and just meet me down there if I'm not already back," he suggested.

I nodded, and Romero got into the cruiser and took off down the road. I worked on Jackie's tire quietly, mumbling curse words under my breath about the situation, about the tire, about anything I could be mad about.

"Kyle, please," she said, "I know you're upset, and I am too. I'm sorry."

The Fight No One Wins | 289

I finished working on the tire and tossed the jack and tire iron in her trunk, letting the anger I'd been holding back flow through me again. "Sorry" was feeling pretty damn pathetic right about now, and I was pissed enough to tell her so.

"Your 'sorry' right now is not enough," I said bitterly. "Are these boxes of paper worth dying for? I told you not to come here alone. I asked you to wait three fucking days so that I could come with you, and you just couldn't do it, could you?"

"I didn't want to waste your time," she tried to explain.

"Waste my time? Good job there! I'm wasting my fucking time right now fixing this hunk of shit car of yours because you didn't want to wait. How is that any better?" I spat back.

"It's not, but–" she replied, her face reddening.

"Why can't you just let me help you? Why can't you just listen to me when you know I'm right? God, Jackie, you've had people leaving threatening notes on your car warning you to stop digging into this. Did you think they wouldn't find you here too?" I demanded.

"It was stupid, okay? Is that what you need to hear?" she shot back defensively.

"That's a good start," I bellowed back, crossing my arms over my chest.

"Fine, Your Highness. I was stupid, and it was wrong to come here. Never mind that I have to live every day with the weight of my testimony that put my own parents in jail five years ago. A testimony that may have been based on false documents, meaning that two people that I love, two people that gave me life, are sitting in jail on false charges, their lives ruined," she sobbed. "What else? What else...oh, let's throw this back into the fight... you still have not forgiven me for the choices I made in the wake of this. Choices that kept us apart for five years. Let's get that out in the air too, huh? It's not fair that you only ever think of the toll it took on you. Do you EVER stop and think about what that time did to me? Nonni was the only person I had once I left for Chicago. Did you know I lived on leftovers from the bakery I worked at for the last year and a half because every penny I made went to paying for Nonni's care and the apartment we lived in? At the end of it, I was left with a year and a half of schooling, a student loan that is still in deferment and the clothes on my back. Nonni's final expenses just broke even."

Her admission was heartbreaking. I didn't know that her situation in Chicago was so dire, but I wished she had told me sooner. The D'Marco family had been well off before everything happened. Better than my family, so I just assumed that Nonni had some money for them to live off. I felt like such an asshole for not asking her more about her time in Chicago.

"Now let's just talk about you for a second and the damage YOU did to this relationship. Every anniversary, every birthday, I get a voicemail or a text from you, and those mean the world to me even though each one breaks my heart a little more each time. But when I needed someone the most, the day Nonni died, what did you do? You left me this gem," she said, pulling her phone from her pocket and queuing up a voicemail I had left her.

My disembodied voice slurred over her phone's speaker. "Jackie, it's me again. I just wanted to let you know I'm glad you never called me back. I'm glad you left. You know why? Because love isn't real. It's some bullshit they make up for the fairy tale books. And that shit isn't real. So, this birthday, I wished I would find another girl to fuck around with. It doesn't matter anyway, right? We were just two stupid kids who thought love was real a lifetime ago, but now it's clear that never mattered..."

The phone made a few crackling noises before my voice came back. Clearly the phone was in my pocket at this point and added, "Hey, Baby, nice rack! You wanna fuck later?"

My eyes locked with hers, and I couldn't bear the agony I saw there. I remembered that night, but I don't remember calling her. It was the night of my twenty-second birthday. I was beyond drunk, and I didn't even remember calling her until I heard that message. Acid rose up my throat. I desperately wanted to pluck each of the words out of the air between us.

"Jackie..." I began and went to reach out to her. She recoiled from me, and I hated that feeling, but I dropped my arm to the side.

"Don't," she sniffled, "clearly there are things neither of us has forgiven."

My heart sank. She hadn't forgiven me for that? Did the time we had been back together mean nothing to her? We stood quietly staring at each other, our heaving breaths coming out in cloudy puffs in the cold December air. I wasn't sure what I could say to take the sad look from her eyes. She huffed and got in her car and drove off. I stood in the cloud of dust left behind, regretting my callous words to her in that message. I was still mad at her, but now I am mad at myself too.

A few minutes later, Oscar pulled back into the lot where I stood.

"Did Jackie go home?" Oscar asked me through the open cruiser window.

"I hope so," I said, still staring off in the direction her car had gone.

I just saw her leaving, and all I could do was hope that she would go home and we could talk this out when I got home after my shift. If she were gone again...well, I couldn't even finish the thought; it was already twisting my insides.

"What happened?" Oscar asked.

"I was an idiot," I sighed and picked up the tire I'd taken from Jackie's car. "Pop the trunk."

Oscar opened the trunk, and as I went to carry Jackie's damaged tire to the trunk, I saw my phone crushed on the ground. It must have fallen out of my pocket when I was changing the tire and got run over by her car when she left.

"Fuck," I growled, bending down to pick up the dead phone and putting it in my pocket. Maybe the SIM card would still be salvageable. I had my last phone at home. I could try to put the SIM card in later to see if it would work.

"What's wrong?" Oscar asked.

"My phone is busted," I complained, hefting the tire from the ground and carrying it to the back of the car.

I swung the tire into the trunk and closed the lid. I got in on the passenger side, and Oscar met my gaze.

"What did Herrington have to say?" I asked, trying to refocus my mind.

"Nothing very helpful," Oscar replied. "The neighbor was there and could verify the time he arrived to visit his mother. The timeline was close, but as best I can tell, he would have been long gone before whoever did this came through. He said the only other person he saw here was Jackie."

I nodded as our next call came in over the radio. I had to set aside my fight with Jackie so that I could finish out my workday. I just hoped I had the chance to work it out with her later. I knew she wouldn't be ready to talk to me yet. I needed to let someone know my phone was busted so that they could tell her.

"Romero, can I borrow your phone?" I asked.

"Help yourself," he replied, turning onto the street from the parking lot.

I dialed my sister's number, knowing that when Jackie was ready to talk to someone, Francine would be the one she reached out to.

"Oscar? Is Kyle okay?" she asked, worry laced through her tone.

"It IS Kyle," I reassured her, "and I'm fine."

"Oh, thank God," she sighed. "Why are you calling from Oscar's phone?"

"My phone is busted," I explained. "I can't talk long, but I just wanted to let you know so that you could reach me if you needed to until I can pick up a new one."

"Oh, okay," she replied, a note of suspicion in her words. "Are you sure you're alright?"

My sister knew me well. I wouldn't normally call about something like this. She had Oscar's number if she was trying to reach me and couldn't. The call was wholly unnecessary, except for what I really needed to tell her.

"I'm fine. Jackie and I just had a terrible argument, and I figured she would reach out to you when she cooled down," I admitted.

"We have a date to go shopping this afternoon, so I should see her then unless she calls to cancel," Francine stated. "What happened?"

"She went to the storage place without me, and her car was vandalized," I relayed to her.

"Is she okay?" Francine asked, worried for her friend.

"Yeah, she was just a little shaken up about it, but she never even saw who did it," I explained. "They tagged her car and slashed one of her tires and ran off while she was inside the building."

"I'm so glad she's not hurt," Francine sighed. "I'll text Oscar to let you know if she meets up with me at lunch as planned. I'm sure everything will be fine between you."

"Thanks, Frannie. I've got to go," I said.

"Okay, be safe. I love you," she said.

"I love you too, sis," I replied and hung up the phone.

"Smart move, calling your sister," Oscar remarked.

"She's going to text your phone later. She and Jackie have a shopping date planned this afternoon, so she's going to let me know if Jackie shows up for that," I said.

"Carrollton answering service at your...service," Oscar chuckled at his own joke.

I shook my head at him, but it brought out a small smile.

"Is your head back in the game? We're almost to the scene of that call we got," Oscar asked seriously.

"Yeah, I'm all here," I said, determined for that to be true.

CHAPTER 27

Christmas Shopping with Francine

Jackie
December 6, 2017

"Oh my God, Jackie, your car!" Francine exclaimed as we met outside of the parking garage of the building where she worked.

She had been waiting outside for me, and I had seen her horrified face as I drove up. As horrified as I had been by the mess the vandals had made of my car, I was even more horrified by the horrible things I had said to Kyle. I was so ashamed that I threw that stupid message in his face. I didn't even know why I had kept it!

"It was vandalized at the storage unit," I explained.

"Kyle told me. Are you alright?" she asked.

Kyle had called her and not me? I felt a pinch in my chest. I'm sure he was too angry to even try to speak to me at that moment.

"What did he say?" I asked, wincing at what he would say to her.

"He just said that your car was vandalized and that you guys had an argument," she shrugged as we started walking down the street to the shops.

"That was it?" I prodded.

"Yeah, pretty much," she answered and then tried to dig out the truth from me with her piercing blue eyes. "Why, was it worse than that?"

I let out a huff. Was it worse than that? She didn't have any idea.

Francine frowned. "I bet he was pissed."

"That's an understatement," I replied miserably. "We got into a huge fight about it."

"I'm sorry," she commiserated. "He does not fight fair. I know that from experience."

"I was the one who didn't fight fair," I admitted.

"What do you mean?" she asked as we entered the first store.

I wished I could forget what I had done. I should have deleted that message the day he left it. I definitely shouldn't have used it as a weapon in our argument!

Francine looked sympathetically at me over the racks of clothing.

I sighed and pulled out my phone and cued up my voicemail so that all she had to do was hit play.

She did, and as she listened to the phone, her eyes widened, and her mouth dropped. When she handed back the phone, I tucked it back into my purse.

"That message came on the day Nonni died," I whispered, a single tear streaking down my cheek at the memory, "I had put my phone down while I was at her bedside saying goodbye to her and I didn't touch it again until I was alone after the coroner and hospice had left."

Francine's eyes welled, and she pulled me into a hug I didn't deserve but so desperately needed. I hugged her back and released her so we wouldn't look like complete weirdos in the high-end store we had walked into.

"I was so excited at first to see he had left me a message. I thought it was a parting gift from Nonni. Like she was returning my heart to me, since she had returned to hers," I laughed ruefully.

"Oh, Jackie, what horrible timing!" she sighed. "Kyle can be an asshole sometimes, but he never would have left that message if he'd have known what was going on."

"I know, but it didn't hurt any less," I acknowledged.

"Of course not," she agreed. "But why hold on to that? I thought you still wanted to be with him?"

"Of course I do. He's my soulmate. Honestly, I don't know why I held onto the message. I thought about deleting it so many times. Since I played it for him, I wish I had deleted it." I replied miserably. "I love him so much. I want to be with him more than anything! I want to forgive him for that message, but I don't think I did. Deep down, I knew he hadn't fully forgiven me for leaving, and somewhere in my mind the message made us even, I guess."

"Jackie," Francine sighed, "You both have to decide either to forgive each other or let each other go. If you don't, you'll never be truly happy with one another."

I nodded, taking in her words as we shopped in the store.

"Can you promise me something?" Francine asked, vulnerability shining in her blue eyes.

"Anything," I replied, and I meant it.

Francine took a fortifying breath and said, "If you and Kyle break up, promise me that doesn't mean I won't see you again. It was too hard being without you, and I don't want to do it again."

I rubbed at the part of my chest that ached with all the time I lost with my best friend. I nodded and replied, "I promise. It was too hard for me too."

She smiled and hugged me again. I pulled her back in when she was about to end our hug, and it made her laugh, which was what I wanted.

When I let go, we both laughed at our emotional selves and wiped away any remnants of tears before we started shopping. We were facing one another, combing through the opposing sides of the same clothing rack.

"Do you think your mom would like this?" I asked, holding up a lovely green sweater.

"Ooh, she'd love that," Francine nodded. "She's been obsessed with green lately."

"Good, I think this is what I'm going to get for her then," I smiled, trying to put the earlier part of the day behind me.

"Good choice," Francine replied encouragingly. "What are you getting for Kyle?"

I deflated when she asked her question. I had no idea what to get him. I wanted to get him something that would mean a lot to him. Even though a piece of me was still upset with him, I wanted to work it out with him, that is, if he was willing to work it out with me.

Christmas Shopping with Francine | 299

"I'm not sure," I admitted.

"Damn, I was hoping you had some good ideas," Francine laughed.

"Sorry, I know he could use a couple of new uniform shirts—some are getting worn out," I suggested.

"Perfect! He appreciates gifts that are useful," Francine latched onto the idea.

"He usually gets them over at the Uniforms and More store," I stated.

"Maybe we can head over there before we finish up for the day?" she suggested.

I agreed and continued browsing the store. I saw a warm cream-colored sweater that my mom would love, and I ran my fingers over the shoulders of the fabric.

"My mom would love this," I admired.

"She would," Francine agreed, looking over at the garment.

I took it off the rack and draped it over my arm with the sweater I had picked up for Mrs. C. Francine shot a look my way but didn't say anything.

"I miss them," I said in answer to the question she hadn't asked.

"How could you not?" she asked carefully.

"I haven't bought either of them a present in five years," I said mournfully.

"You know they are limited in what they can have there, right?" Francine said in a low tone so that only I could hear.

I nodded. "I just need to do this, okay?"

"Okay," she replied supportively, squeezing my shoulder.

I took a deep breath and took my purchases up to the counter to check out. Francine didn't understand, but this was my way of showing that I believed my parents were innocent.

I felt Nonni guiding me toward something today, both when I was at the storage unit and again toward that sweater. It wasn't a feeling I could explain exactly, but I was certain I was closer to uncovering something that would explain how to free my parents.

"Do you mind if we stop in for some coffee?" Francine asked, interrupting my thoughts and gesturing at the coffee shop a few doors down from the store we had stopped in.

My body shot a plea for a hot chocolate to warm me from the cold December air.

"Let's go," I replied, linking my arm with hers as we walked down to the little shop.

We stopped at the coffee shop, and ahead of me were my cousin Drew and his boyfriend, Luis. Chills prickled down my spine at the coincidence. Kyle had still been suspicious of the two of them. It made me wonder now if they could have been the ones who vandalized my car this morning. That was ridiculous, though, neither of them knew I was going to be there, or here for that matter. Despite my brief suspicion, I was excited to see my cousin.

"Drew!" I called out and waved when he turned to face me.

"Jackie!" he smiled when our eyes met. "What are you doing here?"

He wrapped me in a hug, and I knew I had been wrong to suspect him. There was nothing but his warm, loving nature coming through as he smiled at me.

"Christmas shopping," I said, holding up my bag.

"Same," he smiled, holding up a similar bag.

"Francine, this is my cousin, Drew, and his boyfriend, Luis," I introduced my friend.

"I remember you, Drew, but it's been a long time," she smiled and extended her hand to shake.

"Right, we came into town a couple of times and you were over to visit Jackie," Drew smiled, shaking her hand.

"Yep, that was me!" she confirmed with a bright smile.

"Cousin Jackie!" Robbie called, causing several patrons of the coffee shop to turn in his direction.

"Robbie, it is so good to see you!" I called back, rushing forward to hug him and walk back with him to our spot in line.

"You too," he answered, keeping his arm wrapped around me as we walked. His smiling face was exactly what I needed to see that day.

"Come meet my friend Francine," I said to him. "She's Kyle's sister."

We caught up to our respective groups, and Francine smiled widely at him. She had heard me talk about Robbie before, but she hadn't yet met him.

"Robbie, this is my friend Francine. Francine, this is Robbie, my cousin and Drew's brother," I introduced.

"I am so pleased to finally meet you," Francine said, holding her hand out to shake Robbie's.

Robbie, being the smooth man that he was, took her hand and kissed the back of it.

"Nice to meet you," he replied, his cheeks pinkened, "You're very pretty."

"You probably say that to all the girls," Francine giggled, pleased by the compliment.

"Only when I mean it," Robbie insisted.

"What have you girls gotten into today?" Drew asked, switching the topic abruptly.

He was a little guarded when Robbie got flirty with girls. He had seen too many times where people took advantage of Robbie's kindness or made fun of him for being a little too enthusiastic.

"Well, my day started off with my car getting vandalized at the storage unit," I sighed, "but after I put in the police report I met up with Francine to do some shopping and then we came here."

"Oh, Jackie," Drew clucked his tongue, "how bad is it?"

"There's a bunch of profanity spray-painted on my car, and I'm going to have to replace a couple of tires and windows. More than the car is worth," I chuckled ruefully.

"You know, Luis has been looking for a project car. Why don't we buy it from you so he can fix it up and you can get something new or put the money aside and take the subway now that you're back in Brooklyn," Drew suggested.

"Are you actually interested in that rust bucket?" I asked, giving Luis a skeptical look.

"If it's still running, that puts me ahead of the game a bit, even if it has some problems," Luis said, finally joining the conversation.

"Do you want to look at it before you decide?" I asked.

"Yeah, okay, maybe we could grab our coffee to go and get a look at it?" Luis asked.

"Okay," I replied, excited by the prospect of having one less bill to pay.

When I looked at Francine's disappointed face, I felt like an absolute jerk. I opened my mouth to apologize, but she cut me off.

"Why don't you go do your thing with the car, and we can go shopping again tomorrow? Kyle will be out with the boys anyway." Francine suggested.

"Are you sure?" I asked, sad that I might be disappointing my friend.

"Yeah, this could be a good thing for all of you, and truly, I just wanted to stop at the uniform place for today. I need to regroup and think of some gift ideas for everyone else," she shrugged.

I hugged her and squealed, "You are my very best friend, you know? Coffees on me."

We made our way to the counter, everyone placed their orders, and I paid for it.

"Where did you park?" Drew asked.

"Grant Street parking garage back a few blocks," I said, taking the hot cocoa I had ordered from the barista.

"Oh, here," Francine said, pulling a visitor pass from her purse. "I grabbed one from our stash at work; it gives you a free parking pass for two hours or less."

"Thanks, Francine," I smiled at her. "We'll figure out a time for tomorrow later, I promise."

"I'll hold you to that," she warned.

Robbie, Drew, Luis, and I left the coffee shop and walked a handful of blocks back to the parking garage.

Christmas Shopping with Francine | 303

CHAPTER 28

Venmo Love Notes

Jackie
December 6, 2017

I knew next to nothing about Drew's boyfriend, and he had said the most words today that he ever had in the time I'd known him, so I tried to continue the conversation.

"Do you take on project cars often?" I asked Luis.

"No, I just got into derby racing, and the car I have been using got pretty beat up in the last event. I need something new so that I can keep competing," he replied.

"Oh, I didn't know you were into racing," I remarked. "Kyle likes to watch NASCAR sometimes."

Luis nodded, and we continued walking toward the garage. I was parked on the first level, so we didn't have far to go.

"Woah!" Drew remarked, getting a look at the car in its present condition.

"Ugh. It's worse than I remember," I groaned.

"Actually, I've seen worse, and it's just going to get beat up doing the derby," Luis shrugged. "Can I drive it around?"

"Of course," I replied, pulling my keys from my handbag.

We all got into the car, Luis taking the driver's seat, Drew at his side and me and Robbie in the back seat.

"The seats are in good condition," Luis remarked as he turned the key and let the engine warm up a little.

"Our Nonni owned this car before she passed, and she took great care of the interior," I said. "The outside would have been in better shape, but it's been through several Chicago winters and was parked outside."

Luis nodded and drove like an expert out of the parking lot, showing the visitor pass Francine had given us. He tested various things about the car as he drove.

"It actually drives pretty great for all it's been through today and having the donut tire on," Luis commented, "Are you sure you want to sell it?"

I nodded. "It costs me more in upkeep than it would if I got a subway pass. There's only a handful of places I go regularly."

"I'd like to buy it from you then," Luis said. "Would you take two grand for it?"

"Yes, that's great!" I cheered.

This was a great solution. What Luis had offered was more than the car was worth with the current damage, based on its value at the time Nonni passed. Now that I was living in Brooklyn again, I didn't need a car, and for the few times I did, I could borrow Kyle's personal vehicle or rent one.

"Can I take you home so we can sign over the title? You own it free and clear, right?" he asked.

"Yes, I own it free and clear," I replied.

I wasn't ready to face Kyle just yet, but I had the car's title at our apartment, so we needed to go there anyway. Besides, he wouldn't be home for a few hours yet.

Drew guided Luis to the apartment while I sat with my insides twisting anxiously. Robbie, being very empathetic, must have been sensing my anxiety too because he was telling one of his number stories over and over again, barely loud enough that I could hear him.

"Agent 890 is our double-O 17. Our mission is to bring back agent 570," Robbie said repeatedly as we drove up to my apartment.

For some reason, that series of numbers sounded familiar to me. I was trying to think of what those numbers could mean. A phone number? Maybe it was just a game code Drew had been working on? Knowing Robbie, it could be anything!

Luis pulled the car into a spot just down from my apartment building. The four of us got out of the car and walked up to my apartment.

I opened the door and saw Toby for two seconds before he skittered off to hide from the unexpected visitors. He would likely come check everyone out before they left; he was just a little shy at first.

"Please sit anywhere you like. Can I get anyone anything?" I asked, my instinct to host my guests taking over.

They each murmured some variation saying they didn't need anything.

"I'm going to go pull out the title. I'll be right back," I explained.

I walked into our bedroom and went to the closet where I kept my fireproof file box with important documents and shuffled through. I saw a letter with Nonni's shaky handwriting and stopped at it. Mr. Driscall had given it to me at Nonni's funeral. I was so sad about losing her and the voicemail that Kyle had left; I wasn't ready to open it at the time. I had put it in the firebox with the title for the car and forgot all about it. I wondered what she had to say. I took the title for the car and the letter with me to read after the boys left. I wanted to be alone with Nonni's last words to me.

"Jackie, can I send the money to you by Venmo?" Drew asked as I joined them in the living room.

"That's fine," I replied, pulling up the app since I could never remember my handle on the app.

When I pulled up the app, the last payment there was from Kyle. We had been sending the same $25 back and forth for various things: one of us would pick up a special treat for the other or dinner that night. After a while, it changed to a way for us to flirt with one another, like the one I had sent him one Thanksgiving night that said, 'Grateful for your fine ass.'

This last one though, he had sent to me this morning. It said, 'I love you forever.' His words made my heart skip a beat when I read them. Would he still feel that way after I had been so terrible to him this morning?

"Jackie, are you ready?" Drew asked.

"Oh, sorry, yes," I smiled politely, shaking the wayward thought from my mind.

Drew sent through the payment, and as soon as I confirmed it went through, I signed over the title to Luis.

"I'm really excited to get started on this," Luis said, the first genuine smile I'd ever seen on his face.

"I'd love to see it when you have it done," I replied, giving him a genuine smile.

"Maybe we can have you and Kyle come out to the first derby," Drew suggested.

"And me," Robbie insisted.

"Yes, of course," Drew smiled indulgently at his brother.

I nodded and said, "I'd like that."

I just hoped it was possible. Kyle may never want to be in the same room with me again.

"Why don't we bring in those boxes for you, and then we'll take off," Luis suggested.

"Oh yes, I will help," I insisted.

Four boxes for four people would be easier. The four of us went back out to my car—well, Luis' car now—and each took a box inside. I asked them just to stack them at the corner of the kitchen, and I would take it from there.

Robbie and I took the last two boxes from the trunk and closed the lid.

"890 is our double-O 17 mission to bring back agent 570," Robbie said repeatedly as we walked up to the apartment.

It was the same numbers he had been chanting before. Whatever the numbers were, they meant something to him. I tried to think if he might have just seen those numbers somewhere when we went to Coney Island together a few weeks ago. Again, nothing came to mind.

Once the boxes were in my apartment, I hugged the boys before they left. The day had been a whirlwind, so I plopped on the couch and put my feet up on the coffee table. It wasn't long before Toby popped out of his hiding spot and came to curl up in my lap. I ran my hand down the long orange fur of his back over and over, both of us finding comfort in it.

"I really messed up, Toby," I said to him.

He let out a small meow of acknowledgment and rubbed his face against my chin. I wasn't sure how he did it, but his tail caught the letter from Nonni that I had set on the end table and flipped it up between his face and mine. Startled, he ran off, leaving the letter on my lap.

I took a deep breath in and let it out as I held the envelope, feeling the weight of the letter in my hands. Nonni had beautiful handwriting before her stroke, and it was markedly shakier when she wrote this. I missed her so much, but at the same time, I wasn't sure I was ready for the finality that knowing the contents of this letter would bring. I will always remember what this letter said after today.

Careful not to tear anything inside the envelope, I tore open the top and pulled out the bundle of folded pages. When I unfolded the bundle, another envelope fell from the center into my lap, but when I caught the greeting on the letter, I wanted to read first. My eyes welled instantly when I saw she had addressed it to her dearest Stellina, her little star. I hadn't heard her call me that in so very long.

I wiped the tears from my eyes with a tissue. When I was able to see it again, I started reading her letter.

My Dearest Stellina,

You have always been the brightest star in my sky. I've always felt a closeness with you, and I have treasured it since the day you were born. Here, at the end of my life, I am so very grateful to you for caring for me. That is why it breaks my heart to write this to you now.

I never meant to keep you from your love this way. I only meant to protect you, and then I fell ill, and you became stuck with me. I hope when I am gone, you and Kyle can find your way back to one another. In fact, I have included a letter for him I want you to give to him for me.

I also need you to forgive me for not seeing sooner that your mother and father were innocent. I was so angry and ashamed of the way my sons had fought each other over money when Nonno died. There was so much talk of material possessions, and I saw greed in both my sons that I had never seen before.

When your Uncle Masso came to see me, he told me that an awful man, Reese Clearwater, had broken into the computers of your parents' company and forged documents that allowed the money to be moved to a private account in the Cayman Islands. Mr. Clearwater is cunning and knows how to hide his tracks well, but he showed your uncle how he could make it look as though Masso was behind the embezzling and using it to grow DMarco Italiano. That devil even tricked your cousin Drew into moving the money around through coding what he thought was a new game so that he could blackmail Masso if he needed to. Your uncle is stuck in the middle and only wants to protect his sons. If anyone can fix this mess and set your parents free, I know it is you.

I have included the documents that I found before I fell ill. The documents show when Mr. Clearwater first attempted to steal from the investment group. Take these to the police. They will help you free your parents.

Please be careful, my little Stellina. This man is very dangerous and will strike like a viper if he senses you are trying to turn him in.

Ti amo più della mia vita,
Nonni

All this time, all my searching, and the proof of my parents' innocence was in my possession. I was sick to my stomach and, perhaps for the first time in my life, I understood why Kyle seemed angry all the time. There were too many emotions swarming in my mind, and anger was the prevailing feeling. It spread hotly through my veins to all my limbs at once.

I looked over the documents that Nonni had included. One was a record of IP addresses that had accessed the system the day that the first transfer was made to the Cayman Island account. It also showed the routing number: 890 0017 570.

This was the number from Robbie's story earlier! 890 is our double-O 17 mission to bring back agent 570. But what did it mean that he knew the number too? I wasn't going to be able to breathe until I found out what was going on. If Clearwater had tricked Drew into helping him, what would he do with someone as innocent as Robbie? I had to talk to Masso face to face and find out what we were up against before I turned in this evidence.

I snapped pictures of the documents and put them in an email to Kyle just in case something happened to the originals.

I pulled up the Venmo app and sent him $50 this time. In the memo field, I wrote:

> Please forgive me for today. I know that it will take me a lifetime to make up for the way I behaved this morning, but I hope you will allow me to. I will bring your car back soon. Ti amo infinitamente.

Having sent off the message with the money, I stood, and the envelope with the note to Kyle fell to the floor, but I was too determined to find out what Masso had to say. I took the keys from the hook by the door and raced out of the apartment to see my uncle. He would not get away with not answering my questions this time!

CHAPTER 29

The Day from Hell

Kyle
December 6, 2017

T his day has been a shit sandwich with extra flies. The last thing I wanted to do was sit at the station and file our reports. I had been without my phone all day, which normally wouldn't bother me. However, since the roller coaster of a morning Jackie and I had, I desperately wanted to send her a text or see if she had sent one to me. It felt juvenile, but I hadn't gone this long without talking to her since she came back into my life, and it was unsettling.

"Carrollton, you're shaking the whole damn desk," Oscar scolded me.

I looked down at my leg and made the connection that my bouncing leg was the cause of his frustration, so I stopped.

"Why don't you take off, and I can handle the reports for today?" Oscar suggested, not looking up from his computer.

"What?" I asked, not sure I had heard him correctly.

"Go home," he demanded, meeting my eyes. "You need to straighten things out with Jackie."

"I don't have a car here," I answered dumbly.

"Take the patrol car; Maria can come pick me up," he replied, going back to his hunt-and-peck method of typing that drove me nuts.

I nodded and stood to leave.

"Carrollton," Oscar called, stopping me in my tracks.

"Yeah?" I asked, turning back toward him.

"Don't let her go this time," he ordered.

My heart took off at full sprint. She wouldn't really leave after one argument, would she? Not again. I gave a nod to him and ran out the door to go home and hoped like hell she was there. At the very least, I could see if the SIM card from my phone would work in the old phone I had at home until I could go get a new one the next day, after things were resolved.

My chest ached from the weight of worry I had carried all day. When Francine texted me to say that Jackie had joined her for their planned shopping excursion it brought some temporary relief, but all day I had just wanted to go home and hold her and apologize to her and tell her she was the only one that I wanted forever.

Ten minutes to cross town seemed like two hours in the hustle of the city with commuters and Christmas shoppers out in full force. I was tempted to turn on my lights and sirens just to get home sooner, but I knew there was no real need for it, other than my impatience.

When I finally got home, Toby was the only one there. While I was happy to see my furball, I really wanted to see my girl and fix things. I hung the keys to the cruiser on the hook by the door and noticed my keys were gone. Jackie must have borrowed the car to go shopping with Francine.

In front of the coat rack sat a stack of four boxes from D'Marco's Investments. Jackie had been here and left again. I'm not sure why, but those boxes sent relief coursing through my tense muscles. If she left them here, then she would be back, and we could talk.

I took a deep breath and went back to our bedroom to change out of my uniform and lock up my service weapon. On our bed was Jackie's fireproof lock box, the top flopped open. Chills raced down my spine. What would she have needed to get out of there?

I didn't know the contents of the box well enough to know if anything was missing or not, but likely she had pulled out something to do with the car-insurance paperwork maybe-to see if they would cover anything. Still, I didn't touch the box. I took it as another good sign that she would be back, since it looked like there were still important documents like her passport in there.

I stripped off my holster and put my gun in the lock box I kept it in when I was off duty. I stripped out of my uniform and put on a pair of jogging pants and a t-shirt I had worn so often that the fabric had gone soft. We were likely to have a long talk tonight, so I might as well be comfortable.

From the other room, Toby was making a 'brrrr-wow' sound. He usually made that sound when he pretended to stalk his prey and it wasn't cooperating. I just hoped that didn't mean we had a mouse in the apartment. Jackie would absolutely freak out.

I walked, barefooted, out into the living room space to see what he was after. Lying down on my belly on the floor next to him, I looked under the couch and I couldn't see anything.

"I think you're seeing things, Pal," I told him and started to get up.

"Brrrr-wow," Toby called again, trying to coax his victim out of hiding.

I laid down flat on the floor again to try to see what it was he was after. There were a few things that had been pushed under the sofa: a yarn ball that was barely a ball anymore, a sock, a toy mouse, a ring from an old milk jug, and a thick rubber band. I pulled the items out one by one, but Toby resumed his pose ready to pounce, his tail twitching excitedly. Frustrated with the process and the day, I stood and shoved the couch toward the coffee table to see if I could get a better look. As soon as I did, a white envelope dropped to the floor, and Toby lunged for it, his furry body covering it completely.

I didn't have a clue what was in it, but it could be important, so I wrestled it away from him. He gave me his death glare, yowled at me, and bounded off for the kitchen to eat his feelings. I pushed the couch back to its normal position and sat down on it to look at what Toby had been after.

My name was scrawled on the back of the envelope in a shaky hand. It didn't look like Jackie's handwriting, but if she was scared, maybe? My pulse thudded in my veins as I carefully ripped open the top of the envelope to see what was inside.

Kyle,

I hope this letter finds you well. I'm probably one of the last people you want to hear from, but I have something to say before my time in this world is over. You are the only person who has loved my Jackie as much as I have. I hope you can forgive me for taking her from you, but you must understand. I needed to keep her safe.

I want you to know I was never against you proposing to her. You are a fine young man and come from a wonderful family. I was only against the timing. You are still very young and need more time to understand who you will be. Still, I should not have taken the decision into my hands.

When I am gone, I hope that you and Jackie will find your way back to one another. You are a good man, and I know she will be safe with you. Please don't hold my mistake against her. She didn't want to leave you, but I convinced her it would be safer for all of us.

My attorney has put some things in a safety deposit box for the two of you. I hope you will use it to start your lives together. It requires both of you to come to Brooklyn National Bank. Mr. Drury does have permission to allow Jackie soul access if you no longer want to share your life with her. If you're the man I think you are, that won't be necessary.

Please love her as much as I do for the rest of your lives.
Nonni Vittoria

What could Nonni possibly have left us both? Jackie had indicated that there wasn't really any kind of inheritance. Could it just be something of a sentimental nature?

Whatever it was, I wouldn't be able to resolve my curiosity until she and I went to the bank together to see what was there. For now, we just needed to see if our relationship was going to make it. We had a lot of work to do, but I was willing to put in the effort. Jackie was it for me. She always had been.

I put the letter back in the envelope and put it in the drawer of the nightstand next to the sofa so that Toby wouldn't try to take it again. I also pulled out the old phone I had from the drawer and plugged it in to charge. While I waited, I pulled out the SIM card from my broken phone and put it into the old phone. It at least fit, now I just needed to wait for the phone to charge enough to turn it on.

My stomach rumbled, reminding me I hadn't eaten anything at lunch. In the refrigerator, I found a leftover container of lasagna that Jackie had made two nights ago. There were two servings worth, so she could have the other portion when she got home if she wanted. I didn't know what her secret was to making lasagna that tasted better than any restaurant I'd ever eaten at, but Jacks knew her way around a lasagna. The smell took over the entire kitchen by the time it warmed all the way through in the microwave. It was like a siren song to my stomach, which was still growling its call in return. I settled on a stool at the kitchen island, like I used to before Jackie moved in, and took the first bite. It was incredible, arguably better than the night she had made it. Toby circled my ankles, hoping I would give him a little taste.

"Sorry, man, this is too spicy for you," I said.

Truth was, he probably could handle it. I just didn't want to share. Every bite was going to me. I considered licking the plate, but that was just a step too far even for me. Toby eventually settled back on the couch, recognizing he was not going to get any. As soon as he settled in, the phone I had plugged in started going wild with notifications from being out of pocket all day. Toby swatted at the phone in irritation and then swaggered off to the bedroom for some peace and quiet.

I took the last bite of lasagna and rinsed the plate before adding it to the dishwasher. I wasn't sure I was ready to see what messages I had missed throughout the day, but I was hoping to see Jackie had sent me something. When her temper was riled, her Italian heritage came out in full force. While she was angry, she was bound to say anything. I reminded myself of this so that I wouldn't overreact to something she might have sent hours ago.

I was disappointed to see she hadn't left a voicemail or sent me a text. Either she was still mad, or she was afraid that I was. As I went to check my other messages, Jason's call rang through, so I swiped to answer.

"Kyle, about time you answered your phone," Jason said. "I've been trying to reach you for a few hours now."

"Sorry, my phone broke today, so I just got my old phone running again. Is everything alright?" I asked, concerned.

"I was just trying to see what time you wanted to go Christmas shopping tomorrow or if you were still coming with us?" he asked.

"I'm not sure. Jacks and I got in a pretty big fight today, and she's not home yet. Before I go away for the weekend with you and Ben, I have to set things right with her," I explained. "Can I text you back later tonight to let you know?"

"Sure," Jason said, but his tone told me what he was thinking.

"Just say what you want to say, Jason," I grumbled.

"Are you sure she's coming back?" he asked, his tone cautious.

"Well, she has to at least bring my car back. Otherwise, she'll be arrested for grand theft auto," I answered sarcastically.

"Look, I love Jackie. She's like my second sister. I just don't want to see you hurt the way you were the last time. You had some pretty dark nights back then," he reminded me, concern laced through his tone.

"I remember," I sighed, "but this time is different."

"Different how?" Jason asked, genuinely curious.

"We made plans together for the future. And not just one of us talking about our individual plans while the other tries to figure out how that will work. We've made a little family of ourselves with the two of us and Toby. We've talked about financial goals and career goals. We are stronger than we were five years ago," I insisted.

As I thought back to all those conversations in the dark before we went to sleep each night, I felt certain that we would fix this and we would be better for it. Yes, we both screwed up and hurt one another, but the way we learn to recover from this will only teach us how to love each other better.

"Kyle, I want you to have the life you want with her. I really do. I just don't know that I could trust her so soon if I were in your shoes," Jason admitted.

"Good thing you're not then," I replied coldly. "Listen, I need to go. I'll text you later to let you know about tomorrow."

"Yeah, okay, I'll check in with you later," Jason surrendered.

We hung up with each other, and I saw a notification from Venmo. I opened the app to read it.

Fifty dollars from DragonGrlJackieD for: Please forgive me for today. I know it will take me a lifetime to make up for the way I behaved this morning, but I hope you will allow me to. I will bring your car back soon. Ti amo infinitamente.

I was happy that she had at least sent me a message this way. We would be okay, I was certain. I love you endlessly too, Jackie. I will take my lifetime making sure you know it.

CHAPTER 30

Holy Cannoli It's Her

Kyle
December 6, 2017

M y phone rang in my hand. I was disappointed to see Romero's name flash on the screen. I had been hoping it was Jackie.

"Do you need me to come back to the station?" I asked.

"Yes, Brady just stopped by looking for you," Romero replied, unbothered by my lack of greeting.

"What did he want?" I wondered.

"They were able to pull some surveillance footage from the building across the street from Brooklyn U. It's pretty grainy, but I want you to take a look to see if you recognize either of these two," Romero explained.

"Two?" I asked, puzzled. "Send me the footage."

"I just hit send on it," he replied.

I waited, my pulse racing, until the footage came through. I hit play and watched as an older man and a young woman walked around the front of Jackie's car. Romero was right; the footage was very grainy, and even when I tried to zoom in, it was hard to tell for certain, but when the pair walked away, the man had a familiar limping gait.

"I can't tell who the woman is," I said to Romero, "but I have no doubt at all...that man is Pete Billings."

"That's what the guys here thought too," Romero replied. "Do you think he was just trying to warn her?"

"Maybe," I conceded.

"Speaking of Jackie, how are things? Did you patch things up with her yet?" Romero asked.

"She's not back home yet," I answered. "But she sent me a Venmo."

"For what, your phone?" he asked, confused.

"It's a thing we do," I smiled, "kind of a running gag between us."

"Well, that's a good sign," he encouraged.

"I think so too," I replied.

"So, I do need to ask you a favor, buddy," Romero said. "Can you come back and take me home? Maria can't pick me up after all. The baby has a stomach bug and has been reenacting *The Exorcist* all afternoon."

"Yeah, sure. I will just let Jacks know I'll be back home soon," I sighed, figuring it would keep me from going crazy waiting for her to come home.

"Thanks, man, I'll see you," Romero replied before hanging up.

I tried to call Jackie, and the phone went straight to voicemail. Today just wasn't a good day for either of our phones, it seemed. Her phone was older than dirt and probably had run out of battery. I had planned to replace it for her as part of her Christmas gift. I guess I would be buying both of us new phones now instead.

I took a page from the back of our grocery notepad and scribbled out a note to her.

Dearest Jackie,

I am going to pick up Romero and take him home. I'll be back soon.

Check your Venmo.

Love,
Kyle

I pulled up the Venmo app and sent back one hundred dollars. In the memo I wrote:

> I'm sorry too. We both have a lot of making up to
> do, and I have a few ideas. I love you always.

I went back to the bedroom and changed back into my uniform and put my gun back in my holster. As I walked to the door, I grabbed the keys and drove back to the station. Romero was waiting for me outside when I pulled up.

"Thanks so much for doing this," he said. "I just couldn't ask Maria to bring the kids out with the baby sick at home."

"It's no problem. I would have just been sitting around at home pacing until Jackie came home anyway," I shrugged.

"Do you know what you'll say to her?" Romero asked.

"I think I might just need to listen at first," I said.

"A bold choice," he teased.

"Yeah, well, maybe I'm growing up," I laughed.

"Good. She's good for you," he smiled.

Jackie was good for me. I knew that even when we were kids.

I pulled in front of Romero's house.

"Do you want to come in and have dinner with us?" Romero asked.

"Thanks, but I'll pass on the exorcist baby. I have already met my quota of cleaning vomit for this year," I laughed.

"Fair enough," he chuckled. "I'll see you later, then."

I held up my hand in a wave and drove off to go back home. As I was driving down Walnut Street, where Holy Cannoli was, I spotted Jackie's car in the drive-thru, pulling out ahead of me. My heart raced at the chance to pull her over again, the way I had when she first came back to town. It would be something she would call romantic, and I'm sure that would earn me bonus points. It was too bad I didn't have a bag of donuts in the car or a bouquet of flowers.

Holy Cannoli It's Her | 329

As before, I flicked on my lights and weaved around the cars that pulled over to make way for me as I moved in closer to the little red sedan with the Tennessee-shaped rust spot on the back, now marred with graffiti. When the car pulled over, I tucked my cruiser in behind it. I couldn't wait to see her beautiful face.

As I approached the car, I saw that there were two people in there. Francine must be in the car too. Well, it wouldn't be the first time my sister saw me make an ass of myself over Jackie D'Marco. I nearly jumped backward into the street when I got to the window, and it was not who I had expected.

"Why are you in Jackie's car?" I asked.

"Kyle?" Drew asked from the passenger seat.

"Where is Jackie?" I demanded.

"We dropped her off at the apartment," Luis replied, his jaw tight.

"When?" I asked.

"A couple of hours ago. Why don't you just call her?" he shot back. "She sold the car to me, and I took her home."

"She wasn't there. Do you know where she was going?" I asked, trying to check my frustration.

"The last we talked to her, she was going to wait there for you," Drew answered, "We dropped her off and took Robbie back home and then came back here to work on the car at the garage Luis works out of."

"Fuck," I grumbled, "I tried to call her earlier and her phone was dead."

Drew's phone rang loudly.

"You can answer it," I said, but stayed at the window.

"Hey Rob!" Drew answered his phone.

Worry etched his face.

"Slow down, I can't understand you," Drew said loudly into the phone.

My blood ran cold. What had happened?

"Rob, you need to hang up and call 9-1-1," Drew explained.

"Jesus, what is going on?" I asked.

"The restaurant is on fire," Drew explained, covering the mouthpiece.

"Wait, what?"

Drew's eyes grew what I would call comically wide if I weren't already freaking out.

"Kyle, you need to go to the restaurant now," Drew ordered. "Jackie was there."

"What do you mean 'was'?" I demanded.

"Robbie doesn't know where she is, but he remembers her being there and arguing with my dad, and then the next thing he remembers is waking up surrounded by flames," Drew relayed to me. "I need to go with you. Rob is freaking out, and he doesn't know where my dad is."

I was going to be sick...did Masso hurt her and then start a fire to cover it up? My mind raced with ever-sickening ideas of what could have happened.

"Get in the cruiser; we need to go now," I ordered.

"Go home, Luis; I will call you when we figure out what's going on," Drew said, pecking a kiss to Luis's lips.

"Be safe," Luis replied.

Drew rushed back to the cruiser with me. I turned on my siren and lights and took off down the road. I called into dispatch to have them get the fire department out to the restaurant and prayed that Jackie and Robbie were alright.

CHAPTER 31

The Truth

Jackie
December 6, 2017

I don't think I ever made it from Brooklyn to Bayonne in less time than I did that day. Masso had a lot of explaining to do! As I pulled into the parking lot of the restaurant near their closing time, I looked around and didn't see my uncle's car, but he and Robbie didn't live far from the restaurant and walked over from time to time. I got out of the car, my feet pounding against the pavement as I walked to the back entrance. When I was ready to reach out for the door handle, it opened, and Robbie stepped out with a bag of trash in each hand.

"Jackie?" Robbie asked, the trash bags falling to the ground.

"Hi Robbie," I replied, catching the door so that it didn't close on him.

"Did you come for dinner?" he asked. "We're closing."

"No, I came to talk to your dad. Is he in his office?" I asked.

"No," Robbie answered and bent down to pick up the two trash bags that he had dropped in his earlier surprise.

It was my turn to be momentarily frozen in surprise, so I stood still as Robbie weaved past me with his trash bags to put them in the dumpster. When I regained my composure, I decided to just wait for him rather than shout across the parking lot.

Robbie made his way back and smiled at me when he saw I was still standing by the back door. I couldn't help but smile back at him.

"Robbie, do you know when your dad will be back?" I asked as he got back to my side.

"Soon," Robbie answered. "Come on, you can wait for him inside."

I was grateful that I would be going inside. Though I was heated with anger, the cold air of December was chilling even through my thick coat.

"You can go to his office," Robbie offered.

"Thanks. Can you let him know I'm here if you see him?" I requested.

"Okay," he replied and pushed his way through the kitchen door.

I took the hallway to the back office that I hadn't been in since before Nonno died. It was too hard to go to the restaurant when he was gone, but Nonni insisted Masso should take the office and redecorate it to his liking, since he was going to be running the restaurant.

Very little about the small office had changed, much to my surprise. The only difference that tore at me was the framed photos of my parents and me that had been removed and replaced with Masso's college degree.

I sat in the guest chair, waiting for Masso to return from his errand, when a piece of mail caught my attention. The familiar logo for Driscoll and Associates was on the open envelope. My curiosity got the better of me, and I picked it up and pulled out the papers. A gasp escaped my lips.

The letter said that they had investigated his inquiry about my parents' old house, the house I grew up in, and it was owned by an LLC registered with Nonni as the sole proprietor. She had filed the paperwork with a different attorney based out of Brooklyn, and that is why it hadn't been uncovered previously. Mr. Driscoll's team had found that the LLC was to transfer ownership upon her death to me!

My heart raced. I own my childhood home now? How had Nonni done this and why hadn't she told me? I picked up my phone and texted Francine.

Jackie: I own my family's home.

I waited a moment, and when she didn't reply, I put my phone in my pocket. I picked the letter back up and reread it again.

The letter had been dated November 1st. Masso knew this when I saw him at Thanksgiving, and he didn't tell me! My anger toward Masso bubbled in my chest. Not only did he know my parents were innocent, but he didn't tell me I had the means to live rent-free or sell the place and buy something smaller so that I could pay for school.

"You came to see me?" Masso called from the doorway.

Startled, I tossed the letter down onto the desk and whirled around to face him.

"Why didn't you tell me?" I asked when I had regained my composure.

"Tell you what?" he countered, taking the seat at the desk to face me.

"About my house," I replied, "About my parents."

"It was for your own good," he replied simply.

"How was any of this for MY good?" I demanded.

"I thought you had all the answers," Masso mused. "Believe it or not, what I did WAS for your own good."

"Why don't you tell me what you know then?" I needled.

"When Nonno died, Nonni created Nonni D Properties LLC and transferred both the restaurant and the house you grew up in under its umbrella. She did this to even out what your father and I received from our father's estate. She paid off your family home and was negotiating a land contract with your parents to allow them to continue making payments toward the house until it was paid off. They could pay any amount they wanted to as long as they paid something each month. As for the restaurant, I was allowed to do the same, paying off as much of the land contract each month as I could until the same amount was paid in by each brother for their respective properties."

He paused and picked up the letter from Driscoll's office and held it up between us.

"This letter confirms that she left the LLC to you. Which means..."

"I own both the house and the restaurant," I whispered.

He nodded grimly and put the paper back down on the desk.

"Yes, between that and you snooping around, you are in greater danger," he sighed.

"Danger, but why? What kind of danger?" I asked.

"Reese Clearwater is not the partner I led you to believe he was," Masso explained. "You see, I made a horrible error in judgment when I was working for your parents at D'Marco Investments. I was too eager to prove myself as an investor and took a huge risk with Clearwater's investment and lost over half of it. That is why I stopped working for your parents. He insisted I be fired for my actions."

"So why partner with him later?" I asked.

"Your parents worked together to make investments that brought Clearwater back up to his starting balance in about six months. When he heard I was going to take over the restaurant, he approached me and apologized for overreacting. He befriended my boys and even me. Then, once I thought we had actually become friends, he let me know he was interested in helping me improve the profitability of D'Marco Italiano. It would allow me to pay off the restaurant and have full ownership of it, so I took him up on it. I thought I could prove myself to our family and make Nonni proud. Only after he was involved, the true reason he wanted to partner with me became clear."

"What did he want?" I wondered.

"He wanted to ruin our entire family. Burn everything we had down to the ground and forced us to watch it slip from our fingers," he answered grimly.

"How?" I asked, chills racing down my spine.

"First, he got close to me and the boys. We spent hours talking about business and what goals I had. He brought video games that were still in development for the boys and let them play them and give him feedback. He even started teaching Drew some of the programming. Once he built our trust, he used Robbie's love of numbers to sink his claws into D'Marco Investments. He got Robbie to give the IP address for your dad's computer and hacked in from there, telling Robbie it was so that he could put the video game he loved on the computer so that he could play while he was there. That's when the small amounts of money drained out little by little, and every bit of it was tied to your mom and dad," Masso explained.

My heart sank. I had so desperately wanted to believe my parents had been innocent, but all the evidence pointed to them. Clearwater did an excellent job of covering his digital tracks.

"When D'Marco Investments went under, Clearwater was thrilled that it was uncovered by other members within our own family. In his eyes, we were self-imploding, and he couldn't ask for anything better. By then, I had already accepted his investment in D'Marco Italiano. The timing was suspicious, and I was pulled into the investigation. He refused to come forward as my silent partner for a long time, letting me squirm under the pressure," Masso explained, "But, at the eleventh hour he came forward. It was after that he told me what he had done to take down my brother's business. It wouldn't take much to do the same to me, but he wasn't done playing cat and mouse with me yet."

"What do you mean?" I prompted.

"He had employed Drew for the summer and hired him on full time. During his summer internship, he taught Drew how to program what he thought was a game. Instead, it was programming a series of steps that would move the money he had taken from D'Marco Investments through crypto currency, back out and into a shell company and then broke down the shell company, sent it through crypto currency again and several other back-and-forth steps like this before it was invested into D'Marco Italiano. All done under Drew's IP address so that it would appear he was the one that hacked the system," Masso explained.

"Oh my God!" I gasped.

"Knowing he had both of my sons involved in this and could point to them without too much trouble, he came to me and told me to keep my mouth shut and he wouldn't destroy the rest of us. I had a sinking feeling he wasn't done, but the last couple of years until your Nonni died had been peaceful. He hadn't made any big declarations of framing us for any wrongdoing. I couldn't end our partnership until I had paid back what he had invested with 15% interest according to our agreement. With Nonni gone, though, he's been looking to find out who had a controlling interest in the restaurant. The will filed with Mr. Driscoll didn't say who took over the LLC, and we didn't know where it had been filed, so it went into my custody temporarily since I had a land contract on one of the properties. Now that you've been named, and he's heard you were looking into your parents' case, you have been in danger. You need to stop looking."

"We need to turn this guy in," I insisted.

"With what evidence?" Masso asked, "He covered his tracks well."

"Nonni found something that points back to him," I explained, handing the envelope of papers Nonni had sent me. "I have the proof."

"I'm going to need you to give me that proof, then," a voice said from the doorway.

Masso and I both looked in horror to see Reese Clearwater standing in the frame of the door. My blood ran cold. This man had been dismantling my family, and for what? My parents had helped him recover the money he had lost. Who would be that vindictive?

He met my eyes with a terrifying calmness and held out his hand expectantly. With shaking hands, I put the envelope in his hand. My heart pounded in my chest. I hadn't considered that the plot against my parents was so sinister and that I would come face to face with the man behind it all while I was confronting my uncle. The man I was looking at wanted to ruin my entire family because my uncle had wronged him a decade ago. My parents had even done their best to make it right, and he took them down first. What kind of man was he?

"Very good, Jackie," he sneered. "You're not as foolish as I suspected."

"Why do all this?" I asked.

"Because no one makes a fool of me. What your uncle neglected to tell you is that he 'borrowed' some of my funds for his own purposes. Didn't you, Masso?"

I looked back at Masso and saw that his face flushed red and he dipped his head in shame.

"What did you do?" I demanded of my uncle.

"It was for Robbie's surgery. I altered the contract to show our fees were a higher percentage on his copy than on the copy I turned into the office so that I could take the difference and pay for Robbie's surgery without being a burden on my family," he admitted, a tear rolling down his cheek.

Instead of asking his family, he stole from a man who now wanted to destroy his entire family. I couldn't believe Masso had done this. He should be the one in jail right alongside this monster.

"My brother claimed it was a clerical error to save me from being prosecuted and refunded Clearwater the difference, but it wasn't enough for him," Masso said, giving the other man the coldest look I'd ever seen him give anyone.

So, my father had protected his brother and still ended up in the crossfire. I was sick to my stomach. Where did it stop?

"Now that we're all on the same page, let's just put an end to all of this animosity," Clearwater smiled ominously.

I could see Masso's posture go rigid out of the corner of my eye, and my body automatically stiffened as well.

"Why are you all back here?" Robbie asked, oblivious to the nightmare unfolding in the room.

"Robbie, run!" I shouted.

To my horror, he stood in place, confused.

"He doesn't need to run," Clearwater's voice was ice cold.

Robbie looked between all of us, growing fearful of what he didn't understand. When my message finally caught up with his mind, he started to run, and Clearwater tripped him with his foot, sending Robbie headfirst into the wall and knocking him out cold. Blood trickled from the corner of his mouth as he lay on the hard ground.

I sobbed over the fact that Clearwater could be so cruel to someone as innocent as Robbie. I stood to go to Robbie, and Clearwater pulled a gun from his waistband and aimed it at me. I stopped in my tracks and my entire being was numb with dread.

I prayed silently to my Nonni. I begged her to intervene in this and save our family. I had to be able to go back home to Kyle after this. If I died like this he would never recover.

"You two are coming with me," Clearwater said. "We're going to get rid of those files once and for all. First, Masso, will you do the honor of burning these?"

He held out the documents to Masso. Masso took them and pulled out the lighter he kept in his top drawer and lit the papers on fire.

"Just put those down on the desk and step out now," Clearwater ordered. "We're going for a little ride."

The burning papers ignited the other paperwork on Masso's desk until there was quite a fire going.

"What about Robbie?" I asked, scared of the answer.

"You don't need to worry about him," Clearwater answered coldly, firing a shot into Robbie's back.

I screamed in shock and horror.

"Move!" Clearwater ordered.

Masso and I walked single file down the narrow hallway in front of Clearwater and through the kitchen. Clearwater turned up the gas on the stove as we walked out the back entrance toward a black town car with a waiting driver.

"Sir?" the driver asked.

"We're going to Brooklyn," Clearwater ordered, forcing Masso and me into the back seat of the town car.

"Yes, sir," the driver complied.

The driver made eye contact with me in the rearview mirror, and I couldn't shake the feeling he looked familiar. I couldn't place him, but I definitely knew this man. He gave me a look that I could tell was meant to communicate something, but I was so scared, I wasn't sure if it was reassurance or menace.

As the car pulled away from the restaurant, I could see flames shooting out of the window to Masso's office, and I began gasping for air that wouldn't come. A panic attack.

"Don't worry, Jackie, this will all be over soon," Clearwater promised.

I wanted to cry, but tears would not come. I felt Masso's hand wrap around mine, and I knew he was just as scared as I was. I looked up at him, and he mouthed, 'I'm sorry.'

While I appreciated his apology, it wouldn't get us out of this mess. I just wanted Kyle to swoop in and save the day, but I didn't tell him where I was going. He was probably still on duty and hadn't checked the email or the Venmo message yet. By the time he did, I was afraid it would be too late.

CHAPTER 32

Where is She?

Kyle
December 6, 2017

First responders and fire trucks surrounded D'Marco Italiano when I pulled up, my lights and sirens blaring. Smoke billowed overhead, but the flames were out. I had made it to Bayonne in record time, but the damage had already been done.

"Oh my God," Drew gasped from beside me.

When I put the car in park, we both exited the car and ran up to the scene. I flashed my badge and explained that Drew was family to one of the officers blocking the scene from reporters and onlookers. He nodded and let us through.

Robbie was being loaded into an ambulance. Drew ran up alongside the stretcher.

"That's my brother! Will he be alright?" Drew demanded, panicked.

"He's been shot, but it appears to be a superficial wound. You can ride along to the hospital if you want," the EMT explained.

"Was anyone else inside?" I asked, catching sight of my car in the parking lot, my heart sinking to my toes.

"No, he was the only one," they answered.

"Robbie," I said, "do you know where Jackie and your dad went?"

He coughed and shook his head.

"Dammit," I muttered.

"Clearwater," Robbie said, his voice hoarse.

"She's with Clearwater?" I asked.

Robbie nodded.

I raced back to my car and requested an APB be put out for Clearwater and any of his known vehicles. In record time, someone reported a sighting of a town car driving erratically that matched the description of one of Reese Clearwater's vehicles. I drove at breakneck speed to catch up with the car. If Jackie was still with him, I needed to catch up to him soon.

Blood pounded an anxious rhythm in my ears as I drove closer to where Clearwater's car had been last seen. Jackie had to be okay. I would never forgive myself if I had let our last words be our fight earlier.

My eyes burned from being forced to remain open too long. I didn't want to drive past them. Over the sound of my siren, I could hear horns honking and the sound of squealing tires straight ahead of me. I was on 440 headed toward the Bayonne Bridge when I finally spotted the town car swerving from lane to lane going around other vehicles. Three police cars were already in pursuit. At times it made it hard to see the car they were tailing, but I just kept following them.

The town car must have hit a patch of ice or something when it began to cross the bridge because it spun all the way around and slammed into one of the bridge posts. I saw a body slam through the windshield and fly several feet from the car. I wanted to throw up. The car was practically folded in half by the impact. The police cars surrounded the scene, and got out of their cars, guns drawn. I did the same as I parked my cruiser.

One of the officers pried open the driver's side door to check on the passengers. I could hear a man's voice screaming out in pain. Another officer walked carefully up to the figure laying on the pavement, the driver that had been ejected.

"He's alive!" the officer called back to the others. He radioed for EMS to come to the scene.

Two men: Clearwater, Masso...

"Is there a brunette woman in the car?" I called out to the officer speaking to the man in the car, who was still screaming in agony.

"No, there's no one else in the car," he hollered back.

I pushed my way through the other officers and looked in the car to see Clearwater was the one screaming.

"Where the hell is she?" I demanded, grabbing Clearwater by the tie.

The other officers on the scene took hold of my arms and pulled me off the other man.

"Who are you looking for?" One of them demanded, "You're not in your jurisdiction."

"My fiancé," I answered, "This man kidnapped my fiancé."

I didn't know why I called her my fiancé instead of my girlfriend, but when I found her, I was going to ask her. I was done waiting. I was done keeping her at arm's length. I wanted her to know that I wanted her forever. I always had.

"Just before the crash they were tossing things out of the car," a petite female officer said from the side, "maybe it was your fiancé making her escape."

"Where?" I asked desperately.

"Just before the bridge," she answered.

I took off in a sprint in the direction that the officer had pointed. Acid rose in my throat as I made it to the edge and saw the steep embankment. There was a mass that could be a person or just trash; it was hard to tell, but I alternated sliding and walking down. When I got closer, Masso's lifeless body lay atop Jackie. Her bottom jaw was dislocated on the right side, hanging at an unnatural angle. Her eyes were closed, and her hair was matted in blood.

"No!" I screamed in horror.

With shaking hands, I rolled Masso from his position on top of her. He had been shot, but he had a thready pulse.

"Get some of the EMS guys down here," I called to the female officer that had pointed me in the right direction.

She ran back up and flagged down the EMS team.

I touched Jackie's neck and choked back a sob of relief upon finding that she had a pulse.

"Baby, please don't leave me," I begged her, "I love you and I want to marry you."

She lay unresponsive, but I watched her chest rise and fall, and it brought me some comfort that she would recover. She had to.

The medical responders carefully made their way down with stretchers.

"I'm going with her," I insisted as they put her in a brace to stabilize her neck and they transported her back up the hill. "This man is her uncle. Will they be going to the same hospital?"

"Yes, sir," the EMT carrying Masso responded.

"I will alert his son, and he will meet you at the hospital," I said.

I sent a quick text message off to Drew and climbed into the ambulance with Jackie. We were taken to Bayonne Medical Center. I believe that is where he and Robbie were headed too.

I held Jackie's hand as the EMT monitored her during the ride. When we were halfway to the hospital, Jackie's eyes fluttered open, and she began screaming and crying for help. It was a bloodcurdling sound that made every muscle in my body tense.

"Sweetheart, you're safe," I yelled over her screaming, stroking her hand.

She stopped screaming, met my eyes, and began sobbing.

She tried to speak, but with her dislocated jaw and her emotional state, the words were too muddled to begin to understand.

"We're taking you to the hospital," I explained as calmly as I could. "They will help you. For now, just try to stay quiet."

Tears streamed down her face, and I felt useless. I knew she was in pain, and there wasn't a damn thing I could do about it. I cried too, for the first time since she disappeared five years ago.

"Jackie, I know this isn't the time or place either of us imagined, but I can't wait or pretend anymore. I love you with everything I am. Will you marry me?"

Her eyes went wide, and a tear rolled down her cheek. Her lips tugged at the corners with what would have been a smile if she could.

She made a sound that came out as "yah."

My smile was so wide it hurt my cheeks. I held her hand up to my lips and kissed each finger. When she was better, I would kiss every inch of her, not in a sexual way, but in a way of gratitude that she was still here and still mine.

When we pulled up at the hospital, they asked me to go to the waiting room so that they could examine her and get X-rays. I pulled my phone out of my pocket and saw dozens of messages from my sister.

"Let me guess, you're just now checking your fucking phone," a familiar voice said to me.

"Francine! What the hell are you doing here?" I demanded.

"I've been trying to reach you to tell you how to find Jackie. She called my phone, and I could hear everything. It's all recorded, Clearwater's confession, all the way up to her being shoved out of the car to the ambulance ride," she said, "Only you would ask a girl to marry you when she can't speak!"

Francine laughed and wrapped me in a hug I didn't know I needed. I was surprised she came but so grateful to have her there.

"When I heard Robbie had been shot and left in the burning restaurant, I grabbed my work cell and called 9-1-1. I ran out the door without another thought and caught a cab," she explained. "I knew Robbie would need someone until his family could be tracked down."

"You are the best sister," I said, squeezing her in a hug again.

"I know. I'm so glad you both made it through this," she said.

I released her, and we sat down in the waiting room.

"How is Robbie?" I asked.

"He was being taken to surgery. The bullet went clear through and didn't seem like it had hit any vital organs or arteries. They expect he will have a full recovery," she answered.

"Have they said anything about Masso?" I asked, realizing I had been so focused on Jackie that I hadn't really checked him over.

"It wasn't looking good when he came in," she admitted. "I heard they did CPR on him throughout the ride here. He was rushed back for emergency surgery. He's still back there."

"Where is Drew?" I asked.

"There's a separate waiting room for surgery. He's up there waiting for Robbie and Masso," Francine answered.

My brothers burst into the room, running toward us.

"Is Jackie alright?" Jason asked.

"What happened?" Ben asked.

I gave the two of them a quick rundown of the events of the day.

"Jay, do you think you could go up to the surgery waiting area and sit with Drew? He may need some help understanding all the medical jargon when his family comes out of surgery. And he really shouldn't be alone," I asked.

"Yes, of course," Jason said, standing to go to the surgical wing.

He stopped and looked back at me with a questioning look on his face.

"We're good, Jay," I said, giving him a reassuring nod. I knew he was worried about what he had said to me earlier.

He smiled, nodded, and continued toward the other waiting area.

I sat back down in the chair. My body began to shake, coming down from the adrenaline that had been pumping through my body for the last few hours.

I could see the worry in my sister's eyes. Just as I was about to explain, Ben piped in.

"It's okay, Frannie. It's what happens after an intense adrenaline rush," Ben said, squeezing her hand.

She looked at our little brother and then back at me, and I nodded to confirm what Ben had told her was true.

"Are you Jackie D'Marco's family?" A middle-aged woman in scrubs asked us.

"Yes," I replied, standing and whirling quickly in her direction.

"She wanted me to bring her fiancé back to the room. Can you two wait out here, please?" She explained.

My siblings nodded, and I followed the nurse, my heart racing a million miles a minute. The hall seemed to stretch on forever with patients in each one, none of them my girl.

Finally, we came upon a room with the curtain drawn, and my pounding heart crawled into my throat. I was desperate to see her but terrified. What if she wanted to change her mind about marrying me? What if she wasn't okay?

The nurse pulled back the curtain, and my heart slowed, relaxing in Jackie's presence. She reached out for me, and I took her hand, glad to touch her and see that she was still okay.

A female doctor came in behind me and started pulling up Jackie's files on the computer.

"Hello, I'm Dr. Valentino," she said. "I've been working to get Jackie feeling better. She came in with some trauma to her head, mandible, and abdomen. The jaw is broken, so she will need to undergo surgery for that and will probably have her mouth wired shut for a few weeks with the location of this break being so close to the joint where it connects to the skull."

I looked over at Jackie, and she was listening intently to the doctor, so I turned back and did the same.

"The head injury was just some cuts. We will put a couple of stitches in while you're under for the jaw surgery, but those are minor," Dr. Valentino explained.

I nodded, the tension slipping from my muscles with each piece of information she gave us.

"The other thing we found is that Jackie has some deep bruising in her abdomen, particularly around her uterus. This could cause scarring or for her fallopian tubes to close off, but it is too soon to tell how her body will handle the recovery. We did see some anomalies around her right ovary on her scans, so we will refer her to a gynecologist to have this investigated further," Dr. Valentino said, "this isn't anything we think needs to be operated on today and should be looked into by a fertility specialist."

My heart sank. I knew how much Jackie wanted to be a mother. I knew there were many ways to achieve that, and I wasn't worried about having biological children. Still, I knew her well enough to know she would feel like she was letting me down.

"I'm sorry; I know that is a lot to take in. I will give you a few moments alone, and then we will come in to prep Jackie for her surgery," Dr. Valentino announced and stepped out of the room.

Tears were flowing down Jackie's cheeks. I pulled a scratchy tissue from the box on the table and carefully dabbed her cheeks.

"Jackie, none of what we just heard changes anything for me. I still love you. I always have. Please don't change your mind," I pleaded. "Children or not, I only want you."

She cried harder, and I felt miserable. I so desperately wanted to fix this, but I couldn't. Someone had put a pad of paper and a pen on Jackie's tray next to the bed. She picked it up and wrote on it and the backside too.

You deserve to be happy. and so do I.

My mind racing at what she could mean, I looked her in the eyes, begging her not to break up with me. She took the paper from me, turned it over and handed it back to me.

Nothing makes me happier than loving you.
Yes. I want to marry you!

"Could you lead with that next time?" I asked with a relieved laugh, "I was sweating over here."

I kissed the top of her head and brushed a wayward lock from her face.

"I'm happiest when I am loving you too," I admitted.

CHAPTER 33

I Hate Hospitals

Kyle
December 6, 2017

An orderly led me down endless hallways from Jackie's emergency room to the surgical waiting room when she had been taken to surgery. I was given a pager that would go off when she was in recovery. My insides twisted with worry, even though the doctor assured me there were minimal risks involved. I would have taken every ounce of pain for her if it were humanly possible.

When the double doors opened, I saw my brother, Jason, hugging Drew tightly with tears in his eyes. I raced over to the two of them, my stomach flip flopping.

"What happened?" I demanded.

"My dad...he died in surgery," Drew sniffed and with a sob choked out, "he's gone."

I couldn't find words. I just wrapped my arms around my brother and Drew. I could feel that Drew's legs were about to give out on him, so I helped Jason guide him to a chair.

"Any word on Robbie?" I asked.

"He came out of surgery and will make a full recovery," Jason answered.

"How am I going to tell him?" Drew asked, his body still racking with sobs.

"We'll help you," Jason offered.

My heart squeezed. My brother didn't know Drew really at all, and he had offered his help without a second thought. I squeezed Drew's shoulder as confirmation that I would help him too.

"What about Jackie?" Drew asked, sucking in a ragged breath.

"She is having surgery on her jaw. It's broken, and they believe it will need to be wired shut for a few weeks due to where it broke. They don't expect any complications. She does have some internal trauma, but they didn't see anything that would require surgery at this time," I answered.

"I'm so glad to hear she wasn't hurt worse," Drew said.

"Me too," Jason agreed, meeting my eyes.

I nodded, understanding that Jason really did mean it, despite the conversation we had earlier in the day.

My phone vibrated in my pocket. I excused myself and stepped out of the room to answer my phone. Romero was calling.

"Romero?" I answered.

"Carrollton, am I glad to hear your voice!" he exclaimed.

"I'm glad to hear yours too," I answered. "It's been one Hell of a day."

I truly was happy to hear from Romero. I hadn't expected him to call, but I considered him my brother.

"Are you and Jackie alright? The news coverage has been limited. Dispatch said our cruiser was taken to the Bayonne PD Garage," Romero explained.

"I'm fine," I said. "Jackie is in surgery, though. She broke her jaw."

"Shit. I hope everything goes well with the surgery," Romero said.

"Me too," I replied. "We just found out her uncle died in surgery. She doesn't know yet. Her cousin Robbie, the one you met at the station was shot, but he is in good condition and came through surgery just fine."

"Have you heard anything about Pete Billings?" Romero asked.

"What do you mean?" I asked, my muscles clenching.

"He was the driver, the one ejected from the car," Romero explained. "I heard he was taken to Bayonne Medical Center. I just assumed he came in with the rest of you guys."

"He may have," I replied, "but I had come in with Jackie and stayed pretty close to her until they took her back for surgery."

"None of us have been able to figure out what he was doing there," Oscar said, "I know he said he was driving people around, but we don't know if he was helping Clearwater or if he was trying to gather evidence. It's such a mess."

I couldn't imagine a world where the kindhearted but gruff Pete Billings that I knew would be helping someone like Reese Clearwater, but you don't always know everything you think you do about people. Masso had certainly kept some big secrets, and look where that had gotten him.

"You can say that again. I'll see if I can find out anything here. I need to go, but please tell Maria and the kids to take care and I'll come see them soon," I said.

"I will, take care man," Romero replied.

I hung up with Romero and turned to go back into the waiting room. The female officer who had helped me find Jackie was walking up to the waiting room. Seeing her again, there was something familiar about her I just couldn't place.

"Officer Carrollton, how is Jackie?" she asked, stopping in front of me.

"She's in for surgery now; her jaw was broken," I answered.

Damn, even her voice was familiar.

"I'm Officer Candice Williams," she said, extending her hand, "I am the one that helped you out at the scene."

"I remember," I replied, my eyebrows still furrowed.

"I also met you at Thanksgiving," she said, cluing me in on who she was.

"Wait," I said, "you're Clearwater's wife?!"

"Well, he thought so," she smiled. "We did a fake wedding, never turned in the paperwork to make it legal."

"So, you were undercover?" I asked and winced as I realized how stupid I sounded.

"Yes," she answered, "I had been investigating him for some other crimes we had suspected him of, and that seemed the only way he would let me even get close to him."

"Wow," I said.

My mind was blown. The Candi that I had met at Thanksgiving was done up like a blond bombshell, but Officer Williams, while still a lovely woman, would never have made me think she could pull off that look.

"I can't believe you're the same person," I huffed.

"I'm here to follow up on Pete Billings' condition," she said, "He was torn up pretty badly after the accident and might lose his leg."

I winced. "Right or left?"

"What?" she asked, her brow now the one wrinkled.

"Which leg?" I asked.

"The left," she answered, perplexed by my question.

I blew out a breath. "Pete's going to be pissed. That was his good leg."

She gave me a small smile.

"Do you know what he was doing there?" I asked, though I was afraid of the answer.

"Pete had insisted on being part of the investigation on Clearwater," she explained, "he had a suspicion that Jackie's parents were not guilty of the crime, but while he was working with Brooklyn PD, he couldn't ever string together enough evidence to confirm his suspicions. He got word that I was looking into Clearwater, and he thought that maybe he could find some clues from that direction. He had suspected Jackie's Uncle Masso until he started working as Clearwater's driver and picked up on some of the conversations he was having. I tried to get him to go home to his wife and let me handle things, but he insisted that we try to warn Jackie to stop looking. I hired the boys to mess up her car, hoping it would scare her away from the storage units."

"Even that didn't scare her off completely," I shook my head, though I couldn't help but smile about how brave my girl was.

"We even tried leaving the note on her car at the university," Candi continued.

"So that was you with Billings?" I nodded, finally putting all the pieces together.

"You saw us?" she asked.

"Surveillance cameras from across the street caught you. I recognized Pete's limp right away, but couldn't tell who was with him," I said.

She nodded.

The waiting room door opened, and Jason stuck his head out.

"Excuse me, I'm sorry to interrupt, but Robbie is in recovery. Did you want to come back with us to see him?" Jason asked.

"Yes, I would like to," I answered. "Officer Williams, can I follow up with you if I have any questions?"

"Of course," she replied and handed me her card. "Please tell Robbie I hope he gets well soon and that I will come to see him tomorrow."

I gave her a nod and went with Jason and Drew back to the recovery area to see Robbie. He looked so small on the bed, but for all he had been through he didn't look nearly as scary as Francine had when I saw her in the hospital.

Robbie looked around at us and gave a weak smile.

"What are you all doing here?" Robbie asked hoarsely from being intubated during surgery.

"Hey Rob, how are you feeling?" Drew asked carefully.

"Tired," Robbie answered.

Drew nodded and squeezed Robbie's hand.

"You can rest," Drew encouraged. "We just wanted to see how you felt after surgery."

The beeper in my pocket began to vibrate, so I asked one of the nurses working with Robbie where Jackie was.

"We actually have her just over here," the nurse smiled and led me to the curtained section next to Robbie. "The doctor will come talk to you in a bit, but everything went really well."

I was relieved. The nurse pulled back the curtain, and there she was, my beautiful fiancé. Her face was swollen, but her jaw was no longer mashed over to the side like it had been, which was comforting. I walked up beside her bed and took the hand that didn't have the IV into mine.

"Hi Sweetness, the nurse said your procedure went well," I told her.

She parted her lips and pointed to her mouth, showing me that they had wired her mouth shut. All I could see was metal covering her beautiful teeth.

"I'll try to stick to yes or no questions," I smiled at her. "Robbie's out of surgery, he's in the recovery bay next to you. He's going to make a full recovery."

She gave a tired nod, and through her wired jaw she asked, "Masso?"

I hung my head. I didn't know how to tell her he was gone. She squeezed my hand, and I looked up. Tears were glistening in her eyes. I shook my head, and the tears slid down her cheeks.

"I'm so sorry," I said.

My words felt inadequate, but it was all I could think of saying. She wiped away her tears and looked at the curtain separating her from Robbie.

"Do you want to see Robbie?" I asked.

"Yes," she replied.

I slowly pulled the curtain separating them.

"Hey Robbie, somebody wanted to see you," I said.

Robbie turned his head, and his smile was dopey from the lingering anesthesia, but genuine.

"Jackie," he said, stretching out his hand.

Jackie stretched her hand toward him, and they were just able to touch fingertips.

"Hey, Sis," Jason said, crossing around to her bedside and kissing the top of her head, "Francine and Ben are in the waiting room waiting to hear about how you're doing."

She parted her lips and showed him her wired shut mouth as she had done to me earlier.

"Still one of the most beautiful girls I know," he insisted, "they'll be happy to see you."

She nodded slowly.

One of the nurses came up to us to tend to Robbie and then Jackie.

"We're going to be taking them to their rooms soon. Jackie will be going to room 396, and it looks like Robbie will be going to 325," she said. "Why don't you all go get something to eat and come back in about an hour. We should have them cleaned up and moved into their respective rooms."

I didn't want to leave either of them, but I knew that the nurses had a job to do, and it was easier to do when there weren't extra people hanging around. I gave her hand a squeeze and kissed her forehead.

"I'll be back, and then I'm staying the night with you," I promised.

She squeezed my hand and looked into my eyes lovingly.

CHAPTER 34

Can You Hear Me Now?

Jackie
December 22, 2017

My heart raced as Kyle carried me bridal-style up the steps to my childhood home. His tender gaze held mine. I was heavy, too heavy for him to do this, but he didn't seem to be straining at all. I was so impressed with his strength and so in love with him.

When I got home from the hospital, I found that he had replaced his sofa at our apartment with two matching recliners, since I had to sleep sitting up while my jaw healed. He slept next to me every night, even though it wasn't nearly as comfortable as our bed.

We contacted Nonni's attorney here in Brooklyn, Mr. Lawrence Drury, and gained access to the security deposit box she had written to us about. Inside had been the deed to my childhood home, the deed to the restaurant, and the set of wedding rings she and Nonno had exchanged on their wedding day. There was also a bunch of cash, along with a copy of the will that left all these items to me to distribute how I saw fit. The final item was a cooking pan that she had brought over from Italy when they came to the USA all those years ago. I think it was my favorite item.

Kyle put me down just inside the door of the house, and we looked around at the bare walls.

"The timing is amazing," Kyle remarked. "The tenants that have been living here moved out just as you realized you own the place."

I hum my agreement. My doctor removed the wiring at my last appointment. My mouth only had to be wired shut for 2 weeks, thankfully, but I was already used to speaking less. My jaw was healing well, but my face still had some of the ugly yellow color from the fading bruises.

"I'm so sorry I can't stay and make plans for the house with you right now. Are you sure you don't want to go to the party with me? Romero will kill me if I don't at least make an appearance at his holiday party," Kyle smiled.

"Go, I'll be fine," I replied, smiling back at him.

Kyle wrapped me in a warm hug and kissed my forehead, still afraid of hurting me.

"I'll be home in a few hours," he said.

"I'll be here," I replied. "I love you."

"I love you too," he said.

Kyle opened the door, and Francine was standing on the other side, hand raised to knock on the door.

"Hey, Frannie, come on in!" he said, stepping aside to let his sister in. "I've gotta run to Romero's for a few hours, but I'll be back soon."

"Okay, see you then," Francine replied.

We both watched Kyle leave, and then she turned toward me, a basket of goodies in her hand.

"Happy housewarming!" She smiled cheerfully.

"I don't know," I admitted. "We may just sell it."

"Why?" Francine asked. "You're within walking distance of me and you love this house!"

Francine was right, I did love the house, but I could sell it and buy us a smaller house and pay for my tuition and still have a little money in the bank.

"I have a lot of expenses coming up: the restaurant, college tuition, medical bills..." I answered pragmatically.

"Jackie, consider this: your house is paid for in full right now. You could take out a mortgage on it and take care of all the expenses you have coming up and be able to live here if that's what you both want," Francine suggested.

I hadn't considered that, but it was definitely an option to talk to Kyle about. I nodded and walked out to the kitchen with the basket that Francine had brought. It had some things that needed to be put in the refrigerator. I was relieved to find that the house did still have all the kitchen appliances and the set of stools at the kitchen island that I used to sit at with my parents every morning to have breakfast.

"Kyle told me the lawyers are still hoping to get your parents released by Christmas," Francine said, compassionately.

"I don't understand what is taking so long," I said, frustrated by the whole situation. "They have the recording!"

"I don't quite understand either, but he said it is all part of the process to make sure they dispel any of the prior evidence used against them," she explained.

Francine sat down on one of the stools at the counter. I sat down and joined her.

"So, what is the plan for today?" Francine asked.

"I want to take stock of what is here and any repairs or cleaning that needs to be done to get this place ready to live in," I answered.

"Okay, I am here. Let me help you with that," she smiled.

"Thanks," I replied, smiling back at her.

We went around the first floor, going over every detail with a fine-toothed comb. I asked Francine to note anything she saw, and I made a separate list of the things that I noticed, and we would compare our two lists at the end of our inspection.

"Let's head upstairs," I suggested when we both agreed the first floor was complete.

Francine's phone had buzzed in her pocket several times, and she pulled it out to check it.

"I'm right behind you, I just have to answer this text message from work," she said, typing out a message to one of her colleagues.

I went up the stairs, and the first room to the right was my old bedroom. My dad had measured my height each year on my birthday at the end of my door so that it wasn't as noticeable. The marks were still there and hadn't been painted over, to my relief.

I noted in my inspection that if the house were to be sold, this door would be replaced. It was coming with me to our new house. It was sentimental and silly, but it was what I was going to do.

Francine came up the steps a minute or two later.

"Is everything okay?" I asked, jotting down a note about repainting my old bedroom to something more neutral if we were selling.

"Oh, it's fine," Francine replied. "They just had a question about one of my clients."

We went back to writing down all the little things that needed fixed in each room upstairs. As we were finishing, I realized that I hadn't examined the steps and the banister, so I paid close attention to each bit of the staircase as we went back down to the first floor. As I made it to the final step, I bumped into a warm body.

"Sorry, I–" I said, and looked up to see Kyle. "You're back. I didn't hear you come in."

"Good, I wanted to surprise you," he smiled. "Can you close your eyes for me?"

I gave him a suspicious look but put my hand over my eyes, playing along with whatever he was up to. Kyle took my hand in his and wrapped his other arm around my waist to guide me to his surprise.

"Okay, stand right here, but don't uncover your eyes just yet," he said.

I took a deep breath, nerves dancing through my belly. I heard him moving in front of me, but I couldn't tell what he was doing.

"You can look now," he said.

I lifted my hand from my eyes, and the family room had been decorated with a Christmas tree and the old couch from our apartment and a few accent chairs. Ben, Shreya, Jason, Francine and Seth, Mr. and Mrs. Carrollton and Oscar and Maria were all huddled to the side of the Christmas tree.

"Who wants cookies?" a voice called from behind me.

The voice was one I hadn't heard in years but knew to my core. I whipped around, and there she was...my mother. Her hair was longer than mine and had silver strands, but it was her! She smiled widely at me, and my father came up behind her with a second tray of cookies.

"Ciao, Cara," my father said, his smile as wide as my mother's, "We've missed you so much."

Cara is what my father called me. It means "beloved" in Italian. I never thought I would hear him call me that when I sent him to jail all those years ago.

I ran to them and nearly knocked the cookies out of their hands when I wrapped them both in a hug. Someone took the tray of cookies from them, and we all held each other for the longest time.

"My poor girl, look how bruised your face is," my mother whimpered as she examined me.

"The bruises will fade," I dismissed her worries, "I am just so happy you're here!"

"Kyle helped to speed up the process. He petitioned for our release and kept pushing them until we were free," my father explained.

My heart melted. I had no idea he had done any of that. He never told me, but I was so grateful that he had.

I turned to face Kyle, and he sank down to his knee and took my hand.

"Jackie, the first time I asked you wasn't how either of us planned, and that was okay. It was still magical and perfectly us. Now, I have a second chance to make it special, and I'm taking it. The second time is always sweeter with you. Each time we come back to each other, it is better than the first, and that tells me that our lives are only going to get better and better if we keep coming back to each other. You are the best thing in my life, and I want this, us, forever. Jacqueline Christine D'Marco, will you marry me?" Kyle asked.

My heart was racing from the surprise, from his sweet words, from my love for this man and for what he had done to help me feel whole again.

"Yes, Kyle, I will marry you," I managed to choke out, tears of joy slipping down my cheeks.

He slipped my Nonni's ruby engagement ring onto my finger and got to his feet to peck a gentle kiss on my lips. Everyone in the room cheered.

Francine handed out champagne flutes, and we toasted the future. It was such a lovely moment. We passed around cookies and talked.

"When's the big day?" Mrs. C asked.

"We haven't picked one yet," Kyle answered.

"I actually wanted to talk to you about that," I said, squeezing his torso for support in what I was about to ask.

"Oh?" he asked.

"Would it be okay if we waited until I graduated?" I asked hopefully.

"That's a couple years off," Kyle said. He didn't sound upset, just more contemplative.

"Yeah, is that okay?" I asked, nervously.

"Of course it is," he replied, "that doesn't mean you want to move away from me though, right?"

I looked nervously at my parents, and they just smiled, waiting for me to respond. I had fully expected them to have disapproving looks on their faces.

"No, I want to keep living together," I answered honestly.

Kyle let out the breath he had been holding and smiled. "Good. I thought we could move here when the lease is up at the apartment."

"Really?" I asked, surprised.

He nodded. "Your parents and I have been talking a lot about ways we can make it work."

I looked over at my parents, and they nodded their approval. I was thrilled. Having gone through the house today with Francine, I had so many ideas of what I wanted to do if we decided to keep the house. I couldn't wait to tell Kyle all about it.

The bunch of us found places to sit in the living room, and I soon noticed everyone had gift bags at their feet.

"Are we doing Christmas now?" I asked.

"No sweetheart, this is our housewarming," Kyle answered, carefully kissing my cheek.

"Here, open mine first!" Francine said, excitedly handing us each a wrapped gift from the bag in front of her.

Kyle and I looked at each other and unwrapped our respective packages. Inside there were brand new iPhones.

"Thanks Frannie," Kyle stood and hugged his sister.

"Thank you," I said, giving her a hug too.

"Well, I guess I need to return what I got you guys," Jason said.

He pulled out a pair of phones from the bag in front of him with a rueful laugh.

"No way, me too," Ben laughed, lifting his bag to show he had gotten them a set of phones too.

The room burst out in laughter.

"Maybe we should keep them. You never know when Jackie will run over my phone again," Kyle laughed.

I gave him a playful smack on the knee and laughed. There was a knock at the front door and Ben went to see who it was.

"Hey look who I found," he announced.

Robbie and Drew came in, and everyone greeted them.

"Aunt Susan! Uncle Davide! You're home!" Robbie called out to my parents excitedly.

"Oh Robbie, you look so well!" my mother cooed and gave Robbie and Drew each a kiss on the cheek.

"Boys, it is so good to see you," my father greeted them. "I'm sorry I wasn't there to support you when your father passed."

My heart sank at the memory. Masso had died in surgery. He had massive internal bleeding. They found that the car had run him over when he jumped out of the car behind me.

Masso was the reason I had survived. When the car had started to lose control, he took the opportunity to push me out, and when he tried to follow, Clearwater had fired a shot at him. Masso, despite what he had done wrong, had been my guardian angel that day. If I had stayed in the car, I likely would have been crushed against the bridge post. Masso had his faults, but he was my uncle and my godfather, and I would always miss him terribly.

"We're just glad you are free, and the right person is behind bars," Drew replied.

Drew had been far too stoic since Masso had died. I knew he was heartbroken on the inside, but he had a lot on his plate too with becoming Robbie's primary caregiver and losing his job. When Mr. Clearwater was sent to jail, his companies crumbled, and his employees were left jobless.

"Kyle, what happened to Peter Billings?" Drew asked.

Peter Billings, I recalled, was the mentor that Kyle had. The guy who convinced Kyle to become a police officer not only was the one who had left the note on my car at the college, he also was the driver that was ejected from the car that Reese Clearwater had taken me and Masso in.

"Pete is recovering," Kyle answered. "It turns out, Pete was onto Clearwater and what had happened. When he couldn't get anyone to reopen the case with the evidence he had, he took a job as Clearwater's driver to try to collect more evidence on the guy. He's the reason I was able to push through Susan and Davide's release."

"I'm so glad he didn't let Clearwater get away with it!" my mother declared. "He put himself at risk to save my daughter, and I am eternally grateful."

"I just wish he could have saved my brother too," my father sighed. "I never got to apologize to him for the way I acted when our father had died."

"He knew," Drew said, reassuring my father.

Davide gave him an appreciative nod.

The room grew quiet, an unplanned silent moment for Masso.

Robbie was the first to break the silence and asked, "Jackie, are you going to marry Kyle or what?"

"Yes, I'm going to marry him," I smiled and held up my hand to show him Nonni's ring on my finger.

"It looks different," Robbie noted.

I looked down at my hand and saw that Robbie was right.

Kyle cleared his throat and said, "Your dad said it was okay, but I took your Nonni's ring and the ring I had bought for you 5 years ago and had a jeweler combine the two. I thought it was a nice representation of our second chance. The two rings were very different, but they came together so nicely."

It was beautiful what the jeweler had done. I didn't know what the second ring looked like before, but it must have had some kind of vine-like design to it that was brought over to the new ring and accented the ruby beautifully in its new setting.

"I love that," I said. "It's special to us now."

My heart swelled in my chest with all the love Kyle had shown to me. Even though we had lost Masso, it felt like my family was growing again and Kyle made that all happen.

"I'm never happier than when I am loving you," he said, kissing my hand.

I wrapped him in a hug and held on. He was mine, and I was his, forever.

EPILOGUE

The Best Gift

Kyle
Sunday, May 5th, 2019

❝ Are you sure you want me to take it now?" Jackie asked, nervously holding the box of pregnancy tests. "What if it's negative again?"

"What if it's not?" I asked, squeezing her shoulders.

We weren't officially trying, but we weren't "not trying" if you catch my drift. She was two weeks away from graduating with her bachelor's degree, so it wouldn't be the worst timing if she were to take a year off at this point.

"I don't want to ruin your birthday," she said, giving me a sad look.

"No matter what this little stick says, you could never ruin my birthday," I insisted. "If it's a no, it just means I get to have you all to myself a little longer."

She smiled up at me and tip-toed to peck a kiss on my lips. "You really are wonderful, you know?"

"I just love you," I said. "If it is only ever us for the rest of our lives, that is all I want. Anything else is a bonus."

I meant it. I wanted kids, of course I did, but if that wasn't something we ever had, I would still be the happiest lovesick idiot on the planet with her at my side.

"We need to get ready soon," she said. "Don't forget we're having lunch with our family."

"So, stop stalling," I teased her and gave her a playful swat on the butt, "go take the test."

She took a steadying breath, went into our bathroom, and closed the door behind her. I stood on the other side of the door, pacing excitedly. She was late, but her cycles were never regular. Surely, this time we'd get the news we'd been waiting for. It was my birthday after all. It could be a lovely present for both of us.

"Fuck!" she called out.

My heart pounded in my chest.

"What's wrong?" I asked.

"Just a minute," she replied.

I put my ear up to the door when she didn't come out right away. I could hear rustling wrappers and the sink turning on and off. I stepped back from the door just before she opened it.

"My period started," she sniffed, her eyes glistening with tears that hadn't yet fallen.

"Oh, Sweetheart," I said, wrapping her in a hug and holding her tight.

"I just wanted to give you a positive test today," she sobbed into my shoulder.

"I've got all I wanted right here in my arms," I said, but I couldn't help the tear that slid down my cheek.

My heart hurts for her more than for myself. When she was injured trying to escape Clearwater's car a few years ago, the anomalies they saw on the scan of her abdomen had created scar tissue around her right ovary. We'd been to several specialists over the last two years, and they said that it would decrease her fertility and may mean that we would need to do IVF or IUI in the future if we wanted to have a biological child. Even though we knew this, we still hoped for a miracle.

"I wouldn't blame you if you didn't want to marry me," she said on a hiccupping sob.

"Jackie, look at me," I ordered, pulling back from her and holding her by her shoulders.

I didn't hide the tears that had fallen down my cheeks. I just looked deeply into her brown eyes as soon as she looked up at me.

"There is no one, and I do mean no one, that will ever be my wife, but you," I said. "If it's not you, there will not be anyone else."

"But I'm broken," she sniffled.

"And together we make each other whole," I answered. "Please Jackie, I know this makes you so sad. Why don't we just put a hold on trying to have a baby for now? We could go on vacation somewhere after graduation. Just the two of us."

"I would like that," she said with a wobbly smile.

"Good," I said, pulling her in again and hugging her.

Toby let out a meow at our feet, trying to get in on the hug.

"What will we do with Toby when we go?" she asked, stepping out of my hug to pick up Toby.

He rubbed his face on hers and left a few hairs in the trails of her tears. We both laughed as I tried to remove them between Toby leaving a few more behind.

"One of my brothers can stay with him, I'm sure," I said.

She nodded.

"Here, I'll take Toby so you can take a shower," I offered.

She passed the fur ball over to me and went back into the bathroom to take her shower.

"Come on buddy, let's go get you a snack," I said.

Toby licked my nose with his sand-papery tongue. I carried him downstairs to the kitchen and pulled his treats out of the pantry. I put him down on the floor and gave him one of his stick treats that he loved to kick while he chewed on the other side. He looked ridiculous when he did it, but it made him happy.

I went back upstairs and pulled out a lightweight button-down shirt and dress slacks. We were going to Chevy's Steakhouse for lunch with our family, so I had to look halfway decent. I used the second bathroom to take my shower and get ready so that Jackie wouldn't feel rushed.

Within an hour, we made it to Chevy's, and Jackie held my hand as we walked in.

"Hi, we're here for the Carrollton party," she said to the host.

"Right this way," the host replied and led us to the back of the restaurant where the stairs led to the rooftop area.

"We're eating on the rooftop?" I asked excitedly.

"Yeah, I thought it would be a nice throwback to our first time here," Jackie blushed.

"Prom night," I smiled.

She nodded, and we walked up the stairs together.

"Surprise!" all our family yelled out when we got to the top. "Happy Birthday!"

It wasn't a surprise at all that they were there, so I wasn't sure why they yelled that out, but I was a good sport. I had my best girl with me, and that's all that mattered.

"Uncle Kyle, I lost my tooth!" Carmen, Romero's daughter said to me, tugging on my pants leg.

"I see that," I said, picking her up and looking in her little mouth at the gap on the top row.

"I got a dollar!" she squealed excitedly.

"Wow, that must have been a really clean tooth! I only ever got a quarter for mine," I complained.

"Your teeth are a little yellow," she scrunched her face, looking at my teeth as though she was going to report me to the tooth fairy herself.

"That's what happens when you get old, like this guy," Romero said, busting my chops.

"Yeah, I'm REALLY old," I laughed.

"How old are you?" she asked.

"Twenty-five," I answered matter-of-factly.

"Woah!" she said, her mouth falling open as though I had told her I was from the year 25 B.C.

"I know. I better put you down so I can pick up my cane," I teased. "You're getting pretty heavy."

I tickled her, and when she squealed. I put her on the ground, and she ran off to tell her sister how very old her Uncle Kyle was.

"You still look good to me," Jackie whispered and gave me a suggestive wiggle of her eyebrows.

"That's all that matters," I replied, wrapping my arm around her and pressing her into my side.

"Carrollton, I just heard some of the Mackenzie kids are in foster care again. Lorna's not recovering as well as everyone first thought. She's back into drugs again," Romero said when I let Jackie go ahead of me to her seat.

I let out a sad sigh. Those kids deserved to have a mother and father they could count on. I really thought that since Timothy was gone, Lorna would clean up her act.

"That's too bad. Did they get placed together this time?" I asked.

"No, there weren't any foster families that were willing to take all six of them," Romero answered.

My heart sank. I had a big family and couldn't imagine going through what they had and being separated on top of that.

Romero and I found our seats when the wait staff came up to take our drink orders and to bring fresh bread to eat. I noticed my sister sitting by herself to my left.

"Where's Seth? Off pumping iron at the gym?" I teased her.

Seth Easton was my least favorite person that my sister had ever dated. It would be my birthday wish come true if she finally dumped him. He was a leech that was draining my sister financially and emotionally. I get that he was a good-looking guy, but she could do so much better if she just cut him loose for good.

"He's probably balls deep in the new female trainer at the gym," she said bitterly, "we broke up."

"I'm sorry," I managed to say without grinning from ear to ear.

Jackie and I shared a look, and I could see that she was just as happy about it as I was. The drinks and bread were brought up and lunch orders were taken. When the wait staff went back downstairs to put the order in with the kitchen, the table started clinking their glasses.

"Speech!" Ben called out encouragingly.

The rest of the table followed and chanted, "Speech! Speech!"

I stood and raised my glass, and they quieted.

"Thank you all for coming to celebrate my birthday with me. My twenty-fifth year on this planet has been one of the best yet and that's because of this lady to my right," I said, looking down at Jackie.

Jackie stood smiling and said, "I hope you all will indulge me for just a moment and let me give Kyle his birthday gift."

"Just remember there are small children present," Ben teased.

"Not that kind of gift," she laughed.

She handed me an envelope. It was deep red. I grinned, excited to see what she had gotten me. I carefully opened the envelope and pulled out the card inside.

Mr. and Mrs. Davide and Susan DMarco
ARE PLEASED TO ANNOUNCE THE UPCOMING
WEDDING OF THEIR DAUGHTER

Jacqueline Christine DMarco
TO
Kyle Anthony Carrollton

SON OF
Mr. and Mrs. Charles and Constance Carrollton

SAVE THE DATE
FEBRUARY 14, 2021

Wedding invitation to follow

My heart skipped in a wild rhythm. She had been dragging her feet to set the date, wanting to finish school, but here, in my hand, was the date that would allow me to call her my wife for the rest of our lives. I put my drink down on the table and engulfed her in a hug.

"Best birthday gift ever," I grinned.

"What is it?" the Romero children yelled excitedly.

"We're getting married!" I replied.

"We know," various people at the table said.

"I set the date," Jackie answered with a laugh. "You all have cards in the mail. It will be ten years to the day of our first date."

The table erupted into cheers and congratulations. She was right; I had taken her to a Valentine's Day dance. I told her I would take her to it because she helped organize it but didn't have a date, and she shouldn't miss the party she spent weeks planning. What I was too scared to tell her then was that I had been in love with her for years. My heart overflowed with all the love I had for her.

As I held her in a tight embrace, I whispered in her ear, "What do you think about taking in six foster kids at one time?"

She pulled back from me in surprise with her head angled to the side, asking me without words if I was serious. We had talked about adoption and fostering before, but we hadn't committed to the idea. Taking on six kids at once certainly hadn't been discussed, but the story of the Mackenzie kids tugged at my heart, and I felt called to help them.

"Let's talk about it when we get home," I said, letting her know I was serious.

She grinned and squeezed me tight. I didn't know what this next chapter of our lives would bring, but I knew I was ready for anything with Jackie at my side.

The End

ACKNOWLEDGMENTS

Thank you to my family and friends for your unending support and love. I would not be the woman I am today without you. You've fostered all of my crazy ideas of what I wanted to do with my life, and I appreciate you all so much.

To Shonda Ramsey, your ability to take my book and turn it into a masterpiece with your beautiful cover work and book formatting is nothing short of brilliant. Thank you for also stepping in to act as editor and business coach as I get things off the ground.

To Angela Pralle, I'm so glad that you joined our writing group in 2024 and have continued on with us. You are a great writing buddy, and I can't wait to get my hands on your book when it is ready!

To those kind enough to follow my nonsense on social media, thank you for taking this journey with me! I know it's been a wild ride at times, but I hope you enjoy this book and continue to follow me for the next one!

Last but certainly not least, thank you to you, the reader. We live in a strange world, and maybe you feel a little lost in all of it. If so, you are who I write for. I hope that you find something you can relate to in the pages and feel seen in this world. Your voice matters too.

ABOUT THE AUTHOR

J. Lynn Million is an author of poetry and contemporary romance novels for adults. Writing has been her salvation and greatest joy throughout her life. This love began with a love of reading, fostered by her mother, who read to her children nightly.

Her educational background is unique and provides an interesting landscape from which to write. She has an Associate of Arts degree in Theater Performance and a Bachelor's Degree in Applied Psychology. She is a Customer Service Supervisor at the company she has worked at for over 20 years.

J. Lynn Million is a pet momma to Stella the dog, Webster the cat, and Myrtle the turtle. She is an aspiring health nut and completed her first 5K race, coming in 2nd place in her age group.

She loves to travel, spend time with friends and family, watch reruns of old favorite shows, listen to audio books and music, and of course write. She likes to prove that even though she's an "old dog," she can still learn new tricks by learning new languages.

Connect With Me!

Visit my website www.jlynnmillion.com or follow me on social media for the latest info and sneak peeks on upcoming projects.

You can also scan the QR code below to connect with me across all platforms!

JOIN MY STREET TEAM!

If you want to see more of my work going forward, I need your help. I'm looking for people to join my street team and spread the word about my book. In exchange you will have access to exclusive behind the scenes details and early sneak peeks of upcoming works before they go up on social media.

Go to www.jlynnmillion.com/street-team or scan the QR code.